Charles Adolphus Buchheim

Elementary German Prose Composition

Charles Adolphus Buchheim

Elementary German Prose Composition

ISBN/EAN: 9783337367022

Printed in Europe, USA, Canada, Australia, Japan

Cover: Foto ©Andreas Hilbeck / pixelio.de

More available books at **www.hansebooks.com**

ELEMENTARY
GERMAN PROSE COMPOSITION

BEING PARTS I. AND II. OF

"Materials for German Prose Composition"

SELECTED AND ANNOTATED BY

C. A. BUCHHEIM, Phil. Doc., F.C.P.

*Professor of the German Language and Literature in King's College, London
Examiner in German to the University of London, &c.*

WITH A VOCABULARY

BASED UPON DR. BUCHHEIM'S KEY

LONDON
GEORGE BELL AND SONS
AND NEW YORK
1894

TABLE OF CONTENTS.

TABLE OF CONTENTS.

EXTRACT FROM THE PREFACE

TO THE THIRTEENTH EDITION

OF

Materials for German Prose Composition.

THE great success with which this book has met wherever
German is taught through the medium of English,
and the great educational progress which has taken
place almost throughout the civilized world, relieve me
from the necessity of dilating on several topics which
required to be specially pointed out when this book was
first issued in 1868.   I need no longer dwell on the importance of German as a discipline of the mind, and as
a medium of enlightenment and refinement, or on the
numerous advantages which a knowledge of the language
offers both from a practical and utilitarian point of view.
All this is now universally admitted.   Nor is it needful
to send forth a special plea on the utility, nay, necessity,
of translating from our own language into the foreign
idiom, if the latter is to be thoroughly mastered.   This
fact too may now be considered as an axiom.   Under
these circumstances it seemed to me expedient to omit
the bulk of the former Prefaces, and to confine myself,
in issuing the present *Thirteenth Edition,* to a mere
description of the book.

In the first instance, I have to state that I made myself all the extracts contained in this volume from the works of the respective authors, and that I did *not* take them "ready cut" from any other compilations. I imposed this arduous task upon myself, partly because I wished to give such passages only as seemed to me best suited for bringing out the idiomatic differences between English and German, and for illustrating the structure of the German sentence and the niceties of the language, and partly because I was anxious to avoid all those hackneyed extracts and "professional" anecdotes, of which both teachers and pupils must be heartily tired. In making the selections I have, besides, confined myself to *modern* authors, as it seemed to me impossible to learn to write modern German by translating those old English writers who deserve our admiration, but whose style nobody would now-a-days imitate. It has, finally, been my endeavour to give interesting extracts only—mostly of an instructive kind without being dull —and to furnish specimens of nearly every branch of prose writing, thus practically illustrating the narrative, descriptive, epistolary, scientific, critical, and conversational style. Though merely extracts, the pieces are mostly complete in themselves; and where this is not absolutely the case, I have given the necessary explanations in a foot-note. I have, besides, explained everything which seemed to me necessary for a full understanding of the text; which is, after all, a primary condition before any translation is to be attempted at all.

The *First Part* consists of easy detached sentences and *minor extracts*, taken from English standard works, which are to serve for practice in the order of words and the less complicated construction of sentences. The *Second Part* contains short but complete sketches, chiefly historical. The *Notes* to the first two Parts have this in common, that they contain, besides copious renderings of single expressions and idiomatic phrases, also numerous philological remarks and grammatical rules. This section of the work contains, in fact, almost the *whole of the German Syntax*.

The *Introductory Part* consists of three chapters. The *first chapter* gives what I ventured to designate as *Essentials of Syntax*, containing as it does a general recapitulation of some of the most important features of German syntax. Frequent references have been made throughout the book to this chapter, a thorough knowledge of which will greatly facilitate the student's task of translating from English into German. The *second chapter* gives the principal rules for *Punctuation* in German. A proper knowledge of this subject is absolutely necessary for composition in any language. I believe I am not overrating the importance of punctuation if I assert, that he who knows how to place his *commas* in German, shows that he has an accurate knowledge of the grammatical structure of a German sentence. In fact, the two topics, *Punctuation and Construction of Sentences*, supplement each other in German, which, as I have repeatedly pointed out in my educational works, is a strictly *grammatical* language. The *third chapter* relates to the *Division of Words in German*. Those who have had occasion to read the German compositions of a number of pupils or examinees, will be aware of the fact that most students of German have not the faintest idea of how to divide German words; and yet a knowledge of this subject forms part and parcel of the knowledge of any language. Both the last-named subjects, viz. *Punctuation* and *Division of Words*, are, as a rule, fully treated in the German grammars written for the use of Germans, and it seems therefore doubly desirable to include them in a German manual destined for non-Germans.

C. A. BUCHHEIM.

KING'S COLLEGE, LONDON,
January, 1890.

I have to express my sincerest thanks for permission to reprint some of the following Copyright Extracts :—to Lady Trevelyan, Messrs. A. and C. Black, Messrs. Blackwood and Sons, Messrs. Longmans and Co., Messrs. Macmillan and Co., Mr. John Murray, and Messrs. Smith, Elder, and Co.

GRAMMATICAL INTRODUCTION.

GERMAN is a strictly grammatical language, and this circumstance forms the basis of the construction of German sentences. The grammatical inflections, which have not been lost in German as in English, claim inexorably their right, but offer at the same time the great advantage of effecting a distinctness which leaves room neither for a real nor for a merely grammatical ambiguity. Apart from these formal exigencies, there is the same freedom of movement in the expression of thought in German as in English—a freedom which is of incalculable advantage to prose, but still more so to poetry.

The German language possesses, besides, an adaptability which most other languages lack, and to which the fact may be attributed that German can boast—as has been universally acknowledged—of unrivalled translations from foreign languages, especially from the English. The fact just pointed out may serve as an encouragement to English students of German, proving, as it does, that the difficulties of translating into German are by no means so overwhelming as is generally asserted, more particularly by those whose knowledge of the language is only superficial. Any one who has a fair knowledge of German, and is familiar with the Grammar, will, by the help of a comprehensive Dictionary, be able to produce such a translation as, though not elegant, would not be stamped as absurd or as 'un-German,' since the mode of expression is by no means prescribed by implacable laws. There is, it is true, a peculiarly German order of words; but this order can easily enough be learned by means of certain rules : and so can the peculiarity of the construction of German sentences in general, especially if it is constantly borne in mind that German is, as has been stated before, a strictly grammatical language, and requires all the various relations between subject, object, &c. to be pointed out with grammatical distinctness.

The following general recapitulation of some of the most important features of German Syntax will fully bear out my assertion as regards the thorough grammatical character of the language.

I. One of the chief characteristics of German construction is that of placing the qualifying expressions and clauses before the qualified term; which mode of expression gives great vigour and compactness to the sentences. For example : Ein auf bem Hügel ſtehenbes Haus, *a house standing on the hill*. This mode of construction enables us to avoid the too frequent use of relative clauses which, in German, cannot be contracted by the omission of the relative pronoun.

The student of German should, however, be very cautious in forming such adjective sentences. They should never be too long, and it is far better to make use of relative clauses than to compress a number of clauses into one protracted adjective sentence. It is in this respect, before all, that modern German prose has materially improved, and the present *Guide* has been arranged in accordance with that improvement.

II. *Participial Constructions*, so very frequently employed in English, are in German generally turned by a different form. This important topic has been fully explained in the present volume, and one Extract (part ii. page 82, No. xxx.) has been inserted for special practice in the various rules referring to the Present (or 'Imperfect') Participle. The most important of the rules alluded to are here recapitulated.

(a) In adverbial clauses of time *participial Constructions are* usually changed into a regular clause with a conjunction indicating time, (as: inbem, während, *whilst;* als, ba, *when;* nachbem, *after*, etc.) and a finite verb *e.g.; (while) speaking with me, he saw, etc.*, während (or inbem) er mit mir ſprach, etc. Tenses and conjunctions must be employed according to the sense of the passage.

(*b*) The Present Participle which qualifies a preceding noun or pronoun is generally changed into a regular relative clause; that is to say, the Present Participle is changed into a finite verb and is introduced by a relative pronoun or adverb. The sense of the passage will generally show which tense is to be used. Thus we should turn *retaining* in Extr. 19 by 'which had retained,' because it refers to the past; and *enabling* in Extr. 21 by 'which enable,' because it contains the notion of the present tense.

(*c*) When the Present Participle expresses a logical cause, it is changed into a regular sentence, and introduced by da; e.g. *Not finding him at home, I went away,* da id) iþn nidjt zu Haufe fanb, fo ging id) weg.

(*d*) Present Participles having the force of an adjective, are, in some cases, actually changed into attributive adjectives, (cf. p. xiv. I).

(*e*) Present Participles are often turned by a finite verb, and connected by *and* with a preceding clause. Cf. p. 28, l. 12.

(*f*) A very convenient way of rendering briefly the Present Participle is the employment of adverbial expressions with which the German language abounds. This expedient has been resorted to in various passages of the present volume, as page 112, where the clause *having sustained considerable losses* has been briefly rendered by the adverbial expression, mit großem Verluſte.

(*g*) In one case the Present Participle may also be used in German, more particularly in elevated diction,—viz. when it denotes an action which is represented as taking place simultaneously with the action expressed by the predicate ; e.g. Dies alles bei mir denkend ſchlief ich ein (*Sch.*), *thinking on all these matters I fell asleep*, i.e. 'whilst I thought of all these matters I fell asleep.' Cf. Extract 42, note *b*.

In common prose, however, we generally use a finite verb introduced by indem (and sometimes by da), as : *in walking through the town, I observed, etc.* indem ich durch die Stadt ging, etc., (Cf. above II. *a*).

III. The construction of the *Accusative with the Infinitive*, so frequently occurring in Latin, Greek, and English, is inadmissible in German, since the verb governs in such a construction two objects of a perfectly different *grammatical* character—if we may say so ; a process quite adverse to the character of the German language, which requires all grammatical relations to be logically and distinctly pointed out. We must, therefore, generally change the accusative into the nominative, the infinitive into a finite verb, and introduce the sentence by the conjunction baß. For instance: *I wish you to write the letter immediately*, ich wünfche, baß Sie ben Brief fogleich fchreiben.

The Infinitive may, however, be used in German with some verbs, as fehen, hören, finden, fühlen, haben, etc., and also with the intransitive verbs gehen, reiten, fahren, bleiben; but all these and similar verbs form with the infinitive a kind of compound verbal expression, expressing one idea only, as: *I see him coming*, ich fehe ihn kommen; *we go for a walk*, wir gehen fpazieren. In these examples the verbs kommen fehen and fpazieren gehen express one notion only. Cf. Extract 17.

The reason stated with reference to the inadmissibility of the Accusative with the Infinitive in German may, in some measure, also explain the circumstance that verbs of choosing, appointing, declaring, considering, etc. do not govern in German *two* accusatives, as is the case in Greek, Latin, and English; but put the suffering or direct object alone in the accusative, and the word expressing the office to which a person has been appointed, or that which a person or thing is declared to be, is preceded by the preposition zu with the dative (after the verbs of choosing, electing, and declaring), and by the accusative with the prepositions als or für (after verbs of considering and declaring): e.g. *They appointed him president of the society,* fie ernannten iljn jum Präfibenten ber Gefellfdjaft; *I esteem it a favour,* idj betradjte es als eine Gunft.   Cf. page 36, note 4, and page 85, note 2.

IV. The rule with reference to words in *Apposition* requires in German the greatest attention.

A noun (or its substitute, viz. a personal pronoun) or adjective or ordinal number is said to stand in the relation of *Apposition,* when it qualifies or explains another noun previously mentioned.

The *Apposition* agrees, for the sake of grammatical distinctness, with the noun qualified, in gender, number, and case.   Thus, in the extract No. 17, page 4, we must render the sentence, *The flax plant is composed of three distinct parts, the wood, the fibres, and the gum resin,* &c., by ber Fladjs beftel)t aus brei verfdjiebenen Xljeilen, bem Holje, ben Fafern unb bem Harje, &c.   The terms Holj, Fafern, and Harj stand here in *apposition* to Xljeilen, and must therefore, like the latter expression, be used in the dative case.   See page 85, note 9.

The rule that the *Article* must be repeated before nouns of different gender or number—which is merely owing to the requirements of grammatical distinctness—may here appropriately be appended to the rule concerning the *Apposition*.   See page 42, note 9.

V. Grammatical distinctness requires in German —though not rigorously—that the place of the object be supplied in the principal clause by the pronoun es when the leading verb governs the accusative case, and the object consists of a whole clause or a supine; e.g. *He had ventured to go in secret*, &c. (see page 17, note 7), er hatte es gewagt, ſich heimlich aufzumachen, &c.

If, however, the verb or adjective in the principal clause require a preposition, the latter is added to the demonstrative pronoun da or dar; e.g. *This castle is remarkable as containing* &c. (see page 97 note 2), dieſes Schloß iſt dadurch merkwürdig, daß &c.

Words printed in *italics* in the text are not to be translated.

When two words are separated by a dash (—) in the Notes, the German rendering refers to the whole clause of which the first and last word are given.

When words are separated by dots (...), the German rendering in the Notes is the equivalent for these words only, and not for the intervening expressions.

In Part I. the rules and renderings referring to each Extract are given in a single Note.

I.

ON GERMAN PUNCTUATION.

THE rules of punctuation are, in general, the same in German as in English, more especially as regards the employment of *Stops, Colons, Points of Interrogation,* etc. There is, however, a considerable difference between the use of the *Comma* in the two languages; and some in the use of the *Semicolon.*

GENERAL RULE.—A *Comma* is required in German after every distinct part of a sentence, whether it be a whole clause, or a single term, such as nouns, adjectives, or verbs, placed side by side.

A *Comma* is, in particular, placed in German:

1. Between nouns, adjectives, or verbs, placed side by side without being connected by unb or ober, as: Männer, Frauen, Kinder, Alles eilte herbei:—Er ist ein bescheidener, tapferer und edler Mann. Der Knabe konnte reiten, fechten, tanzen und schwimmen, aber nicht lesen.

2. Between co-ordinate clauses, having different subjects, as: Der Vogel fliegt, der Fisch schwimmt, die Schnecke kriecht. Sowohl meine Bücher, als auch meine Bilder sind angekommen.

3. Before dependent clauses, as: Hier ist das Buch, das ich gekauft habe.—Er sagte, daß er morgen abreisen werde.—Sie glaubt, sie habe Recht.

4. Before a principal sentence, preceded by a dependent clause, as: Wer nicht wagt, gewinnt nicht.

b

5. Before clauses beginning with unb, when they have not the same subject as the preceding clause, as: Ich gehe aufs Land, und mein Bruder reist nach Deutschland. But we write: Ich gehe aufs Land und werde morgen zurückkehren.

6. Before adversative clauses beginning with ober, as: Soll ich das Buch behalten, oder es zurücksenden? But we should write: Sage Ja ober Nein!

7. Before and after parenthetical clauses, as: Kommt, rief er, laßt uns die Stadt vertheidigen.

8. Before substantive clauses containing a *Supine* [cp. p. 2, Extract 9, (*a*)], as: Er eilte herbei, um sie zu retten.

9. Before and after appositions, as: Hermann, der Befreier von Deutschland, war ein Cherusker.

NOTE.—The German equivalents of *however, moreover* (indeſſen, überbies), and of several similar words which are separated in English by *Commas* from the clauses preceding or following them, require no *Commas* in German, as: He said he would come late; he came, however, very early.—Er sagte, er würde spät kommen; er kam indeſſen sehr früh.

The *Semicolon* is chiefly required in German between co-ordinate sentences which are rather extended, or contain themselves several clauses, as: Es ist nicht genug zu wiſſen, man muß auch anwenden; es ist nicht genug zu wollen, man muß auch thun.

ON THE DIVISION OF WORDS IN GERMAN.

GERMAN words, consisting of more than one syllable, are, in general, divided in accordance with their pronunciation, and not as is done in English, chiefly according to etymological derivation. The principal rule is therefore in German: DIVIDE AS YOU SPEAK.

EXAMPLES :—Frei-heits-liebe; Va-ter-land.

SPECIAL RULES :—

1. Compound nouns are divided in accordance with their component parts, as: Zimmer-thüre; Dinten-faß.

2. Final consonants are placed at the end of the first line, as: Faul-heit; Freund-schaft; Mäd-chen.

Conformably with the above rules, compound words are divided in accordance with their component parts, even if the division should not strictly coincide with the pronunciation, as: war-um; dar-in; vor-aus; be-ob-achten (although pronounced beo-bachten); voll-enden; Inter-esse.

Some Grammarians divide, however, in accordance with the pronunciation: wa-rum; da-rin, etc.

3. A consonant occurring between two vowels is placed in the second line, as; ge=ben; lau=fen.

4. The compound letters ch, ph, sch, th, dt, are placed in the second line, because they form one sound only, as: Sa=che; brau=chen, Or=tho=graphie; Men=schen; Stä=dte.

5. When two consonants occur before a vowel one consonant is placed on each line. For example: Freun=de; bef=fer, Laf=ten (or Las=ten); Knof=pe (or Knos=pe); klop=fen; Ach=fel.

6. The double consonant ck is changed, when divided, into k k; thus bücken should be written bük=ken; and the double consonant ß is simply reduced into its component parts; thus kratzen should be divided krat=zen.

7. The double consonants x (= ks) and z (= ts) are always placed in the second line, as forming one syllable only; for example, Ta=xe; rei=zen.

The sign of division in German is a double hyphen at the end of the line, viz. (=).

There is a curious practice current in this country of dividing German words in writing, by putting hyphens both at the end and at the beginning of the lines; the latter being of course quite superfluous.

GERMAN PROSE COMPOSITION.

PART I.

1. TIME is an important element in the action of force.

2. The hearing of birds is most acute.

3. The dome of St. Paul's Cathedral is built of wood.

4. The silver fir was introduced into England in the seventeenth century.

[1] *Important*, in the sense of affecting considerably some result, wid𝔗tig; *element* denotes here an 'essential condition,' and is to be rendered by Umstand, or by the more scientific term Moment, *n. ; action* signifying 'effect of power' is rendered by Wirkung and *force* denoting 'active power' by Kraft. —Use the word *time* with the definite article, which is frequently required in German with *abstract nouns*, when the abstract idea is expressed in a *general* sense.

[2] *Hearing*, (the sense of), Gehör; *most*, here äußerst; *acute*, with reference to the senses, scharf. — Use *birds* with the definite article, because *common names* denoting 'an aggregate whole or entire genus,' require in German the definite article.

[3] *Dome*, denoting 'cupola,' (It. and Engl.), Kuppel; *St. Paul's Cathedral*, die Paulskirche; cf. p. 59, n. 3; *wood*, (the substance) Holz. The prep. *of* referring to a material of which a thing is made, is translated by aus or von; by the former more generally when a verb is used at the same time, and by the latter when the verb is understood.

[4] *Silver fir*, Silbertanne; *to introduce into*, here bringen nach; *century*, Jahrhundert. (a) Adverbial expressions of time precede in German adverbial expressions of place. Construe therefore: was in the seventeenth century into England, &c. (b) Use the verb bringen in the imperf. of the passive voice. This form is always required in German when the suffering of an action by the subject is to be expressed. In the preceding sentence the action is represented as completed; we must, therefore, use the auxiliary verb sein in order to express the 'state' of the subject; but in the present instance we represent the subject as suffering the action, and have therefore to employ the auxiliary verb werben.

B

5. Water in the act of freezing becomes electrical.

6. The Assyrians, like the Egyptians, appear to have had organized and disciplined troops.

7. When hair becomes very fine and crisp, it is termed wool.

8. The last years of John Locke's existence were spent at Oates in Essex.

9. The Berber language has no terms for expressing ab stract ideas, and is obliged to borrow them from the Arabic.

10. Green is a common colour in the vegetable kingdom; it is very rare in the mineral kingdom. ✔

---

[5] *In—freezing*, im Gefrieren. (a) When the entire genus of a material is to be expressed, we generally use the definite article. (b) When a sentence begins with the subject, the assertion, *i. e.* the verb containing a personal inflection, is, as a rule, placed immediately after the subject; construe, therefore, (the) *water becomes in, &c.*

[6] *Assyrians*, Affyrer; *like*, gleich, which adjective governs the dative; *to appear*, scheinen; *organized*, organisirt; *disciplined*, disciplinirt; *troops*, here Armeen.—In this sentence the subject stands first, and *appear* forms the assertion.

[7] *Fine*, fein; *crisp*, traus. Render *it is termed* by so nennt man es. For the rendering of the term *hair* compare Extr. 5 n. *a.*, and for the place of wird (becomes) cf. Extr. 12 n. *b.*—The conjunction so is here used in accordance with the rule that, when a sentence, expressing a condition, precedes a principal clause, the latter is generally introduced by the expletive so, and given in an inverted form.

[8] According to the rule mentioned in n. *b* to Extr. 4, we ought to use here the passive voice; but this form is generally changed into the active voice when the agent from whom the activity proceeds is, on account of its greater importance than the subject suffering the action, to be made more prominent. Turn, therefore, the above sentence by 'John Locke spent (brachte...zu) the last years of his existence (Lebens) at (zu) Oates, &c.'

[9] The Berber language (Berbersprache) is spoken in the mountainous districts of the north coast of Africa by the aborigines. *Arabic* (das Arabische) is spoken by the Arabs in the adjoining plains. When *term* is synonymous with 'word' or 'expression,' it must be rendered by Wort or Ausdruck; *to be obliged*, müssen: to borrow (*from*), entlehnen. (a) Render *for expressing* by um auszudrücken, because the *Supine*, *i. e.* the infinitive with the preposition zu before it, is required in German with verbs expressing a purpose, or forming the object of a clause. Frequently the preposition um, 'for,' is made to precede the *Supine*. (b) The verb entlehnen governs the dative of the indirect object—here *Arabic*—like many other inseparable compound verbs.

[10] *Vegetable Kingdom*, Pflanzenreich; *rare*, selten; *mineral kingdom*, Mineralreich. Adjectives denoting colour in general, are used in German as neuter substantives and require the definite article.

11. The prose of Dryden, says Sir Walter Scott, may reckon with the best in the English language.

12. In the reign of Elizabeth the town *of* Brighton was situated on that tract where the chain-pier now extends into the sea.

13. We command nature, according to the saying of a philosopher, by obeying her laws.

14. The swiftest and most agile quadrupeds, as well as the most graceful and beautiful, also those which are most useful to man, belong chiefly to the old continent.

15. Demosthenes felt such delight in the history of Thucydides, that to obtain a familiar and perfect mastery of his style, he copied his history eight times.

16. The inhabitants of the Marianne Islands pretended to be the only people in the world.

11 *May reckon with,* kann zu... gerechnet werden. (a) Turn *the prose of Dryden* by 'Dryden's prose,' in accordance with the rule that, when a proper name occurs in the genitive case, it is generally placed before the noun which it qualifies. (b) Cf. for *Sir,* p. 31, n. 7.

12 The preposition *in* referring to *reign* (Regierung) is rendered in German by unter. For the construction of *In—Elizabeth,* cf. n. a to preceding Extr.; *to be situated,* sich befinden; *on,* here auf; *tract,* Stelle. The *chain pier* here alluded to refers, of course, to the old Brighton pier, which, being a 'landing bridge projecting into the sea,' may be rendered by the abbreviated form Kettenbrücke (omitting the word Landungs between the two nouns); *extends into,* sich... hinaus erstreckt. (a) When a clause does *not* begin with the subject, the assertion must be placed before it; put therefore *was situated* before *the town.* (b) The verb erstreckt must here be placed at the end, the clause being a dependent one.

13 To *command,* here beherrschen; *according to,* nach; *saying,* here Ausspruch. Place *nature* with the def. art. after *philosopher,* and turn *by obeying* by 'whilst (indem) we obey.' Cf. Int. p. xv. II. *a.*

14 *Swift,* schnell; *agile,* behend; *quadruped,* Vierfüßler; *as well as,* sowie; *graceful,* here zierlich; *as also,* wie auch; *most useful,* am nützlichsten; *to belong,* angehören; *chiefly,* vorzüglich; *continent* = world.—*Man* denotes here human being; use therefore the noun Mensch, which corresponds to the Latin *homo* and the Greek ἄνθρωπος. Cf. the *note* to Extr. 2.

15 *Felt—in,* war von...so sehr entzückt; *to—style,* um dessen Stil vollständig in seine Gewalt zu bekommen; *eight times* is a reiterative numeral. (a) The genitive case is with *foreign proper names* ending in a sibilant, generally pointed out by means of the definite article. (b) The pronoun *he* in the above sentence should be placed after *that,* because, as a rule, *inversions do not take place in dependent sentences,* or with other words, the subject is placed immediately after the word, introducing the dependent clause; when the subject is to be made more emphatic, it takes the place of the principal object after one or more objects.

16 *Inhabitant,* Bewohner; or here

17. The flax *plant* is composed of three distinct parts : the wood, the fibres, and the gum resin, which causes the fibres to adhere.

18. No body is so black as to reflect no light at all, and to be perfectly invisible in a strong light.

19. A loaf was found in a baker's shop at Herculaneum still retaining its form, and with his name stamped upon it.

20. It is *well* known that if one in a troop of lions is killed, the others take the hint, and leave that part of the country. ✔

21. A great number of seeds are furnished with downy and feathery appendages, enabling them, when ripe, to float in the air, and to be wafted easily to great distances.

Ureinwohner. The *Marianne Islands*, Marianen or Ladronen, (from the Spanish 'ladrones,' *i.e. thieves;* hence also the German name, Diebes-inseln) are a group of islands in the N. Pacific Ocean. *To pretend,* behaupten, which verb must here be followed by the Supine. Render *people* by Menschen.

[17] *Flax plant,* Flachs; *to be composed of,* bestehen aus; *distinct,* verschieden; *fibre,* Faser; *gum resin,* Harz n. ; *to cause,* bewirken; *to adhere,* zusammenhalten. (*a*) For the rendering of *the wood, &c.,* see Int. p. xix., IV., and for the constr. of the *accusative with the infinitive* ('the fibres to adhere') see ib. p. xvii., III.

[18] *Body,* denoting 'matter as opposed to spirit,' Körper; *no . . . at all,* gar kein ; *perfectly,* vollständig. When an infinitive is preceded by *as* and refers to the demonstrative *so,* thus implying a condition, it must generally be changed in German into a regular sentence with a finite verb in the conditional mood. Render therefore, *as to reflect,* by als daß er . . . zurückwürfe, and *to be,* by daß er . . . wäre.

[19] *A loaf,* ein Laib Brod, or simply ein Brod; *Herculaneum,* Herculanum; *to retain,* beibehalten; *its form,* die form ; *to stamp,* stempeln. Arrange 'at Herculaneum was in the shop of a baker,' &c. For the rendering of *was found,* compare n. *b* to Ext. 4; and for *still retaining,* which qualifies the noun *loaf,* see Int. p. xvi., *b*; turn *with—it* by 'upon which (worauf) his name was stamped.'

[20] *Known,* bekannt; *in,* here aus ; *troop,* (of animals), usually Trupp; *take the hint,* here es sich zur Warnung dienen lassen; *to leave,* verlassen. The prep. *of* in *troop of lions* is not translated, because 'of' denoting in general the partitive relation, is not expressed in German after nouns denoting *number, weight,* or *measure.*

[21] *Number,* here Menge; *seeds,* Samen; *furnished,* versehen; *downy,* flockicht; *feathery,* gefiedert; *appendage,* Anhängsel; *to enable,* in den Stand setzen; *when ripe* = when they are ripe; *to float,* schweben; *to be wafted,* getragen werden; *to great,* say : in weite; *distance,* Entfernung. (*a*) The rule given in note 20 with reference to the omission of the prep. *of* in partitive relations, refers also to the word Menge. (*b*) Cf. for *enabling,* Int. p. xvi., *b*; and for *to float* and *to be wafted.* n. *a* to Ext. 9.

22. Among the Dyaks, aborigines of Borneo, no man is allowed to marry till he can show the skull of a man whom he has slain.

23. There is reason to suppose, from the quantity of light emitted by the brightest stars, that some of them are much larger than the sun.

24. In the marsh of Curragh, in the Isle *of* Man, vast trees are discovered standing firm on their roots, though at a depth of eighteen or twenty feet below the surface.

25. During the hundred and sixty years which preceded the union of the Roses nine kings reigned in England. Six of these nine kings were deposed. Five lost their lives as well as their crowns.

26. The modern system of music is one of the few

²² *Among*, referring to nations in a general sense, as is the case here, is rendered by the prep. bei. The *Dyaks* (Diaken) are a fierce people with very savage customs; *aborigines*, Eingeborne; *to be allowed*, dürfen; *to marry*, (to take for wife or husband) heirathen; *to show*, here vorzeigen; *skull*, Schädel. (a) Insert the dat. plur. of the def. art. before *aborigines*, and compare for the reason Int. p. xix., IV. (b) *Is allowed* cannot here be rendered by ist or wird erlaubt, because erlauben belongs to that class of verbs which govern besides a direct object in the accusative, an indirect object in the dative. Similar verbs are often construed with man or rendered impersonally, as *I am told*, man hat mir gesagt, or es ist mir gesagt worden.

²³ *Reason*, denoting 'ground or cause of opinion,' Grund; *to suppose*, here annehmen; *to emit*, ausstrahlen; *of them*, say: derselben. Construe 'from the quantity of light (nach der Lichtmasse zu urtheilen), which is emitted by (von) the brightest stars, one has reason to suppose that some, &c.' The relative pronoun cannot be omitted in German; insert therefore, 'which is' before *emitted*.

²⁴ *Marsh of Curragh*, Curraghmarsch; *in* with reference to *isle* or *island*, generally auf; *vast*, sehr groß, or mächtig; turn *are discovered* by 'one finds,' *on their* by 'with the,' and *though at a depth* by 'though they are (sich befinden) at a depth.' (a) The prep. *of* is not expressed in German when standing between the common names, Insel, Land, Stadt, Königreich, &c., and the respective proper names, as: *the Isle of Man*, die Insel Man. (b) Cf. for *standing*, Int. p. xvi., b, and for *feet* Extr. 32, n. d.

²⁵ *To precede*, vorangehen; *union*, Vereinigung; *to reign*, regieren; *to depose*, (kings, &c.) entthronen. (a) The verb vorangehen governs the dative case, like many other verbs compounded with the separable prefixes an, auf, bei, vor, &c. (b) For *were deposed*, cf. Extr. 4, n. b. (c) The expression Leben does not admit of the plural, when used in a general sense. Turn, therefore, *lost—crowns* by 'lost as well (sowohl) the life as (als) the crown.'

²⁶ Retain the terms *modern* and *system; science*, Wissenschaft; turn *if —called* by 'if one can so call it (viz. the system); *to owe*, verdanken; *improvement*, here Ausbildung; *the Middle Ages*, das Mittelalter. (a)

sciences, if so it may be called, which owe their improvement to the Middle Ages.

27. It seems impossible, says a' great botanist, in the present state of our knowledge to give a complete and perfect definition of what is to be considered an animal, in contradistinction to what is to be looked upon as a plant.

28. In the reign of William the First the penalty for killing a stag or a boar was loss of the eyes ; for William loved the great deer, says a Saxon Chronicle, as if he had been their father.

29. When a body is once in motion it requires no foreign power to sustain its velocity.

30. Etna appears to have been in activity from the earliest times of tradition, for Diodorus Siculus mentions an eruption which caused a district to be deserted by the Sicani before the Trojan war. ✓

31. The art of painting in oil was first discovered by

For *music* cf. the note to Extr. 1. (*b*) The *partitive genitive*, which signifies the whole of which anything is a part, as here in *of the few*, is generally rendered by von.

²⁷ *In*, here bei; *state*, Zuſtanb; *knowledge*, Wiſſenſchaft; *complete*, vollſtänbig; *perfect*, genau; *definition* Definition; *of what*, von bem was; *to be considered*, zu betrachten iſt; *in contradistinction*, im Gegenſatz; *to what*, zu bem was; *to be looked upon*, say : man...anſehen muß. Cf. on the English passive participial constructions, p. 45, n. 20.

²⁸ *Killing*, say bie Tödtung; which is to be followed by the genitive case ; turn *was loss* by ' consisted in the loss (Berluſt); *great deer*, Hochwilb, is to be used in the singular only, like all nouns denoting unlimited plurality ; *says*, transl. wie...bemerkt, *i.e.* observes ; *Saxon*, ſächſiſch; *their*, say beſſen. (*a*) For *in the reign*, see Ext. 12. (*b*) The title, *the First*, stands here in *apposition* to *William ;* cf. Int. p. xix.,IV. (*c*) The first clause does not

begin with the subject, see Ext. 12, n. *a*. (*d*) For the conj. *for* see p. 89, n. 8.

²⁹ For *body* see Ext. 18; *motion*, Bewegung; *to require*, bebürfen which governs the genitive case ; *power*, here Kraft; *to sustain*, aufrecht erhalten; *its*, say beſſen; *velocity*, Schnelligkeit. For the rendering of *it requires*, see note to Ext. 7, and for that of *to sustain*, n. *a* to Ext. 9.

³⁰ *Activity*, Thätigkeit; *from—tradition*, von ber früheſten Sagenzeit an. Turn the clause *which—war*, by ' which before the Trojan war, caused (veranlaßte) the Sicani (Sicanier) to desert a district (einen Lanbſtrich).' Diodorus Siculus was a Greek historian and a contemporary of Cæsar and Augustus. He wrote a large work entitled Βιβλιοθήκη Ἱστορική, *i.e.* Historical Library. — Use the definite article with *Etna*, in accordance with the rule that the names of mountains require the definite article

³¹ *First*, here zuerſt; *to discover* may here be rendered by erfinben

Van Eyck of Bruges, towards *the* end of the fourteenth century. It has now become almost the only manner in which paintings of magnitude are executed.

32. The Urceola Elastica is to be found in abundance in the islands of the Indian Archipelago, and can, without being injured, yield by tapping *from* fifty to sixty pounds *of* caoutchouc in one season.

33. In our island the Latin appears never to have superseded the old Gaelic speech, and could not stand its ground against the German.

34. Sir Robert Cotton, one day at his tailor's, discovered that the man was holding in his hand, ready to cut up for measures, an original Magna Charta, with all *its* appendages of seals and signatures; and an original Magna Charta is preserved in the Cottonian Library exhibiting marks of dilapidation.

Goethe sanctions, however, the use of entbecfen in similar instances by speaking of the Entbecfung ber Rupferftidje. *Bruges,* Brügge; *has—become,* say: ift jetzt; *manner,* Weife; *of magnitude,* say: von Bebeutung; *to execute,* ausführen. (*a*) Render *of painting,* by zu malen, because similar verbal forms in — *ing,* preceded by *of, instead of, for,* or *without,* are rendered in German by the *Supine.* (*b*) For *was* and *are* see n. *b* to Ext. 4.

[32] Retain the Latin term *Urceola Elastica* with the original feminine gender and use for *is to be found* the present of the passive voice; *in abundance,* in großer Menge; for *in* see Ext. 24; *the Indian Archipelagus,* ber inbifche Archipel (usually abbreviated from Archipelagus); *to be injured,* befchäbigt werben; *yield by tapping,* burch Einfchnitte...liefern; *caoutchouc,* Feberharz, or usually Rautfchuf; for *season* see p. 99, n. 11. (*a*) The expression *in abundance* is to be put after *Archipelago,* because *adverbial expressions of manner are placed after all other adverbial expressions.* (*b*) Construe the remaining clauses: 'can in

one season, without being injured, fifty to sixty pounds of caoutchouc yield by tapping.' (*c*) When *to* between two cardinal numerals denotes an amount approximately, it is rendered by bis. (*d*) Use *pounds* in the singular, because masculine or neuter nouns, being preceded by a numeral and employed as terms of weight, measure, or number remain unchanged.

[33] *The Latin,* bas Lateinifche; for the position of *appears,* cf., n. *a* to Ext. 12; *to supersede,* verbrängen; *the old Gaelic speech,* bas Altgälifche; supply es before *could; to stand its ground,* fich behaupten; *the German,* bas Deutfche.

[34] *One day,* eines Tages; *at his tailor's,* bei feinem Schneiber; *ready,* im Begriff; *to—measures,* als Maß zu zerfchneiben; *an—Charta,* say ein Driginal ber Magna Charta; *appendages,* Zubehör, (*sing.*); *seal,* Siegel; *signature,* Unterfchrift; *to preserve,* aufbewahren; *Cottonian,* Cottonifchen; *to exhibit,* here an fich tragen; *marks of dilapidation,* Spuren ber Verftümmelung. (*a*) Construe 'when Sir Robert Cotton was one day at his tailor's, he discovered, &c.,' and

35. Practice must settle the habit of doing without reflecting on the rule.

36. During the eruption *from the crater* of the Tombora *mountain*, in Sumbawa, the darkness occasioned by the ashes in the day-time was so profound, that nothing equal to it was ever witnessed in the darkest night of Java.

37. A piece *of* caoutchouc or india-rubber is very elastic, but not perfectly *so*, for it becomes permanently elongated by stretching. Glass, on the contrary, is perfectly elastic, for it will retain no permanent bend ; when drawn into a fine thread, it may be twisted round upon its axis many times without breaking, and when set free always returns to the point from which it set out. ✓

38. Dr. T. Fuller had such a wonderful memory that

place after *signatures* the words from *was* to *measures*. (*b*) Turn *his hand* by 'the hand' in accordance with the rule *that the definite article is usually employed in German*, (as is the case in Greek and French) *instead of the possessive pronoun when the context clearly shows who the possessing object is*. (*c*) Cf. for *is preserved*, Ext. 4, n. *a*, and for *exhibiting*, Int. p. xvi., *b*.

35 *Practice*, Uebung; *to settle*, here verleihen; *habit*, (i.e. aptitude,) Fertigkeit; *of doing*, say etwas zu vollbringen; *to reflect on*, nachdenken über; *rule* (the precept or maxim), Regel. (*a*) *Abstract nouns denoting actions require in German the definite article*. (*b*) Cf. for the term, *without reflecting* Ext. 31, n. *a*.

36 *Eruption*, Ausbruch; *darkness*, Finsterniß; *to occasion*, verursachen; *by*, durch; *in the day-time*, am Tage; *profound*, tief; *that—witnessed*, wie man nie was Aehnliches...wahrgenommen; *dark*, dunkel; *of*, here auf. (*a*) The above sentence does not begin with the subject, see Ext. 12, n. *a*. (*b*) Turn *occasioned by the ashes*, (which words qualify the term darkness) by 'the by the ashes occasioned,' and see Int. p. xiv., L

(*c*) Render *ashes* in accordance with the rule that *names* of material are, commonly, not used in the plural. (*d*) The above Extract refers to the eruption of the volcano of Tombora in 1815, when the ashes were wafted from the isle of Sumbawa to that of Java.

37 *India-rubber*, Gummi Elasticum; *perfectly*, vollkommen; *for*, here denn; *permanently*, bleibend; *by stretching*, durch Ausziehen; *on the contrary*, here hingegen; *to retain*, beibehalten; *bend*, Biegung; *when drawn into*, wenn man es zu...ausdehnt; *fine*, here, dünn; *thread*, Faden; *be—upon*, um...gedreht werden; *many times*, vielmals; *to break*, zerbrechen, *when set free*, wenn es losgelassen wird; *returns*, say schnellt es...zurück; *point*, Punkt; *set out*, ausging. (*a*) For *glass*, cf. Ext. 5, n. *a*. (*b*) Turn *it will retain* by 'it retains.' (*c*) For *when* see p. 41, n. 9. (*d*) When *may* is a synonym of *to be able*, it is rendered by können.

38 *Such a wonderful*, ein so außerordentliches; render *could* by im Stande war; *unconnected*, unzusammenhängend; turn *after—them* by 'after he had heard them twice;' *to recite*, here hersagen; *the—signs*.

ne could repeat five hundred unconnected words after twice hearing them, and recite the whole of the signs in the principal thoroughfares of London after once passing through and back again.

39. It was the just boast of Schiller that in his country no Augustus, no Lorenzo, had watched over the infancy of poetry. The rich and energetic language of Luther, driven by the Latin from the schools of pedants, and by the French from the palaces of kings, had taken refuge among the people.*

40. The Philippine Islands were discovered by Magellan in the first voyage *that was made* round the world. They were first called the Archipelago of St. Lazarus: this was in the year 1520. In the year 1565 a Spanish

sämmtliche Schilder; *principal thoroughfares,* Hauptstraßen; *after — again,* nachdem er durch dieselben hin- und zurückgegangen war. If the activity expressed by a verb is represented as something which *can* or *should* be done, we use in German the supine. It is, therefore, required after im Stande sein, and should be used here with the verb *repeat* and *recite.* Dr. T. Fuller, the historian, lived from the year 1608 to 1661.

39 *It—Schiller,* Schiller war mit Recht stolz darauf; *to watch over,* bewachen; *poetry,* Poesie; *energetic,* kraftvoll; *driven,* verdrängt; *by,* durch; *pedant,* Pedant; *the French,* das Französische; *taken refuge,* ihre Zuflucht genommen; *among,* here zu; *people,* Volk. When the word *country* refers to a man's land of nativity, we generally use in German the expressive term Vaterland. The same is done in almost all Teutonic languages. Thus the Swedes speak of their Fäderneland, the Danes of

their Fædreland, &c.; Greek and Latin scholars will find analogous terms in πατρις, *patria,* from which the Romance expressions *patria, patrie, &c.,* currently used in Italy and France, are derived.

40 *The Philippine Islands,* die Philippinen; *in,* here auf; *round,* used as a preposition, um; *colony,* Colonie; *to found,* gründen; *there,* daselbst; *command,* Anführung; *to name,* here benennen. (a) For *were discovered, were...called, was founded* and *were named,* cf. Ext. 4, note b. (b) Use the genitive of the def. article before *Legaspi,* because with *foreign proper names,* even if not ending in a sibilant, the case is sometimes pointed out by means of the def. article. (c) The prep. *of* is generally rendered by von, when the name of a place, but more especially of a country, follows the noun by which it is governed. as in the present instance: *Philip II. of Spain.*

* The above extract, from Macaulay's Essay on Frederick the Great, refers to Schiller's poem, " Die deutsche Muse," the first verses of which run—

'Kein Augustisch Alter blühte,
Keines Mediçäers Güte
Lächelte der deutschen Kunst,' &c.

colony was founded there under the command of Legaspi, and the islands were named after Philip II. of Spain.

41. A bitter plant with wavy sea-green leaves has been taken from the sea-side, where it grew like wild charlock; it was transplanted into the garden, lost its saltness, and has become metamorphosed into two distinct vegetables, as unlike to each other as is each to the parent-plant—into the red-cabbage and the cauliflower.

42. Camoens, the celebrated poet of the Lusiads, was wrecked at the mouth of the *river* Mekon, and with difficulty reached the shore, swimming with one hand and bearing his poem above the water in the other, the only treasure which he had saved, and which was dearer to him than his life. ✓

43. Sir Humphry Davy relates, that a friend of his, having discovered under the burning sand of Ceylon the eggs of an alligator, had the curiosity to break one of

---

[41] *Wavy*, (in botany) wellenförmig; *sea-green* seegrün; *sea-side*, Meeres-küste; *like*, wie; *charlock* is the general English name for Ackersenf or wilber Senf; *to be transplanted*, verpflanzt werden; *saltness*, Salzge-schmack; for *distinct* see Ext. 17; *vegetables*, here Gemüsearten; supply 'which are.' before *as unlike* (so unähnlich); *as is each*, say: wie jebe berselben. (a) Use for *has been taken* the passive imperf. of nehmen. (b) Render *has become metamorphosed* by the imperf. of sich ver-wandeln; the reflective form being, in German, preferred to the passive voice, when the agent from whom the activity proceeds is not mentioned. The plant alluded to in the above extract is the wild cabbage or *Brassica oleracea*.

[42] *Celebrated*, berühmt; *Lusiads*, Lusiaben, *pl.*; *to be wrecked*, Schiffbruch leiben; *mouth*, (of a river) Mündung; *Mekon* is a river in Cochin China; *with difficulty*, mit Mühe; *to reach*, erreichen; *shore*, Ufer; *with one*, say: mit ber einen; *to bear*, here empor-halten; *poem*, Gebicht; *treasure*,

Schatz; to save i.e., 'to rescue,' retten; *dear*, theuer. (a) Place *reached* before *with difficulty*. (b) For *swim-ming* and *bearing*, cf. Int. p. xvii., *g*, and construe *swimming — other*: 'with the one hand swimming and in the other his poem,' after which clauses place the words *above the water* and *bearing*. (b) Camoens, the greatest Portuguese poet, was born in 1524. His great epic poem, *Os Lusiadas*, (i.e. 'the Lusitanians,' as the Portuguese are called) des-cribes Vasco di Gama's expedition to India, and the brilliant exploits of his countrymen.

[43] *To relate*, erzählen; turn *that—under*, by 'that one of his friends who had discovered in;' *burning*, here glühenb; retain the word *alli-gator*; turn *had—them* by 'from (aus) curiosity one of the same broke (zerbrach);' *came forth*, heraus-kroch; *perfect*, say: vollständig...ausge-bilbet; *passions*, here Triebe; *hatched*, ausgehectt; *influence*, Einwirkung; *sun-beams*, Sonnenstrahlen; *it made towards the*, eilte er bem...zu; *proper*, eigentlich; *element*, Element; *when*

them, when a young alligator came forth perfect in its motions and its passions; for although hatched in the sand under the influence of the sunbeams, it made towards the water, its proper element : *when* hindered, it assumed a threatening aspect, and bit the stick presented to it.

44. Several of the British forests which are now marshes, were cut down at different periods by order of the English Parliament, because they harboured wolves and outlaws. Thus the Welsh woods were cut and burnt in the reign of Edward I., as were many of those in Ireland by Henry II., to prevent the natives from harbouring in them and harassing his troops.

45. A grain *of* musk is said to be divisible into three hundred and twenty quadrillions *of* parts, each of which is capable of affecting the olfactory nerve.

46. Our knowledge of the origin and affinities of European languages has been, within the last forty or fifty years, greatly increased and improved by the labours of German scholars.

hindered, aufgehalten; *to assume,* annehmen; *aspect,* Aussehen; supply 'in' after *bit* and render *presented to it,* by ben man ihm vorhielt.

44 *Several,* mehrere ; *to cut (down) a forest* or *wood,* einen Wald umhauen; *period,* here Zeit ; *by order,* auf Befehl; *to harbour* used transitively, denoting 'to give shelter,' is rendered by Zuflucht gewähren ; when employed intransitively, denoting 'to seek shelter' it is translated by Zuflucht suchen ; *Welsh,* wallisisch ; *Welsh woods* may also be turned by 'woods in Wales;' *to burn,* nieberbrennen ; turn *as—those* by 'as also many ;' *to prevent,* verhinbern ; *natives,* Eingeborne ; *to harass,* here belästigen. (*a*) For *in the reign* see Ext. 12. (*b*) The verb verhinbern would here require the prep. an; cf. p. 97, n. 2.

45 *Grain* (weight), Gran ; *each of which,* von benen jeber ; *to be capable,* können ; *to affect,* here afficiren, from

the Latin *afficere ; olfactory nerve,* Geruchsnerv (e). (*a*) When the phrases *it is said, they say,* are used to report the assertion of others—like the Latin *dicitur*—they must be rendered by the requisite tense of sollen. (*b*) *Of affecting* ought according to the rules given before to be rendered by the *Supine ;* the infinitive without zu is, however, always required in German after the auxiliary verbs of mood können, mögen, bürfen, wollen, sollen, müssen, and also after a few other verbs, as sehen, hören, finben, &c. Cp. the English usage of omitting the prep. 'to' before infinitives after those verbs.

46 *Knowledge,* Kenntniß ; *Origin,* Ursprung ; *affinities,* Verwantschaft, *sing.* ; transl. here *within* by in, or by bis, *greatly* by bebeutenb, *increased* by bereichert and *improved* by erweitert ; *labour,* Arbeit ; *scholar.* Gelehrte. When *by* is a synonym of 'through,' denoting the means

47. At the battle of Solway, in the time of Henry VIII., 1542, when the Scotch army, commanded by Oliver Sinclair, was routed, an unfortunate troop of horse·driven by *their* fears, plunged into a morass, which instantly closed upon them. The tale was traditional, but *it* is now authenticated; a man and a horse in complete armour having been found by peat diggers in the place where it was always supposed the affair had happened. The skeleton of each was well preserved, and the different parts of the armour easily distinguished.

48. The works of Milton cannot be comprehended or enjoyed unless the mind of the reader co-operate with that of the writer.

49. The town of Guatemala was founded in 1742 on the side of a volcano, in a valley about three miles wide, opening on the South Sea. Nine years afterwards it was destroyed by an earthquake, and again in 1773, during an eruption of the volcano. The ground on which the town stood gaped open in deep fissures, until at length,

by which an effect is produced, it is generally rendered by burd).

47 *At*, in; *the battle of Solway* is called in German die Schlacht bei Solway Moß; *in the*, zur; *to command*, befehligen; *by*, von; *to be routed*, zersprengt werden; *a troop of horse*, ein Trupp Reiter; *to plunge*, stürzen; *instantly*, here sofort; *to close upon*, sich schließen über. *The tale was traditional*, say: das Ereigniß war als Sage bekannt; *to be authenticated*, als authentisch erwiesen; *armour*, Rüstung; *peat digger*, Torfgräber; *it was always supposed*, wo, wie man stets annahm; *to happen*, sich zutragen. *The skeleton of each*, say die beiden Skelette; *to preserve*, here erhalten; *distinguished*, transl. zu erkennen. (a) Begin the German version with als (*when*). (b) The words *commanded by Oliver Sinclair*, qualify the expression *Scotch army*, cf. Int. p. xiv., I. (c) The word *fear* being an abstract noun which denotes a 'state' is used in German in the singular only. (d) Turn *a man, &c.*, by 'since a man and (sammt) a horse, &c. was found.' (e) The verb *had* may be left out in the translation, the omission of *the auxiliary verbs of tense* haben and sein, being sanctioned in dependent sentences, especially when occurring in compound tenses.

48 *Work*, (literary composition) Werk; *to comprehend*, verstehen; *to enjoy*, genießen; *unless*, wenn…nicht; *mind*, here Geist; *writer*, here Verfasser; *to co-operate*, zusammenwirken. Cf. for the—*Milton*, Ext. 11, n. *a*, and for *be*, Ext. 4, n. *b*.

49 *Side*, (of a hill, &c.) Abhang; *about*, ungefähr; *wide*, here breit; *opening on*, das…gegenüber lag; *to be destroyed* zerstört werden; *again*, here abermals; *ground*, Boden; *to gape open*, aufklaffen; *fissure*, Spalte; *to open*, here sich öffnen, comp. the French 's'ouvrir;' *with all its treasures*, sammt all ihren Schätzen:

after five days, an abyss opened, and the city with all its riches and eight thousand families was swallowed up. Every vestige of its former existence was entirely obliterated, and the spot is now indicated by a frightful desert four leagues distant from the present town.

50. In modern times little may be thought of the gratifications arising from motion. Yet we read that the greatest of the Greeks and even of the Romans, studied elegance in their attitudes and movements. Their apparel favoured that display of grace, while their exercises and games contributed to encourage elegance of movement. The dances they performed were not exhibitions of mere exuberance of spirit and activity. It was their pride to combine harmony in the motion of the body and limbs with majesty of gait.

to be swallowed up, verschlungen werden; *vestige,* Spur; *to be obliterated,* vertilgt werden; *spot,* Stelle; *indicated by,* bezeichnet durch; *desert,* Wüste; *leagues,* Meilen; *distant,* entfernt. (a) For *was founded,* cf. Ext. 4., n. *b.* (b) If the prep. *in* before the date of a year is expressed in German, the words 'the year' must be supplied after it. (b) The words *three miles wide* qualify the term *valley,* cf. Int. p. xiv. I.

50 *Modern,* say neuer; *little—of,* mag man...gering achten; *gratifications,* Genuß, *sing.* ; *to arise from,* entstehen aus; *of the Greeks,* unter den Griechen; *Roman,* Römer; *to study,* here sich befleißigen; *which*

verb requires the genitive; *elegance,* Anmuth; *attitude,* Stellung; *movement,* Bewegung; *apparel,* Kleidung; *display of grace,* Entfaltung von Grazie; *exercises,* here Leibesübungen; *contributed,* say dazu beitrugen; *to encourage,* here befördern; *to perform,* (a dance, &c.) aufführen; *exhibitions—activity,* Kundgebungen von bloßem Uebergefühl des Daseins und der Thatkraft; *it—pride,* sie waren stolz darauf; *harmony,* die Harmonie; *limb,* Glied; *majesty,* Majestät; *gait,* Gang. (a) When the word *times* is employed in a general sense to express a historical period, it is used in German in the singular only. (b) Cf. for *motion,* Ext. 35. n. a.

PART II.

I.

THE DEFENCE OF A FORD.

1.

The good king, Robert Bruce, who was always watchful and vigilant,[1] had received *some* information of the intention of this party to come upon him suddenly and by night. Accordingly he quartered[2] his little troop of sixty men on the side of a deep and swift-running river that had very steep and rocky banks. There was but one ford by which this river could be crossed in that neighbourhood,[3] and that ford was deep and narrow, so that two men could scarcely get through abreast. The path which led upwards from the water's edge[4] to the *top of* the bank was extremely narrow and difficult.

2.

X Bruce caused[5] his men to lie down to take some sleep

---

[1] *Vigilant*, vorſichtig; *information*, Kunde; *intention*, Vorhaben; *party*, Partei; *to come upon*, here überfallen; *by night*, zur Nachtzeit, or in ter Nacht. The party alluded to were a number of Galloway men, who set out to attack Bruce by surprise, taking with them some bloodhounds in order to track his steps.

[2] *To quarter*, in the sense of 'to station,' ſtationiren. Cf. for *men*, Ext. 32, n. *d;* render *on the side of* simply by the prep. bei; *swift-running*, reißend; turn *that had*, &c. by 'whose banks (Uſer) were, &c.'

[3] Turn *there — neighbourhood* briefly by 'the river had only one ford in that neighbourhood' (Gegend). *Narrow*, ſchmal.

[4] *Edge*, (border) Rand; *difficult*, here ſchwierig. Turn *water's edge* by 'edge of the water,' because the genitive ought in common prose not to precede the word which it qualifies; cf. Ext. 11 n. *a*.

[5] *To cause*, synonymous with 'to order,' 'to make,' &c. is rendered by laſſen; *men*, here and further on Leute; *to lie down*, ſich niederlegen; turn *to—sleep* by 'to sleep a little;' and *distant*, by 'which (to be placed before *about*) distant was;' *attendant*, Begleiter; *to pass*, (through a ford) gehen. Render *they* by er, because the word *enemy*, used as a military term, generally occurs in German in the singular only.

at a place about half a mile distant from the river, while he himself, with two attendants, went down to watch the ford, through which the enemy must ~~needs~~ pass before they could come to the place where King Robert's men were lying. He stood *for* some time looking[1] at the ford, and thinking how easily the enemy might be kept from passing there, ~~provided~~ it was bravely defended, when he heard at a distance the ~~baying of~~ a hound, which was always coming nearer and nearer. This was the ~~blood-~~ hound[2] which was tracing the king's steps to the ford, and the two hundred Galloway men were along with the animal, and guided by it. Bruce at first thought[3] of going back to awaken his men; but then he reflected that it might be only some shepherd's dog.

3.

So[4] he stood and listened; and by and by, as the cry of the hound came nearer, he began to hear a trampling of horses and the voices of men and the ringing and clattering of armour, and then he was sure the enemy were coming to the river side. Then the king thought, "If I go back

[1] *Looking at,* ſich beſehend; *think-ing,* here bei ſich denkend; *might be kept,* davon abgehalten werden könnte; turn *from passing there* by 'to go through the same,' and *provided* by 'if,' to be followed by the expletive nur; *to defend,* (a place) vertheidigen; *when,* als; *at a distance,* in der Ferne; *the baying,* das Bellen, because the English verbal forms in *ing* used substantively, are generally rendered in German by the simple infinitive used as a neuter noun.

[2] The German expression for *bloodhound* is: Schweißhund, because the blood of wounded animals is called with sportsmen Schweiß. *To trace steps,* die Spuren verfolgen; Render the expression *Galloway men, men of Galloway* by die Männer von Galloway. *Along with,* here bei; turn *guided by it,* by 'were guided (geführt) by the same.'

[3] When *to think* expresses intention or purpose, it is rendered by gedenken, and followed by the *Supine.* *To reflect,* sich überlegen; render here *might* by dürfte, because it expresses a supposed possibility; *shepherd's-dog* Schäferhund.

[4] Render *so* by alſo, and supply da after *stood; to listen,* (hearken) horchen; *by and by as,* say bald darauf wie. Use for *the cry,* das Gebell, which is the frequentative substantive of bellen, and form in the same manner frequentative nouns from trampeln, for *trampling,* from klirren for *ringing* and from raſſeln for *clattering.* Render here *men* by Menſchen; *then—sure,* by dann ward es ihm zur Gewißheit, and supply daß before *the enemy were* (see p. 14, n. 5); *river side,* Ufer.

to give my men the alarm,[1] these Galloway men will get through the ford without opposition ; and that would be a pity since it is a place so advantageous to make defence against them." He therefore sent his followers[2] to waken his men, and remained alone by the bank of the river.

4.

In the meanwhile[3] the noise and trampling of the horses increased, and the moon being bright, Bruce beheld the glancing arms of about two hundred men, who came down to the opposite bank of the river. The men of Galloway, on their part,[4] saw but one solitary figure guarding the ford, and the foremost *of them* plunged into the river without minding him. But as they could only pass the ford one by one,[5] *the* Bruce, who stood high above them on the bank where they were to land, killed the foremost *man* with a thrust of his long spear, and with a second thrust stabbed the horse. In the confusion five or six of the enemy were slain, or, having been borne down the current,[6] were drowned. The rest were terrified and drew back. But when the Galloway men looked[7] again and saw that they were opposed by only one man, they themselves being so many, they cried out that their honour would be lost for ever if they

---

[1] *To—alarm,* um meine Leute zu den Waffen zu rufen. Cf. for the next clause the *note* to Ext. 7. *To get,* here kommen; *without opposition,* ungehindert ; *that—pity,* bas wäre Schabe. Render *it* by dieselbe, cf. for *so advantageous* (günstig) which qualifies *place,* Int. p. xiv., I. and transl. *to—them* briefly by zur Vertheibigung.

[2] *Followers,* Begleiter ; *to waken,* wecken ; use the supine ; *by the,* am.

[3] *In the meanwhile,* unterdessen; *to increase,* zunehmen; for *being,* cf. Int. p. xvi., *c ; to behold,* erblicken; for *men,* cf. Ext. 32, *note d* ; *opposite* here jenseitige.

[4] *On their part,* ihrerseits ; *but,* here nur ; *solitary figure,* einzelne Gestalt ; *to guard,* bewachen; see Int. p. xviii. ; *the foremost,* Vorderste ; *to mind,* (any one) sich um (Jemand) kümmern ; see *note a* to Ext. 31.

[5] *One by one,* je einer; *to land,* here ans Land steigen ; *to stab,* erstechen.

[6] Place *having — current,* von der Strömung fortgerissen after *were drowned,* which latter verb is here used intransitively.

[7] *Looked,* say : hinblicken; turn *they—man* by 'that only one man stood opposite (gegenüber) to them ;' *they themselves being,* während ihrer... waren *for ever,* auf immer; *did—way,*

did not force their way, and encouraged each other, with loud cries, to plunge through and assault him. But by this time[1] the king's soldiers came up to his assistance, and the Galloway men retreated and gave up their enter-prise.—WALTER SCOTT, *Tales of a Grandfather.*

II.

SCHILLER'S FLIGHT FROM STUTTGART.[2]

Schiller's embarrassments[3] became more pressing[4] than ever.[5] With the natural feeling of a young author,[6] he[7] had ventured to go in secret[8] and witness the first representation[9] of his tragedy at Mannheim. His incognito

say : nicht ben Uebergang erzwängen : cries, Geschrei, sing. ; to plunge through, burchzuwaten.

[1] Avoid the Anglicism bei tiefer Zeit for *by this time* which should be rendered by jetzt or nun ; or here by the more emphatic schon ; came—assistance, famen...bemselben zur Hülfe herbei.

[2] For the benefit of those who are not acquainted with the life of Schill , we will briefly add that, after having been educated at the Military Academy at Stuttgart, later called „Die Karlsschule," after the founder, Duke Karl of Würtemberg, he became military surgeon, and continued to be kept under strict military discipline. Having been refused permission to visit Mannheim in order to witness the performance of his first drama, Die Räuber. he did so clandestinely, and was put under arrest for a fortnight, and forbidden to write in future on anything except on medicine. He then threw up his post and freed himself by flight.

[3] *Embarrassment*, Verlegenheit.

[4] *Pressing*, bringenb.

[5] When the adverb *ever* signifies 'at any time' past or future, it is rendered by jemals, or the more expressive je. Compare the French *jamais* and the Latin *unquam.*

[6] *Author*, Autor or Schriftsteller.

[7] When the object of a sentence is a supine or a whole clause, and the leading verb in the principal sentence governs the accusative case, we generally add—to that principal sentence—the accusative of the pronoun es, in order to supply the direct object ; more particularly when the emphasis is laid on the governing verb : *e.g.* Wer wagt es, Rittersmann oter Knapp, zu tauchen in biefen Schlund ? *Who ventures, knight, or squire, to dive into this gulf ?* *

[8] *To — secret*, sich heimlich aufzumachen; *to witness*, i.e. to see by personal presence, beiwohnen.

[9] *Representation*, here Aufführung.

---

* According to our opinion, the pronoun es, in the above application might properly be called the *grammatical object.*

C

did not conceal him ; he was put under arrest during a week[1] for this offence ; and as the punishment did not deter him from again transgressing[2] *in a similar manner,* he learned[3] that it was in contemplation to try more rigorous measures with him.   Dark hints[4] were given to him of some exemplary[5] as well as imminent severity ; and Dalberg's aid, the sole hope of averting[6] it by quiet means, was distant and dubious.   Schiller saw himself reduced to extremities.[7] Beleaguered[8] with present distresses and the most horrible forebodings on every side, roused to the highest pitch of indignation,[9] yet forced to keep silence[10] and wear the face of patience, he could endure this maddening[11] constraint no longer.

He resolved to be free, at whatever risk ;[12] to abandon advantages which he could not buy at such a price ; to quit his stepdame[13] home, and go forth, though friendless and alone, to seek his fortune in the great market of life.[14] Some[15] foreign duke or prince was arriving at Stuttgart ; and all *the people* were in movement, occupied with seeing the spectacle of his entrance : Schiller seized this opportunity of retiring from[16] the city, careless whither he went, so[17] he got beyond the reach of turnkeys and

---

[1] *He—week,* ihm wurde. . .eine Woche Arreſt auferlegt ; *offence,* Vergehen.

[2] **When** *to transgress,* is used transitively, it must be rendered by ſich eines Vergehens ſchuldig machen. Use here deſſelben instead of eines.

[3] *To learn,* here erfahren. Transl. *it was in contemplation* by man be= abſichtigte.

[4] *Hint,* here Anreutung ; *given* = made.

[5] *Of some exemplary,* von einer exemplariſchen ; *imminent,* nahe be= vorſtehend.

[6] *To avert,* abwenten ; use Supine.

[7] *Reduced to extremities,* aufs Aeußerſte getrieben.

[8] The expression *beleaguered* must here be rendered freely, since we cannot say in German that a man is von Ahnungen belagert or umgeben. The term heimgeſucht, 'afflicted,' would here be a suitable expres-

sion. *Distresses,* Nöthen ; *on,* von.

[9] *Roused—indignation,* bis auf den höchſten Grad entrüſtet.

[10] *To keep silence,* ſtill zu ſchweigen ; *face,* here Maßte.

[11] *Maddening,* transl. ihn bis zur Raſerei treibenten.

[12] *At—risk,* auf jete Gefahr hin *abandon* = give up.

[13] *Stepdame,* ſtiefmütterlich ; *to go forth,* fortzuwantern ; *to seek,* here verſuchen.

[14] We use in German the meta= phor ter Jahrmarkt des Lebens.

[15] *Some,* irgenb ein ; *occupied with seeing,* nur barauf bebacht . . . mit an= zuſehen ; *entrance,* Einzug.

[16] *Of—from,* aus . . . zu flüchten ; *careless,* unbekümmert.

[17] *So,* used in the sense of 'pro= vided that,' is rendered by wofern ; wenn nur ; *got—reach,* aus tem Bereich …käme.

grand-dukes and commanding officers.   It was in the month *of* October, 1782. * * *

Schiller was[1] in his twenty-third year when he left Stuttgart.   He says he " went empty away[2]—empty in purse and hope."   The future was,[3] indeed, sufficiently dark before him. * * * Yet his situation, though gloomy enough, was not entirely without its brighter side.[4]   He was now a free man—free, however poor.—CARLYLE, *Life of Schiller.*

III.

SILHOUETTES.

Etienne de Silhouette was Minister of State in France in[5] 1759.   The treasury[6] was in an exhausted condition, and Silhouette endeavoured to save the country by ex-cessive economy.   At first the Parisians pretended[7] to take his advice, merely to laugh at him :[8] they cut their coats shorter, and wore them without sleeves ; they turned[9] their gold snuff-boxes into rough wooden ones ;[10] and the new-fashioned portraits were now only profiles[11] traced by a black pencil round the shadow of a profile cast by candle on white paper.[12]   These portraits retained[13] since those times the name *of* Silhouette.

---

[1] *Was* = *stood.*

[2] *Away,* hinweg; *in,* an.   These are Schiller's own words.

[3] *Was,* say . fag.

[4] *Its brighter side,* Lichtseite.

[5] Cf. Ext. 49, n. *b*; Ext. 4, n. *a.*

[6] *Treasury,* Schatzkammer ; *was,* befand sich; *condition,* Zustand; *by,* durch ; *economy,* Sparsamkeit .

[7] *To pretend,* sich stellen; *to take* = as if they....followed.

[8] *To—him,* um sich über ihn lustig zu machen.

[9] *To turn into,* vertauschen mit.

[10] When *one* is used after adjec-tives, as a substitute for a noun previously mentioned, or merely understood, it is suppressed in German.   *Rough,* roh.

[11] *Were—profiles,* bestanden nun bloß aus Profilen.

[12] *Traced—paper.*   The above sentence must be given in German in a thoroughly different form, viz. 'which with a pencil round the through a candle on white paper cast shadow of a profile were traced' (gezeichnet). For *round,* cf. Ext. 40; *on,* auf governs here the accusative.

[13] *To retain,* beibehalten; for *times,* cf. Ext. 50, n. *a.*

IV.

PERHAPS IT WAS HIS UNCLE.

We were towing[1] through high reeds this morning, the men invisible, and the rope mowing over the high tops of the grass,[2] when the noise disturbed a hippopotamus from his slumber, and he was immediately perceived close to the boat. He was about half-grown,[3] and in an instant about twenty men[4] jumped into the water in search of him, thinking him a mere baby;[5] but as he suddenly appeared, and was about three times as large as they had expected, they were not very eager to close. However, the reis[6] Diabb pluckily led the way,[7] and seized him by the hind leg, when[8] the crowd of men rushed in, and we had a grand tussle. Ropes were thrown from the vessel, and nooses *were* quickly slipped over his[9] head; but he had the best of the struggle,[10] and was dragging the people into the open river. I was therefore obliged to end[11] the sport by putting[12] a ball through his head. He was scored all over[13] by the tusks of some other hippopotamus that had been bullying[14] him. The men declared that his father had thus misused[15] him; others were of opinion that it was his mother; and the argument ran high, and

[1] *To tow,* bugfiren; *reeds,* Schilf, *sing.; mowing,* say: fuhr ... dahin.

[2] *Tops—grass,* Grasſpitzen.

[3] *Half-grown,* halb ausgewachſen.

[4] *About...men,* an...Mann; *in—him*=in order to seek it.

[5] *Thinking — baby,* da ſie es für ein bloßes Kind hielten; *appeared,* say: auftauchte; *eager to close,* begierig es anzugreifen.

[6] *Reis* means in Turkish the captain of a merchantman.

[7] *Pluckily—way,* ging muthig voran.

[8] *When—in,* worauf die Männer nachſtürzten.

[9] *Slipped over his,* ihm ... über den ... gezogen.

[10] *To have the best of a struggle,* die Oberhand bekommen.

[11] *To end,* here ein Ende machen; *sport,* Jagd.

[12] *By putting,* indem ich... jagte; *ball,* Kugel; *his*=the.

[13] *Was—over,* war über und über wie gekerbt; *tusk,* Hauzahn.

[14] There is no single equivalent in German for the comprehensive term *to bully.* The expressions given in the Dictionaries are mostly quite inappropriate. We should suggest here the idiomatic phrase daß ihm übel mitgeſpielt hatte.

[15] *To misuse,* mißhanteln; *to be of opinion,* der Meinung ſein.

became hot.[1] These Arabs have an extraordinary taste[2] for arguments upon the most trifling points. I have frequently known my men argue[3] throughout the greater part of the night, and recommence the same argument on the following morning. These debates generally end in a fight; and in the present instance the excitement of the hunt only added to[4] the heat of the argument.

They at length agreed to[5] refer it to me,[5] and both parties approached, vociferously advancing their theories;[6] one half persisting[7] that the young hippo had been bullied by his father, and the others adhering to the mother as the cause.[8] I being[9] referee, suggested[9] that "perhaps it was his uncle." "Wah Illahi sahé!" (By Allah, it is true!) Both parties were satisfied with the suggestion.[10] Dropping their theory, they became practical, and fell to[11] with knives and axes to cut up the cause of the argument.—Sir S. W. Baker, *The Albert N'Yanza.*

V.

A ROMAN STRATAGEM.[12]

The place near the Mulucha was a rocky eminence in the midst of a plain. On the summit[13] there was just room enough for a small town. The sides[14] of this hill-

[1] Turn *the—hot* by 'the dispute (Streit) became loud and violent.

[2] *Taste*, here Vorliebe; *argument*, Discuffion; *trifling*, geringfügig.

[3] *I—argue*, ich habe es oft erlebt, daß meine Leute...disputirten; *debates*, Debatten; *instance*, Fall.

[4] *Only—to*, erhöhete...nur noch.

[5] *To—me*, mich zu befragen.

[6] *Advancing their theories*, indem sie ihre Meinungen...vorbrachten.

[7] Render *one half persisting*, by die Einen bestanden darauf?

[8] *And—cause.* More briefly, in German, während Andere die Mutter als die Ursache angaben.

[9] *Being*, say als; *suggested*, meinte.

[10] *Suggestion*, Ansicht; *dropping*, indem sie...aufgaben.

[11] *Fell to*, machten sich daran; *to cut up*, zu zerlegen.

[12] The above is an episode from the famous Jugurthine war, at the time when Marius was in command of the Roman army in Africa. The learned author from whose work the extract is taken conjectures that the siege of the fort *near the Mulucha*, (unweit der Mulucha) took place in 106 B.C.

[13] *Summit*, Gipfel; *just*, gerade.

[14] *Sides*, here Abhänge.

fort[1] were steep and very high, and there was only one
narrow approach to the town, for all the rest[2] of the
mountain was as precipitous as if it had been made so
by the hand of man.[3] This place contained Jugurtha's
money,[4] and Marius was very eager to get possession of it.
But this was not an easy undertaking. The place had
sufficient men[5] to defend it, a good supply of provisions[6]
and a spring of water.[6] It could not be attacked in the
usual way, by raising earth-banks and towers,[7] and employing[8] other military contrivances. The[9] single road by
which the place was reached[9] was not only very narrow,
but steep on both sides, either naturally so,[10] or[11] the
ground had been cut away. * * *

Many days · passed, and nothing was done, when a
lucky accident[12] helped Marius out of his difficulty. A
Ligurian,[13] who belonged to the auxiliary cohorts,[14] and

---

[1] *Hill-fort*, Bergfeſte; *there—approach*, nur ein ſchmaler Weg führte.

[2] *The rest*, der übrige Theil.

[3] Translate *hand of man*, by the
compound word Menſchenhand. The
student of German will soon discover that that language possesses
greater facilities in compounding
words forming one notion into a
single term than any other modern
language. Great vigour and poetic
colouring is thus imparted to words
which, when merely linked together by means of adverbs and
prepositions, produce no particular
effect; and as an additional advantage afforded by these compounds, may be mentioned the
possibility of avoiding the frequent
repetition of the genitive relation,
a drawback from which even the
Latin is not free. Nobody should,
however, coin new compound terms
without having mastered the language. Special rules and hints for
forming compound substantives
will be given in the course of the
present work.

[4] *Money*, say: Schatz; *eager*,
begierig; *to—it*, ſich deſſen zu bemächtigen; *not an*, kein.

[5] *Sufficient men*, hinlängliche
Mannſchaft. [6]*A—provisions*, Vorräthe
genug; *spring of water*, Brunnen.

[7] *By—towers*, durch die Errichtung von Dämmen und Thürmen.
The military expressions are Ver-
theidigungsdämme and Wandelthürme,
i.e. 'walking towers.'

[8] *Employing*, transl. durch die
Anwendung; *contrivance*, Vorrichtung.

[9] Turn *the—reached* by 'the only
way which led to the place.'

[10] *Naturally so*, say: von Natur.

[11] Supply the conjunction weil;
to cut away, here abtragen.

[12] *Accident*, here Zufall.

[13] There are various forms in
German for the proper name *Ligurian*, all of which have the same
form in both numbers. In accordance with the Greek Λιγυες we have
the word Ligyer; whilst the forms
Ligurier, Ligurer, and Ligurianer, are
derived from the Latin *Ligur*.

[14] The expression *auxiliary cohorts* may be turned in German
into one compound term by omitting the letter *y* in the first, and
replacing *s* by en in the second
word.

had gone out of the camp to fetch water, saw some snails crawling[1] among the rocks on the back[2] of the hill-fort. He picked up one or two; and as he went on picking more,[3] he came at last almost to the top of the hill. Being[4] curious to reach the very[5] summit, he made his way up[6] with some difficulty, and had a full view of the flat on which the town was built; for all *the* Numidians[7] were engaged on the opposite side, where the fight was going on.[8] Having well examined[9] the place, and carefully observed[10] the way down, he reported his discovery to Marius, and urged him to make an attempt[11] on the fort by the part[12] where he had climbed up, offering to lead the way. Marius sent a few men who were about him, *and* the Ligurian with them,[13] to examine the track that had been discovered. The reports of the men varied.[14] Some said that the thing was[15] easy, and others that it was difficult. However, the general had some confidence that the plan would do.[16] Accordingly, he selected five trumpeters and hornblowers,[17] the most active[18] that he could find, and four centurions[19] to look after them. * * *

The little company[20] were directed to obey the Ligurian as their[21] guide, and the next day was appointed for the

---

[1] Cf. Int. p. xviii.

[2] *Back*, Rückſeite.

[3] Turn *he—more*, by 'whilst he picked up always more.'

[4] See Int. p. xvi.*c*; curious, begierig.

[5] The word *very*, in the sense in which it is used here, must be rendered in German by ſelbſt.

[6] *Made—up*=went up.

[7] *Numidian*, Numidier.

[8] *Was going on*, ſtattfand.

[9] *Having well examined*, say: nachdem er...genau beſichtigt.

[10] *Carefully observed*, say: ſich... gut gemerkt hatte; *down*, here hinunter.

[11] *Attempt* = attack.

[12] *By the part*, von der Seite aus. Two prepositions are frequently used in German, as is the case here, in order to express direction, or the course of a motion.

[13] Render *with them* by ſammt, placing this preposition before the words *the Ligurian*.

[14] *Varied*, lauteten verſchieden, *i.e.* 'sounded contradictory.'

[15] See page 29, note 3.

[16] The verb *to do* is here a synonym of 'to succeed.'

[17] The Romans are known to have had two kinds of military musicians, viz. trumpeters and hornblowers.

[18] *Active*, here energiſch.

[19] The plural of Centurio is, in German, Centuries, or more usually Centurionen; *to—them*, auf ſie Acht zu geben.

[20] *Company*, here Truppe; *were directed*, turn by 'received the order;' *to obey*, here folgen.

[21] Use here the dative.

ascent. The snail-picker[1] had no doubt often climbed his native rocks and mountains; but his companions were less expert than himself. However, after a good deal of trouble and much fatigue,[2] they reached the summit, at the back of the town. They found all quiet, for the men, as on previous occasions, were fighting with the Romans on the opposite side. ✗ Marius had kept the Numidians actively engaged all that day[3] up to the time when he was informed that the Ligurian and his party had reached the summit of the hill. He then came out from under the vineæ,[4] and cheering[5] his men, ordered them to advance to the wall with their[6] shields interlaced over their heads in the manner which the Romans named "testudo," or tortoise. At the same time the enemy were[7] assailed with missiles from the engines, and with arrows and slings. The Numidians, who had often destroyed and burnt the vineæ, did not fight from the walls, but[8] confidently came out in front of them.[9] While the battle was raging, all at once the sound of horns and trumpets was heard at the back of the town. The women and children, who had crowded to[10] the front to see the fight, fled back in alarm; they were followed by those who were nearest to the wall;[11] and at last all the Numidians turned their backs.[12] The Romans pressed upon them,[13]

---

[1] *Snail-picker*, Schneckensammler; *native*, here heimathlich. The Italian district formerly called 'Liguria' is traversed by the Maritime Alps and the Apennines. *Climbed*, erklommen.

[2] *After—fatigue*, nach vieler Mühe und Anstrengung.

[3] *Had—day*, hatte die Numidier den ganzen Tag im Kampf beschäftigt.

[4] The Latin term *vineæ* may be rendered by Lauben- or Laufgang-hütten, or by the more expressive Laufhallen, *i.e.* running halls.

[5] *Cheering* = encouraging.

[6] Turn *with their* by 'the;' *interlaced*, transl. zusammengehalten.

[7] Use the singular number.

[8] When the adversative conjunction *but* merely limits the antecedent, it must be rendered by aber; when, however, it denies entirely the antecedent, it is to be translated by sondern, which was in Middle High German 'sunder,' a form still existing in English, with a cognate signification.

[9] *Confidently—them*, rückten muthig vor dieselben hinaus.

[10] *To crowd to*, strömen nach which, being a verb denoting motion, is conjugated with sein; *alarm*, Bestürzung.

[11] Turn *they — wall* by 'those who were nearest to the wall followed them.'

[12] *Turned their backs* = fled.

[13] *Pressed upon them*, drangen auf sie ein.

and passing over[1] *the bodies of* the killed and wounded, made their way[2] to the wall without stopping to plunder,[3] as we are told,[4] though we cannot conceive[5] that a poor Numidian had anything upon him that was worth taking.[6] —GEORGE LONG, *Decline of the Roman Republic.*

VI.

A SIGN OF THE TIMES.

There was,[7] at all events, one class by which the memory of Joseph II. was long and fondly cherished;[8] and it was that to the sympathies of which he would have best loved to make his appeal.[9] The Austrian peasantry[10] of German blood are *at once* an eminently loyal race, and one on which[11] affection and kindness are rarely thrown away. They were never misled in their judgment of him. Even when[12] kneeling before the carriage of the pope,[13] they had no idea[14] that they were

---

[1] *Passing over*, inbem fie über... bahin fchritten.

[2] *Made their way*, famen fie.

[3] *Without—plunder*, ohne fich mit Plünbern aufzuhalten.

[4] *To tell* belonging to that class of verbs mentioned in Ext. 22, note *b*, we cannot use it in the passive voice in German unless we employ it impersonally; as, *I am told*, mir wirb gefagt. Here we might render *as we are told* by wie uns berichtet wirb.

[5] *Though—conceive*, obwohl wir uns nicht benfen fönnen; *upon him*, bei fich.

[6] *That—taking*, bas bes Nehmens werth gewefen wäre.

[7] The impersonal phrases *there is, there was*, are rendered by es gibt, es gab, when existence is to be expressed in an indefinite manner,

as is the case here (compare the French *il y a*); but if existence is to be expressed in a definite manner, we must use the corresponding form of the verb fein.

[8] *By—cherished*, bei ber Jofeph ber Zweite lange in theurem Anbenfen ftanb.

[9] Render *to—appeal*, by an beren Sympathie er am liebften hätte appelliren mögen.

[10] *Peasantry* = peasants; *blood*, here Abfunft; *a—race*, eine außerorbentlich lovale Raffe.

[11] *And—which*, bei ber.

[12] See page 41, note 9.

[13] Pope Pius VI. visited Vienna in 1782 with a view to persuade the emperor to desist from his ecclesiastical reforms.

[14] *No idea*, transl. feine Sbee bavon.

assuming an attitude of opposition to[1] their friend and emperor. No royal name lives among them at this day in reverential tradition so truly[2] as that of Kaiser Joseph.

Their estimate[3] of him cannot be better expressed than in the simple apologue[4] which is still current in Austria. The peasantry of a Styrian[5] village are met[6] to discuss the news of Joseph's death. They will not believe it.[7] It is a lie of the Court nobles,[8] the lawyers, the lazy friars. While they are debating,[9] information is brought of the arrival, bit by bit,[10] of the old order of things: the Carthusians[11] have returned to the neighbouring abbey; the Capuchins have resumed their rounds;[12] the Forstmeister[13] and the gamekeeper have reoccupied[14] their lodges; and the[15] steward is sitting at the receipt[15] of feudal dues. The oldest peasant rises and takes off his hat: "Then Joseph is dead indeed; may Heaven have mercy[16] on his soul."—H. MERIVALE, *Historical Studies.*

---

[1] *An—to,* eine feindliche Stellung gegen; *royal,* here fürstlich.

[2] *Lives — truly,* erfreut sich bei ihnen bis auf diesen Tag einer solchen traditionellen Ehrfurcht.

[3] If we do not wish to render the above sentence freely, we must translate the term *estimate* by Meinung, *expressed* by bezeichnet, and turn *in* by 'through.'

[4] *Apologue,* Sage; *is—current,* noch im Umlauf ist.

[5] *Styrian,* steierisch.

[6] Use the perfect of sich versammeln; *to discuss,* besprechen.

[7] Translate this and the following *it* by the neuter pronoun, the same referring to a statement in general.

[8] *Court nobles* = courtiers.

[9] *To debate,* debattiren; *information,* die Nachricht.

[10] *The—bit,* say: die allmähliche Einführung;' *order,* here Ordnung.

[11] *Carthusians,* Karthäuser.

[12] *Have—rounds,* machen wieder ihre Runken.

[13] The Germans in Austria use commonly for Forstmeister the term Waldmeister, which expression, however, might be objected to because it is the name of some plants, more particularly of the *Asperula odorata* or 'woodroof.' For the term *gamekeeper* there is in German no general expression which would denote the same rank in all parts of Germany. It may often be rendered by Förster, and in the present instance by Jäger.

[14] *To reoccupy,* wieder Besitz nehmen (von); *lodge,* here Försterhaus.

[15] *The — receipt,* der Verwalter beaufsichtigt die Einnahmen; *feudal,* feudal; *dues,* Abgaben.

[16] *May...have mercy.* Use the present conjunctive (subjunctive) of sich erbarmen, this mood being required in clauses containing a prayer, request, wish, hope, &c.

VII.

THE SHAKERS'[1] DINNER.

These Shakers dine in silence.[2]   Brothers and sisters dine[2] in a common[3] room, at tables ranged[4] in a line, a few feet[5] apart.   They eat at six in the morning,[6] at noon,[7] at six in the evening; following[7] in this respect a rule which is all but uniform[8] in America, especially in the western parts of this continent, from the Mississippi *River* to the Pacific Ocean.   They rally to[9] the sound of a bell; file[10] into the eating-room in a single line, women going[10] up to one end of the room, men to the other, when[11] they drop on their knees for a short and silent prayer; sit down and eat, helping[12] each other *to* the food.   Not a word is[13] spoken, unless a brother should need some help from a brother, a sister from a sister.[14]

[1] The *Shakers* are a religious sect in America, the chief home of which is the village of Mount Lebanon, situated in the upper country of the Hudson River. The English term *Shaker* may be retained in German, although it is translated by some writers by the coined expression Schütter-Quäfer. or the more euphonic Zitterer.

[2] *Dine in silence*, essen schweigend zu Mittag; *dine*, speisen.

[3] *Common* is here to be rendered by gemeinschaftlich; the simple form gemein would signify 'mean.'

[4] Turn *ranged, &c.*, by 'which are ranged (aufgestellt) in a line, (Reihe), some feet apart, (von einander).'

[5] Cf. Ext. 32, note *d*.

[6] Similar adverbial expressions are expressed in German by the genitive case, with or without the definite article, when they denote an habitual occurrence of an action.

[7] *At noon*, um die Mittagsstunde; turn *following* by 'they follow; *respect*, here Hinsicht.

[8] Turn *a —uniform* by 'a custom which is almost general.'

[9] *To rally to*, sich versammeln auf.

[10] *To file*, here sich begeben; *single*, einfach; *women going* = the women go; place *end—room* after *other*.

[11] *When*, worauf.

[12] There is no single equivalent for the expression *to help*, and its derivatives, in the sense of 'to present to at table.' It may be rendered by sich bedienen, anbieten, or reichen. The last term should be used here. *food*, see p. 65, *n*. 6.

[13] See Extr. 4, note *b*.

[14] In accordance with the remark made in the last note but one, we must turn the above by 'except when (außer wenn) a brother from a brother, or a sister from a sister, should want something to be reached' (etwas gereicht haben wollte).

A whisper serves.[1] No one[2] gossips with her neighbour, for every one is busy with her own affairs. Even the help that any one may need is given and taken[3] without thanks;[4] such forms of courtesy[5] and politeness not being considered necessary in a family of saints. ⁷

Elder[6] Frederick sits at the end, not at the head, of one table;[7] Elderess Antoinette at the other end. The food,[7] though it is very good of its[8] kind, and very well cooked,[9] is simple, being[9] wholly, or almost wholly, produce of the earth; tomatoes, roast apples, peaches, potatoes, squash,[10] hominy, boiled corn, and the like. The grapes are excellent, reminding me of those of Bethlehem; and the eggs—hard[11] eggs, boiled eggs, scrambled eggs[11]—are delicious. The drink[12] is water, milk, and tea. Then we have pies,[13] tarts, candies,[14] dried fruits, and syrups. For my own part,[15] being a Gentile and a sinner, I have been indulged[16] in cutlets, chickens, and home-made wines.[17]

"Good food and sweet[18] air," says Frederick, "are our

[1] *To serve* being here a synonym of 'to suffice,' translate by genügen.

[2] The assertion referring to the female portion of the company, we must employ the feminine of Rein, and of the corresponding term, Jeder, for *every one*. Transl. *with—affairs* by mit sich selbst.

[3] Here again we must express the whole phrase by some other turn, viz. 'even when something is reached to any one, it is offered and accepted.'

[4] *Thanks,* say: Förmlichkeiten. Dant might here imply that the help offered was ungratefully or ungraciously received.

[5] *Courtesy,* feiner Anstand.

[6] *Elder,* Aeltester. The article may here be omitted in accordance with the rule, that common names used as titles before proper names require no article. *Elderess,* Aelteste.

[7] Turn *at—table* by 'at the lower, not at the upper, end of the one table.' *food,* say: Speisen.

[8] Turn *of its* by 'in their.'

[9] Well cooked, sorgfältig zubereitet; *being,* say: da sie...aus...bestehen.

[10] *Squash,* Kürbiß; *corn,* here Mais; *the like,* dergleichen.

[11] *Hard—eggs,* hart- und weichgekochte Eier, Rühreier.

[12] *Drink,* Getränk; *is,* besteht aus.

[13] *Pies,* when not made of meat, as is evidently the case here, retain the English name in German; *meat pies* are called Fleischpasteten, or simply Pasteten.

[14] *Candy,* Zuckerwerk, is used in German in the singular only; and the equivalent of *syrup,* denoting the sweet juice of fruits, is Fruchtsaft. The word Sirup is employed in German for *treacle.*

[15] *For my own part,* was mich betrifft; *being,* da ich...bin.

[16] Use the passive imperfect of regaliren (mit).

[17] We use in German for the expression *home-made wine* the general term Obstwein, *i.e.* 'fruit-wine.'

[18] Turn here *sweet* by 'fresh.'

only medicines." The rosy flesh[1] of his people, a tint but rarely seen in the United States, appears to answer very well for his assertion,[2] that in such a place no other physic is required.[3]

No words[4] being spoken during meals,[5] about twenty minutes serve [6] them amply for repast. One minute more, and the table is swept bare of dishes ;[7] the plates, the knives and forks, the napkins, the glass,[8] are cleaned and polished ; every article[8] is returned to[9] its proper place, and the sweet, soft[10] sense of order is restored.— HEPWORTH DIXON, *New America.*

VIII.

BEN JONSON.[11]

Ben Jonson had written conjointly[12] with Chapman and Marston a comedy which contained some passages reflecting[13] on the Scottish nation. The authors were thrown into prison, and threatened[14] with the loss of their ears

---

[1] *Flesh,* transl. Teint, *m.* (from the Latin *tingere*), to be pronounced in German as in French ; *the United States,* die Vereinigten Staaten.

[2] *To—assertion,* die Wahrheit seiner Behauptung zu bestätigen.

[3] *To be required,* nöthig sein. The assertion being here a quotation from another person (*oratio obliqua*), the verb must be used in the *conjunctive* (called by some grammarians *subjunctive*) mood, which mood we should also use in Latin.

[4] Use in German the singular. Cf. Int. p. xvi., *c,* and Ext. 4, n. *b*

[5] The term *meals* must here be turned by 'the eating,' to avoid the unnecessary repetition of the same expression in one and the same short sentence.

[6] *Serve,* here genügen. See p. 2, Extr. 7. Render *more* by noch.

[7] *Swept—dishes,* say briefly abgedeckt.

[8] *Glass* must be rendered by Glasgeschirr, if it is to denote in general the various articles made of glass. Render *article* by Stück.

[9] *Is—to,* befindet sich wieder an.

[10] For *sweet* and *soft* we should prefer in German the epithets ' beautiful,' ' friendly ;' *sense,* here Gefühl.

[11] Ben Jonson was a contemporary of Shakespeare, to whom he is considered second as a dramatist.

[12] *Conjointly,* gemeinschaftlich ; *passage* (in a book), Stelle.

[13] Turn *reflecting* by the present participle of ' to blame,' using it as an attributive adjective.

[14] The simple verb drohen would here be inapplicable, since it is an intransitive verb, and could

and noses. Jonson had no considerable share in[1] the composition of the piece,[2] and was, besides, in such favour,[3] that he would not have been involved;[4] but he voluntarily accompanied his two friends to prison, determined to share their fate. They were not tried;[5] and when Jonson was set at liberty, he gave an entertainment[6] to his friends. His mother was present on this joyous occasion, and she produced[7] a paper of poison, which, she said, she[8] intended to have given[9] her son in his liquor[10] rather than he should submit to personal mutilation and disgrace, and another dose, which she intended[11] afterwards to have taken herself.[11]

IX.

A MAIDEN SPEECH.[12]

The season[13] had hardly commenced when the "Bill[14] for regulating Trials in Cases of High Treason"[15] was

therefore not be used in the passive voice. But this verb can assume a transitive meaning by means of the prefix be.

[1] *To have a share in anything*, an einer Sache Antheil haben; *composition*, here Abfassung.

[2] The piece alluded to was called *Eastward Hoe.*

[3] The idiomatic expression is, in German, 'to *stand* in favour.'

[4] *Involved*, in die Sache verwickelt, to be used here in the passive voice.

[5] *To try*, here vor Gericht stellen.

[6] *Entertainment* being here synonymous with 'feast, banquet,' transl. Gastmahl.

[7] *To produce*, here zeigen; *of* = with.

[8] Turn *which—she* by 'which she, as she said.'

[9] *Intended—given*, hätte geben wollen.

[10] *Liquor*, here Getränk; *than—submit*, als daß er sich...unterwürfe; *another dose*, eine zweite Dosis.

[11] *To intend*, beabsichtigen; *to—herself*, say: selbst zu nehmen.

[12] As the nearest approach to the idiomatic English expression *maiden speech*, there has been coined the term Erstlingsrede, *i.e.* 'firstling-speech,' in the same way as we say Erstlingslied for the first song written by a poet or set to music by a composer. Some dictionaries translate *maiden speech* by erste Rede only, which is neither a characteristic nor a convenient general expression. The literal translation, Jungfernrede, coined by some contemporary German writers, does not grammatically convey the same meaning as the English expression.

[13] The 'Parliamentary' *season* is called in German Session.

[14] Retain the English expression, using it as a fem. noun.

[15] *For—Treason*, um das Gerichtsverfahren in Hochverrathssachen zu reguliren; *Commons* = House

again laid on the table of the Commons. Of the debates
to which it gave occasion[1] nothing is known except one
interesting circumstance,[2] which has been preserved[3] by
tradition. Among those who supported the Bill appeared
conspicuous[4] a young Whig of high rank, of ample[5]
fortune, and of great abilities, which had been assiduously
improved by study.[6] This was Anthony Ashley Cooper,
Lord[7] Ashley, eldest son of the second Earl of Shaftes-
bury, and grandson of that renowned politician[8] who
had, in the days of Charles the Second, been at one time
the most unprincipled *of* ministers,[9] and at another the
most unprincipled *of* demagogues.[9] Ashley had just
been returned to Parliament[10] for the borough of Poole,
and was[11] in his twenty-fifth year. In the course of his
speech[12] he faltered, stammered, and seemed to lose the
thread of his reasoning.[13] The House—then, as now,
indulgent to[14] novices, and then, as now, well aware
that, on a first appearance,[15] the hesitation which is the
effect[16] of modesty and sensibility[17] is quite as promising
a[18] sign as volubility of utterance and ease of manner[19]—

[1] *Occasion*, here Veranlaſſung.

[2] The term *circumstance* being
here a synonym of 'incident,' we
must render it by Zwiſchenfall.

[3] *Has been preserved*, transl. auf
uns gekommen iſt.

[4] *Appeared conspicuous*, zeichnete
ſich beſonders . . . aus.

[5] Turn *ample* by 'great,' and
the subsequent adjective *great* by
bedeutend. Intelligent students will
soon find out that it is not always
possible or advisable to use the
same epithets in all languages.

[6] Turn *which—study* by 'which
had been improved (gepflegt worden
waren) through industry and study.'

[7] Titles like *Lord, Lady, Earl,*
&c., should be retained in German.

[8] *Politician* = statesman.

[9] Use in both cases the nominative singular; *unprincipled*, gewiſ-
ſenlos.

[10] *To be returned to Parliament,*
ins Parlament gewählt werden.

[11] Turn *was* by 'stood.'

[12] When the term *speech* is a
synonym of 'discourse,' 'oration,'
it must be rendered by Rede; but
when denoting the 'faculty of
uttering articulate sounds,' it is in
German Sprache. *To falter*, ſtocken.

[13] For *reasoning* we may use
here the expressive term Gedanken-
gang; *then*, here damals.

[14] *To*, gegen; *well aware*, überzeugt.

[15] *On—appearance*, beim erſten
Auftreten; *hesitation*, Stocken.

[16] Turn *effect* by 'consequence,'
and use the indefinite article.

[17] *Sensibility*, here Schüchternheit,
i.e. 'timidity.'

[18] Whenever the article is used
with an attributive adjective, it
must, in German, precede the
same. *Quite as* is here to be rendered by eben ſo, and *promising*
by vielverſprechend.

[19] Translate *volubility of utterance*
by the compound expression Zun-
gengeläufigkeit, and *ease of manner*

encouraged him to proceed. "How can I, Sir,"[1] said the young orator, recovering himself,[2] "produce[3] a stronger argument in favour of this Bill than my own failure?[4] My fortune,[5] my character, my life, are not at stake. I am speaking to an audience[6] whose kindness might well inspire me *with* courage. And yet, from[7] mere nervousness, from mere want of practice in addressing[8] large assemblies, I have lost my recollection;[9] I am unable[10] to go on with my argument. How helpless, then, must be a poor man who, never having opened his lips in public,[11] is called upon[12] to reply, without a moment's preparation,[13] to the ablest and most experienced advocates in the kingdom, and whose faculties[14] are paralysed by the thought, that if he fails[15] to convince his hearers, *he will* in *a* few hours die on a gallows, and leave beggary and infamy to those who are dearest to him!"[16] It may

by Leichtigkeit im Vortrag ; *to proceed,* fortfahren.

[1] Retain the English word, or say Herr Präsident, which expression would be used in a German Parliament.

[2] *To recover oneself,* sich sammeln.

[3] *To produce,* here verbringen. The term *argument*—to be pronounced as a German word—may be retained.

[4] The term *failure,* in its comprehensive signification, has no single equivalent, neither in German nor, I think, in most other modern languages. Here the word Mißgeschick, *i.e.* 'ill-fate,' might properly be used.

[5] *Fortune* standing here for 'possessions,' 'wealth,' is to be rendered by Vermögen ; *character,* Ruf; are, &c., stehn nicht auf dem Spiele.

[6] When the word *audience,* refers, as is the case here, to an assembly consisting of regularly appointed members, we generally use the word Versammlung; when referring to an assembly of promiscuous listeners, it may also be rendered by Publikum, and an assembly consisting more particularly of students, &c. is called Auditorium or Zuhörerschaft.

[7] *From,* aus ; *nervousness,* transl. Aengstlichkeit.

[8] *In addressing* = to speak before.

[9] *My recollection,* transl. Fassung, or, less literally, den Faden, *i.e.* the thread.

[10] *To be unable,* nicht im Stande sein ; *argument,* here Gegenstand.

[11] *Who—public.* Turn the whole clause briefly by 'who has never spoken publicly,' connecting it with the following clause by und nun.

[12] *To be called upon,* aufgefordert werden. Place *to reply* after *kingdom.*

[13] In order to translate the phrase *without a moment's preparation* with literal faithfulness, we should be obliged to spin it out to 'without that one grants him even (auch nur) a moment to his preparation;' but we can easily avoid this turn by simply saying ohne irgend welche Vorbereitung.

[14] *Faculties,* Geisteskräfte.

[15] *That—fails,* daß er, wenn es ihm nicht gelingt; *on a,* am.

[16] *And—him.* This clause will best be turned by 'and will leave behind those who are the dearest

reasonably be suspected[1] that Ashley's confusion and the ingenious[2] use which he made of it had been carefully premeditated.[3] His speech,[4] however, made a great impression.—MACAULAY, *History of England.*

X.

A SELF-DUBBED[5] MESSENGER.

On the evening of the battle an officer[6] of the Ziethen Hussars, who were forward[7] in the pursuit, rode as far as[8] the gates of Königgrätz,[9] and, finding[10] there were no sentries outside, rode[11]in ; the guard, immediately on seeing[11] him in his Prussian uniform, turned out[12] and seized him, when,[13] with a ready presence, he declared he had[14] come to demand[15] the capitulation of the fortress. He was conducted to the commandant, and made the same demand to[16] him, adding that[17] the town would

to him in poverty and disgrace.' The superlative *dearest* is to be used substantively : bie Theuerften.

[1] *It—suspected.* Turn here by ' one can well assume with reason' (mit Grund annehmen).

[2] *Ingenious,* here genial.

[3] *Had—premeditated,* planmäßig vorbereitet war.

[4] See page 31, note 12.

[5] *Self-dubbed,* selbsternannt.

[6] *Officer* is here the subject of the sentence, and *rode* the assertion. *Ziethen Hussars,* Ziethen'sche Husaren.

[7] *Who were forward,* say : bie sich ... vorgewagt hatten. Supply the words 'of the enemy' after *pursuit.*

[8] The literal translation of *as far as* would here be an Anglicism ; transl. the same by bis zu.

[9] Königgrätz is a fortress on the Elbe, in Bohemia. The battle alluded to was fought near that place on 3rd July, 1866.

[10] *Finding—outside,* say : ba er keine Schildwache daselbst vorfand.

[11] Supply 'he;' *the—seeing,* so wie bie Wache ihn...erblickte.

[12] *Turned out,* trat sie ins Gewehr.

[13] *When,* here worauf; *a ready presence,* rasche Geistesgegenwart.

[14] Use the perfect conjunctive, and remember that *to come* is a verb denoting motion.

[15] *To demand,* fordern.

[16] *To make a demand to any one,* an Jemand eine Forderung stellen.

[17] By omitting here the conjunction *that* we obtain a more rhythmical construction, since the sentence assumes by this omission the form of a direct principal clause, and the inharmonious accumulation of verbs is thus avoided. Good writers have often recourse to this expedient, a circumstance which the student of German should bear in mind.

D

be bombarded if not surrendered[1] within an hour; the commandant, unconscious[2] that he was not dealing[3] with a legitimate messenger, courteously refused to capitulate; but[4] the Hussar was conducted out of the[4] town, passed through[5] the guard at the entrance, and got off safely[6] without being made a prisoner.—H. M. HOZIER, *The Seven Weeks' War.*

XI.

DON JOHN OF AUSTRIA[7] AT LOUVAIN.

Meantime Don John of Austria came to Louvain. * * * The object[8] with which Philip had sent him to the Netherlands,[9] that he might[10] conciliate the hearts of the inhabitants by the personal graces[11] which he had inherited from his imperial father, seemed in a fair way of accomplishment;[12] for *it was*[13] not only the venal applause of titled[14] sycophants *that* he strove to merit, but he mingled gaily and familiarly with[15] all classes of citizens.

[1] *If not surrendered,* wenn die Uebergabe nicht . . . erfolgte.

[2] *Unconscious,* transl. nicht ah= nend, *i.e.* 'not suspecting.'

[3] *To deal,* here unterhandeln; *legitimate,* say: officiellen.

[4] By placing *but* after *Hussar* the assertion becomes more em- phatic. *Out of the,* zur . . . hinaus.

[5] *Passed through,* passirte; *at the,* am.

[6] *To get off safely,* glücklich davon kommen. See page 36, note 4.

[7] Don John of Austria, fre- quently called Don Juan d'Auftria, son of the Emperor Charles V., was born at Ratisbonne in 1546, and died at the fortified camp of Namur in 1578. In 1576 he had been appointed Governor to the disaffected Netherlands by his brother, Philip II. *Louvain,* Löwen.

[8] *Object,* here Abficht.

[9] Insert the expletive 'namely.'

[10] Use the pres. cond. of mögen, and turn *conciliate* by win.

[11] *Graces,* transl. Liebenswürdigkeit.

[12] Turn *in—accomplishment* by 'upon a good way to be accom- plished.' *To accomplish,* erfüllen.

[13] The English usage of making a *verb* emphatic by *it is, was, &c.,* that, is not required in German, where the emphasis can be suffi- ciently marked by inverting the regular order of words, and begin- ning with the term to be em- phasized.

[14] *Titled,* transl. vornehm.

[15] *To mingle—with,* here sich an= schließen. See page 24, note 8; *gaily,* fröhlich; *familiarly,* vertrau= lich.

Everywhere his handsome face and charming manner[1] produced their natural effect. He dined and supped[2] with the magistrates in the Town-house; honoured[3] general banquets of the burghers with his presence; and was affable and dignified, witty, fascinating, and commanding,[4] by turns.

At Louvain the five military guilds[5] held a solemn festival. The usual invitations were sent to the other societies and to all the martial brotherhoods the country round.[6] Gay and gaudy processions, sumptuous banquets, military sports, rapidly succeeded each other.[7] Upon the day of the great trial of skill[8] all the high functionaries[9] of the land were, according to custom, invited, and the Governor was graciously pleased[10] to honour[11] the solemnity with his presence. Great was the joy of the multitude when Don John, complying with the habit[12] of imperial and princely personages in former days, enrolled himself, cross-bow[13] in hand, among the

---

[1] *Charming manner*, einneh-mentes Wesen.

[2] *He—supped*, er speiste zu Mittag und zu Abend.

[3] *To honour* means both ehren and beehren; but there is a very nice distinction between these two verbs. Ehren signifies 'to entertain feelings of respect,' *i.e.* to revere, to esteem, &c., as *Honour thy father and thy mother*, Ehre Vater und Mutter. Beehren means 'to show *marks* of civility and respect,' *i.e.* to favour a person or thing by any outward distinction, as '*Favour me with a visit*,' Beehren Sie mich mit einem Besuche. Here the Prince favoured the burghers with his presence: we must therefore say, Er beehrte die Bankette, since er ehrte, &c. would signify 'he revered the banquets.' The present case may aptly serve to illustrate the great advantage which the German language derives from the inseparable prefixes, there having been achieved here, as in innumerable other instances, a characteris-

tic nicety by means of a simple prefix; *general*, here öffentlich.

[4] *Commanding*, ehrfurchtgebietend; put *by turns*, abwechselnd, after *was*.

[5] *Military guild*, Schützengilde; *to hold* (a festival), begehen.

[6] *The country round*, in der Umgegend; *gay*, heiter; *gaudy*, bunt.

[7] *To succeed each other*, auf einander folgen.

[8] *Trial of skill*, Kunstprobe.

[9] *Functionary*, Beamte.

[10] *Was graciously pleased*, ließ sich gnädig herab.

[11] See above, note 3. *Solemnity*, here Festlichkeit.

[12] *Complying with the habit* and *in former days*, is to be rendered by the clause dem ehemaligen Gebrauche ... nachkommend.

[13] Use the definite article both with *cross-bow* and *hand*, and retain the elliptical construction, which is generally used in German when the accusative is followed, as is the case here by an adv. exp. of place, viz., *enrolled, etc.*, sich die Armbrust in der Hand...aufnehmen ließ.

competitors.　Greater still was the enthusiasm when the conqueror[1] of Lepanto[2] brought down[3] the bird, and was proclaimed[4] king of the year amid the tumultuous hilarity of the crowd.　According to custom, the captains of the guild suspended a golden popinjay[5] around the neck of his Highness, and, placing themselves in procession,[6] followed[7] him to the great church.　Thence,[3] after the customary religious exercises,[8] the multitude proceeded[9] to the banquet, where the health of the new king of the cross-bowmen[10] was pledged in deep potations.[11]—MOTLEY, *Rise of the Dutch Republic.*

XII.

WORSE THAN HIS REPUTATION.

I have, while[12] in England, heard and read more than once of the " docile[13] camel."　If " docile " means stupid,

[1] When the word *conqueror* is synonymous with 'victor,' it is rendered by Sieger.

[2] Don John gained the great naval battle of Lepanto against the Turks in 1572.

[3] *Brought down*, transl. herab-schoß.

[4] Trnsl. *was proclaimed* by zum... ausgerufen wurde, in accordance with the rule that verbs of choosing, appointing, declaring, considering, and the like, do not govern in German, as is the case in English, Latin, and Greek, *two* accusatives, but express the office or dignity to which a person has been appointed, &c. by zu with the dative.　The person appointed is alone put in the accusative, unless the passive construction be employed—as is the case in the above sentence—when the nominative is used.

[5] Turn here *popinjay* simply by ' bird.'

[6] *Placing—procession*, transl. in-dem sie eine Procession bildeten.

[7] The third person plural of the personal pronoun must here be inserted.

[8] *Thence*, von da aus; *religious exercises*, Andachtsübungen.

[9] *To proceed*, here sich begeben.

[10] *Cross-bowmen*, Armbrustschützen.

[11] *Was—potations*, in starken Zügen getrunken wurde.

[12] If the word *while* is translated, we must give the sentence in a complete form, *i.e.* 'while I was in England.'　We can, however, construe the clause in a still more elliptical manner by omitting that adverb altogether, since the adverbial expression of place is in similar cases quite sufficient in German, viz., *I have in England.*

[13] When *docile* refers to the temper of animals, it is rendered by sanft; *to mean*, here bedeuten.

well and good ;[1] in such a[2] case the camel is the very[3]
model of docility.   But if the epithet is intended[4] to
designate an animal that takes *an* interest in[5] its rider, so
far as a beast can ;[6] that in some way[7] understands his
intentions, or shares them in a subordinate fashion ;[8] that
obeys from[9] a sort of submissive or half fellow-feeling
with his master, like the horse and elephant ; then I say
that the camel is by no means docile : very much the contrary.[10]   He takes no heed of[11] his rider; pays no attention[12] whether he be on his back[13] or not ; walks straight
on when once set a-going, merely because he is too stupid
to turn aside ;[14] and *then*, should some tempting thorn[15] or
green branch allure him out of [16] the path, continues[17] to
walk on in this new direction simply[18] because he is too
dull to turn back into the right road.   His only care is to
cross[19] as much pasture as he conveniently can while
pacing mechanically onwards, and for effecting[20] this his
long flexible neck sets him at great advantage ;[21] and a

[1] *Well and good,* here ſo mag
es hingehen.

[2] Turn here *such a* by ' this.'

[3] Here the word *very* is synonymous with ' real,' ' true ' — the
French *vrai.* In German the adjective must here be. preceded by
the indefinite article.

[4] *But —intended,* say briefly : ſoll
aber ber Ausbruck (*i.e. expression*).
The supine is not used after the
auxiliary verbs of mood.

[5] The preposition *in,* referring to
take interest, is rendered by an.

[6] Turn *as—can* by ' it is possible
to a beast.'

[7] *In some way,* gewiſſermaßen.

[8] The above clause will best be
rendered idiomatically by translating *shares them* by auf bieſelben
eingeht, and *fashion* by Grab.

[9] *From,* transl. aus.   The term
fellow may here be rendered by the
adjective kameratſchaftlich; but then
with should be turned by ' for.'

[10] *Very—contrary,* ganz im Gegentheil.

[11] *To take heed of,* here ſich kümmern um.   Kamel being neuter in
German, the corresponding pronoun should be used throughout.

[12] *Pays no attention,* render
achtet nicht barauf.

[13] *Be—back,* ihm auf bem Rücken
ſitze; *set a-going,* in Bewegung ge-
bracht.

[14] *To turn aside,* um abzulenken.

[15] *Thorn,* here Dornbuſch.

[16] *To allure out of,* ablocken von.

[17] The verb *to continue,* referring
to an infinitive, as above, is generally expressed by the adverb weiter,
and sometimes by fort. The infinitive is in this case used in the
same tense as the verb *to continue.*
Supply ' it' after the finite verb.

[18] *Simply* = merely ; *dull* =
stupid ; *into,* here ' upon.'

[19] *To cross,* say : über... zu gehen:
pasture, Weiteplatz, to be used here
in the plural ; *conveniently,* mic
Bequemlichkeit.

[20] *To effect,* bewerkſtelligen.   See
Extr. 9, note *a.*

[21] *To set at advantage,* Vortheile
gewähren.

hard[1] blow or a downright[2] kick alone has any influence *on him* whether[3] to direct or impel. He will never attempt to throw you[4] off his back,[5] such a trick being far beyond[6] his limited comprehension ; but if you[6] fall off, he will never dream[7] of stopping[8] *for you*, and walks on just the same,[9] grazing while he goes,[10] without knowing or caring an atom[11] what has become of you.[12]   *If* turned loose,[13] it is *a* thousand to[14] one that he will never find his[15] way back to his accustomed home or pasture, and the first comer[16] who picks him up[17] will have no particular shyness to get over ;[18] Jack or Tom are all the same[19] to him; and the loss of his old master and of his former cameline[20] companions gives him no regret,[21] and occasions no endeavour to find them again.   One only symptom will[22] he give that he is aware[23] of his rider, and that is[24] when the

[1] The literal translation of *hard* with reference to *blow* is also used in German, but mostly when the word is employed figuratively ; used in the primitive sense, the usual German epithet is ſtarf.

[2] *Downright*, here entſchieren, *i.e.* 'decided ;' *kick*, Fußtritt.

[3] Turn *whether* by 'be it,' and transl. *to impel* by anſpornen.

[4] The pronoun *you*, used in English colloquial speech indefinitely for 'one''any one,' is usually rendered in German by man, Jemand, or Niemand; by the two latter, more generally, when *you* occurs in the accusative, as is the case here.

[5] Suppress in German the words *his back*, the verb *to throw off* fully indicating the action. *Trick*, Streich.

[6] Turn *far beyond* by 'much too high for;' *comprehension*, here Verſtand. Turn *you* by 'the rider.'

[7] *He—dream.* We use in German the idiomatic expression es fällt ihm nicht im Traume ein.

[8] *To stop*, here ſtehen bleiben.

[9] *And—same*, ſondern es ſchreitet ruhig weiter.

[10] *While he goes* may be briefly turned in German by im Gehen, to be placed before *grazing*, weidend. Cf. Int. page xvii., *g*.

[11] *Caring an atom*, translate ſich im Geringſten carum zu fümmern.

[12] Turn here *of you* by ' of (aus) his rider.'

[13] *Turned loose*, losgelaſſen.

[14] *To*, here gegen.

[15] See Extr. 34, note *b*. *Accustomed home*, here gewöhnlichen Aufenthaltsort ; *pasture*, Weideplatz.

[16] *The first comer* is idiomatically rendered in German by ter Erſte Beſte.

[17] *To pick up*, here aufgreifen.

[18] *To get over*, figuratively überwinden; *Jack, &c.*, say Hans oder Peter.

[19] *Are—same*, gilt ihm gleich.

[20] Omit the adjective *cameline*. Generally it would be rendered by the noun Kamel, which is, however, not applicable here.

[21] *To give regret*, Kummer machen.

[22] This emphatic future not being used in German, the principal verbs must be rendered by the present indicative.

[23] *To be aware*, here ſich bewußt ſein, which governs the genitive.

[24] Turn *and that is* by ' namely.'

latter is about to mount[1] him; for on such an[2] occasion he will bend back his long snaky neck towards his master, open his enormous jaws to bite, if he dared,[3] and roar out a tremendous sort of groan,[4] as if to complain of[5] some entirely new and unparalleled injustice about to be done him.[6] In a word,[7] he is from first to last an un-domesticated[8] animal.—W. G. PALGRAVE, *Narrative of a Year's Journey through Central and Eastern Arabia.*

XIII.

SPEEDY[9] PROMOTION.

A remarkable anecdote is related[10] by Voltaire of[11] the circumstance that obtained for Leonard Torstenson[12] his first commission.[13] He had been in close attendance on[14] the King of Sweden[14] during the campaign in Livonia in 1624,[15] and it happened,[16] at a moment of importance,[17]

[1] *To mount* is rendered by steigen when it is used intransitively, but it assumes a transitive meaning by means of the inseparable prefix be, which possesses the faculty of transforming intransitive verbs into transitive ones.

[2] *On such an*, bei biefer.

[3] *Dared*, say ben Muth bazu hätte.

[4] *And—groan*, unb stößt eine Art schrecklichen Gestöhnes aus.

[5] *As — of*, als ob es sich beflagen wollte über. When an infinitive is preceded by *as if*, we generally express the condition by als ob… wollte; *unparalleled*, beispiellos.

[6] *About — him*, bie man ihm anthun will.

[7] We say in German 'with one word;' *from—last*, transl. burch-aus.

[8] *Undomesticated*, ungeselliges, *i.e.* unsociable.

[9] *Speedy*, schnell

[10] *To relate*, erzählen.

[11] Turn *a—of* by 'Voltaire relates a remarkable anecdote (Anefbote) of (in Bezug auf).'

[12] Turn *that — Torstenson* by 'through which L. T. obtained.' General Torstenson, born 1603 at Forstena, in Sweden, was one of the principal generals in the Thirty Years' War. He particularly excelled as a strategist, and as such he gave—as related above—an early proof under the command of Gustavus Adolphus.

[13] *Commission* (in military affairs), Offizierstelle. Less briefly, but more elegantly, we might render it here by Ernennung zum Offizier.

[14] Place *he—Sweden*, befanb er sich stets um ben König von Schweben after '1624.' *Livonia*, Liefland.

[15] Cf. Extr. 49, note b.

[16] *To happen*, here sich fügen.

[17] Turn in German the above

that his Majesty had no staff officer near him.[1] Accordingly he entrusted[2] an order for an important movement to *the hands of* his squire, who, seeing a change in the enemy's plan of attack as he rode along,[3] took upon himself[4] the bold responsibility of making a corresponding[5] change in the directions that his sovereign directed him to give.[6]

" Sire,"[7] said the youth on[8] his return to his royal master's side, " forgive[9] me *for* what I have done ; but when I saw the enemy was changing his line, I made a corresponding change in your[10] Majesty's orders."

Gustavus made no answer at the time ;[11] but in the evening, when the page was about[12] to serve the table,[13] as was his wont,[14] he was commanded to sit down at the king's side,[15] when the good-humoured monarch, threatening[16] *him* with the hand, said : " Young man, what you

---

expression by 'in an important moment.' The pronoun *his* before names of titles, as *Majesty, Excellency,* &c., is in German turned by the abbreviated form Se. = Seine: the pronoun Ihre, however, is in such cases rendered in full.

[1] *Near him,* bei sich.

[2] Render here *to entrust* by anvertrauen, *for* by zu, and *squire* by Page; in which last word the letter g is pronounced soft, as in French, and the e short, as in Freude.

[3] Turn the clause *who—along* by ' who, when he as he rode along (beim Dahinreiten) a change in the plan of attack (Angriffsplan) of the enemy saw (here bemerkte).'

[4] *Took upon himself,* übernahm.

[5] *Corresponding,* entsprechend.

[6] Turn *in — give* by ' in the order which the king had given him for delivery ' (zur Bestellung).

[7] This term, derived from the Latin *senior,* is also used in German in addressing kings, &c. ; the i is pronounced as in German, but the e is mute.

[8] Render here *on* by the prep. bei, and *to. . . side* simply by zu.

[9] Use the 2nd pers. pl. of vergeben,

and supply the conjunction ' that ' after *saw. Line,* here Stellung.

[10] The pronoun Euer was formerly written Ewer; which obsolete mode of spelling is still officially retained before titles, but is generally given in the abbreviated form Ew., which stands for all the respective forms of Euer.

[11] Turn *made — time* by ' answered nothing in the moment ;' *in the,* here am.

[12] The phrase *to be about,* denoting near futurity, is rendered in German by im Begriff sein, and sometimes by wollte, which latter expression corresponds, in this sense, to the English *wanted.*

[13] *To serve the table,* bei Tafel aufzuwarten.

[14] Turn *as was his wont* simply by ' as usual,' and *was commanded* by ' received the order.' Why the verb befehlen, which governs the dative of the person and the accusative of the thing, cannot be used in the passive voice will be seen from Ext. 22, note *b.*

[15] *At. . . side,* neben ; *when,* here worauf ; *good-humoured,* gutgelaunt.

[16] See Int. p. xvii., *g.*

did this[1] morning might have cost you your life ; but I
see *in you* that you have the qualities of a great general,
and I make you an ensign[2] in a company of my Guards."[3]
—Sir Edw. Cust, *The Warriors of the Thirty Years' War.*

XIV.

GOETHE AT THE AGE OF TWENTY.[4]

Goethe reached Strasburg on the 2nd April, 1770. He
was now turned[5] twenty ; and a more magnificent youth
never, perhaps,[6] entered the Strasburg[7] gates. Long before celebrity[8] had fixed all eyes upon him he was likened
to an Apollo ; and once, when[9] he entered[10] a dining-room,
people[11] laid down *their* knives and forks to stare at[12] the
beautiful youth. Pictures and busts, even when most
resembling,[13] give but[14] a feeble indication of that which
was most[15] striking in his appearance : they give the form

[1] Render *this* by ȟeute, the time
of morning having already passed ;
and render *might* by the infinitive
fönnen.

[2] See page 36, note 4.

[3] *Guards*, here Leibwache.

[4] Supply the word ' years.'

[5] Transl. *turned* by über ; *magnificent*, ȟerrlich.

[6] Use here the adverb wohl, which
indicates more forcibly than vielleicht
the probability of an event. That
adverb is generally placed before
the word which has the principal
accent,—here the term *never*. *Entered*, fam...burch.

[7] Use the genitive case, and see
Extr. 11, note *a*.

[8] *Celebrity*, ber Ruhm. Turn *fixed*
—*him* by 'drawn the eyes of all
(Aller) upon him.'

[9] *When* can, as a rule, be rendered in four different ways :—
1st, by als, when it denotes an occurrence that has once taken place,
—in this sense it corresponds to the
French *lorsque;* 2nd, by wenn, when
it denotes an indefinite or habitual
occurrence,—in this sense *when*
is equivalent to ' whenever;' 3rd,
by wann, in questions, signifying
'at what time;' 4th, by worauf,
when standing for ' upon, or after
which.'

[10] *To enter*, treten (in).

[11] When *people* signifies persons
in general, in the sense in which
it is used here, we render it in
German by Leute; when, however,
it denotes the 'commonalty,' we
translate it by Volf, as in French
by *peuple*, and in Latin by *popu-
lus.*

[12] *To stare at*, here anstaunen.

[13] *Even — resembling*, selbst bie
ähnlichften.

[14] When *but* is synonymous with
only, it is rendered by nur; when
with *merely*, by bloß. *Indication*,
transl. Begriff.

[15] *Most striking*, am auffallenbften ;
appearance, say äußern Erscheinung.

of the features,[1] but not the play of features; nor[2] are they very accurate as to the form.

His features were large[3] and liberally cut, as in the fine sweeping lines[4] of Greek art. The brow was lofty and massive;[5] and from beneath it shone large lustrous brown eyes of marvellous beauty, their pupils[6] being of almost un-exampled size. The slightly aquiline[7] nose was large, and well cut. The mouth was full, with a short, arched, upper lip, very sensitive and expressive;[8] the chin and jaw[9] boldly proportioned; and the head rested on a handsome and muscular[10] neck.

In stature[11] he was rather above the middle size: but although not really tall, he had the aspect[12] of a tall man; and is usually so described, because his presence[13] was very imposing. His frame[14] was strong, muscular, yet sensitive. Dante says this contrast is[15] in the nature of things, for

"Quanto la cosa è più perfetta,
Più senta 'l bene, e così la doglienza." *

[1] *Feature* (of a face), Zug; *play of features*, Mienenspiel.

[2] When *nor* introduces a sentence, it is rendered by auch...nicht; and when it follows the negative *neither*, by noch. *Accurate*, genau; *as to*, was...betrifft.

[3] Render here *large* by kühn, and *liberally* by edel; *cut*, here gebildet.

[4] *The — lines*, den schön geschwungenen Linien.

[5] *Massive*, here gewölbt; *from beneath it*, unter derselben hervor; *of*, here von.

[6] *Pupil* (of the eye) is in German Pupille. We have also two genuine Teutonic words for the same thing, —viz. the homely Augapfel, *i.e.* the apple of the eye; and the poetical Augenstern, *i.e.* star of the eye. *Size*, here Größe.

[7] There is in German no exact equivalent for the adjective *aqui*-line. The expression *aquiline nose* would be rendered by Adlernase, whilst *a slightly aquiline nose* must be somewhat freely translated by eine leichtgebogene Nase. *Well*, here fein.

[8] *Very—expressive*, äußerst sensitiv und ausdrucksvoll.

[9] The article must be repeated before Kinnbacken (*jaw*), since, being masculine, it differs in gender from the noun Kinn. *Boldly proportioned*, in kühnen Proportionen.

[10] *Muscular*, muskulös.

[11] *In stature*, von Gestalt; *rather*, here etwas; *middle size*, Mittelgröße.

[12] *Aspect*, Aussehen; turn *tall* by 'tall-grown;' transl. *so* by als solcher.

[13] *Presence*, here persönliche Erscheinung; *imposing*, imponirend.

[14] *Frame*, in the sense in which it is used here, means in German Körperbau. Transl. *yet* by und doch.

[15] Use here the verb liegen.

* Longfellow translates the above with literal faithfulness by—
"As the thing more perfect is,
The more it feels of pleasure and of pain."
DANTE'S *Inferno*, Canto VI. v. 107. &c.

Excelling[1] in all active sports,[2] he was almost a barometer in sensitiveness[3] to atmospheric influences.

Such, externally, was[4] the youth who descended at[5] the hotel *Zum Geist*, in Strasburg, this[6] 2nd April, and who, ridding himself of[7] the dust and "ennui" of a long imprisonment in the diligence,[8] sallied forth[9] to gaze at the famous cathedral,[10] which made a wonderful impression on him as[11] he came up to it[12] through the narrow streets.— G. H. LEWES, *Life of Goethe*.

[1] The present participle implying here a concession, turn it by 'though he excelled;' and insert in the principal clause, to be given in an inverted form, the conj. doch after *he*. To excel, here fich auszeichnen.

[2] There does not exist in most continental languages a single equivalent for the comprehensive term *sport*. The English term has been adopted abroad, but more in reference to horse races. Render here *active sports* by Leibesübungen, and see the note to Ext. 7. page 2.

[3] Transl. *in sensitiveness* by in feiner Empfindlichkeit, and turn *to* by 'against.'

[4] Transl. *such — was* by so war das Aeußere, and put *youth* in the genitive case.

[5] *To descend at* (an hotel, &c.), absteigen in. Goethe makes use of this identical verb in relating his arrival at Strasburg in his autobiography „Wahrheit und Dichtung." The hotel alluded to he simply calls Wirthshaus.

[6] Transl. here *this* by an dem besagten; and see for the construction of the above sentences Extr. 4, note *a*.

[7] Render here *ridding—of* by abschüttelnd; *ennui*, die Langeweile.

[8] The expression *diligence* is also

used, with the French pronunciation, in German. The words Eil- or Schnellwagen are also employed as equivalents for that term.

[9] *Sallied forth*, transl. fort eilte; *to gaze at*, here besehen.

[10] *The cathedral* (of Strasburg) is commonly called in German der (Straßburger) Münster; which term being derived from the Græco-Latin expression *monasterium*, is sometimes also used in the neuter gender.

[11] The conjunction *as* may generally be translated in the following ways:—1st, in comparisons by als or wie; by the latter more generally when perfect equality is to be expressed. In this case *as* is frequently rendered by so wie, more particularly when two actions are compared: e.g. *He acts as he speaks*, Er handelt so wie er spricht. 2nd, when it occurs twice—before and after an adjective—the first *as* is generally rendered by so: e.g. *As cold as ice*, So kalt wie Eis. 3rd, when it stands for 'if' it is rendered by wenn; when for 'since' by da; when for 'because' by weil; when for *whilst* by da, wenn, indem, and sometimes by wie; and when for the conj. *when*, as above, by als.

[12] *Came—it*, vor demselben ankam.

XV.

THE PILGRIMS.[1]

The[2] next day they rose at five: their morning prayers[3] were finished, when,[4] as the day dawned, *a* war-whoop and a flight[5] of arrows announced an attack from Indians.[6] They were[7] of the tribe of the Nausites, who knew the English[8] as kidnappers; but the encounter[9] was without further result. Again[10] the boat's crew give thanks to God,[10] and steer their bark along the coast for the distance of[11] fifteen leagues. But no convenient harbour is[12] discovered. The pilot of the boat, who had been in these regions before, gives assurance of a good one,[13] which may be reached before night; and they follow his guidance.

[1] The Pilgrims alluded to in the above extract were a number of Covenanters who, being persecuted under James I. for their opposition to the Church of England, emigrated to Holland. But being desirous to remain under English rule, and to do service to their native country as loyal citizens, they left Holland in 1620, in order to found an English settlement in America.

[2] Use the accusative case.

[3] Render *morning prayers* by the compound Morgenandacht, to be used in the singular only; *finished*, here verrichtet.

[4] *When* is here to be rendered by da, and the verb *announced* placed immediately after that adverb; *as—dawned*, bei Tagesanbruch.

[5] The term *flight*, referring to arrows, is rendered by Schauer, *i.e.* 'shower.'

[6] There exists in German a very convenient mode of distinguishing the natives of East India from those of the West Indies or of the American continent. The former are called Indier or Inter, and the

latter Indianer. As regards the adjectives indisch and indianisch, the same distinction is made, but is not quite so strictly adhered to.

[7] Translate *were* by gehörten ... an, and *of—Nausites* by dem Stamm: der Nausiten.

[8] Turn *who knew the English* by 'to whom the English were known;' *kidnapper*, here Menschenräuber.

[9] Transl. *encounter* by the frequentative noun formed from fechten, and turn *was without further result* by 'had no further consequences.'

[10] Turn *again — God*, by 'the boat's crew (Schiffsmannschaft) thanks God anew (von Neuem);' crew requires in German the sing. only.

[11] Translate *for the distance of* simply by weit, placing this adverb at the end of the sentence. The term *league* may here be turned by 'mile,' though, arithmetically speaking, a German mile is longer than a *league* by 1·63 of an English mile.

[12] See the note to Ext. 8, and use the third person plural.

[13] The above elliptical construction is not admissible in German.

After some hours' sailing,[1] a storm of snow and rain[2] begins; the sea swells:[3] the rudder breaks—the boat must now be steered[4] with oars. The storm increases; night[5] is at hand: to[6] reach the harbour before dark, as much sail[7] as possible is borne; the mast breaks into three pieces; the sail falls overboard; but the tide is favourable. The pilot, in[8] dismay, would have run the boat on shore[9] in a cove[10] full of breakers. "About with her,"[11] exclaimed a sailor, "or we are cast away!"[12] They get her about[13] immediately, and passing[14] the surf, they enter[15] a fair sound, and shelter themselves[16] under the lee of a small rise of land.[17] It is dark, and the rain beats furiously;[18] yet the men are so wet *and* cold and weak, they[19] slight the danger to be apprehended[20] from the savages, and after great difficulty[21] kindle a fire on shore.

where it would be necessary to supply before *a good one* the words 'that there was;' but we can contract the above clause with the following one, turning them briefly by 'assures that they could reach (erreichen) a good *one* before night.'

[1] Use the third person plural of *to sail* in the pluperfect tense.

[2] The expression Schneesturm sounds like an Anglicism, though we use Hagelsturm, and some modern German writers have coined the word Regensturm. Turn, therefore, the above clause by 'a storm rises, accompanied by snow and rain.'

[3] *Swells*, geht hoch.

[4] *To steer*, here lenken.

[5] Use the definite article, and render *at hand* by rückt heran.

[6] See Extr. 9, note *a*. *Dark*, here Dunkelwerden.

[7] Use in German the plural number, and render here *to bear* by aufspannen. See also Extr. 4, note *b*.

[8] Supply here the pronoun *his*, and see for the construction of the clause Extr. 5, note *b*.

[9] Render the clause *would—shore* by hätte...das Boot...stranden lassen.

[10] *Cove*, here Bucht; *of breakers*, brandender Wogen.

[11] *About with her*, wendet!

[12] The nautical expression *to cast* or *to be cast away* is rendered in German an ten Strand treiben.

[13] Translate *to get about* by umwenden, *immediately* by sofort, and omit the pronoun *her*.

[14] Render here *passing* by indem sie ... durchschiffen.

[15] *To enter*, here gelangen (in); *fair sound*, ruhige Meerenge.

[16] *To shelter oneself*, Schutz finden; *lee*, Leeseite, pronounced entirely as a German word, it being a genuine Teutonic expression.

[17] *Small rise of land*, sanfte Erhöhung.

[18] *Beats furiously*, here strömt heftig nieder.

[19] In similar constructions the conjunction *that* cannot be omitted in German. *To slight*, here verachten.

[20] The English passive participial constructions, expressing relations of possibility or necessity, are generally changed in German into the active form by means of the supine. Here *to be apprehended* = which was to apprehend (befürchten).

[21] Turn *after great difficulty* by 'with great trouble' (Mühe).

Morning, as it dawned, showed the place to be[1] a small island within the entrance[2] of a harbour. The day was required[3] for rest and[4] preparations. Time was precious; the season advancing;[5] their companions were left in suspense.[6] The next[7] day was the "Christian Sabbath." Nothing marks[8] the character of the Pilgrims more fully, than that they kept it sacredly,[9] though every consideration demanded haste.[10]

On Monday the[11] 11th *day of* December, old style,[12] the exploring party[13] of the forefathers land at Plymouth. * * * The spot, when examined,[14] seemed to invite a settlement;[15] and in[16] *a* few days the *Mayflower* was safely moored[17] in its harbour. In memory of[18] the hospitalities[19] which the company had received at[20] the last English port from which they had sailed, this oldest New England colony[21] obtained the name of Plymouth.—GEORGE BANCROFT, *History of the United States.*

[1] Turn *Morning — be* by 'when the morning dawned (graute) it was discovered (zeigte es sich) that the place was.'

[2] *Within the entrance,* am Eingang.

[3] *Required* may here be rendered by the predicative adjective nöthig.

[4] Since the term Ausruhen (*rest*) requires the definite article, here contracted with the preposition zu, and the word Vorbereitungen (*preparations*) does not require the article, on account of its being used in a general sense in the plural number, the preposition zu must be repeated before *preparations.*

[5] We should use here in German the past participle, vorgeschritten, *i.e.* advanced. *Companions,* Gefährten.

[6] *Left in suspense,* in banger Ungewißheit zurückgelassen.

[7] The word *next* should in the above phrase be turned by 'following.'

[8] *Marks,* here bezeichnet; *more fully* = better.

[9] *To keep sacredly* might be rendered literally, or in accordance with Luther's translation of the Fourth Commandment, by heiligen.

[10] Turn *every — haste* by 'all considerations (Rücksichten) urged to the (zur) haste.'

[11] See page 44, note 2.

[12] Retain the corresponding foreign term, and use the genitive case.

[13] *Exploring party,* Expedition.

[14] *When examined,* bei genauer Untersuchung. For the construction of the whole clause see Extr. 5, note *b.*

[15] In German the accusative case would not be used here; we must therefore supply the preposition zu after *invite.*

[16] Turn here *in* by 'after.'

[17] *Was ... moored,* lag ... vor Anker. Retain the name of the boat—*Mayflower*—using it as a fem. noun.

[18] *In memory of,* zur Erinnerung an.

[19] Use the singular of *hospitalities,* and turn *received* by 'enjoyed.'

[20] *At,* in; *port,* Hafen.

[21] Turn *this — colony* by 'this oldest colony in New England.'

XVI.

THE SLAVE-MAKING[1] INSTINCT OF ANTS.

This remarkable instinct was first discovered in [1]the *Formica (Polyerges) rufescens*[2] by Pierre Huber, a better observer even[3] than his celebrated father.[4] This ant is absolutely dependent on its slaves; without their aid the species[5] would certainly become extinct in a single year. The workers, though most energetic and courageous in capturing slaves,[6] do no other work. They are incapable of making[7] their own nests, or of feeding their own larvæ.

When[8] the old nest is found inconvenient, and they have to[9] migrate, it is the slaves which determine[10] the migration, and actually[11] carry their masters in their jaws. So utterly helpless are the masters, that when Huber shut up[12] thirty of them without a slave, but with plenty[13] of the food which they like best, and with their larvæ and pupæ to stimulate[14] them to work, they did nothing; they would not even feed themselves, and many perished[15] of

---

[1] A literal translation of the epithet *slave-making* would here be inapplicable; we must therefore turn the above by ' the instinct of the ants to make slaves.' *In*, say bei.

[2] The *Formica rufescens*, or ' red ant,' is called die röthliche Ameise. The suffix lich modifies, like the English *ish*, the intensity of colours.

[3] Turn *a—even* by ' a (use dative) yet sharper observer.'

[4] Supply here *was*. The father of the naturalist Pierre Huber was Francis Huber, born at Geneva in 1750.

[5] *Species*, Art; *become extinct* = die out.

[6] *In capturing slaves*, im Sclaven-fange ; *do*, here verrichten.

[7] We say in German ' to build a nest.' See Extr. 9, note *a*.

[8] See page 41, note 9.

[9] *Have to* = must.

[10] Supply here the preposition über, and see for the construction of *it is*, &c. page 34, note 13.

[11] *Actually*, thatsächlich, or, more idiomatically, factisch. Use for *jaws* the singular of ' mouth.'

[12] *To shut up*, einsperren ; *of them*, say derselben.

[13] *With plenty*, mit einer Menge; *food*, Nahrung; *and with*, say sammt.

[14] *To stimulate*, anregen; use *supine* with um. *To work*, zum Arbeiten.

[15] *Perished* = died; *of* in the above phrase is rendered by vor, or it may be omitted in the transla-

hunger.　Huber then introduced[1] a single slave[2] (*Formica fusca*[3]), and she instantly set to work,[4] fed and saved the survivors, made[5] some cells and tended the larvæ, and put all to rights.[6]　What can be[7] more extraordinary than these well-ascertained[8] facts.　If we had[9] not known of[10] any other slave-making[11] ant, it[12] would have been hopeless to have speculated[13] how so wonderful an[14] instinct could *have been* perfected.[15]—DARWIN, *The Origin of Species.*

tion, and the term *hunger* put in the genitive case.

[1] Render here *introduced* by gesellte dann zu ihnen.

[2] Use the masculine form of *slave*, but retain the feminine pronoun *she*, the same referring to 'ant' in general.

[3] The *Formica fusca* is called in German die schwarzgraue Ameise.

[4] *To set to work*, sich an die Arbeit machen.

[5] Turn *made*, as with nests, by the verb 'to build;' *to tend*, here pflegen.

[6] *To put all to rights*, brachte Alles in Ordnung.

[7] Turn here *be* by 'give,' supplying the pronoun es before it.

[8] *Well-ascertained*, völlig erwiesen. When the word *fact* denotes 'a deed or action,' it must be rendered in German by That; and when it is synonymous with 'event,' as is the case here, by Thatsache. The term Factum, which has in the plural the two forms Facta and Facten, is sometimes used for *fact* in both significations.

[9] It is a matter of course that the conditional mood is also to be used here in German, because a supposition is expressed which is contrary to reality.　The conjunction *if* may, however, in similar cases be omitted in German (as also in English), and the condi-

tional clause given in an inverted form : *e.g.* Wären diese Lords wie Ihr sie schildert, verstummen müßt ich; hoffnungslos verloren wär' meine Sache, sprächen sie mich schuldig.—*Schiller. If these Lords were as you represent them, I must remain silent; my cause would be hopelessly lost if they pronounced me guilty.*　From the two last clauses will also be seen that the hypothetical clause may be placed after the principal one.

[10] *To know of* means here 'to have a knowledge of,' and may, therefore, be rendered by wissen von.

[11] Here we might employ for *slave-making* the expression knechtend, *i.e.* to enslave, to enthral ; or turn the expression by 'an ant which makes slaves.'

[12] See the note to Ext. 7

[13] In German we can avoid the frequent repetition of the auxiliary verb haben by using the supine of nachdenken, preceded by the adverbial compound darüber.

[14] The words *so wonderful* qualify in the above clause the term *instinct*.　See, therefore, page 31, note 18.

[15] The agent performing the action not being expressly mentioned, we ought to use here, according to the rule mentioned in Ext. 41, n. *b*, the reflective form of *to perfect*—here ausbilten—in the infinitive.

XVII.

THE BATTLE OF[1] THE ALMA.[2]

The French seized[3] the empty ground which divided[4] the enemy from the sea, and then undertook to assail the enemy's[5] left wing; but were baffled[6] by the want of a road for Canrobert's artillery, and by the exceeding cogency[7] of the rule which forbids them[8] from engaging[9] their infantry on open ground without the support of cannon.[10] Their failure[11] placed them in jeopardy; for they had committed[12] so large a[13] proportion of their force to the distant part of the West Cliff[14] and the sea-shore, that

---

[1] The preposition *of* before the name of a place near which a *battle* was fought is generally rendered by the preposition bei when the place is a town, village, island, &c.; by the preposition an when the place is a mountain, hill, stream, river, &c.: e.g. *the battle of Leipzig,* die Schlacht bei Leipzig; *the battle of the Katzbach,* die Schlacht an der Katzbach.

[2] The proper name *Alma* is, like that of most rivers, feminine.

[3] *To seize,* the military expression, is in German sich bemächtigen; *the — ground,* des freien Terrains.

[4] When *to divide* is synonymous with 'to keep apart,' render it by trennen; undertook, machten sich daran.

[5] See page 14, note 4.

[6] The verb *to baffle,* in the sense in which it is used here, cannot be applied in German to persons, since vereiteln is applicable to actions only, and not to the agents performing them. We can, therefore, say of a plan that it has been vereitelt, but not of a person. For this reason we should supply here the words 'their plans' before the verb.

[7] *Exceeding cogency,* übermäßiger Zwang. For the translation of the preposition *by,* occurring above twice, see the note to Ext. 46.

[8] The German construction of the above sentence will be greatly simplified by omitting the pronoun *them,* and by construing *which forbids their infantry,* &c.

[9] *From engaging,* sich . . . auf einen Kampf einzulassen; *open ground =* free field.

[10] When *cannon* denotes artillery in general, it is rendered by the collective noun Geschütz, and by Kanone when it signifies the guns considered singly.

[11] One rendering of the comprehensive term *failure* has been given page 32, note 4. Here, however, it may be rendered by vereitelter Versuch.

[12] *Committed =* sent.

[13] The article must in German be placed before the adjective, and the adverb. expression qualifying the same. *Proportion,* here Anzahl; *force =* troops.

[14] The expression *West Cliff* forms in German a compound term. The Cliff, which lies near the sea-shore, is a height measuring 350 feet.

E

for[1] nearly an hour they lay much at the mercy[2] of any[3] Russian general who might have chosen[4] to take advantage of their severed condition.[5]

But instead of turning to his own glory[6] the mistake the French had been making, Prince Mentschikoff hastened[7] to copy it, wasting[8] time and strength in a march towards the sea-shore and a counter-march[9] back to the Telegraph.[10] Still the sense[11] the French had of their failure,[12] and the galling fire which Kiriakoff's two batteries were by this time bringing to bear on them,[13] began to create[14] in their army a grave discontent and sensations scarce short of despondency.[15] Seeing[16] the danger to which[17] this condition[18] of things was leading, and becoming for[19] other reasons impatient, Lord Raglan determined to order the[20] final advance of the English infantry, without waiting any longer for[21] the time when[22] Canrobert and Prince Napoleon should be established on

[1] Turn *for* by 'during.'

[2] *Lay — mercy*, fich ganz in ber Gewalt...befanben.

[3] When the pronoun *any* is used in the sense of 'every,' it must be rendered by jeber.

[4] *Who — chosen*, bem es beigefallen wäre.

[5] *Severed condition*, ifolirte (or vereinzelte) Stellung.

[6] Place the clause *of turning* (auszubeuten) *to his own glory* after *had been making*.

[7] *To hasten*, here fich beeilen; *to copy*, say: zu wieberholen.

[8] *To waste*, vergeuben. Cf. Int. p. xv., II., *a*, and use the imperfect.

[9] We use also in German the military expression Contremarsch.

[10] The *Telegraph* or *Telegraph Height* is a height joined on to the West Cliff, which was crowned during the time of the war by an unfinished turret, intended for a telegraph.

[11] *Sense* = consciousness. See the note to Ext. 23, and, further on, note 13.

[12] Render *of their failure*, by vom Mißlingen ihres Planes, *i.e.*, ill success of their plan;' *galling* by läftig.

[13] *Were—them*, jetzt auf fie richteten. The imperfect *began* is here the principal verb, and since the sentence does not begin with the subject itself, it should be placed after *still* (bennoch).

[14] *To create* (feelings), hervorrufen. erwecken.

[15] Turn *sensations—despondency* by 'feelings which nearly bordered on despondency.'

[16] Turn *seeing...Lord Raglan* by 'since Lord Raglan...saw.'

[17] *To which*, wohin.

[18] We should use in German in phrases like the above the term Lage for *condition*.

[19] Render the preposition *for* in the above phrase by aus, before which the adverb auch should be placed by way of expletive.

[20] Turn *to order the* by 'to give the order to the;' *final*, enblich.

[21] *To wait for*, here abwarten.

[22] The adverb *when*, referring in general to any period of time, may also be rendered by wo.

the plateau.[1] So the English infantry went forward,[2] and in *a* few minutes[3] the battalions which followed Codrington had not only defeated one of the two heavy "columns of attack"[4] which marched down to assail them, but had[4]stormed and carried[5] the Great Redoubt.

From that moment the hill-sides[6] on the Alma were[7] no longer a fortified position ; but they were still a battle-field, and a battle-field on which, for a time,[8] the combatants were destined to meet[9] with checkered fortune : for[10] not having been supported at the right minute, and being encompassed by great organized numbers, Codrington's disordered force was made to fall back[11] under the weight[12] of the Vladimir column; and its retreat involved[13] the centre battalion[14]of the brigade of Guards.[15]

Nearly at the same time Kiriakoff, with his great "column of the eight battalions," pushed[16] Canrobert down from the crest[17] he had got to, obliging or causing him[18] for a time to hang back[19] under the cover of the steep.

At that time the prospects of the Allies were overcast.[20] But then the whole face of the battle was suddenly changed[21] by the two guns which Lord Raglan had brought

[1] *Should — plateau,* baß Plateau beſetzt hätten.

[2] *So ... went forward,* demgemäß rückte ... vor.

[3] The clause does not begin here with the subject.

[4] *Column of attack,* Angriffs-colonne. Supply 'also' after *had.*

[5] *To carry* (a place, &c.), einnehmen. *The Great Redoubt* — Große Redoute — was a breastwork thrown up by Prince Mentschikoff at a distance of about 300 yards from the river, on the jutting rib which goes round the front of the Kowrgané hill.

[6] *Hill-sides,* Hügelabhänge.

[7] Turn here *were* by 'formed,' and *fortified* by 'firm.' The term *position* may be retained in German.

[8] *For a time,* eine Zeitlang.

[9] *Were — meet,* zuſammentreffen ſollten; *checkered,* here abwechſelnd.

[10] Turn *for—force,* by 'for since Codrington's disordered (in Unordnung gerathene) troops were not supported at the right moment and were encompassed by great organized numbers (organiſirten Maſſen).' Use *to support,* (unterſtützen) in the passive voice, but not the verb *to encompass* (einſchließen).

[11] *Was—back,* so wurden ſie (*i.e.* the troops) ... zurückgedrängt.

[12] *Under the weight,* durch die Wucht.

[13] *Involved,* zog auch...mit hinein.

[14] *Centre battalion,* here Centrum.

[15] *Brigade of Guards,* Leibgarden-Brigade.

[16] *Pushed,* transl. drängte.

[17] *Crest,* Gipfel; *to get to,* erreichen.

[18] *Obliging—him;* und zwang, oder veranlaßte, ihn.

[19] *To hang back,* zu zögern; *cover,* Schutz.

[20] *Overcast,* trübe.

[21] Turn the clause *But—changed*

up[1] to the knoll; for not only did their fire extirpate[2] the Causeway batteries,[3] and so lay open the pass,[4] but it tore through[5] the columns of Prince Mentschikoff's infantry reserves, and drove them at once from the field. This discomfiture of the Russian centre could not but govern the policy of Kiriakoff,[6] obliging him to conform[7] to its movement of retreat;[7] and he must have been the more ready to acknowledge to himself[8] the necessity of the step he was taking,[9] since by[10] this time   he had suffered the disaster[10] which was inflicted upon[11] his great "column of the eight battalions" by the French artillery. He retreated without being molested[12] by the French infantry, and took up[13] a position at a distance of two miles from the Alma.   Meanwhile, after a sheer[14] fight of infantry, the whole strength[15] that the enemy had on the Kowrgané hill[16] was broken and turned to ruin[17] by the Guards and the Highlanders.   Thenceforth the

---

by 'but suddenly the battle assumed another face' (Geſtalt).

[1] *Had brought up,* hatte...bringen laſſen.   We use here laſſen for gelaſſen, in accordance with the rule that the auxiliary verbs of mood—dürfen, mögen, fönnen, müſſen, wollen, ſollen, and laſſen—are generally used in the infinitive instead of in the past participle when immediately following another infinitive.

[2] *To extirpate,* here vernichten.

[3] *Causeway batteries,* Chauſſée Batterien.   This refers to the two batteries which were placed by Prince Mentschikoff "astride the great road, and disposed along the chain of hillocks which runs across the pass, looking down on the bridge."

[4] *So—pass,* machte auf dieſe Weiſe ten Paß frei.

[5] *Tore through,* zerſprengte; *infantry reserves,* Infanttiereſerve.

[6] *Could—Kiriakoff,* mußte natürlich Kiriakoffs Strategie beeinfluſſen.

[7] *To conform,* here ſich anſchließen; *movement of retreat,* rückgängige Bewegung.

[8] *To acknowledge to himself,* ſich eingeſtehen.

[9] The whole of the above sentence might in German be condensed by turning it by 'and he must the more readily (um ſo eher) acknowledge to himself the necessity of this step.'

[10] *By—disaster,* er von dem Unheil ſchon betroffen war.

[11] *To inflict upon,* zufügen, which v. governs the dat. of the person.

[12] Use the supine.

[13] *To take up,* here einnehmen; *at—from,* zwei Meilen weit von... entfernt.

[14] *Sheer,* here bloß. The two following nouns form in German a compound term.

[15] *Strength,* here Macht.

[16] The troops stationed on the Kowrgané hill were to oppose the Guards, the Highlanders, and the Light Division.

[17] *To turn to ruin,* here vernichten. The preposition *by* is rendered by von when it refers to the agent or cause from which an action or effect proceeds.

slaughter[1] that is wrought by artillery upon retreating[2] masses was all that remained to be fulfilled.[3]—KINGLAKE, *The Crimean War.*

XVIII.

THE APOSTLE OF THE GOTHS.

Ulphilas,[4] the Bishop and Apostle of the Goths, acquired their love and reverence by his blameless life and[5] indefatigable zeal; and they received with implicit[6] confidence the doctrines of truth and virtue which he preached and practised.[7] He executed the arduous task of translating[8] the Scriptures[9] into their native tongue,[10] a dialect of the German, or Teutonic, language; but he prudently[11] suppressed the four Books of Kings, as[12] they might tend[13] to irritate the fierce and sanguinary[14] spirit of the barbarians.

The rude, imperfect idiom[15] of soldiers and shepherds, so ill qualified[16] to communicate *any* spiritual ideas, was improved and modulated[17] by this genius; and Ulphilas,[18]

---

[1] *Slaughter* (in fights, &c.), Ge= meßel; *is wrought...upon*, unter... angerichtet wird. For the rendering of *by* see page 52, note 17.

[2] *Retreating* = fleeing.

[3] *That — fulfilled*, was noch zu thun übrig blieb.

[4] Ulphilas, the son of Christian captives from Cappadocia, was born about the year 318. Ulphilas, signifying in Gothic 'Little Wolf,' is spelt in German as in English, but sometimes the letter f is substituted for ph. The Gothic spelling was, to judge from Jornandes, *Vulfila.*

[5] It is almost a matter of course that the possessive pronoun must here be repeated, on account of the difference of gender of the qualified nouns.

[6] *Implicit*, unbedingt.

[7] *To practise*, here ausüben.

[8] Use the Supine.

[9] *The Scriptures*, die heilige Schrift, or die Bibel.

[10] *Native tongue*, Muttersprache.

[11] *Prudently*, vorsichtiger Weise.

[12] See page 43, note 11.

[13] *Might tend*, translate dazu beitragen könnten; *to irritate*, aufregen.

[14] *Sanguinary*, lit. blutig, blutgierig; transl. here kriegerisch.

[15] We use the same expression in German.

[16] *So ill qualified*, das sich so schlecht dazu eignete; *to communicate* = to express; *spiritual*, here abstract.

[17] *To modulate*, here verfeinern.

[18] Insert here the words *was obliged*, and turn *frame* by 'make.'

before he could frame his version, was obliged to compose[1] a new alphabet of twenty-four letters, four[2] of which he invented to express the peculiar sounds[3] that were unknown to the Greek and Latin pronunciation.

The character of Ulphilas recommended him to[4] the esteem of the Eastern[4] Court, where he twice appeared as the minister of peace;[5] he pleaded the cause[6] of the distressed Goths who implored the protection of Valens;[7] and the name *of* Moses was applied[8] to this spiritual guide, who conducted his people[9] through the deep waters of the Danube to the Land of Promise.[10] The devout shepherds, who were attached to his person and tractable to his voice,[11] acquiesced in their settlement at the foot of the Mæsian[12] mountains, in a country of woodlands and pastures,[13] which supported[14] their flocks and herds,[15] and enabled[16] them to purchase the corn and wine of the more plentiful provinces.[17] These harmless barbarians multiplied[18] in obscure peace and the profession[19] of Christianity.—GIBBON, *Decline and Fall of the Roman Empire.*

[1] *To compose,* here bilben.

[2] Place the numeral *four* after *he.*

[3] *Peculiar sounds,* eigenthümliche Laute; *unknown,* say fremb.

[4] Turn *The — to* briefly by ' Ulphilas gained by his character.'— *Eastern,* here : oftrömifch.

[5] *Minister of peace,* Friebensbote.

[6] *To plead a cause,* eine Sache führen; *distressed,* here bebrängt.

[7] Proper names—especially those of foreign origin—terminating in a sibilant, *i.e.* s, ß, x, sch, z, are not declined, but have the case pointed out by the definite article.

[8] *To apply* (a name), beilegen; *spiritual,* here geiftlich.

[9] See page 41, note 11. *Waters,* Gewäffer.

[10] The Biblical expression for *the Land of Promise* is in German bas gelobte Land; *devout* = pious.

[11] *Tractable—voice,* translate auf feine Stimme hörten;·*acquiesced—the,* ließen fich ruhig nieber am.

[12] *Mæsian,* möfifch.

[13] The expression *of woodlands and pastures* may be rendered by the terms walbig unb wiefenreich, used as attributive adjectives before the noun *country.*

[14] *To support,* here nähren.

[15] The two synonyms *flocks* and *herds* might here be rendered by the single expression Herbe, though the term Rubel is also used for *herd,* especially when referring to deer and pigs.

[16] *To enable,* here in ben Stant feßen.

[17] *Plentiful provinces* = blessed countries.

[18] *To multiply,* here fich vermehren. *obscure,* unbeachtet.

[19] *Profession,* Bekenntniß.

XIX.

THE PRAIRIE.[1]

In truth there is nothing[2] to describe about the prairie except its vastness, and that is indescribable. * * * East,[3] west, north, and south—on the right *hand* and on the left—in front and behind—stretched[4] the broken, woodless upland. Underneath the foot a springy[5] turf, covered with scentless violets and wild prairie roses; overhead[6] a bright, cloudless sky, whence the sun shot down beams that would have scorched up the soil long *ago* but for[7] the fresh, soft prairie breeze blowing from across the Rocky Mountains;[8] low, grassy slopes on every side, looking like waves òf turf[9] rising and falling gently. Not a tree to be seen[10] in the far distance; not a house in sight,[11] far or near; not a drove[12] of sheep or a herd of cattle; no sign of life except the dun-coloured prairie chickens[13] whirring through the heather as we drove along,[14]—nothing but the broken, woodless upland.

[1] The term *prairie* is also used in German, where it retains the original feminine gender.

[2] *There is nothing*, transl. es läßt fich...nichts; *about*, here von.

[3] Supply nach before *East; in—behind*, vor uns und hinter uns.

[4] *To stretch*, here fich ausdehnen; *broken*, with reference to land, uneben; *woodless*, waldlos.

[5] Turn *underneath—springy* by 'under the feet elastic.'

[6] *Overhead*, say: über dem Haupte.

[7] The expression *but for*, referring to a present participle, must be turned by 'if not,' and the present participle changed into the conditional. The sense of the passage must determine which tense is to be employed. Here we should use the present conditional, *i.e.* 'if ...did not blow.'

[8] *From — Mountains*, von dem

Felfengebirge her. The original English name *Rocky Mountains* is not unfrequently met with in German books. Humboldt employs it in his „Ansichten der Natur."

[9] Turn *waves of turf* by the compound 'grass-waves,' using *rising and falling gently* (sanft auf- und niederwogend) as an attributive clause.

[10] Turn *to be seen* by 'is to see.'

[11] *In sight*, sichtbar. For *far and near* we use in German the alliterative expression weit und breit, to which the English 'far and wide' corresponds.

[12] *Drove*, Trieb, from treiben, *to drive.*

[13] *Prairie chickens*, amerifanische Feldhühner. The word *dun-coloured* may here be rendered by dunfelfarbig; whirring, die ... fchwirrten.

[14] *To drive along* and, further on, *to pass on*, dahinfahren.

So we passed on, coming from time to time upon[1] some break[2] in the monotony of the vast, dreamlike[3] solitude. Sometimes it was a prairie stream, running[4] clear as crystal between *its* low, sedgy banks, through[5] which our horses forded knee-deep, and then again the broken, woodless upland; sometimes it was a lone Irish shanty,[6] knocked up roughly with[7] planks and logs, and wearing a look[8] as though it had been built by shipwrecked settlers[9] stranded on the shore of the prairie-sea. Farther on we came upon[10] a herd of half-wild horses, who as we approached dashed away[11] in *a* wild stampede; then upon a knot of trees,[12] whose[13] seeds had been wafted from the distant forest, and taken root[14] kindly on the rich prairie soil; now upon an emigrant's team, *with* the women and children under the canvas awning,[15] and the red-shirted and brigand-looking miners[16] at its side, travelling across the prairie in search of[17] the land of

---

[1] *To come upon* (anything), ftoßen auf. See Int. page xv., II., *a*.

[2] *Break*, here Abwechßlung.

[3] *Dreamlike*, traumhaft.

[4] *Running* may here be rendered by the present participle bahinfließend, placing it after *banks*.

[5] *Through...forded*, burchwateten.

[6] *Shanty*, Blockhaus or Hütte. Some German writers employ the English expression. *Knocked up*, translate zusammen gezimmert. The verb zimmern is applied to work done by carpenters.

[7] Translate *with* by aus; cf. the note to Extr. 3.

[8] *To wear a look*, aussehen.

[9] The German for *settler* is Ansiebler, but the English word is also used; *shipwrecked*, schiffbrüchig.

[10] See above, note 1.

[11] *To dash away*, fortstürzen. Render the Americanism *stampede* — from the Spanish *estampido* — denoting a sudden scamper of large bodies of cattle or horses on the prairies, by Flucht.

[12] *Knot of trees*, Baumgruppe.

[13] In German we could not use here the relative pronoun, because it would imply that it was the seeds which the trees themselves had produced that were wafted from the distant forest. We should therefore, in order to avoid an ambiguity, render *whose — wafted*, freely by bie ihr Dasein bem Samen verbankt, ber...hergetragen worben.

[14] *To take root*, Wurzel fassen; *kindly*, here schnell, and *rich*, üppig; *emigrant's team*, Auswanbrergespann.

[15] *Canvas awning* (of vehicles), Plane. In some parts of Germany people say Plaue.

[16] There are no single equivalents for the adjectives *red-shirted* and *brigand-looking*, and the expression *miners* could not be rendered here by Bergleute, as this term is generally applied to professional miners only. The whole clause must, therefore, be turned by 'the gold-diggers with their red shirts and brigand-like appearance' (räuberhaftem Aussehen).

[17] *In search of*, um... aufzusuchen; *land of gold* forms in German a compound term.

gold ; and then again the silent solitude and the broken, woodless upland.—E. DICEY, *Six Months in the Federal States.*

XX.

CHIVALRY[1] IN SPAIN.

Spain was indeed the land of chivalry. The respect for the sex[2] which had descended[3] from the Visigoths[4] was mingled[5] with the religious enthusiasm which had been[6] kindled in the long wars with the Infidel.[7] The apotheosis[8] of chivalry in the person of their apostle and patron, St. James,[9] contributed still further to this exaltation of sentiment,[10] which was maintained[11] by the various military orders, who devoted themselves, in the bold language of the age, to the service "of God and the ladies." So that the Spaniard may be said to have put in action[12]

---

[1] *Chivalry*, here baß Ritterthum, or baß Ritterwesen, and not tie Ritterschaft ; for the latter denotes the 'body or order of knights,' whilst the former expressions signify the 'system or practice of knighthood.'

[2] The expression *sex*, alone, cannot be used in German, as is done in English, to denote 'womankind ;' the adjectives 'female' or 'fair' must, therefore, be supplied before the noun.

[3] *To descend*, herstammen.

[4] The Visigoths have, like all other members of the great German family, at all times displayed the deepest respect towards women, to whom they attributed an almost sacred character. *Visigoths*, Westgothen.

[5] Turn *was mingled* by the reflective form 'united itself.'

[6] See Extr. 4, note *b ; to kindle*, fig. anfachen ; use the imperf.

[7] The term *Infidel*, used here collectively for unbelievers, is in German employed in the plural.

[8] Retain here the corresponding foreign term. *Patron*, Schutzheilige.

[9] *St. James* standing here in apposition to the preceding nouns, we must render it by Sanct Jago or teß heiligen Jacub. The patron of the Spanish knights was the Apostle St. James (Spanish *Jago*), said to be buried in the Spanish town called after him Santjago di Compostella. The *shrine* (Schrein) of the patron is in that place.

[10] The whole clause *contributed —sentiment* must in German be rather freely paraphrased by trug noch mehr bazu bei, diesem Gefühle einen höhern Aufschwung zu verleihen.

[11] *To maintain*, here nähren ; *orders*, here Orben ; *to devote oneself*, sich wibmen ; *age*, here Zeit ; *ladies*, Damen.

[12] Turn *so—action* by 'so that one can say that the Spaniard put in action.' *To put in action*, thatsächlich ausführen.

what, in other countries, passed for the extravagances[1] of the minstrel. An example of this[2] occurs in the fifteenth century, when[2] a passage of arms was defended[3] at Orbigo, not far from the shrine of Compostella, by[4] a Castilian knight, named Suero de Queñones, and his nine companions, against all comers,[5] in the presence of John the Second and his court.

The object was[6] to release the knight from the obligation, imposed on him by his mistress,[7] of publicly wearing an iron collar round his neck[8] every Thursday. The jousts[9] continued *for* thirty days, and the doughty champions[10] fought, without shield or target,[11] with weapons bearing points of Milan steel.[12] Six hundred and twenty-seven encounters[13] took place, and *one* hundred and sixty-six lances were broken,[14] when the emprise[15] was declared to be fairly achieved. The whole affair[16] is narrated with becoming[17] gravity by an eye-witness, and the reader may fancy himself[18] perusing the adventures of a Launcelot or an Amadis.—PRESCOTT, *History of the Reign of Ferdinand and Isabella.*

[1] *Passed—extravagances,* für die Ueberschwenglichkeiten...galt.

[2] *Of this,* hievon; *to occur,* vorkommen. See page 50, note 22.

[3] *A—defended,* ein Ritterkampf... aufgenommen wurde.

[4] See page 52, note 17.

[5] Transl. *all comers* by alle Welt.

[6] *The object was,* dies hatte zum Zweck; *to release,* befreien.

[7] Turn the clause *the—mistress* by 'the on him by his lady imposed obligation (auferlegten Verpflichtung).

[8] *Collar round his neck,* say simply Halsband.

[9] *Joust,* Turnier. Use here the singular only. *Continued* = lasted.

[10] *Champion,* here Kämpe.

[11] The term *target* denoting here a shield, formerly used as a defensive weapon, must be rendered by Tartsche.

[12] *Bearing — steel,* deren Spitzen aus Mailänder Stahl waren.

[13] *Encounter,* here Kampf.

[14] *To break,* here brechen.

[15] Translate *emprise,* by Aufgabe; and render *to be fairly achieved* by für vollständig gelöst.

[16] When the expression *affair* is synonymous with 'incident,' it is rendered by Ereigniß; when with 'occurrence,' by Vorfall; and when with 'event,' as is the case here, by Begebenheit.

[17] *Becoming,* here geziemend. The corresponding foreign term of *gravity* may here be retained.

[18] Transl. *may fancy himself* by könnte glauben, and turn the present part. *perusing* by 'that he reads.'

XXI.

CHARLES THE GREAT.

. 1.

CORONATION OF CHARLES[1] AT ROME.

Charles remained in the city for[2] some weeks; and on Christmas-day, A.D. 800, he heard mass in the basilica *of* St. Peter.[3] On the spot where now the gigantic dome of Bramante and Michael Angelo towers[4] over the buildings of the modern city, the spot[5] which tradition had hallowed as that of the Apostle's martyrdom,[6] Constantine the Great had erected the oldest and stateliest[7] temple of Christian Rome.

Out of the[8] transept a flight *of* steps led up to the high altar,[9] underneath and just beyond the great arch, the Arch of Triumph,[10] as it was[11] called: behind in the semi circular apse[12] sat the clergy, rising tier above tier

[1] See Ext. 11, note *a*.

[2] The literal translation of the preposition *for* would here be an Anglicism, duration of time being generally expressed in German, as in Latin, by the accusative only. Sometimes the word lang is added, if the length of time is to be denoted emphatically, as: vierzig Jahre lang, *for forty years*. For the constr. of *in—weeks*, cf. Ext. 4, n. *a*.

[3] Turn here *the—St. Peter* by 'the St. Peter's Church.' The abbreviation *St.* is in accordance with the Latin *sanctus*, for which it stands, pronounced in German 'Sanct;' *gigantic dome*, Riesendom.

[4] *To tower*, emporragen.

[5] *The spot*, say : an jener Stelle.

[6] Turn *which — martyrdom* by ' which the tradition *has* hallowed as that where the martyrdom of the Apostle *has* taken place.' According to tradition, the Apostle Peter was crucified on that spot A.D. 67.

[7] *Stately*, here prächtig.

[8] *Out of the*, vom.

[9] *High altar* is in German a compound substantive ; and the principal member—that is, the component which determines the other—being an adjective, it is joined without any inflection to the subordinate member. Place *out—transept* before *up to the* (bis zum ...hinauf); *just beyond*, gerade hinter.

[10] Turn *Arch of Triumph* by the compound term 'triumph-arch.' In German compound expressions the principal, or qualifying, member always precedes the other, as is also the case with the English compounds forming one word.

[11] See Extr. 4, note *b*.

[12] *Semi circular apse*, halbkreisförmige Apsis. The word *apsis* is

around its walls ;[1] in the midst, high above the rest,[2] and looking down, past the altar, over[3] the multitude, was placed[2] the Bishop's throne, itself[4] the curule chair of some[5] forgotten magistrate.[6] From that chair the Pope now rose,[7] as the reading of the Gospel ended,[8] advanced to[9] where Charles—who had exchanged his simple Frankish dress for the sandals and the chlamys[10] of a Roman patrician—knelt in prayer by[11] the high altar ; and as in the sight[12] of all he placed upon the brow[13] of the barbarian[14] chieftain the diadem of the Cæsars, then bent in obeisance[15] before him, the church rang to the shout[16] of the multitude,[17] again free, again the lords[18] and centre of the world : *"Karolo Augusto, a Deo coronato, magno et pacifico Imperatori, vita et victoria."*[19]

In that shout, echoed by the Franks without,[20] was

sometimes rendered by Chœrnische, *i.e.* niche of the choir, or by Abfeite, off-side ; *clergy*, Geistlichkeit.

[1] Render the clause *rising—walls* by in aufsteigenden Reihen an den Wänden herum.

[2] Transl. *high above the rest. . was placed*, by stand, alles Andere überragend.

[3] *Looking—over*, über den Altar hinweg .... übersehend.

[4] The pronoun *itself* should here be rendered freely by ehmalig, 'former,' to be used as an attributive adjective, with the definite article. *Curule*, curulisch.

[5] *Some* is here synonymous with 'any one,' and is to be rendered by irgend ein.

[6] Translate here *magistrate* by Staatsbeamten ; the *curule chair* having been the seat of honour of the highest dignitaries of the ancient Roman State.

[7] *To rise*, in the sense of 'to get up from a seat, &c.' is rendered in the more elevated style by sich erheben, instead of aufstehen.

[8] *As—ended*, transl. so wie das Evangelium verlesen war.

[9] Render *advanced to* by schritt bis zu dem Platze vor ; *Frankish*, fränkisch.

[10] There is no exact and single

German equivalent for the Greek term *chlamys*. We may retain the original expression, die Chlamis, or render it by Staatsmantel.

[11] Turn *knelt—by* by 'praying knelt at :' *as*, here wie.

[12] *Sight*, here Angesicht.

[13] *Brow*, transl. Haupt, which is the more dignified expression for Kopf, *head.*

[14] The adjective *barbarian* would in German be too strong an epithet here: use, therefore, the less harsh expression Barbarenhäuptling for *barbarian chieftain*. Turn *diadem* by 'crown.' *Cæsars*, denoting 'Emperors,' is in German Cäsaren.

[15] *Bent in obeisance*, sich tief... verneigte.

[16] *To ring to the shout*, von dem Rufe erschallen.

[17] Turn *multitude* by 'people, and add 'which was.'

[18] For *lords* use Beherrscher, in the singular only ; *centre*, Mittelpunkt.

[19] Turn the above Latin phrase by 'Long life and victory to Charles Augustus, the crowned by God, great and peace-loving Emperor.' *Vita* might also be rendered here by Heil, *i.e.* hail.

[20] *Echoed—without*, in welchen die

pronounced the union, so long in preparation,[1] so mighty
in its consequences, of the Roman and the Teuton, of the
memories[2] and the civilization of the South with the fresh
energy of the North, and from that moment modern[3]
history begins.[3]

· 2.

CHARACTER OF CHARLES THE GREAT.

No claim can be more groundless[4] than that which the
modern French, the sons of the Latinised Kelt, set up to[5]
the Teutonic Charles. At Rome he might[6] assume the
chlamys[7] and the sandals, but at the head[8] of his Frankish
host he strictly adhered to[9] the customs of his country,
and was beloved by his people as the very[10] ideal of their
own character and habits.[10] Of strength and stature almost
superhuman,[11] in swimming and hunting[12] unsurpassed,
steadfast[13] and terrible in fight, to[14] his friends gentle and
condescending, he was[15] a Roman, much less a Gaul, in

Franken von außen einstimmten. The
literal wiederhallen, for *to echo*, cannot
be used with reference to persons.

[1] Turn *in preparation* by 'prepared,' and render *so mighty in its
consequences* by the expressive compound term folgenreich; placing
both adjectives as attributes before
union (Verbindung); *of—Teutons*,
'between the Romans and Teutons.'

[2] *Memories*, say : historischen Vergangenheit.

[3] Render *from that moment
modern···begins*, by von diesem Augenblicke an datirt die neue.

[4] *Groundless*, here unbegründet;
Latinised, latinisirt.

[5] *To set up a claim to anything*, einen Anspruch auf etwas machen.
Recent historical investigations
have conclusively proved that
Charles the Great was born in the
country formerly called *Austrasia;*
consequently, on genuine German
soil.

[6] Use here for *might* the imperfect
of mögen; *to assume*, here anthun.

[7] See page 60, note 10.

[8] We say in German, in the
above and similar phrases, an der
Spitze ; *host = army*.

[9] *To adhere strictly to anything*,
streng an etwas halten.

[10] *Very* may here be rendered
by the expressive term verförpert.
i.e. embodied. Cf. p. 42, n. 9.

[11] Turn *of—superhuman* by 'of
nearly superhuman strength and
stature (Statur).

[12] See page 15, note 1.

[13] *Steadfast*, standhaft.

[14] *To* is here to be rendered by
the preposition gegenüber, which is
put after the noun to which it
refers ; *gentle*, milde.

[15] The expression *in nothing* is
to be placed in the translation
after *he was*, and the indefinite
article before *Roman* and *Gaul*
omitted.

nothing but[1] his culture and his width of view,[2]—otherwise
a Teuton. The centre of his realm was the Rhine; his
capitals Aachen and Engilenheim;[3] his army German; his
sympathies, as they are shown[4] in the gathering of the old
hero-lays,[5] the composition[6] of a German grammar, the
ordinance against confining prayer to[7] the three languages
—Hebrew, Greek, and Latin—were all for the race from
which he sprang,[8] and whose advance,[9] represented by the
victory of Austrasia, the true Frankish fatherland,[10] over
Neustria and Aquitaine, spread a second Germanic wave[11]
over the conquered countries.—JAMES BRYCE, *The Holy
Roman Empire.*

XXII.

LOVE OF[12] FLOWERS.

Perhaps it may be thought, if we understood flowers
better, we might love them less.[13]　We do not love them

[1] *But,* referring here to the term
nothing, is to be rendered by als,
and the preposition *in* repeated
after it.

[2] *Width of view,* umfaſſende Anſchauungsweiſe; otherwise, ſonſt

[3] *Engilenheim,* now called *Ingel-
heim,* lies between Mentz and Bin-
gen, not far from the left bank of
the Rhine.

[4] *Are shown,* transl. ſich kundgeben.

[5] *Hero-lay,* Heldenlied.

[6] *Composition,* transl. Ausarbei-
tung, *i.e.* elaboration. We might
also use the infinitive verfaſſen substantively, and render *the* by im.
It may not be quite superfluous to
remark here, that although the
verb *to compose* (a book) is rendered
by verfaſſen, we rarely use the
noun Verfaſſung for *the composition*
(of a book), but employ it for the
'state or mood of the mind,' and
more particularly for the political
constitution of a country.

[7] *The—to,* in der Verordnung das
Gebet nicht bloß auf...zu beſchränken.

[8] *Were—sprang,* waren ſämmtlich
für die Raſſe aus welcher er ſtammte.

[9] Translate *advance* by Ausdehnung, and *represented* by wie ſie...
bezeichnet wird. *Austrasia,* Auſtraſien.

[10] *The—fatherland,* dem eigentlichen
Heimatland der Franken. *Neustria,*
Neuſtrien; *Aquitaine,* Aquitanien.

[11] *Wave,* in the sense in which it
is used here, Woge.

[12] The objective genitive, *i.e.* the
genitive which stands as an object
of some action or feeling, is frequently expressed in German by a
preposition, in order to avoid all
ambiguity. The governing substantive or the verb from which
it is derived will in such instances
show which preposition is required. The noun *love* is in
German followed by the preposition zu.

[13] Turn *Perhaps—less* by 'one

much as it is.[1] Few people care about[2] flowers. * * *
I have never[3] heard of a piece of land which would let
well on a building lease remaining unlet because it was[4]
a flowery piece. I have never heard of parks being kept
for[5] wild hyacinths, though often of their being kept[6] for
wild beasts. And the blossoming time[7] of the year being
principally spring, I perceive it to be the mind of most
people[8] during that period to stay in towns.

A year or two ago[9] a keen-sighted and eccentrically-
minded friend of mine[10] having taken it into his head[11] to
violate this national custom, and go to *the* Tyrol in spring,
was passing through a valley near Landeck with several
similarly headstrong companions. A strange mountain
appeared[12] in the distance, belted about its breast with a
zone of blue,[13] like our English Queen. Was it a blue
cloud? * * * Was it a mirage—a meteor? Would it stay
to be approached?[14] (Ten miles of winding road[15] yet

could perhaps believe, that we
should love the flowers less if we
understood more of them.'

[1] Translate *as it is* by aud̄ fo, and
place the same at the beginning of
the clause.

[2] *Care about*, in the above sense,
mad̄en fid̄ etwas aus.

[3] Supply here bavon, and turn *of*
—*unlet* by 'that a piece of land
which would let well on a building
lease (bas fid̄ zu Bauzweden gut ver-
mietḥen liese) remained unlet.'

[4] Use here the present tense, and
translate *a flowery piece* by ein
blumenreid̄er Boden.

[5] Turn here *for* by 'on account
of,' and construe the clause according to note 3 above.

[6] Turn *of their being kept* by
'that one kept them.'

[7] *Blossoming time*, Blüthezeit. See
Int. page xvi., *c*, and supply im
before *spring*. *To perceive*, bemerfen.

[8] Turn *it—people* by 'that most
people like' (mögen).

[9] Turn the above clause by 'before
one or two years;' and in construing the following clauses remember
that the sentence does not begin

with the subject, and that the expression *was passing through* (fam...
burd̄) contains the principal verb.

[10] *A—mine*, ein sd̄arffid̄tiger unb
ercentrisd̄er Freund von mir. In similar
phrases the dative is used in German for the genitive.

[11] *To take anything into one's
head*, fid̄ etwas vornehmen; *to violate*,
here entgegen handeln.

[12] *To appear*, here fid̄ zeigen.

[13] *Belted—blue*, in ber Mitte mit
einem blauen Gürtel gesd̄müdt; *like*,
here wie.

[14] *Would—approached*, wirt es
bei ber Annäherung nid̄t versd̄winben?
i.e. will it not disappear at our
approaching it? Some free version
of the kind is necessary in German,
partly because *to approach* is an
intransitive verb, and cannot be
used in the passive voice, and partly
because it seems more in accordance with the genius of the German
language to ask whether the *blue
zone* will not disappear, as a rain-
bow would, than to inquire whether
it would stay, since this verb would
imply a voluntary action.

[15] *Of—road*, einer fid̄ hinwindenben

between them and the foot of its mountain.)   Such questioning[1] had they concerning it.   My keen-sighted friend
alone maintained it to be substantial;[2] whatever it might
be, it was not air, and would not vanish.   The ten miles
of road[3] were overpassed, the carriage left,[4] the mountain
climbed.   It stayed[5] patiently, expanding[6] still into richer
breadth and heavenlier glow[7]—a belt of gentians.   Such
things[8] may verily be seen among the Alps in spring, and
in spring only.[9]   Which being so,[10] I observe most people
prefer going in autumn.—JOHN RUSKIN, *Modern Painters.*

XXIII.

LIFE[11] AMONG THE BEDOUINS.

1.

If a Bedouin tribe[12] be moving in great haste before an
enemy,[13] and should be unable to stop for many hours,[14]
or be making a forced march to avoid pursuit over[15] a
desert where the wells are very distant from each other, the

Straße.   Supply lagen before *yet*
(noch), and turn *its* by 'the.'
   [1] *Questioning* = questions; *had
—it,* ſtellten ſie darüber auf.
   [2] *Substantial*, transl. etwas Wirk-
liches.   Cf. Int. page xvii., III.
Whatever—was, was immer es auch
ſei, ſo war es.
   [3] Turn *road* by 'way,' putting
it in the genitive case without
any article; *overpassed,* zurückgelegt.
Here the action may be considered
as quite past.
   [4] Supply here the imperfect of
werben; *to climb,* erklimmen.   The
prefix er denotes here the achiev-
ing of an action.
   [5] *Stayed,* transl. lag...ba.
   [6] Use in German the reflective
form, retaining the present participle; *into richer,* zu vollerer.

   [7] *Heavenlier glow,* transl. tieferer
Himmelsbläue; *gentians,* Enzianen.
   [8] *Such things,* Dergleichen; *may
verily be seen* = can one verily see.
   [9] *Only* should be placed before
in spring.
   [10] *Which being so,* und ba dies der
Fall iſt; supply 'that' before *most,*
and 'it' before *prefer; going,* zu
reiſen.
   [11] *Life,* here Lebensweiſe; *among*
= of.
   [12] *Bedouin tribe,* Beduinenſtamm.
   [13] Turn *be—enemy* by 'flees before an enemy in great haste.'
   [14] Render *should—hours* by viele
Stunden lang nicht Halt machen kann.
   [15] Turn *be — over* by 'if he, in
order to avoid pursuit (um der
Verfolgung zu entgehen), makes a
forced march (Eilmarſch) through.'

women sometimes prepare[1] bread whilst riding on camels.
The fire is then lighted in an earthen vessel. One woman
kneads the flour, a second rolls out the dough, and a third
bakes, boys or women on foot passing the materials, as
required,[2] from one to the other. But it is very rare that
the Bedouins are obliged to have recourse to this process,[3]
and I have only once witnessed[4] it.

2.

The common Bedouin can rarely get[5] meat. His food[6]
consists almost exclusively of wheaten bread[7] with truffles,
which are found in great abundance during the spring, a
few wild[8] herbs, such as asparagus, onions, and garlic; fresh
butter, curds,[9] and sour milk.

But at certain seasons even these luxuries[10] cannot be
obtained: for months together[11] he often eats bread alone.
The Sheikhs[12] usually slay[13] a sheep every day, of which
their guests, a few of their relatives, and their immediate
adherents partake.[14] The women prepare the food,[15] and
always eat after the men,[16] who rarely leave them much
wherewith to satisfy[17] their hunger.

[1] Cf. the note to Ext. 7.
[2] *Passing — required*, bringen die Sachen so wie sie gebraucht werden.
[3] *Process* being here synonymous with 'proceeding,' is to be rendered by Verfahren.
[4] Turn here *witnessed* by 'seen.'
[5] *To get*, here bekommen.
[6] When *food* expresses in a general sense all that is eaten for nourishment, we use in German Nahrung; but when it is a synonym of *dish*, denoting a particular kind of food, the German equivalent is Speise.
[7] Form here a compound expression from *wheat* and *bread*.
[8] *A few wild*, aus einigen wildwachsenden; *such as*, wie.
[9] *Curds*, Quark, for which the

expression Käsebutter is used in some parts of Germany.
[10] *Luxuries*, here Leckerbissen; *cannot be obtained*, sind...nicht zu haben.
[11] Substitute in the translation 'long' for *together*, and omit *for*.
[12] *Sheikh* is written in German either Scheif or Scheich, and pronounced as a German word.
[13] *To slay* (an animal for eating), schlachten.
[14] *Of which...partake*, transl. an dessen Genuß...Theil nehmen.
[15] See above, note 6.
[16] *Men* denotes here male individuals; we must therefore use the plural of Mann. Compare the Latin *vir* and the Greek ἀνήρ.
[17] Turn *wherewith to satisfy* by 'with which they could satisfy.'

F

3.

The dish[1] usually seen in a Bedouin tent[2] is a mess[3] of boiled meat, sometimes mixed with onions, upon which a lump of fresh butter is placed and allowed to melt.[4] The broad tail of the Mesopotamian[5] sheep is used for grease when there is no butter. Sometimes cakes of bread[6] are laid under the meat, and the entertainer,[7] tearing up the thin loaves into small pieces, soaks[8] them in the gravy[9] with his hands. The Anezza[10] make very savoury dishes of chopped meat and bread mixed with sour curds, over which when the huge platter[11] is placed before the guest is poured a flood of melted butter. Roasted meat is very rarely seen in a Bedouin tent. Rice is only eaten by the Sheikhs, except among[12] the tribes who encamp[13] in the marshes of Southern Mesopotamia,[14] where rice of an inferior quality[15] is very largely cultivated.[16] There it is boiled with meat and made into pilaws.[17]

[1] See page 65, note 6. *Usually seen* = which one usually sees.

[2] *Bedouin tent*, Bebuinenzelt.

[3] *Mess*, here Gericht; *lump* = piece.

[4] Turn *and—melt* by 'which one lets melt.'

[5] *Mesopotamian*, mesopotamisch. By means of the suffix isch — the English *ish*—we form in German adjectives from the proper names of countries, nations, persons, &c., *For*, here als; *grease*, Fett.

[6] *Cakes of bread*, transl. platte Brobkuchen.

[7] *Entertainer*, Wirth; *tearing up*, bricht.

[8] *To soak*, here tunfen. Supply the conjunction unb before *soaks*.

[9] The equivalent for *gravy* is not the same in all parts of Germany. It is called Sauce, Brühe, or Jus. The first term, in which au has the sound of o in grobe, and the e is also pronounced,' is the more usual. The last expres-

sion is pronounced as in French.

[10] The plural is in German Anezzas. *Savoury*, schmackhaft.

[11] *Huge platter*, riesige Schüssel; *flood*, here Strom.

[12] *Among*, here bei.

[13] *To encamp* may here be rendered by the corresponding foreign term, campiren.

[14] Proper names of countries preceded by adjectives generally require in German the definite article. The names themselves are by some authors not declined, in analogy with the rule for the decl. of proper names of persons preceded by the def. art. *Southern Mesopotamia*. Süb=Mesopotamien.

[15] Render *an inferior quality* by eine schlechtere Art, placing this expression before the term *rice*, and omitting the preposition *of*.

[16] *Is—cultivated*, in großer Menge gebaut wirb.

[17] *Made into pilaws*, Pilaws barauf zubereitet.

4.

The Bedouins are acquainted with[1] few medicines. The desert yields[2] some valuable simples, which are, however, rarely used.

Dr. Sandwith hearing[3] from Suttum that the Arabs had no opiates, asked[4] what they did with one who could[5] not sleep. "Do!"[6] answered the Sheikh: "why,[7] we make use of him, and set[8] him to watch the camels."— LAYARD, *Discoveries in the Ruins of Nineveh and Babylon.*

XXIV.

SIR SIDNEY SMITH AT BATH.

Not even a rumour of Sir Sidney's[9] escape had or could have run before him,[10] for at the moment of[11] reaching the coast of England[11] he had started with post-horses[12] to Bath. It was about dusk when he arrived;[13] the postilions were directed[14] to the square[15] in which his mother lived;

[1] *Are acquainted with,* kennen.
[2] *To yield,* liefern; *simples,* Heilfräuter.
[3] *Hearing,* als ... hörte; Sheikh Suttum accompanied the author.
[4] Supply 'he' after *asked; did with one,* mit Jemand thäten.
[5] *Could* is here the conditional of 'can,' and not the imperfect. This remark may seem superfluous; still the distinction between könnte, the imperfect, and könnte, the conditional, of können is very often neglected even by advanced students of German.
[6] Supply 'with him' before *do.*
[7] *Why,* here nun.
[8] Render *make use of,* by benutzen; *set* by lassen, and *watch* by hüten.
[9] That famous Admiral had been

taken prisoner by the French in a naval combat near Havre in 1796.
[10] *Had—him,* war ihm vorangegangen oder hätte ihm vorangehen können. In German the repetition of the verb vorangehen is preferable on account of the different auxiliary verbs which are required in the above clause.
[11] Turn *of—England* by 'when (wo) he reached the English coast.'
[12] *Post-horses,* here Extrapost.
[13] Begin the German version by *he arrived,* and transl. *it—when* by ungefähr in der Dämmerstunde.
[14] Render *were directed* by er ließ ...fahren.
[15] The term *square* denoting a thing peculiar to England, may

in *a* few minutes he was in his mother's arms,[1] and in fifty minutes more[2] the news had flown to the remotest suburb *of the city*.

The agitation[3] of Bath on this occasion was indescribable. All the[4] troops of the line then quartered[5] in that city and a whole regiment of volunteers immediately got under arms,[6] and marched to the quarter in which Sir Sidney lived. The small square overflowed with[7] *the* soldiery; Sir Sidney went out,[8] and was immediately lost to us[9] who[10] were watching for him, in the closing[11] ranks of the troops. Next[12] morning, however, I, my younger brother, and a schoolfellow of my *own* age, called formally upon[13] the naval hero. Why, I know not, unless as *alumni*[14] of the school at which Sir Sidney Smith[15] had received his own education, we[16] were admitted without question or demur;[16] and I may record[17] it as an amiable

be retained in German, and used as a masculine noun. $\mathfrak{Platz}$ would not be the exact equivalent.

[1] Turn 'in the arms of his,' &c.

[2] Turn *in ... more* by 'after; *flown*, transl. $\mathfrak{sich\ verbreitet}$.

[3] *Agitation*, $\mathfrak{Aufregung}$.

[4] The definite article after the numeral *all* is not required in German, except in emphatic speech. For *troops of the line* form in German the compound expression 'lines-troops,' and supply the words 'which were.'

[5] *To quarter*, here $\mathfrak{einquartieren}$; *volunteers*, $\mathfrak{Freiwillige}$.

[6] *To get under arms*, $\mathfrak{ins\ Gewehr}$ $\mathfrak{treten}$; *quarter*, here $\mathfrak{Stadttheil}$ or $\mathfrak{Stadtviertel}$.

[7] *Overflowed with*, $\mathfrak{war\ gedrängt}$ $\mathfrak{voll\ von}$; *soldiery* = soldiers.

[8] *Went out*, $\mathfrak{trat\ heraus}$.

[9] Turn *to us* by 'for us.' The author refers here to himself and his schoolfellows at the Bath Grammar School.

[10] When a relative pronoun refers to a personal pronoun of the first or second person — singular or plural—the personal pronoun must, for the sake of grammatical dis-

tinctness, be repeated after the relative which, in this case, is never to be rendered by $\mathfrak{welcher}$, $\mathfrak{welche}$, $\mathfrak{welches}$, but by $\mathfrak{der}$, $\mathfrak{die}$, $\mathfrak{das}$. The verb in the relative clause agrees in such cases, generally, with the personal pronoun. Render, therefore, *who—him*, by $\mathfrak{die\ wir\ auf\ ihn}$ $\mathfrak{warteten}$.

[11] *Closing*, transl. $\mathfrak{geschlossenen}$.

[12] When *next* refers, as is the case here, to a period of time past, it is usually rendered by $\mathfrak{folgend}$, and when referring to the future by $\mathfrak{nächst}$. See also page 59, note 2.

[13] *To call formally upon*, einen $\mathfrak{förmlichen\ Besuch\ machen}$. For *naval hero* use the compound expression $\mathfrak{Seeheld}$.

[14] *Unless as alumni*, $\mathfrak{es\ sei\ denn\ daß}$ $\mathfrak{wir\ Alumnen....waren}$.

[15] Supply the word $\mathfrak{selbst}$, which will convey the meaning of the word *own* occurring in the original.

[16] *Demur*, $\mathfrak{Aufenthalt}$. Place the words *we—demur*, which form here the principal clause at the beginning of the sentence, viz., before *why, I know not, &c.; admitted,* here $\mathfrak{vorgelassen}$.

[17] *May record*, $\mathfrak{kann...anführen}$.

trait in[1] Sir Sidney, that he received us *then* with great kindness, and took us down with him[2] to the pump-room.[3] Considering, however,[4] that we must have been most afflicting bores[5] *to* Sir Sidney—a fact which no self-esteem could even then disguise from us[6]—it puzzled me at first to understand the principle[7] of his conduct. Having[8] already done more than enough in courteous[9] acknowledgment of our fraternal claims as fellow-students at *the* Bath Grammar School,[10] why should he think it necessary[11] to burden himself further[12] *with* our worshipful[13] society? I found out[14] the secret, and will explain it. A very slight[15] attention to Sir Sidney's deportment in public revealed to me that he was morbidly afflicted[16] with nervous sensibility and with *mauvaise honte.*[17] * * *

And yet there was a[18] necessity that Sir Sidney should gratify[19] the public interest, so warmly expressed, by presenting himself somewhere or other to the public eye.[20] * * *

[1] *In* = from; *kindness,* Freundlichkeit.

[2] Turn *took — him* briefly by 'went with us.'

[3] The expression *pump-room* may be considered as a proper name of the place where the mineral waters at Bath are drunk. The corresponding designation for similar places is in German Trinkhalle, or simply Brunnen.

[4] *Considering, however,* da ich aber in Erwägung zog.

[5] *Must—bores,* äußerst lästig gefallen sein mußten, or, wie entsetzlich langweilig...sein mußten.

[6] Render *a—us* by ein Factum welches wir bei der besten Meinung von uns selbst, uns schon damals nicht verbergen konnten.

[7] *Ii—principle,* so zerbrach ich mir zuerst den Kopf darüber (*i. e.* I racked my brains about) den Grund...zu entdecken.

[8] See Int. p. xvi., c.

[9] Use def. art. before *courteous.*

[10] The English *Grammar School* corresponds in a great measure to the German Gelehrtenschule, which term should here be followed by the words *at Bath.*

[11] *To think anything necessary,* eine Sache für nöthig halten.

[12] *Further* = still longer. *To burden himself* may be rendered literally, or by sich aufbürden lassen.

[13] The expression *worshipful,* used here ironically, may be rendered in German by hochlöblich or hochachtbarlich.

[14] Turn *found out,* and further on *revealed,* by 'discovered.'

[15] Supply 'degree of;' *to,* auf; *deportment in public* = public deportment (Benehmen).

[16] *Was morbidly afflicted,* auf krankhafte Weise...litt; *with,* here an.

[17] The French expression *mauvaise honte* corresponds to the German falsche Scham. The term Befangenheit would here be equally applicable.

[18] Use here the definite article, and place the adverb *there* (vorhanden) after *necessity.*

[19] *To gratify,* here Genüge thun, which governs the dative. The expression *so warmly expressed* (bezeigte) qualifies the term *interest* (Theilnahme). See Int. p. xiv., I.

[20] Turn the whole clause by

The thing[1] was unavoidable, and the sole palliation[2] that it admitted was to break[3] the concentration of the public gaze[4] by associating Sir Sidney with some alien[5] group, no matter of what cattle.[6] We, *the* schoolboys, being three,[7] intercepted and absorbed[8] part of the enemy's fire. —DE QUINCEY, *Autobiographic Sketches.*

XXV.

OF STYLE.[9]

The eloquent Buffon says that the style is the man; by which he means that we may[10] see what the man is when we see his style. If this is true, every man should think[11] well what he is before he begins to write, and whether it is wise to expose himself.[12] It is true that nobody may[13] read his book, and that is often the best[14] luck that may befall him.

The first rule in good writing[15] is to know what you[16] are

' whilst he showed himself publicly in (an) the one or the other place.'

[1] There are two terms in German for the word *thing*, viz. Ding and Sache. For the present purpose it will suffice to mention one characteristic distinction between these synonyms — namely, that when *thing* is synonymous with 'matter, affair,' &c. as is the case here, it must be rendered by Sache, and not by Ding.

[2] *Palliation*, here Erleichterung.

[3] Render *to break* by abzulenken, and retain the term *concentration*, pronouncing it like a German word.

[4] The expression *public gaze* may be rendered, somewhat freely, by allgemeine Angafferei, and *by associating* by indem ... sich ... zugesellte.

[5] *With some alien*, einer fremdartigen.

[6] *No—cattle*, transl. von welcher Art sie auch sei.

[7] Turn *being* by 'were,' and see page 68, note 10.

[8] *Intercepted, &c.*, fingen auf und absorbirten (einen); *enemy's* = hostile.

[9] We should in German say Ueber den Stil, as in French *sur le style*.

[10] *We may*, say: man ... kann.

[11] *To think*, here erwägen.

[12] *To expose oneself*, here sich bloßstellen.

[13] Use here the present conditional of dürfen, and in the last clause that of können.

[14] Turn here *best* by 'greatest;' *to befall*, here widerfahren.

[15] *In good writing*, einer guten Schreibweise.

[16] See page 38, note 4, and render *are going* by will; *to go*, expressing futurity, is generally translated by the corresponding tense of wollen.

going to write about,[1]—a plain,[2] simple rule, but one that[3] is very much neglected. If a man makes a good choice of his subject,[4] he will not fail[5] to have the best words at his command,[6] and to put all in the best order.[7] So Horace says,[8] and he may be right; but it strikes me[9] that a man might[10] choose a good subject and yet[11] spoil it, of which we have notable[12] examples in our own days. The Roman, however, tells us that we must well consider[13] what our shoulders will bear, and what they will not;[14] *and* so[15] the rule is this: choose a good subject, if you[16] are able to handle it. If you are not,[17] need I tell you that you had[18] better let it alone?[19]—*An Old Man's Thoughts about Many Things.**

[1] *What...about*, worüber.

[2] *Plain*, schlicht.

[3] Render *but one that* by die aber. *Much* = often.

[4] Turn *if—subject* by 'if any one chooses a good subject.'

[5] The verb *to fail* cannot, in the sense in which it is used here, be employed personally; we must therefore turn the clause *he will not fail* by 'so it is certain.'

[6] *To have...at his command*, daß ihm...zu Gebote stehen werden.

[7] *To — order*, er Alles aufs beste zusammenstellen wird.

[8] The above and the following allusions refer to the verses of Horace:—

Sumite materiam vestris, qui scribitis, æquam
Viribus; et versate diu quid ferre recusent,
Quid valeant humeri. Cui lecta potenter erit res,
Nec facundia deseret hunc nec lucidus ordo.

(Epist. ii. 3, v. 38.)

[9] The idiomatic phrase *it strikes me* may be rendered here by es will mir scheinen.

[10] When *might* expresses a supposed possibility, it is translated by the indicative of können or by the present conditional of dürfen.

[11] When *yet* is used as a conjunction, and synonymous with 'nevertheless,' it is generally translated by dennoch.

[12] Render *notable* by the corresponding foreign term notorisch (Lat. 'notorius'), and turn *in—days* by 'in our time.'

[13] When *to consider* is a synonym of 'to reflect, to deliberate,' it is usually rendered by überlegen, or by erwägen; the latter expression is here preferable.

[14] Turn *what—not* by 'what our shoulders can bear, and what not.'

[15] Render here *so* by demnach; and transl. *this* by Folgendes, placing it before *the rule.*

[16] In similar apostrophes we use in German the familiar second person singular, unless an author addresses his readers collectively. *To handle* (a subject), behandeln.

[17] Turn *If—not* by 'if thou canst it not;' *to need*, here brauchen.

[18] Use for *had* the present conditional of thun.

[19] The idiomatic phrase *to let a thing alone* is rendered in German by eine Sache sein or bleiben lassen, *i.e.* to let it be, or remain, what it is.

* The above extract is taken from a work full of wit, humour, and original thought, which has been published anonymously, but is attributed to Professor George Long.

XXVI.

THE BORDER FEUDS.[1]

For[2] twenty miles on either side of the Border *there* grew up a population who were[3] trained from their[4] cradles in licensed marauding.[5] Nominal amity between the countries operated as but a slight check upon[6] habits inveterately lawless; and though the Governments affected[7] to keep order, they could not afford[8] to be severe upon offences committed[9] in time of peace [10] by men on whom they chiefly depended for the defence[11] of the frontiers in time of war. The scanty[12] families in the fortified farms

[1] In analogy with the expressions Landfrieg, *war on land*, Seefrieg, *naval war*, &c. we may also form a compound term of the words Grenze, *border*, and Fehde, *feud*, by simply joining them together without any connecting link, after suppressing the final vowel of Grenze.

[2] *For*, here auf; *either* = both.

[3] Collective nouns occurring without any sign of the plural require in German, as a rule, the verb and pronoun referring to them in the singular only. *Trained*, erzogen; *from*, von…an.

[4] See note *b* to Extract 34, and use *cradles* in the singular.

[5] *In licensed marauding*, zu autorisirter Plünderung. *Nominal*, nominell.

[6] *Operated — upon*, that ten… nur geringen Einhalt. Turn the adverb *inveterately* by the adjective eingewurzelt, and place the same, together with *lawless*, zügellos, as attributes before *habits*.

[7] *Affected* being here synonymous with 'pretended,' is to be rendered by sich stellen; *to keep* = as if (ob) they kept.

[8] The verb *to afford* is one of those comprehensive English expressions which can be hardly in any other modern idiom rendered by a single equivalent. Render here, *they — afford*, by so konnten sie es dennoch nicht wagen.

[9] Turn *to — committed* by 'to punish severely offences (Vergehen) which were committed.'

[10] The expressions *time of peace* and *time of war* are to be rendered here by compound substantives formed by adding in the first instance the term *times* to the genitive of *peace*, and in the second instance by adding the term *times* to the genitive of *war*. The first mode of forming compound expressions, *i.e.* by simply joining them together — especially when both members are substantives — has been alluded to before; and the present instances furnish an example of the second mode, which consists in adding the subordinate member to the genitive of the principal one.

[11] *On — defence*, auf welche sie sich…als Vertheidiger…vorzüglich verlassen mußten.

[12] *Scanty* = few.

and granges[1] in Roxburgh and Northumberland slept with their[2] swords under their pillows,[3] and their horses saddled[4] in their stables. The[5] blood of the children by the fireside was stirred by tales of wild adventure in song and story ;[5] and perhaps[6] for two centuries no boy *ever* grew to man's estate[7] along a strip of land forty miles across and joining the two seas[8] who had not known the midnight[9] terror of a blazing homestead,[10] who had not seen his father or brother ride out[11] at dusk harnessed and belted for some night foray, to be brought back before morning,[12] gory and stark, across the saddle, and[13] been roused from *his* bed by his mother to swear with his child's lips[14] a vow of revenge over the corpse.

And the fierce feuds of the Mosstroopers[15] were but an expression in its[16] extreme form of the animosity between the two nations. The English[17] hated Scotland because Scotland had successfully[18] defied them : the Scots hated

---

[1] *Farms,* Farmhäuser; *granges,* Gehöfte.

[2] See page 35, note 13.

[3] Use the singular, and see for the possessive pronouns n. *b* to Ext. 34.

[4] *Saddled,* transl. standen gesattelt.

[5] Turn *The—story* by 'the blood of the children was through narrations by the fire-side (am Herde) of wild adventures in song and story (Sage) stirred up.'

[6] *Perhaps* is to be placed after *centuries,* and *for* turned by 'during.'

[7] *Grew to man's estate,* erwuchs... zum Mannesalter.

[8] Turn *along—seas* by 'upon a forty miles wide and on the two seas (Meere) bordering strip of land' (Landstrich).

[9] Use for *midnight* the attributive adjective mitternächtlich.

[10] *Homestead,* transl. Heimstätte.

[11] *Ride out,* here fortreiten; *harnessed—for,* geharnischt und gerüstet zu; *night* = nightly.

[12] *Before morning,* here vor Tagesanbruch; *across,* transl. über... liegend.

[13] Supply 'who had not.' The verb aufwecken, for *to rouse,* would be here hardly expressive enough. Besides, we should then have to paraphrase the words *from his bed* by 'from his sleep.' But we may properly use here the very expressive and poetical term aufschrecken, somewhat corresponding to the verb *to startle.*

[14] *Child's lips,* kindliche Lippen; *vow of revenge,* Rachgelübde.

[15] The only adequate expression for the term *Mosstrooper,* peculiar to Scotland of bygone times, seems to be Grenzräuber.

[16] Turn *its* by 'the,' and retain the expression *form ; of,* here von, *animosity,* Erbitterung.

[17] When the term *English* stands for 'the people of England,' we must render it by the equivalent of the word 'Englishmen :' when it is used adjectively, however, it is translated by englisch The rule applies to the names of other nations.

[18] Turn *successfully* by 'with success ;' *to defy,* Trotz bieten.

England as an enemy on the watch[1] to make[2] them slaves.
The hereditary hostility strengthened[3] with time, and
each generation[4] added fresh injuries to the accumulation
of bitterness.

Fortunately for mankind,[5] however, the relations between
nations are not eventually[6] determined by sentiment and
passion.[7] The[8] mutual sufferings inflicted by the existing
condition of things[8] produced its effect[9] in minds where
reason was admitted to influence.[10]—FROUDE, *History of
England.*

XXVII.

A GERMAN HAUTBOY-PLAYER.[11]

About[12] the year 1760, as Miller[13] was dining at Pontefract with the officers[14] of the Durham militia, one[15] of
them, knowing his love of music, told him they had[16] a

[1] *On the watch*, translate ber auf
bie Gelegenheit lauerte.

[2] See page 36, note 4.

[3] Turn *strengthened* by 'became
stronger.'

[4] Retain here the term *generation,* pronouncing the same as a
German word ; *to — bitterness,* ber
aufgefammelten Erbitterung...hinzu.

[5] *Mankind,* here Menschheit, to
be used with the definite article.

[6] *Eventually* being here used in
the sense of 'ultimately,' is to be
rendered by schließlich.

[7] Turn *sentiment and passion* by
'feelings and passions.'

[8] The contracted construction
of the above clause *The—things*
makes it in German necessary to
give it in a completely different
form. Turn therefore by 'the sufferings which through the existing order (Thatbestand) of things
were inflicted upon (zugefügt) both
parties.'

[9] *To produce an effect,* eine Wirkung hervorbringen (auf); *mind,* here
Gemüth.

[10] *Was—influence,* Eingang fand.

[11] *Hautboy-player* and, further
on, *performer on the hautboy,* Hoboen-
bläser, or simply Hoboist.

[12] Translate here the adverb
about by um, and turn the sentence
by 'as (als) Miller about, &c.'

[13] The above refers to Dr. Miller,
organist at Pontefract, known as
the historian of Doncaster.

[14] Military and naval *officers* are
called Offiziere, and civil *officers*
Beamte. *Durham militia* = militia
of Durham.

[15] The subordinate clause of the
above sentence preceding the principal one, we must give the latter
in an inverted form, *i.e.* begin with
the principal verb, *told* (him). For
love of music see page 62, note 12.

[16] According to the rule mentioned page 29, note 3, we should

young German in their band,[1] as performer on the hautboy, who had only[2] been *a* few months in England, and yet spoke[3] English almost as well as[4] a native, and who was also an excellent performer on the violin :[5] the officer added[6] *that* if Miller would[7] come into another room this German should entertain him with[8] a solo.

The invitation was gladly[9] accepted, and Miller heard a solo of Giardini's[10] executed in[11] a manner that surprised him. He afterwards took[12] an opportunity of having some private conversation with the young musician, and asked him whether he had engaged himself [13] for any long period to the Durham militia. The answer was,[14] "Only from month to month."[15] "Leave them then," said the organist,

use here the present conjunctive : the preference ought, however, to be given to the present conditional, which is frequently used in dependent clauses containing the quotation, when the verb of the principal clause is employed in the imperfect or pluperfect.

[1] A regimental *band* is called in German Mufikcorps or Mufikbande.

[2] Insert here the preposition feit, *since*, which denotes in German 'the whole period of an event,' including the present time,' and use the aux. verb fein in the pres. conjunctive. *Only*, here erft.

[3] See preceding page, note 16.

[4] *As well as*, eben fo gut wie. It may here be mentioned as a caution that the general similarity between the English words *good*, *well*, and the German gut, wohl, very frequently misleads the students of German in their translations It will in this place be sufficient to point out in general that the German adverb wohl does by no means stand in the same relation to the adjective gut as the English *well* does to the adjective *good*. Gut is in German, like every other adjective, also used as an adverb, and the use of wohl in its adverbial capacity is limited

to a few verbs only, more particularly to those relating to the moral and physical condition of a person ; as, fich wohl befinden, es ift mir wohl, &c. The adverb wohl is, besides, used in compound terms, and still more frequently as an expletive.

[5] *Performer on the violin* = violin-player.

[6] *To add*, here hinzufeßen.

[7] Use the present conditional of wollen.

[8] *Entertain him with*, transl. ihm ein...vorfpielen.

[9] *Gladly*, here mit Freuten.

[10] The genitive being in German expressed with sufficient distinctness by means of the preposition von, *of*, the proper name itself need not be put in the genitive case.

[11] We use in German, in the above phrase, the preposition auf with the accusative.

[12] *To take* (an opportunity), ergreifen; *some private conversation*, eine Privatunterhaltung.

[13] *To engage oneself*, fich binden; *for—period*, auf längere Zeit; *to*, here bei.

[14] *Was*, transl. lautete. Cf. page 23, note 14.

[15] Turn *from month to month* simply by 'monthly;' *them*, here fie.

"*and come* and live[1] with me.　I am a single man,[2] and think we shall be happy together; and doubtless your merit will soon entitle[3] you to a more eligible situation."

The offer was accepted as frankly[4] as it was made: and the reader may imagine[5] with what satisfaction[6] Dr. Miller must have remembered[7] this act of generous feeling when he hears that this young German was Herschel the astronomer.[8]—SOUTHEY, *The Doctor.*

XXVIII.

CRANFORD.

In the first place[9] Cranford is in possession of the[10] Amazons: all the holders[11] of houses above a certain rent

---

[1] When *to live* is synonymous with *to reside,* it is translated by wohnen; *with,* here bei.

[2] *Single man,* Junggeſell. Supply after *and* the first personal pronoun, and turn *think* by 'believe,' as in most cases when it stands for 'to conclude, imagine,' &c.

[3] *Entitle,* transl. verhelfen; *eligible situation,* paſſende Stelle.

[4] *Frankly,* freimüthig.　Construe 'the offer was as frankly accepted as it was made.'　When *as...as* is used to express an equality of two compared actions, we must translate it by ſo or eben ſo...als. When the equality refers to nouns, we generally use wie instead of als.

[5] Turn here *imagine* by the reflective form of 'to think.'

[6] *Satisfaction,* Befriedigung, *i.e.* gratification.

[7] *To remember,* ſich erinnern, governs the genitive; *act—feeling,* transl. großmüthige Handlung.

[8] Place *the astronomer* before *Herschel.*　The celebrated astronomer, Wilhelm Herschel, was born at Hanover in 1738.　His father, himself a musician, gave him instruction in music, and sent him over to this country to seek his fortune.　The Earl of Darlington engaged him for the regimental band of the Durham militia, and afterwards Herschel settled in the neighbourhood of Leeds, Pontefract, and Durham as a teacher of music, devoting himself at the same time to that science which has made his name so illustrious.

[9] *In—place,* vor Allem.

[10] The above clause may serve to illustrate a characteristic difference in the use of the article in German and in English.　The term *possession* requires the definite article, on account of the object being singled out definitely, whilst the expression *Amazons* does not require it, because the statement does not refer to them in a definite manner, but only in a general way, in which case the preposition von is quite sufficient.

[11] *Holders,* transl. Bewohner; *rent* (of houses, &c.), Miethe; Miethzins.

are women. If a married couple[1] come to settle in the town, somehow the gentleman[2] disappears : he is either fairly frightened to death[3] by being the only man in the Cranford evening parties,[4] or he is accounted for[5] by being with his regiment, his ship, or closely engaged in business[6] all the week in the great neighbouring commercial town[7] of Drumble, distant only twenty miles on a railroad.[8] In short,[9] whatever does become of the gentlemen, they are not at Cranford : what could they[10] do if they were there?

The surgeon[11] has his round of thirty miles,[12] and sleeps at Cranford ; but every man cannot be *a* surgeon. For keeping[13] the trim gardens full of choice flowers, without a weed to speck them,[14] for frightening away[15] little boys who look wistfully at the said[16] flowers through the railings, for rushing out at[17] the geese that occasionally venture into the gardens if the gates are left open, for deciding all questions of literature and politics[18] without

[1] *Married couple*, Ehepaar; *come to settle*, briefly fich niederläßt.

[2] Translate the word *gentleman*, standing here for Ehemann, *husband*, simply by Mann. Further on it should be translated by Herr.

[3] *He — death*, entweder es überfällt ihn eine wahre Todesangst; *by being* = because he is.

[4] *Evening parties* = evening-societies.

[5] *He—for*, transl. es heißt. The words *by being* must here be turned by 'that he is ;' *with*, here bei.

[6] *Closely — business*, von Geschäften sehr stark in Anspruch genommen ; *all the* = the whole.

[7] *Commercial town*, Handelsstadt.

[8] *Distant—railroad*, die nur zwanzig Meilen weit an der Eisenbahn liegt.

[9] *In short*, kurz; *whatever*, was auch immer. The adverb *auch* is here an expletive. The emphatic *does* remains in German untranslated.

[10] Here, too, we should make use of the expletive auch.

[11] When the noun *surgeon* is used, as is the case here, in a general sense for a 'medical man,' it must be rendered simply by Arzt, and not by Wundarzt, which latter term corresponds to the word *surgeon* in its primary sense only, viz. 'one who cures by manual operation.' The more dignified expression for the latter signification is now in German Chirurg.

[12] The clause *his — miles* may be freely rendered by eine Praxis die sich auf dreißig Meilen in die Runde erstreckt.

[13] *To keep*, erhalten, to be used here with the *supine* preceded by um. *Trim*, zierlich ; *of choice*, transl. der schönsten.

[14] Turn *without—them* by 'free from every weed.'

[15] *To frighten away*, verscheuchen ; *wistfully*, here sehnsüchtig.

[16] *Said*, in the sense of 'before-mentioned,' besagt.

[17] *To rush out at*, losstürzen auf; *venture*, here sich wagen; *gate*, Thüre.

[18] Turn *of literature and politics* by 'literary and political,' employ-

troubling themselves with[1] unnecessary reasons or arguments, for obtaining clear and correct knowledge of
everybody's affairs[2] in the parish, for keeping their neat
maid-servants[3] in admirable order, for kindness (somewhat
dictatorial) to the poor,[4] and real, tender, good offices to
each other[5] whenever they are in distress,[6] the ladies of
Cranford are quite sufficient.[7] " A man," as one of them
observed to me once, " is *so* in the way[8] in the house ! "

Although the ladies of Cranford know all each other's
proceedings,[9] they are exceedingly indifferent to each
other's[10] opinions. Indeed, as each has her own individuality, not to say eccentricity,[11] pretty strongly developed,
nothing is so easy[12] as verbal retaliation ; but somehow[13]
good-will reigns among them to a considerable degree.
The Cranford ladies have only an occasional[14] little
quarrel, spirted out[15] in a few peppery words and angry
jerks of the head ; just enough to prevent the even tenor[16]
of their lives from becoming too flat.[17] Their dress[18] is very

ing these terms as attributive adjectives to *questions.*

[1] *To trouble oneself with,* here
fid) befümmern um; *reason,* Grund ;
argument, Beweis ; *clear,* say genau.

[2] *Affair,* Angelegenheit; *in the parish,* in ihrem Kirchspiel.

[3] *Maid-servant,* Dienstmädchen;
admirable, transl. musterhaft.

[4] The clause *for — poor* must be
rendered somewhat freely, viz. um
ten Armen (wenn auch auf etwas victa-
torifche Weife) Gutes zu thun.

[5] *Real—other,* um sid) gegenseitig
mahrhaft freundschaftliche Dienste zu
leisten.

[6] *Distress,* Noth.

[7] *To be sufficient,* ausreichen, which
verb is to be preceded here by the
expletive ba3u. *To observe* (*to*),
bemerken (gegen).

[8] *Is—way,* ist einem...so sehr im
Wege. The adverb *so* has been
italicised by the author, and not by
the editor: it has therefore been
translated.

[9] *All—proceedings,* sämmtlich ihr
gegenseitiges Thun und Lassen.

[10] *To each other's,* gegen ihre gegen-
seitigen.

[11] Turn *as—eccentricity* by ' since
the individuality, not to say eccentricity, of each (einer Jeden) is.' The
corresponding foreign forms of
individuality and *eccentricity* may
be retained in German.

[12] Render *so easy* by ihnen nichts
leichter, and *as verbal retaliation* by
als mündliche Repressalien (reprisals)
zu nehmen.

[13] *But somehow,* transl. dennoch
fügt es sid) so; *good-will,* Wohlwollen;
to a considerable = in a high.

[14] *Occasional,* gelegentlid).

[15] *Spirted out,* transl. der sid)...
Luft macht; *peppery* = sharp ; *jerks
of the head,* Kopfbewegungen.

[16] *Even tenor,* ruhige Gang. For
the expression *lives* compare Extract 25, note *c*.

[17] Turn *from—flat* by 'that...be-
comes too flat' (schal).

[18] When the term *dress* stands,
as is the case here, for 'clothing in
general,' we render it by Kleidung.
somewhat corresponding to the

independent of fashion, as they observe, "What does it signify[1] how we dress[2] here at Cranford, where everybody knows us?" And if they go from home,[3] their reason is equally cogent: "What does it signify how we dress here, where nobody knows us?"—MRS. GASKELL, *Cranford*.

XXIX.

BEFORE THE BATTLE OF[4] KÖNIGGRÄTZ.

Long before midnight the troops were all in motion, and at half-past one in the morning[5] the general staff[6] left Kamenitz. The moon occasionally[7] shone *out* brightly, but was generally hidden behind clouds, and then could be distinctly seen[8] the decaying[9] bivouac fires in the places which had been occupied[10] by the troops along the road.

These fires looked like large will-o'-the-wisps as[11] their flames flickered about[12] in the wind, and stretched for many a mile,[13] for there were 100,000 soldiers with the

French *habillement;* but when it signifies a single garment, it is to be rendered by Kleid.

[1] *Does it signify*, liegt daran.

[2] *To dress*, sich kleiden. In German the reflective form occurs far more frequently than in English, there being but few German verbs which can be used both in a transitive and intransitive sense.

[3] *Go from home*, verreisen; *cogent*, triftig.

[4] See page 49, note 1.

[5] Use for the adverbial expression *in the morning* the genitive des Morgens, which case is generally used, with or without the article, when the point of time is indicated in an indefinite manner.

[6] *General staff*, Generalstab.

[7] The idiomatic rendering for *occasionally* is here dann und wann.

[8] The agent from whom the activity proceeds not being expressed, we should not employ here the passive voice in German; but since the reflective form, requisite in similar cases, would not be applicable in the present instance, the active voice, with the indefinite pronoun man, ought to be used.

[9] *Decaying*, here erlöschend. *Bivouac fires* is in German a compound term.

[10] *To occupy* (used as a military expression), besetzen.

[11] *As*, da. Turn *their* by 'the.'

[12] *To flicker about*, hin und her flackern.

[13] *For many a mile*, transl. meilenweit. Turn *soldiers* by 'men,' and see n. d to Extr. 32; *with*, here bei.

First Army alone, and the bivouacs of so great a force[1] spread over a wide extent of country. Day gradually *began* to break,[2] but with the first symptoms[3] of dawn a drizzling rain came on, which lasted[4] until late in the afternoon. The wind increased and blew coldly upon the soldiers,[5] for they were short of both sleep and food,[6] while frequent gusts[7] bore down to the ground the water-laden corn in the wide fields alongside[8] the way.

The main road[9] from Horitz to Königgrätz sinks into a deep hollow near the village of Milowitz. On the side of this hollow furthest from[10] Horitz is placed near the road the village of that name,[11] and on the left of the road, on the same bank, stands a thick fir-wood. A little after[12] midnight the army of Prince[13] Frederick Charles was entirely concealed in this hollow, ready to issue[14] from its ambush and attack the Austrians if they should advance.

Soon after dawn a[15] person standing between the village of Milowitz and the further hill of Dub could see no

---

[1] *Force* will here best be rendered by Truppenmaffe; *to spread*, fich ausbreiten; *extent of country*, Lanbstrecken (pl.).

[2] *To break* (referring to day), anbrechen. Use the imperfect.

[3] *Symptoms*, Zeichen; *drizzling rain*, feiner Regen or Nebelregen; *came on* = began.

[4] *To last*, here anhalten; *in the*, am.

[5] The phrase *blew coldly upon the soldiers* must in German be rather freely rendered by unb bie Soldaten fühlten feine Schärfe, in order to express distinctly that the soldiers felt the wind the more keenly in consequence of want of sleep and food.

[6] The clause *they — food* may be turned by 'they had had neither enough sleep nor food' (Nahrung).

[7] *Gust*, Windstoß; *to bear down to the ground*, briefly zu Boten werfen.

[8] *Alongside*, längs.

[9] *Main road*, Hauptstraße; *to sink*, here fich fenken; *hollow*, Hohlweg.

[10] *Furthest from*, bie von ... am weitesten entfernt liegt; *is placed*, befindet fich.

[11] Render *of that name* by genannte, placing it before *village*. *Stands* = is; *thick*, here bicht.

[12] Translate *a little* in the above phrase by balb.

[13] The German language has two expressions for the word *prince*, viz. Prinz and Fürst. The former title, to be used here, is given to descendants of sovereign princes as long as they do not exercise any sovereign power; and the latter, in a general sense, to all sovereign rulers, as kings, emperors, dukes, &c., and, in a more limited sense, to rulers of principalities, and to those who have been raised to the titular dignity of prince.

[14] *To issue*, hervorbrechen.

[15] See next page, note 1.

armed men[1] except a few Prussian vedettes[2] posted along the Dub ridge,[3] whose lances stood in relief[4] above the summit against the murky sky. A few dismounted[5] officers were standing below a fruit-tree in front of Milowitz, with their horses held by some orderlies behind them.[6] These were Prince Frederick Charles and his staff. All was still except when[7] the neigh of a horse or a loud word of command,[8] as the last division formed, rose mysteriously from the hollow of Milowitz.

Until nearly four o'clock the army remained concealed. * * * To hold the Austrian army in front[9] of the Elbe was absolutely necessary for the success of the Prussian plans,[10] and Prince Frederick Charles resolved with his own army alone[11] to engage the whole of Benedek's forces,[12] and, clinging to[13] the Austrian commander,

[1] *A—men.* The whole of the above clause must be given in German, where we should use the conditional in a different form; arrange therefore: 'would a person (ḥätte Jemand), who between the village of Milowitz and the further hill of Dub (entferntern Dubhügel);' and insert here the verb 'stood' (geſtanden) for *standing*, and *could see* (ſehen könnten) after *men* (Mannſchaft). On the omission of the aux. verb after geſtanden, cf. Ext. 47, n. *c.*

[2] We use also in German the foreign military expressions Vedette for 'a sentinel on horseback,' and poſtirt for *posted*.

[3] *Dub ridge,* Rücken des Dubhügels.

[4] *Stood in relief,* ſtark abſtachen; *murky,* trüb.

[5] The adjective *dismounted* must in German be turned into a regular clause with a finite verb, viz. die von ihren Pferden abgeſtiegen waren. We also use the foreign military expression demontiren, but more in its transitive meaning, *i.e.* 'to unhorse soldiers,' or 'to disable cannon.'

[6] Turn *with — them* by 'whilst some orderlies (Ordonanzen) held their horses behind them.'

[7] See page 41, note 9.

[8] *Word of command,* Commandowort; *as,* während; *to form,* ſich aufſtellen; *rose,* here herausſcholl.

[9] *In front,* transl. dieſſeits.

[10] The German version of the above clause can be made more emphatic by employing the grammatical subject es, which, besides with impersonal verbs—as es regnet, &c.—is used for the sake of emphasis, or to impart more poetic colouring to a construction,—as es heult der Sturm, es brauſt das Meer. The real subject follows in such a case the inflected verb, and sometimes even other far less important parts of the sentence. Turn, therefore, the above clause by 'it was for the success of the Prussian plans absolutely (durchaus) necessary to hold,' &c.

[11] The adverb *alone,* bloß, has in the above clause the emphasis: place it, therefore, at the beginning of the clause, viz. *alone with,* &c. *To engage* = to attack.

[12] *The whole of...forces,* die Geſammtmacht.

[13] *To cling (to),* ſich klammern (an). The preposition an governs here the accusative case.

to hold[1] him on the Bistritz until the Prussian flank attacks[2] could be developed. A few short words passed[3] from the commander of the First Army to the chief of his staff; a few aides-de-camp, mounting[4] silently, rode quietly away; and, as it were by the utterance of a magician's spell,[5] *one* hundred thousand Prussian warriors springing into sight, as if from the bowels[6] of the armed earth, swept[7] over the southern edge[8] of the Milowitz ravine towards the hill of Dub. — H. M. HOZIER, *The Seven Weeks' War.*

XXX.

A DISPUTED[9] BOUNDARY.

A peculiar[10] interest attaches itself at the present time to[11] everything which throws light upon the debated question of[12] the boundary between the two kingdoms;[13] a question which is not less keenly debated[14] among naturalists than that of many a disputed frontier *has been* between adjacent nations.

[1] *To hold,* here feſthalten or beſchäftigen. *Bistritz* is in German feminine, most names of rivers belonging to the feminine gender.

[2] *Flank attacks,* Flantenangriffe; *be developed,* ſich entfalten.

[3] *Passed,* transl. wurden...an... gerichtet; *chief of his staff,* Chef ſeines Generalſtabs.

[4] *Mounting,* beſtiegen...ihre Pferde.

[5] *As—spell,* wie auf den Ausſpruch eines Zauberwortes; *after which* clause ought to be placed the words *springing into sight,* to be turned by 'appeared suddenly.'

[6] *As—bowels,* gleichſam aus dem Schoße.

[7] Transl. *swept* by ſtrömten, connecting it with the preceding clause by means of the conjunction 'and.'

[8] *Edge,* here Abhang; *towards—Dub,* dem Dubhügel zu.

[9] *Disputed,* ſtreitig.

[10] *Peculiar,* here beſonderes.

[11] *Attaches — to,* knüpft ſich jetzt (or gegenwärtig) an.

[12] *Debated question of,* Streitfrage in Bezug auf.

[13] *Kingdoms,* transl. Naturreiche, the expression referring here to the animal and vegetable kingdoms.

[14] *Which—debated,* über die...nicht minder lebhaft geſtritten wird. *That of* must, in accordance with the translation given of the preceding clause, be rendered by über; *disputed,* ſtreitig gemacht; *adjacent* = neighbouring. The auxiliary verb *has been* need not be expressed in the German translation. If it were retained, it would be necessary to supply the verb geſtritten, which would make the sentence much too long.

For many parts of this border-country[1] have been taken and retaken several times ; their inhabitants, so to speak,[2] having[3] first been considered on account of their general[4] appearance to belong to the[5] vegetable kingdom; then in consequence of some movements being observed in[6] them being[7] claimed by the zoologists ; then, on *the* ground of their evidently plant-like[8] mode of growth, being transferred back[9] to the botanical side ; then, owing to the supposed[10] detection of some new feature in their structure or[11] physiology, being again claimed as members of the animal kingdom ; and lastly,[12] on the discovery of a fallacy in these arguments, being once more turned over[13] to the botanist, with[14] whom for the most part they remain. For the attention which has been given[15] of late years to the study of the humblest[16] forms of vegetation has led to the knowledge among[17] what must be 'un-

---

[1] *Border-country*, Grenzland; transl. here *taken* by erobert, and *retaken* by zurückerobert. See page 89, note 8.

[2] Turn here *speak* 'say.'

[3] Compare Int. p. xvi., *c*. The frequent occurrence of the present participle in the above extract will afford the student an excellent opportunity for practice in the construction so commonly occurring in English, and so very rarely in German.

[4] Render *general* by im Allgemeinen, to be placed after the term *appearance* (Aussehen).

[5] *To belong to the*, als zum...gehörig; *vegetable kingdom*, Pflanzenreich.

[6] *To observe in*, wahrnehmen an. Turn *being observed* by 'which one observed.'

[7] The present participle *being*, referring to *claimed* (reclamirt), should be turned by a finite verb, viz. wurden sie, and inserted after *then*.

[8] The term *like*, joined to another expression and employed in its compound form as an attributive adjective, is frequently rendered by mäßig or artig. The latter expression added to the plural of *plant*

ought to be used here. *Mode of growth*, Wachsthum.

[9] *To transfer back*, zurückbringen. The present participle *being* may be omitted in the translation, both in this clause and the next.

[10] *Owing—supposed*, in Folge der vermeintlichen; *feature*, Umstand, *i.e.* circumstance.

[11] The possessive pronoun must here be repeated on account of the difference of the gender of the nouns *structure*, Bau ; and *physiology*, Physiologie.

[12] *Lastly*, schließlich. The following present part. (*being*) should here be inserted according to note 7, above. *On*, bei; *fallacy*, Trugschluß.

[13] *To turn over*, überliefern.

[14] Translate *with* by the preposition bei, and *for the most part* by größtentheils.

[15] Render *has been given* by man ...schenkte, and *of late* by in letzteren.

[16] *Humblest*, here untersten. The expression *forms of vegetation* may be translated by the compound term Pflanzenformen, *i.e.* 'forms of plants.'

[17] For the rendering of the whole clause from *has* to *phenomena* see next page, note 1.

doubtedly' regarded as plants of so many phenomena[1] which would formerly have been considered[2] unquestionable marks[3] of animality, that the discovery of the like phenomena among[4] the doubtful beings in question,[5] so far from being evidence[6] of THEIR animality, really affords[7] a probability of the opposite kind.—DR. W. B. CARPENTER, *The Microscope and its Revelations.*

XXXI.

THOMAS CARLYLE TO GOETHE.*

Craigenputtoch, Sept. 25, 1828.

You inquire[8] with such warm interest[9] respecting our present abode and occupations that I am obliged to say *a few words*[10] about both while there is still room left.[11]

---

[1] Translate the clause *has—phenomena* by ɦat bei bem was unzweifelɦaft als Pflanze angeſeɦen werben muß, zur Erfenntniß ſo vieler Phänomene gefüɦrt.

[2] See page 85, note 2.

[3] *Mark*, here Merfmal; *animality*, Animaliȿmus. .

[4] *Of—among*, transl. ganz äɦnlicɦer Phänomene bei.

[5] Translate *in question* by betreffenb, placing it as an attributive adjective before *doubtful; so far from*, weit entfernt.

[6] *Being evidence*, zu beweiſen. The word *animality* being used after this verb in the accusative case, the preposition *of* must, as a matter of course, be omitted in the translation.

[7] *Affords*, here bartɦut; *of—kind*, bes Gegentɦeils. Compare with the above passage, Ext. 27.

[8] *To inquire . . . respecting*, forſcɦen . . . nacɦ.

[9] *Interest*, here Tɦeilnaɦme; *occupation*, Beſcɦäftigung, to be used here in the singular only. Cf. p. 83, 11.

[10] When the expression *words* denotes 'single, unconnected terms,' it is translated by Wörter, and when it stands for 'connected terms, having a coherent meaning,' as is the case here, by Worte.

[11] *While—left*, ba nocɦ Raum bazu übrig bleibt.

---

* Goethe took such a lively interest in Carlyle, on account of his being one of the first to make his British countrymen acquainted with modern German literature, that the veteran poet wrote a preface to the German edition of his "Life of Schiller," inserting at the same time a translation—of which some use has been made in the notes—of the above letter, chiefly, as it would seem, in explanation of a woodcut, representing the writer's secluded residence in Scotland, which was added to the German edition.

Dumfries is a pleasant town, containing[1] about 15,000 inhabitants, and is to be considered[2] the centre of the trade and judicial system[3] of a district which possesses some importance in the sphere of Scottish activity.[4] Our residence[5] is not in the town itself, but fifteen miles to the north-west,[6] among the granite hills and the black morasses which stretch[7] westward through Galloway almost to the Irish Sea. In this wilderness of heath and rock our estate[8] stands forth a green oasis, a tract of[9] ploughed, partly enclosed,[10] and planted[11] ground, where corn ripens and trees afford[12] a shade, although surrounded by sea-mews and rough-woolled[13] sheep. Here, with no small[14] effort, have we[15] built and furnished[16] a neat, substantial dwelling; here,[17] in the absence of

[1] This present participle might here be rendered according to rule *b*, Int. page xvi.

[2] *To consider*, here anſehen, to be followed by alß, as is the case with betrachten, to consider, and barſtellen, to represent, when used in the signification pointed out page 36, note 4. These verbs require the accusative; but this case is changed into the nominative in passive constructions and after the supine. See page 45, note 20.

[3] *Judicial system*, Gerichtßbarfeit.

[4] *Activity*, here Betriebſamfeit.

[5] When the expression *residence* refers to the private dwelling of an individual, it is rendered by Wohnort, Wohnſiß, or Wohnung; but when signifying the capital of a ruling sovereign, it is in German Reſiſenz or Reſiſenzſtaſt.

[6] *North-west*, norbweſtlich, which is to be followed by bavon entfernt, as an equivalent for the words *to the*. *Granite hills* forms in German a compound expression.

[7] *To stretch*, here ſich ziehen.

[8] Render here *estate* by Beſiß-thum, and *stands forth* by bilſet.

[9] *Tract of ... ground*, Strecke ... Sanbeß, stands here in apposition to *oasis*, and should, therefore, be used

in the accusative, in accordance with the rule that the apposition always agrees with the term which it qualifies in number and case: the apposition agrees also in gender when the qualifying expression is the name of a person, the gender of which is distinctly marked.

[10] *Enclosed*, here umʒāunt, compounded from the noun Zaun, *hedge*, and the preposition um, *round*.

[11] Use here the past participle of bebauen as an attributive adjective.

[12] *To afford*, gewähren, forms here with Schatten a kind of compound verbal expression, thus making the indefinite article superfluous.

[13] *Rough-woolled*, hartwollig.

[14] The epithet *small*, referring to *effort*, is to be rendered by gering.

[15] It is an idiomatic peculiarity of the German language to point out distinctly the subject to the advantage of which an action has been done, by means of the dative of the personal pronoun. Supply here, therefore, the dative unß.

[16] *To furnish* (a house, &c.), einrichten. The expression *substantial* may here be rendered by bauerhaft, or still better by ſoliſ.

[17] The words *we live* are to be inſerted here.

professional or other office,[1] we live to cultivate[2] literature
according to our[3] strength, and in our peculiar way.
We wish *a* joyful growth[4] to the rose and flowers of
our garden ; we hope *for* health and peaceful thoughts[5]
to further our aims. The roses, indeed, are still in
part[6] to be planted, but they blossom already in anticipation.[7]

Two ponies,[8] which carry[9] us everywhere, and the
mountain air,[10] are the best medicines[11] for weak[12] nerves.
This daily exercise, to which I am much devoted,[13] is my
only recreation ; for this nook *of ours* is the loneliest in
Britain—six miles removed from any one likely to visit
me.[14] * * *

I came hither solely with the design[15] to simplify my
way of life,[16] and to secure the independence through which
I could be enabled[17] to remain true to myself. This bit[18]
of earth is our own : here we can live, write, and think,

---

[1] The above clause, *in — office*,
must in German be rendered
freely by in Ermanglung irgend eines
Berufs oder Amtes, where we take
the expression Beruf in the sense
of ‘ professional occupation,’ and
not in that of ‘ vocation.’

[2] *To cultivate* (a science, &c.), sich
befleißigen, or sich befleißen, which
belongs to that class of reflective
verbs which govern the genitive
of the thing, having the reflective
pronoun in the accusative.

[3] *According to our*, transl. nach
eigenen, and use in German the
plural of Kraft for *strength*.

[4] *Joyful growth*, fröhliches Ge-
deihen.

[5] *Peaceful thoughts*, friedliche Ge-
müthsstimmung; *aim*, Streben, to be
used in the singular only.

[6] *Still in part*, zum Theil noch.

[7] Turn *anticipation* by ‘ hope.’

[8] Goethe renders *ponies* by leichte
Pferde, but we use now the word
Ponies also in German.

[9] The primary sense of *to carry* is
in German simply tragen: here, however, we ought also to express the

direction of the action. Add therefore the pronominal adverb hin.

[10] The words *mountain air* form
in German a compound term.

[11] *Medicine*, Arznei. We use in
German also the word Arzt, physi-
cian, figuratively in the sense in
which *medicine* is employed here.

[12] Translate here *weak* by zart,
and *exercise* by Bewegung.

[13] *Devoted*, here ergeben ; *recreation*, Zerstreuung.

[14] *Removed — me*, von einer jeden
Person entfernt, die mich allenfalls
besuchen möchte.

[15] *With the design*, zu dem Zwecke.

[16] *Way of life*, Lebensweise. Translate here *to secure* by erwerben, and
the by the demonstrative pronoun
jene.

[17] The clause *through — enabled*
might be rendered with literal
fidelity by durch die ich in den Stand
gesetzt werden könnte, or, far more
briefly, die es mir möglich machte.
True, in the above sense, treu.

[18] *Bit*, here Stück. The words
our own may be simply turned by
the possessive pronoun ‘ ours.’

as best[1] pleases ourselves, even though[2] Zoilus himself were to be[3] crowned the monarch[4] of literature.

Nor is the solitude of such great importance;[5] for a stage-coach takes us speedily to Edinburgh, which we look upon as our British Weimar. And[6] have I not, too, at this moment piled up[7] upon the table of my little library a whole cart-load of[8] French, German, American, and English journals[9] and periodicals—whatever may be their worth. Of antiquarian studies, too, there is no lack.[10] From some of our heights I can descry, about a day's journey[11] to the west, the hill where Agricola[12] and his Romans left a camp behind *them*. At the foot of it[13] I was born, and there *both* father and mother still live to love me.

[1] The relative superlative (or superlative of comparison) of adverbs is formed by prefixing am = *at the*, and adding en to the simple form of the superlative : *e.g. He runs quickest of all*, er läuft am schnellsten von Allen.

[2] *Even though*, transl. unb wenn. Zoilus lived in the time of Philip. of Macedon. He was celebrated for his carping criticisms, and his name has become proverbial for a cynical, malignant critic.

[3] *Were to be*, werden sollte.

[4] Render here *monarch* by König, and see page 36, note 4.

[5] *Of — importance*, transl. so bebeutenb; *takes* = brings ; *to look upon*, ansehen.

[6] The conjunction *and* may be omitted in translating the above exclamation, which can be made more expressive in German by means of the expletive tenn, to be inserted between *I* and *not*.

[7] *To pile up*, aufhäufen; *cartload*, Ladung.

[8] The preposition *of* is here to be rendered by von, as is frequently the case with *partitive genitives*, viz. when an entire number or quantity, from which a part is taken, occurs in the genitive case.

[9] *Journal*, Journal, pronounced as in French ; *periodical*, Zeitschrift.

[10] *There is no lack*, fehlt es nicht. The objective relation of verbs expressing *want* requires the preposition an with the dative.

[11] Form here the compound term 'day's-journey.' *To the west* = westward.

[12] The Roman Consul Cn. Julius Agricola was governor of Britain from 78 to 85 A.D.

[13] Turn *of it* by 'of the same.

XXXII.

A STURDY SQUIRE.[1]

King David[2] was taken·prisoner on his homeward[3]
retreat, but not without making[4] the most gallant[5] resistance.　When the Queen of England heard that her army
had[6] gained the victory, she mounted on[7] her white
charger,[7] and went to the battle-field.　She was informed
on the way[8] that the King of Scots was[9] the prisoner
of a squire[10] named John Copeland, who had rode off[11]
with him, no one knew whither.　The Queen ordered[12] him
to be sought out, and told[13] that he had done what was
not agreeable to her in carrying off[14] her prisoner without
leave.　Next[15] day Philippa wrote with her own hand[16]

[1] *A sturdy squire*, transl. ein
troßiger Bafall.

[2] The above extract refers to an
incident which occurred in 1346,
after the battle at Nevil's Cross,
which was fought between the
brave Philippa of Hainault (ßen-
negau), Queen of Edward III., and
David Bruce, King of Scotland.

[3] *Homeward*, transl. in bie ßei-
math, to be placed after *retreat*.

[4] In participial constructions
like the above we frequently de-
part in German from the rule re-
quiring the supine by translating
without by oßne baß, and employing
a regular sentence with a finite
verb in the conditional mood. The
sense of the passage will show
which tense is to be used.　In the
present case the verb *to make*, here
leiften, is to be employed in the
perfect conditional.

[5] *Gallant*, here tapfer.

[6] Compare Ext. 47, note *c*.

[7] *Mounted on*, beftieg fie; *charger*,
Schlachtroß.　Use for *went* the imperfect of fich begeben; *to*, here auf.

[8] Turn *She—way* by 'on the way
vas communicated to her.'

[9] See page 29, note 3.

[10] Render here *squire* by Gbel-
mann, and turn *named* by the genitive singular of Mame.

[11] *To ride off*, bavonreiten.　The
assertions *had rode off* and *no one
knew* are included in the indirect
quotations.

[12] *To order*, here ben Befeßl geben,
which is a more dignified expression than befeßlen.　Use the two
following verbs in the supine of
the active voice.

[13] The verb fagen governing the
dative of the person, we must supply here the pronoun ißm before
told.

[14] *To carry off*, wegfüßren.　Construe 'whilst (inbem) he...carried off.'

[15] The point of time of the pre-
dicated action may in German also
be expressed by the preposition an
with the dative.　The definite article should here be used, whether
the accusative or an with the dative be employed; but if the preference be given to the latter, the
adjective *next* might be rendered
here for euphony's sake by folgenb.

[16] The phrase *with her* (*his*, &c.)

to John Copeland, commanding him to surrender[1] the King of Scots to her. John answered in a manner most contumacious[2] to the female Majesty[3] then swaying the sceptre[4] of England with so much ability and glory.

He replied to Philippa that he would not give up[5] his royal prisoner to[6] woman or child, but only to his *own* lord[7] King Edward, for[8] to him he had sworn allegiance,[9] and not to any woman.

Philippa wrote immediately to the King her husband,[10] relating[11] all that had occurred.

When the King had read the Queen's letter, he ordered John Copeland to come to him at Calais, who, having placed[12] his prisoner in a strong[13] castle in Northumberland, set out and landed near[14] Calais.

When the King of England saw the squire, he took him by the hand, saying, "Ha! welcome, my squire,[15] who[16]

---

own hand is, more briefly than in most other languages, expressed in German by the single term eigen-händig, which students of Greek will be able to compare with the compound αὐτόχειρ.

[1] *To surrender,* ausliefern. The verb befehlen always requires the supine, since the verb to which it refers expresses the object of the sentence.

[2] The phrase *in a manner most contumacious* may be turned in German by 'in a most contumacious (trotzige) manner,' or rendered briefly and forcibly by the adverbial expression äußerst trotzig.

[3] The epithet *female* would, in German, not be applicable here, since it would not be considered, as is the case in English, as forming with the noun *majesty* one expression, equivalent to 'Queen,' but merely as an attribute qualifying the noun *majesty.* We may employ, however, the expression königliche Frau as an elegant equivalent for *female Majesty.*

[4] *To sway the sceptre,* den Zepter führen. See note to Ext. 23, and use the verb in the imperfect.

[5] *To give up,* here auszuliefern.

[6] *To...or,* say: weder einer...noch einem.

[7] Translate here *lord* by Herrn, and connect it with *King* by the conjunction 'and.'

[8] *For* used as a conjunction—in which case it is synonymous with 'because'—is rendered by denn, but when occurring as a preposition —corresponding to the French *pour*—it is generally translated by für. The expletive nur may here be inserted after *for.*

[9] *To swear allegiance,* den Lehens-eid leisten. Turn *any* by 'a.'

[10] Render the phrase *to—husband* by the attributive expression ihrem königlichen Gemahl.

[11] Render *relating* by theilte ihm mit, connecting this clause with the preceding one by the conj. 'and.'

[12] *To place,* here unterbringen. Use the pluperfect with the conjunction nachdem.

[13] *Strong,* here fest.

[14] *Near,* transl. unweit or in der Nähe von.

[15] Translate here *squire* as given in page 88, note 1.

[16] See page 68, note 10.

by thy valour hast captured[1] mine adversary, the King of Scots!" John Copeland fell[2] on one knee, and replied, "If God out of[3] His great kindness has given[4] me the King of Scotland, and permitted[5] me to conquer him in arms, no one ought[6] to be jealous[7] of it; for God can, if He pleases,[8] send His grace to a poor squire as well[9] as to a great lord. Sire, do not take it amiss[10] if I did not surrender King David to the orders[11] of my *lady* Queen, for I hold my lands[12] of you, and not of her, and my oath is to you,[13] and not to her—unless, indeed, through choice."[14]

King Edward answered, "John, the loyal[15] service you have done[16] us and our esteem for your valour is[17] so great, that it[18] may well serve you as[19] an excuse; and shame fall on[20] those who bear you any ill-will![21] You will now return home, and take[22] your prisoner, the King of Scotland, *and* convey *him* to my wife;[23] and by way

---

1 *To capture*, gefangen nehmen.

2 *Fell*, transl. ließ sich...nieber.

3 *Turn out of* by 'in;' *kindness*, here Gnabe.

4 *Given*, transl. überliefert.

5 *To permit*, gestatten; *in arms*, transl. die Waffen in der Hand.

6 See the note to Ext. 7.

7 *Jealous* requires in German the preposition auf.

8 *If He pleases*, wenn es ihm so gefällt. The verb *send* may here be rendered by angedeihen lassen.

9 Place in German the adverbial expression *as well* before *to a poor*, &c.; *great lord*, vornehmer Herr.

10 The usual rendering for *to take amiss*, viz. übel nehmen, would not be in keeping with the elevated tone of the above speech : transl. the phrase *do—if* by zürnet mir nicht darob, daß.

11 *To the orders*, auf Befehl.

12 *I—lands*, ich trage meine Güter zu Lehen. The pronoun *you* should be rendered here by the second person plural, which pronoun was used from about the beginning of the thirteenth to about the middle

of the seventeenth century in addressing persons of rank.

13 *Is to you*, transl. Euch habe ich ...geleistet.

14 Turn *unless—choice* by 'it be then out of (aus) free choice.'

15 Retain this identical expression also in German.

16 *To do* (a service), leisten.

17 Use here the plural, since the verb refers to two subjects, viz. *service* and *esteem*.

18 Render here *it* by bies, the abbreviated form of bieses, which is used indefinitely, without regard to the gender or number of the persons or things spoken of.

19 Render *as* in the above phrase by als, without any article, or by the preposition zu contracted with the definite article.

20 *Fall on*, transl. treffe.

21 *To bear anyone ill-will*, Jemand übel wollen.

22 Suppress the verb *take* in the translation, supplying its place by the subsequent verb *convey* (überliefern).

23 *Wife*, here Gemahlin.

of[1] remuneration I assign[2] lands as near your house as you can choose them to the amount[3] of £500 a year for you and your heirs.—AGNES STRICKLAND, *Lives of the Queens of England.*

XXXIII.

THE HISTORY OF SCIENCES.

There is[4] a certain uniformity[5] in the history of most[6] sciences. If we read *such* works as[7] Whewell's "History of the Inductive[8] Sciences" or Humboldt's "Kosmos," we[9] find that the origin, the progress,[10] the causes of failure[11] and success, have been the same for almost[12] every branch of human knowledge. There are[13] three marked periods, or stages,[14] in the history of every one of them,[15] which we may call the 'empirical,' the 'classificatory,' and the 'theo-

[1] *By way of,* say briefly alé.

[2] *To assign,* here anweifen; *lands,* Ländereien. The clause *for—heirs* ought to be placed in German after *to assign,* and *for you* rendered by the dative.

[3] *To the amount,* zu dem Werthe.

[4] Render here *is* by herrscht, *i.e.* reigns.

[5] *Uniformity,* Gleichförmigkeit, which must be distinguished from Einförmigkeit; the latter expression indicating 'monotony,' or 'tedious sameness in all details.'

[6] The superlative *most* requires in German, contrary to the usage in English, the definite article.

[7] Render here *as* by wie.

[8] We use also in German the neo-Latin expression inductiv, derived from the verb *inducere.*

[9] See the note to Ext. 7.

[10] The article must be repeated in German before all substantives, although they are of the same gender, whenever they are placed side by side in a kind of antitheti-

cal order. That it must be repeated here in German before *causes* is, besides, a matter of course, since it is not used in the same number as the preceding substantives.

[11] Translate here *failure* by Mißlingen, and *success* by Gelingen. The antithesis would greatly lose in force by rendering the latter expression by Erfolg.

[12] Place *almost* before the preposition *for,* and *the same* after *knowledge* (Wissen).

[13] See page 25, note 7. *Marked,* transl. bestimmt.

[14] For the expression *stage,* denoting a 'degree of progression in any change of state,' we use the Latin word Stadium, from the Greek στάδιον, denoting fixedness, firmness, and also a fixed standard of length (about 600 ft.), and figuratively a race-course. Neuter nouns having the Latin termination ium take in German ien in the plural.

[15] Render *of them* by the genitive plural of derselbe.

retical.'[1]   However[2] humiliating it may sound,[3] every one of our sciences, however grand[4] their present titles, can be traced back to the[5] most humble and homely[6] occupations of half-savage tribes.

It was not the true,[7] the good, and the beautiful which spurred[8] the early philosophers to deep researches and bold discoveries. The foundation-stone of[9] the most glorious structures of human ingenuity in ages to come[10] was supplied[11] by the pressing wants of a patriarchal and semi-barbarous society.

The names of some of the most ancient departments[12] of human knowledge tell their own tale. Geometry,[13] which at present declares itself free[14] from all sensuous impressions, and treats of its points and lines and planes as[15] purely

---

[1] The above terms are also used in German ; viz. *empirical*, empirifch, *classificatory*, claffificirend, and *theoretical*, theoretifch.

[2] *However*, fo...auch. The verb *may* in the preceding sentence is synonymous with ' can,' whilst here it corresponds to the German mögen.

[3] *To sound*, flingen. The other usual equivalents of *to sound*, as fchallen, hallen, tönen, would not be applicable here.

[4] *However grand*, wie großartig auch; *titles* = names.

[5] The whole of the above sentence might be rendered, almost literally, with grammatical correctness ; but we should obtain a far more elegant version by turning it by ' the trace of all (fämmtlicher) sciences, however grand their present names, can, however humiliating it may sound, be followed back (verfolgt) to the,' &c.

[6] When two or more adjectives, placed side by side, occur in the comparative or superlative degree, the respective termination must be added to each of them.

[7] Abstract substantives, or such as denote things, formed from adjectives, take in German the neuter gender. For the construction *it was...which* see page 34. note 13.

[8] *To spur* (to), anfpornen (zu) Turn here *early* by ' the oldest.'

[9] In phrases like the above we use in German the preposition zu with the dative, instead of the preposition *of*.

[10] The clause *the—come* must be rendered somewhat freely, since the expression *in ages to come* makes it here necessary to supply in German a verb distinctly expressing ' the *future* glorious development of the structures of human ingenuity.' Translate therefore, ten glorreichften Gebäuten des menfchlichen Geiftes, die für alle fünftige Zeiten ba. ftehen follen.

[11] *To supply*, liefern; *by*, von; *want*, here Bedürfniß.

[12] *Department* (referring to sciences, &c.), Fach; *tell their own tale*, fprechen für fich felbft, *i.e.* speak for themselves.

[13] Use the definite article.

[14] Adjectives referring to the verb erflären (or to halten, annehmen, &c.) must be preceded by the preposition für. Cf. page 36, note 4.

[15] The preposition von must here be repeated. Translate *purely* by

ideal conceptions, not[1] to be confounded with the coarse and imperfect representations,[2] as they appear on paper to the human eye,—geometry, as its very name declares,[3] began with measuring a garden or a field. It is derived[4] from the Greek ' gē,' land, ground, earth, and ' metron,' measure. Botany, the science of plants, was originally the science of ' botanē,' which in Greek[5] does not mean[6] a plant in general, but fodder, from ' boskein,' to feed. The science of plants would have been called ' phytology,' from the Greek ' phyton,' a plant.

The founders[7] of astronomy were not the poet or the philosopher, but the sailor and the farmer.[8]   The early[9] poet may have admired the " mazy[10] dance of planets," and the philosopher may have speculated[11] on the heavenly harmonies ;[12] but *it was* to[13] the sailor alone *that* a knowledge of the glittering guides of [14] heaven became a question of life and death.[15] It was he who calculated their risings and settings[16] with the accuracy of a merchant and the shrewdness of an adventurer ; and the names that were given to single stars or constellations clearly[17] show that they were invented by the ploughers of the sea and of the land. The moon, for instance, the golden hand[18] on the

---

rein, and *ideal* by wealen. *Conception*, here Begriff.

[1] Cf. the note to Ext. 23, and page 45, note 20. *To confound*, here verwechseln.

[2] Transl. here *representations* by Figuren. and use the definite article before *paper*.

[3] *As—declares*, wie der Name schon bezeugt; *with measuring a*, mit dem Ausmessen eines.

[4] *It is derived*, derselbe stammt her. Retain the Greek terms, given in inverted commas, also in German.

[5] *In Greek*, im Griechischen.

[6] *To mean*, here bedeuten.

[7] *Founder*, here Begründer.

[8] Translate here *sailor* by Seefahrer, and *farmer* by Landmann.

[9] Turn here *early* by ' old.'

[10] *Mazy*, verschlungen.

[11] *To speculate*, here grübeln (über).

[12] The *heavenly harmonies* are called in German Harmonie der Sphären.

[13] Translate here *to* by für, and place before it the word erst as an equivalent for *alone*.

[14] Render here *of* by am.

[15] Translate *a—death* briefly by zur Lebensfrage.

[16] *Their—settings*, ihren Auf- und Untergang. When two compound expressions having the same subordinate member are placed side by side, the latter is generally omitted in the first expression, the principal member of which is connected with the second compound term by means of hyphens.

[17] *Clearly*, here deutlich.

[18] The word *hand*, denoting the ' index of a watch,' is rendered by Zeiger or Weiser; the latter ex-

dark dial of heaven, was called by them the measurer—-the measurer of time ; for time was measured by[1] nights and moons and winters long before it was reckoned by days and suns and years. — MAX MÜLLER, *The Science of Language.*

XXXIV.

THE WARTBURG.

In the midst of the wild upland tract which forms the centre of Germany, between Frankfort and Leipsic, is[2] one spot[3] distinguished from all the surrounding country[4] by its singular and romantic beauty. The unmeaning[5] downs rise into bold, rocky hills ; the patches of wood[6] sink into unfathomable depths of forest ;[7] and from the midst of these[8] towers the cluster of heights,[9] on the highest of which[10] stands the ancient castle *of* the Wartburg, or Watchtower, of Eisenach.

pression being more used in higher diction, should be employed in the above metaphor.

[1] *By*, referring to 'measure,' is rendered in German by nach.

[2] The verb *to be* is generally rendered by fich befinben, not only when it refers to the state of health of a person, but also when it denotes 'being in a place.' Compare the French *se trouver.*

[3] *Spot*, here Stelle. Turn *distinguished* by 'which distinguishes itself, and *all* by *whole.*

[4] *The surrounding country*, briefly in German, bie...Umgegenb. *Singular*, here eigenthümlich.

[5] *Unmeaning*, unbebeutenb ; *downs*, here Hügelland, to be used in the singular only ; *rise into*, transl. geht...über.

[6] We say also in German ein Fledchen Land for *a patch of ground ;*

but in the above clause the literal translation of *patch* would not be applicable ; we must therefore render the expression *patches of wood* freely by zerstreut liegenben Gehölze. *To sink into*, here fich entfalten zu ; turn *unfathomable* by 'impenetrable.'

[7] *Depths of forest*, Walbesbidicht. Use the singular only.

[8] Turn *of these* by the genitive singular of the pronoun 'the same ;' *to tower*, here emporragen.

[9] Turn *cluster of heights* by the compound term 'mountain-group.'

[10] *On—which*, auf beren höchster Spitze. The above clause offers an illustration of the second instance (compare page 68, note 10) in which we must use the relative pronoun ber, bie, bas, instead of welcher, welche, welches — viz. when the pronoun occurs in the genitive case.

In that castle *there* lived at the beginning of the thirteenth century one of the most saintly characters[1] of the Middle Ages, Elizabeth, Duchess of Thuringia. Her life, which was consumed[2] partly in deeds[3] of unbounded charity to the surrounding[4] poor, partly in patient endurance of[5] oppression and affliction of all kinds,[5] is one of the most instructive records[6] of those times that can be read.[7] It abounds with[8] all the extravagance and superstition which mark[9] the lives of so many *Roman* Catholic saints ; but[10] it is also one of the best examples of[11] the character which marks[12] so many *of the* holy men, and especially *of the* holy women, of the *Roman* Catholic Church, and which is still to be seen[13] in the hospitals of foreign countries[14]—that devotion,[15] namely, which spends[16] itself in the service and condition of the poor,[17] *the* sick, and *the* afflicted. There she lived and suffered, and there her memory[18] was long preserved in the grateful recollection[19] of the Thuringian[20] peasants.

---

[1] *One—characters*, translate eine ter frömmften Perſönlichkeiten. For the expression *Middle Ages*, cf. the note to Ext. 26. *Thuringia*, Thüringen.

[2] Turn *which was consumed* by 'which she passed' (baḥinbrachte). Why the preference is here given to the active voice will be seen from the note to Ext. 8.

[3] *In deeds*, in ber Ausübung.

[4] The attribute *surrounding* cannot be translated literally in the above clause, which must be rendered by gegen bie Armen in ber Umgegenb ; *endurance*, here Ertragen.

[5] *Of — kinds*, jeber Art von Unterbrücung unb Bebrängniß ; *is* = forms.

[6] *Records*, translate Schilberung. For *times*, cf. note *a* to Ext. 50.

[7] Turn *that—read* by 'which one can read.'

[8] Turn *it abounds with* by 'it is full of ;' *extravagance*, here Ueberſchwenglichkeit, to be used in the plural.

[9] *To mark*, here charakteriſiren. For *lives* see Ext. 25, note *c*.

[10] The conjunction *but* is to be placed after *is*.

[11] *Of*, here von.

[12] The verb *to mark* may here be rendered by kennzeichnen.

[13] Render here the verb *to see* by finben, and see page 45, note 20.

[14] For the expression *foreign countries* we have in German the convenient single term Ausland, corresponding somewhat to the French *l'étranger*.

[15] *Devotion*, here Hingebung.

[16] *Spends — condition*, ſich im Dienſte unb in ber Pflege... erſchöpft.

[17] For this and the two following adjectives, employed here substantively, use in German the plural ; *afflicted*, Betrübte.

[18] *Memory*, here Anbenken.

[19] *Recollection*, Erinnerung.

[20] *Thuringian*, Thüringer. Adjectives formed from the proper names of places frequently take the suffix er, instead of the usual adjective suffix, iſch, more particularly if the name consists of more than one syllable.

Up[1] the rugged pathway to that same castle three hundred years afterwards[2] *there* rode at the dead of night a troop of five horsemen, leading behind them[3] in custody a man closely muffled in a cavalier's cloak,[4] who was brought in silence[5] into the court of the fortress, and the gates closed[6] immediately behind him. That[7] man was Luther ; those horsemen were the guard sent [8] by the Elector of Saxony to carry him off on his return from Worms,[9] and conceal him in this lonely and secluded spot[10] till the fury of his enemies was[11] overpast : and there, in what [12] he called his Patmos,[13] he lived[14] unknown and in disguise[15] *for* some of the most critical months of his career, and began that great work of his life—which[16] alone would make his name famous to all after ages[17]—the translation of the Bible[18] into the German *language.*

[1] *Up,* hinauf, to be placed after *castle ; rugged,* rauh. Use in the above clause the accusative case, there being indicated direction together with motion, and turn *pathway* simply by 'way.'

[2] Turn *afterwards* by 'later,' and *at—night* by 'in the stillness of the night.' The German version will read far more elegantly if the clause *up—castle* is placed after the word *night.*

[3] *Leading behind them,* transl. bie...mit sich führten; *closely,* bicht.

[4] Turn *cavalier's cloak* by the compound term 'rider-cloak.' The clause *closely—cloak* qualifies the word *man.* See Int. p. xiv., 1.

[5] *In silence,* stillschweigend.

[6] *To close,* sich schließen.

[7] Turn here *That* by 'this.'

[8] See the note to Ext. 23, and use the pluperfect of the passive voice. *To carry...off,* zu entführen.

[9] The above refers to a well-known incident in the life of Luther, whose personal safety was in danger after his memorable attendance at the Diet of Worms in 1521, before the Emperor Charles V.

[10] *Spot,* here Ort

[11] Use here the present conditional of sein, this mood being generally required in adverbial clauses of time which are introduced by the conjunctions bis, ehe, als, ob, &c. *Overpast,* vorbei. The expression *was overpast* may, however, also be rendered, rather freely and idiomatically, by sich gelegt hätte.

[12] Turn *in what* by 'in the place which ;' *called =* named.

[13] *Patmos,* one of the islands called Sporades, is celebrated as the place where the Apostle John wrote the Apocalypse.

[14] The verb *to live* may here be rendered by the expressive term verleben, which denotes 'to spend a certain time in living.' The prefix ver (compare the Latin præ, pro, and per), expresses 'a consuming, spending, destroying,' &c.

[15] *In disguise,* verborgen.

[16] Insert here the expletive schon, which gives greater force to the word *alone.*

[17] *To—ages,* für alle künftigen Zeiten.

[18] By means of his unsurpassed version of the Bible Luther became the founder of the glorious New-High-German idiom, which has since his times become the general literary language of Germany.

This castle, then,[1] is remarkable[2] as combining[3] *in itself*, more than any other spot, the associations[4] of the old and the new—of the Middle Ages and of the Reformation which destroyed[5] them; and, accordingly, in the popular tradition[6] Luther and St. Elizabeth still hold divided sway.— DEAN STANLEY, *The Reformation.* (*A Lecture.*)

[1] Render here *then* by auф.

[2] Supply the adverb таѕurф before *remarkable*, in accordance with the rule that, if the adjective or verb upon which the objective clause or the supine depends be followed by a preposition, the latter is added to the demonstrative adverb ta or таr, as таrin, таmit, таrauf, таʒu, &c. These compound adverbs are always placed before tne dependent clause; and if a 'verbal form in *ing*' occurs in the latter, it is generally changed into a regular sentence with a finite verb: *e.g. We rely upon your keeping your word*, wir verlaffen unѕ таrauf, таß Ѕie Зhr Ꙃort halten werten. The adjective merfwürtig, in the above clause, requires the preposition turф; it must, therefore, be preceded by таrurф. The reason for the above rule is to be found in the characteristic feature of the German language, to give all constructions with unequivocal grammatical distinctness, and to employ, as a rule, distinct forms and inflections.

[3] Render *as combining* by 'that it...combines' (verbintet), placing the verb after *new*.

[4] *Association*, transl. Ꙃrinnerung (an); *the old*, таѕ Ꙃlte; *the new*, таѕ Ꙃeue.

[5] *To destroy*, verniфten.

[6] *In—tradition*, transl. таѕ Ꙃeiф тer Ꙃolfѕfage. We use here in German the accusative case, because the expression *hold...sway* will, in the above clause, best be translated by the transitive verb beherfфen. Translate *still* by noф immer, and *divided* by gemeinfфaftliф.

VOCABULARY,[1]

WITH

GRAMMATICAL INDEX TO THE NOTES.

---

a *or* an, ein, eine, ein; £500 a year, £500 des Jahres; as an excuse, als *or* zur Entschuldigung; without a weed, frei von jedem Unkraut; not a tree, kein Baum

a *coming between an adjective and noun in English precedes the adjective in German, e.g.* quite as promising a sign, ein ebenso vielversprechendes Zeichen

a (*omitted*): I am a single man, ich bin Junggeselt; to be a surgeon, Arzt sein; it is a thousand to one, es ist tausend gegen eins; in a few minutes, in wenigen Minuten; in a wild stampede, in wilder Flucht; as day dawned, a war-whoop announced, bei Tagesanbruch, verkündigte Kriegsgeschrei

A.D., N.Ch.

abandon (to give up), aufgeben

abbey, die Abtei

ability, die Fähigkeit; das Geschick

able, *adj.* fähig

abode, der Aufenthaltsort

aborigines, die Eingebornen

abound with, voll sein von

about (nearly), ungefähr; about dusk, ungefähr in der Dämmerstunde; about 20 men, an 20 Mann

about (to write about a subject), über; what (you write) about, worüber; there is nothing to describe about the prairie, es läßt sich nichts von der Prairie beschreiben

about: (men who were) about him, bei ihm; to flicker about, hin und her flackern; to get (a ship) about, umwenden; about with her! wendet!

about: to be about (to), im Begriff sein; to be about (to do a thing, to purpose doing it), wollen; an injustice about to be done him, eine Ungerechtigkeit die man ihm anthun will. *See also p.* 40, *note* 12

---

[1] The Vocabulary is based upon Dr. Buchheim's Key to the work, and therefore gives in each case the German word which expresses the meaning of the English word in the special sense in which it is used in the passages selected. This often differs from the ordinary meaning, and the German word given therefore is not always that which is to be found most readily in the dictionaries.

above (more than), über; —— (the summit), über; high above (surrounding persons or things), überragend; high above (higher up), hoch über; rising tier above tier, in aufsteigenden Reihen

abreast, neben einander

absence (of anything), die Ermangelung

absolutely (completely), vollständig; —— (necessary), durchaus

absorb, absorbiren

abstract, abstract

abundance: in abundance, in great abundance = in large numbers, in großer Menge

abyss, der Abgrund

accept, annehmen

accident, der Zufall

accompany, begleiten

accomplishment: in a fair way of accomplishment, auf gutem Wege erfüllt zu werden

according to, nach; gemäß

accordingly, deshalb

account: on account (of), wegen; or he is accounted for, oder es heißt daß er

accumulation of bitterness, die aufgesammelte Erbitterung

accuracy, die Genauigkeit

accurate (exact), genau

Accusative, used in elliptical clauses, 35, *n.* 13

Accusative, with infinitive, construction of, Gr. Int. xvii. III.

Accusatives, two, not used with verbs of choosing, appointing, etc., 36, *n.* 4

accustomed, *adj.*, gewöhnlich

achieve (a task), lösen

acknowledge (to one's self), sich eingestehen

acknowledgment, die Anerkennung

acquaint: to be acquainted with, kennen

acquiesced in their settlement = settled peacefully, ließen sich ruhig nieder

acquire (for one's self), sich erwerben

across (the prairie), durch; (forty

miles) across, breit; across the saddle, über dem Sattel liegend; from across the mountains, vom Gebirge her

act: in the act of freezing, im Gefrieren; act of generous feeling, die großmüthige Handlung

action, die Wirkung; to put in action, thatsächlich ausführen

active (energetic), energisch; active sports, die Leibesübungen

actively: to keep actively engaged, beschäftigen

activity, die Thätigkeit; die Thatkraft; (industry), die Betriebsamkeit

actually, thatsächlich; factisch

acute, scharf

add (to say further), hinzusetzen; hinzufügen; (he) adding that, indem er hinzufügte; add to, hinzufügen; add to (the heat), erhöhen

address = to speak before an audience, vor einer Versammlung sprechen

adhere, zusammenhalten; (to a custom), anhalten; (to an opinion), bei (der Meinung) bleiben

adherent, *sb.*, der Anhänger

adjacent (nations), benachbart

Adjectives denoting colour, use of, 2, *n.* 10

Adjectives, formation of, from proper names; (1) by isch, 66, *n.* 5; (2) by er, 95, *n.* 20

Adjectives referring to erklären, halten, etc., 92, *n.* 14

Adjectives, repetition of terminations of comparative and superlative of, 92, *n.* 6

Adjectives upon which the objective clause or supine depends followed by a preposition, 97, *n.* 2

Adjective Sentences. Caution about the formation of them, Gr. Int. xiv., etc., I.

admire, bewundern

admirable, musterhaft

admit, zulassen; —— (to see a person), vorlassen; (where reason)

was admitted to influence, Ein=
gang fand

advance, *sb.*, das Vorrücken; (spread-
ing out), die Ausdehnung

advance, *vb.*: to order to advance
(*mil.*), vorrücken lassen; to advance (to step forward), vor=
schreiten; (to put forth), vor=
bringen; (the season) advancing
= advanced, vorgeschritten

advantage, der Vortheil; to set at
advantage, Vortheile gewähren

advantageous, günstig

adventure, das Abenteuer

adventurer, der Abenteurer

Adverbial Expressions. I. Place of,
(1) of *manner*, 7, *n.* 32 (*a*), (2)
of *place* and *time*, 1, *n.* 4 (*a*)

II. — of *time*, rendered by
the genitive, 27, *n.* 6

III. Elliptical use of adv.
expres. of place, 36, *n.* 12

Adverbs, relative superlative of,
how formed, 87, *n.* 1

adversary, der Gegner

advice, der Rath

advocate, der Advokat

affable, herablassend

affair (incident), das Ereigniß;
(tournament, &c.), die Begeben=
heit; *see also* p. 58, *note* 16

affairs (everybody's affairs),
Angelegenheiten; busy with his
own affairs (*i.e.* eating and
drinking), mit sich selbst beschäftigt

affect (the nerves, &c.), afficiren;
(to pretend), sich stellen (als ob)

affection, die Liebe

affinity, die Verwandtschaft

afflict: to be afflicted with, leiden
an; to be most afflicting bores,
äußerst lästig fallen; entsetzlich lang=
weilig sein

afflicted (the), die Betrübten

affliction, die Bedrängniß

afford (a shade), gewähren; —— (a
probability), darthun; could not
afford = could not risk (wagen)

after, nachdem; after some hours'
sailing = after they had sailed
some hours, nachdem sie einige
Stunden gesegelt waren

after (great difficulty), mit

after ages, künftige Zeiten

afternoon, der Nachmittag; in the
afternoon, am Nachmittag

afterwards, nachher; (later), später;
(after an event), darauf

again, wieder; (yet again), aber=
mals; to find again, wiederfinden;
to give thanks again, von Neuem
danken; and back again, und
zurück

against, gegen; against all comers,
gegen alle Welt; ordinance against
confining, die Verordnung nicht zu
beschränken

age, das Alter; at the age of, im
Alter von

ages: after ages, ages to come,
künftige Zeiten

agile, behend

agitation, die Aufregung

ago: a year or two ago, vor ein
oder zwei Jahren

agoing: to set agoing, in Bewe=
gung bringen

agree, übereinkommen

agreeable, angenehm

aid, die Hülfe

aide-de-camp, der Adjutant (eines
Generals)

aim (for which one strives), das
Streben

air, die Luft; mountain air, die
Bergluft

alarm: in alarm, voll Bestürzung

Albert N'yanza, der Albert N'yanza

alien, fremdartig

all, all; (everything), Alles; all
the people (were in movement),
Alles; all the Numidians, alle
Numidier; all the holders (of
houses), alle Bewohner; all kinds,
jede Art; all the rest, der ganze
übrige Theil; all the surrounding
country, die ganze Umgegend; all
that day, den ganzen Tag; all the
week, die ganze Woche; all the
(officials), sämmtlich; the troops
were all = all the. (sämmtliche)
troops were; all (their proceedings), sämmtlich; all (together)
sämmtlich; no (light) at all, none

at all, gar fein; all at once (suddenly), plötzlich; all but (almost),
faft; it is all the same to him,
es gilt ihm gleich; to score all
over, über und über ferben

allegiance: to swear allegiance,
den Lehenseid leisten

alligator, der Alligator

allow, lassen; (no man) is allowed,
darf. (*See also p. 9, note* 22 (*b*))

allure it out of the path, es vom
Wege ablocken

ally, der Verbündete

Alma, die Alma

almost, beinah; fast

alone, allein; (solely), bloß; a kick
alone has, nur ein Fußtritt hat;
but it was to the sailor alone,
aber erst für den Seemann; to let
it alone, es bleiben lassen

along (the road, &c.), längs (des
Weges); along (a strip of land)
= on, auf; seeing as he rode
along, als er beim Dahinreiten bemerkte; along with, bei

alongside (the way), längs (des
Weges)

alphabet, das Alphabet

Alps, die Alpen

also, auch

altar, der Altar; high altar, der
Hochaltar

although, obwohl; obgleich

alumni, Alumner (*plur.*)

always, immer; stets

Amazon (female), die Amazone

ambush, der Hinterhalt

American, *adj.*, amerikanisch

amiable, liebenswürdig

amid, unter

amiss: do not take it amiss (if) =
do not be angry with me about
it (if), zürnet mir nicht darob (daß)

amity, die Freundschaft

among, unter; —— (nations, tribes,
plants, &c., in a general sense),
bei; (between), zwischen; among
(the hills), zwischen; had taken
refuge among the people, hatte
ihre Zuflucht zu dem Volke genommen; life among the Bedouins,
die Lebensweise der Beduinen

amount (value), der Werth

ample (fortune), groß

amply, vollständig

ancient (castle), alt

and, und; (slept with their swords
under their pillows) and their
horses (saddled), während die
Pferde ——; a few men and the
Ligurian with them, einige Männer sammt dem Ligurier; a man and
a horse, ein Mann sammt einem
Pferde; (a lump of butter is
placed) and allowed to melt,
welches man schmelzen läßt

anecdote, die Anekdote

Anezza (*plur.*), die Anezzas

angry (jerks of the head), heftig

animal, das Thier

animal kingdom, das Thierreich

animality, der Animalismus

animosity, die Erbitterung

another, ein anderer, &c.; ein Zwei-
ter, &c.

answer, *sb.*, die Antwort; to make
no answer, antworten nichts

answer, *vb.*, antworten; to answer
very well for his assertion, die
Wahrheit seiner Behauptung zu bestätigen

ant, die Ameise

anticipation: (to blossom) in anticipation, in der Hoffnung

antiquarian, antiquarisch

any, irgend welcher, welche, welches;
(every), ein jeder, eine jede, ein
jedes; more than any other spot,
mehr wie jeder andre Ort; for any
long period, auf längere Zeit; not
to any woman (*p.* 89), nicht
einer Frau

any (*omitted*): without waiting any
longer, ohne länger abzuwarten

any one, Jemand; eine jede Person

apart: a few feet apart, einige
Fuß von einander

Apollo, Apollo

apologue, die Sage

apostle, der Apostel

apotheosis, die Apotheose

apparel, die Kleidung

appeal: to make appeal, to appeal, appelliren

appear, erſcheinen; ſich zeigen; ——
conspicuous, zeichnen ſich beſon=
bers aus; —— (above water),
auftauchen; (seem), ſcheinen

appearance (outward), das Aus=
ſehen; (personal), äußere Erſchein=
ung; first appearance, erſtes Auf=
treten

appendage (feathery), die Anhäng=
ſel; (appurtenance), das Zubehör

applause, der Beifall

apple, der Apfel

apply (a name), beilegen

appoint (a day), beſtimmen

Apposition, agreement of, with
the nouns qualified, Gr. Int.
xix. IV., 85, *n*. 9

apprehend (to dread), befürchten

approach, *sb.*, there was only one
approach to, nur ein Weg führt
nach

approach, *vb.*, ſich nähern; Would
it stay to be approached? Wird
es bei der Annäherung nicht ver=
ſchwinden? [April

April: on the 2nd April, den 2ten

apse, die Apſis

aquiline: slightly aquiline (nose),
leichtgebogen

Aquitaine, Aquitanien

Arab, der Araber

Arabic, das Arabiſch

arch, der Bogen; Arch of Triumph,
der Triumphbogen

arched, gewölbt

archipelago, der Archipel

arduous, ſchwierig

argue, disputiren

argument, das Argument; der Be=
weis; (subject of a discourse),
der Gegenſtand; (dispute), der
Streit; die Discuſſion

arise from, enſtehen aus

arm: in his mother's arms, in den
Armen ſeiner Mutter

arm (weapon), das Gewehr; die
Waffe; in arms, die Waffen in der
Hand; passage of arms (be-
tween knights), der Ritterkampf

armed, gewaffnet; armed men (soldiers), gewaffnete Mannſchaft

armour, die Rüſtung

army, die Armee; the First Army,
das erſte Armeekorps

around its walls, an den Wänden
herum

arrest, der Arreſt; a week's arrest,
eine Woche Arreſt

arrive, ankommen

arrival (introduction), die Einführ=
ung

arrow, der Pfeil

art, die Kunſt

article (of table furniture), das
Stück

Article. I. *Use* of def. (1) with
abstract nouns, 1, *n*. 1, and 8,
n. 35 (*a*); (2) with common
names, 1, *n*. 2; (3) with names
of materials, 2, *n*. 5 (*a*); (4)
with names of mountains, 6, *n*.
30; (5) instead of possessive
pronouns, 8, *n*. 34 (*b*); (6) with
names of countries preceded
by adjectives, 66, *n*. 14; (7)
with foreign proper names, 3, *n*.
15 (*a*), and 9, *n*. 40 (*b*); (8) with
adjs. 31, 18; (9) after alle, 68, *n*.
4; (10) before meiſte, 91, *n*. 6
II. Omission of —, with common names used as titles, 28,
n. 6
III. *General definition* of —,
76, *n*. 10
IV. *Place* of —, when used
with adj., 31, *n*. 18; 49, *n*. 13
V. *Repetition* of —, Gr. Int.
xix. IV., 42, *n*. 9; 91, *n*. 10

artillery, die Artillerie

as, als; wie; ſo; ebenſo (*the* as pre-
*ceding the first or only adjective
in a phrase* = ſo *or* ebenſo; *the
second* as = wie *or* als); da;
während, &c.: as an excuse, als
or zur Entſchuldigung; operate as
but a slight check, nur geringen
Einhalt thun; as far as (the gate),
bis zu; as if it had been made
so, als wäre es ſo gemacht; as if
(springing from), gleichſam; as if
to (complain), als ob es wollte
(*see also* p. 39, *n*. 5); as the day
dawned, bei Tagesanbruch; as
(the division formed), während;

(we do not love them) as it is, auch so (*placed at beginning of sentence*) ; as (the reading ended), so wie ; as the thing more perfect is, the = the more perfect anything is, the, je vollkommener Etwas ist, desto ; as to (with regard to), was . . . betrifft ; as well as, sowie ; almost as well as, fast ebenso gut wie, quite as, ebenso. (*See also p. 43, n. 11 ; p. 76, n. 4*)

ascent, die Besteigung

ascertain : well-ascertained, völlig= erwiesen

ashes, die Asche

aside : to turn aside, ablenken

ask, fragen

asparagus, der Spargel

aspect, das Aussehen

assail, angreifen

assault (him), angreifen

assembly, die Versammlung

assertion, die Behauptung

Assertion, placed (1) *after* the subject, 2, n. 5 (*b*) ; (2) *before* the subject, 3, n. 12 (*a*)

assiduously improve (one's abilities), durch Fleiß pflegen

assign, anweisen

assistance, die Hülfe

associate, zugesellen ; beigesellen

associations of (remembrances of), die Erinnerungen an

assume, annehmen ; —— (a dress), anthun

Assyrian, *sb.*, der Assyrer

astronomer, der Astronom ; Herschel the astronomer, der Astronom Herschel

astronomy, die Astronomie

at, zu ; an ; in ; auf ; bei, &c. : at a depth, in einer Tiefe ; at a distance, in der Ferne ; (arrive, be, descend, take place at a town), in ; (to land at a town), bei ; to set at advantage, Vortheile ge= währen ; no . . . at all, none at all, gar kein ; at all events, auf alle Fälle ; at certain seasons, zu gewissen Jahreszeiten ; at dusk, in der Dämmerung ; at first, zu=

erst ; night is at hand, die Nacht rückt heran ; at his side, zur Seite ; at his tailor's, bei seinem Schnei= der ; at length, endlich ; to set at liberty, in Freiheit setzen ; at once, sofort ; at present, jetzt ; at the age of, im Alter von ; at the battle, in der Schlacht ; at the beginning (lived), zu Anfang ; at the foot, am Fuß ; at the head (of an army, &c.), an der Spitze ; to sit at the king's side, sich neben den König setzen ; at the school, an der Schule ; at the moment, in dem Augenblick ; at the right minute, im rechten Mo= ment ; at (the same time), um ; at six (o'clock), um sechs Uhr ; at the time (just then), im Au= genblicke ; at this day (up to this day), bis auf diesen Tag ; at this moment, in diesem Augenblick ; at whatever risk, auf jede Gefahr hin ; at which = where, wo

atmospheric, atmosphärisch

atom : (without caring) an atom, im Geringsten

attach, anhangen ; attach itself, sich anknüpfen

attack, *vb.*, angreifen

attack, *sb.* : flank attack, der Flan= kenangriff ; column of attack, die Angriffskolonne ; plan of attack, der Angriffsplan

attempt (to take a fort), *sb.*, der Angriff

attempt, *vb.*, versuchen

attendance : to be in close atten= dance on him, sich stets um ihn befinden

attendant, der Begleiter

attention, die Aufmerksamkeit ; at= tention (to), Aufmerksamkeit (auf)

attitude, die Stellung ; an attitude of opposition to, eine feindliche Stellung gegen

audience (an assembly of regu= larly appointed members), die Versammlung. (*See also p. 32, n. 6*)

Augustus, Augustus

Austrasia, Austrasien

Austrian, *adj.*, öſterreichiſch

authenticated, als authentiſch er= wieſen

author, der Autor; der Schriftſteller; der Verfaſſer

autobiographi?, autobiographiſch

autumn, der Herbſt

auxiliary cohort, die Auxiliarcohorte

avert, abwenden

avoid, entgehen

awaken, weden

aware: well aware, überzeugt; to be aware of, ſich bewußt ſein

away, hinweg; to be cast away (driven on shore), an den Strand treiben; to dash away (to take flight), fortſtürzen; to ride away, fortreiten

axe, die Art

axis, die Achſe

baby (child), das Kind

Babylon, Babylon

back (*in conjunction with verbs*), wieder——; zurüd——; to go back, zurüdgehen; to turn back, zurüdkehren; to find the way back; den Weg wiederfinden; to trace back, verfolgen; there and back, hin und zurüd

    back, *sb.:* turned their backs (fled), flohen; back (of a building, of the town), die Rüdſeite

bad (worse than his reputation), ſchlimm

baffle (to frustrate), vereiteln. (*See p. 49, n. 6*)

bake, baden

baker, der Bäder

ball, die Kugel

band (music), das Muſikcorps

bank (of a river), das Ufer; (side of a hollow), der Abhang

banquet, das Bankett

barbarian, *sb.*, der Barbar

barbarian chieftain, der Barbaren= häuptling

barometer, der Barometer

basilica of St. Peter, die Peters= kirche

Bath, Bath

battalion, das Battaillon

battery, die Batterie

battle, die Schlacht; battle of, die Schlacht bei, *or an*. (*See p. 49, n. 1*)

battle-field, das Schlachtfeld

baying (of a hound), das Bellen

be, *insep. prefix, transforms intransitive verbs into transitive ones,* 39, *n.* 1

be, ſein; werden (*see p. 1, n. 4 (b)*); ſich befinden (*see p. 94, n. 2*); &c.: the treasury was (in an exhausted condition), die Schatz= kammer befand ſich; to be (to consist of), beſtehen aus; the drink is water, milk, and tea, das Ge= tränk beſteht aus Waſſer, &c.; to be (a strong position, &c), bilden; (her life is (forms) a record), bildet; what can be (more extraordinary), was kann es geben; to be of (to belong to), angehö= ren; to be without result, keine Folge haben; the object was, dies hatte zum Zwed; night is at hand, die Nacht rüdt heran; the answer was, die Antwort lautete; to be (in the nature of things), liegen; the future was, die Zu= kunft lag; to be on the back (of a camel, &c.), auf dem Rüden ſitzen; to be at stake, auf dem Spiele ſtehen; to be (in favour), ſtehen; to be (in one's —rd year), ſtehen

    be: there is, *see* there

    be: being: though the blossoming time being spring, ob= gleich die Blüthezeit im Frühling iſt; I being referee, ich als Schieds= richter; (I) being a gentile, da ich ein Heide bin; which being so, und da dies der Fall iſt; the moon being bright, da der Mond hell ſchien; they being so many, wäh= rend ihrer ſo viele waren; no words being spoken, da kein Wort ge= ſprochen wird; without being made a prisoner, ohne zum Ge= fangenen gemacht zu werden; by being the only man = because he is the only man; he is accounted for by being, es heißt, daß er ſei be (*followed by a past participle*), *see under* Passive Voice; declared to be fairly achieved, für vollständig gelöst erklärt; (the roses) are to be planted, müssen gepflanzt werden; (though he) were to be crowned, gekrönt werden sollte; it may be suspected, man kann annehmen; to be moored (in harbour), vor Anker liegen; not a tree to be seen, kein Baum ist zu sehen

be: it was (*omitted*): but it was to the sailor alone, aber erst für den Seemann. (*See also p.* 34, *n.* 13)

beam (from the sun), der Strahl

bear, *vb.*, tragen; (to hold up), emporhalten; to bear (sail), aufspannen; weapons bearing points of, Waffen deren Spitzen aus . . . waren; to bear down to the ground, zu Boden werfen; borne down by the current, von der Strömung fortgerissen; to bear illwill, übel wollen; to bring (guns) to bear on (a position), aufrichten

beast, das Thier

beat: the rain beats furiously, der Regen strömt heftig nieder

beautiful, schön; beautiful (youth), herrlich

beautiful, *sb.*, das Schöne

beauty, die Schönheit

because, weil; da

become, werden; whatever does become of the gentlemen, was auch immer aus den Herren wird; has become (now), ist jetzt

becoming, *adj.*, geziemend

bed (place of rest), das Lager

Bedouin. der Beduin; —— tribe, der Beduinenstamm

bedürfen, governs genitive case, 6, *n.* 29

befall, widerfahren

befehlen, requires the supine, 89, *n.* 1

befleißen (sich), governs gen. case, 86, *n.* 2

before, *prep.*, vor; *conj.*, ehe; *adv.*

(had been there before), schon früher

beggary (poverty), die Armuth

begin, anfangen; beginnen; from that moment history begins, to begin = datiren; a storm begins, ein Sturm erhebt sich; day gradually began to break = day gradually broke

beginning, der Anfang; at the beginning (lived), zu Anfang

behind, hinter; to lead behind them, mit sich führen; to leave behind, zurücklassen

behold, erblicken

being, *sb.* (creature), das Wesen

beleaguer (to afflict), heimsuchen

believe, glauben

bell, die Glocke

belong, gehören; belong to the vegetable kingdom, zum Pflanzenreich gehörig

beloved, geliebt

below (under), unter

belt, der Gürtel

belted (knight), gerüstet; belted about with a zone of blue = decorated with a blue girdle, mit einem blauen Gürtel geschmückt

bend, die Biegung

bend back, zurückbiegen; bend in obeisance, sich tief verneigen

Benedek, Benedek

Berber language, die Berbersprache

besides, außerdem

best, *adj.*, best; best luck, das größte Glück; to have the best of the struggle, die Oberhand bekommen

best, *adv.*: as best pleases ourselves, wie es uns am besten gefällt; to like the best, am liebsten mögen

better, besser; better (observer), schärfer; to understand flowers better, mehr von Blumen verstehen

between, zwischen

beyond (one's comprehension), zu hoch für; beyond (the arch), hinter; to get beyond the reach, aus dem Bereich kommen

bill (parliamentary), bie Bill
bird, ber Bogel
bishop, ber Bifchof
Bistritz, bie Bifritz
bit, bas Etüd; bit of land, bas
Etüd Panb
bit by bit, allmählich
bite, beißen; to bite a stick, in einen
Etod beißen
bitter, bitter
bitterness (of feeling), bie Erbit=
terung
bivouac, bas Bivouaf; bivouac fire,
bas Bivouaffeuer
black, fchwarz
black (lead) pencil, ber Bleiftift
blameless, tabellos
blazing, brenneub
blood, bas Blut; (descent), bie Ab=
funft
bloodhound, ber Schweißhunb
blossom, vb., blühen
blossoming time, bie Blüthezeit
blow (a knock), ber Schlag
    blow, vb.: but for the wind
    blowing, wenn nicht ber Winb her
    wehte; it (the wind) blew coldly
    upon the soldiers = the soldiers
    felt its keenness
blue, blau
boar, ber Eber
boast: it was the just boast of
Schiller, Schiller war mit Recht
ftolz barauf
boat, bas Boot; boat's crew, bie
Schiffsmannschaft
body, ber Körper; (denoting matter as opposed to spirit), ber
Körper
boil, vb., fochen; boiled, adj., ge=
focht
bold, fühn
boldly, fühn; boldly proportioned,
in fühnen Proportionen
bombard, bombarbiren
book, bas Buch; Books of Kings,
bie Bücher ber Könige
border, bie Grenze; border-country,
bas Grenzlanb; border feud, bie
Grenzfehbe
bore: to be a bore, läftig fallen;
langweilig fein

born, geboren
borough, ber Flecken; borough of
Poole, ber Flecken Poole
borrow, entlehnen
botanical, botanifch
botanist, ber Botanifer
botany, bie Botanif
both, beibe; to be short of both
sleep and food, weber Schlaf noch
Nahrung genug haben
boundary, bie Grenze
bowels (of the earth), ber Schoß
boy, ber Knabe
branch, ber Zweig
bravely, tapfer
bread, bas Brob; cake of bread,
ber platte Brobfuchen
break, brechen; zerbrechen; (to di-
vert), ablenfen; day gradually
began to break = day gradually
broke (to break, anbrechen)
    break (in the monotony), bie
    Abwechfelung
breakers, branbenbe Wogen
breast (of a mountain), bie
Mitte
breeze, ber Winb
brigade of guards, bie Garben=
Brigabe
brigand-looking, mit räuberhaftem
Ausfehen
bright, hell; the moon being
bright, ba ber Monb hell fchien;
bright (sky), flar; bright side
(of affairs), bie Lichtfeite
brightly, hell
bring, bringen; bring back, zurüd=
bringen; bring down (shoot),
herabfchießen; bring up (guns,
&c.) = to cause or to order (guns,
&c.) to be brought up, aufbringen
laffen; bring (guns) to bear on
(a position), aufrichten
Britain, Britanien
British, adj., britifch
broad, breit
broken (land), uneben
brother, ber Bruber
brotherhood, bie Brüberfchaft
brow (forehead), bie Stirn; (head),
bas Haupt
brown, braun

Bruges, Brügge

build, bauen; (land which would let) on a building lease, zu Bauzwecken

building, sb., das Gebäude

bully, vb., übel mitspielen

burden himself, sich aufbürden

burgher, der Bürger

burn (to destroy by fire), verbrennen; burn (down), niederbrennen

burning, adj., glühend

business, das Geschäft; closely engaged in business, von Geschäften sehr stark in Anspruch genommen

bust, die Büste

busy, beschäftigt

but, aber; (following a negative clause), sondern; (only), nur; operate as but a slight check upon, nur geringen Einhalt thun; saw but one, sah nur eins; give but (an indication), geben nur; nothing but, nicht als; but for the wind blowing, wenn nicht der Wind her wehte; but somehow, dennoch fügt es sich so (daß —)

but, transl. of, (1) by aber, or sondern, 24, n. 8; (2) by als, 62, n. 1; (3) by nur or bloß, 41, n. 14

but for, when turned by if not, 55, n. 7

butter, die Butter

buy (freedom), erkaufen

by (whom or what), von; by (means of, or owing to), durch; (knelt) by the altar, am Altar; by the bank (of a river), am Ufer; by (the utterance) = at, auf; by order, auf Befehl; by (referring to measure), nach; (the time was) measured by nights, nach Nächten gerechnet; by Allah, bei Allah; by no means, durchaus nicht; (to make an attack) by the part (of the hill), von der Seite aus; by night, zur Nachtzeit, in der Nacht; by this time, jetzt; nun; schon; by turns, abwechselnd; by way of (remuneration), als

by (followed by a pres. part.): by employing, durch die Anwen-

dung; by raising, durch die Errichtung; by associating him, indem er sich zugesellte; by presenting himself, indem er sich zeigte; by being the only man = because he is the only man; he is accounted for by being = es heißt, daß er sei

by and by, bald darauf

cabbage, der Kohl; red-cabbage, der rothe Kohl

Cæsar, Cäsar

cake of bread, der platte Brodkuchen

calculate, berechnen

call (to name), nennen; was called, wurde genannt; call upon (anyone to do anything), auffordern; to call upon him, ihm einen Besuch machen

camel, das Kamel or Kameel

cameline, Kameel —

camp, das Lager

campaign, der Feldzug

can, können; so far as a beast can, so weit es einem Thier möglich ist; that he could repeat, daß er im Stande war zu wiederholen; it could not but, es mußte natürlich; could, when rendered by konnte, or by könnte, 67, n. 5; cannot be obtained, ist nicht zu haben

candle, das Licht

candy, das Zuckerwerk

cannon (sing.), die Kanone; (collectively), das Geschütz, (See p. 49, n. 10)

canvas awning (of vehicles), die Plane

caoutchouc, der Kautschuk; das Federharz

capable: to be capable of, können

capital (of a country), die Hauptstadt

capitulate, capituliren

capitulation, die Capitulation

captain (of a guild), der Capitän

capture, vb., gefangen nehmen

capturing slaves, der Sklavenfang

Capuchin, der Kapuziner

care, sb., die Sorge

care (to trouble about), sich kümmern um; to care about flowers, sich etwas aus Blumen machen

career, die Laufbahn

carefully (observe), gut; carefully premeditated, planmäßig vorbereitet

careless (indifferent as to), unbekümmert

carriage, der Wagen

carry, tragen; carry (one everywhere), hintragen; carry (a place by storm), einnehmen; carry off (a person), entführen; wegführen

Carthusian, der Karthäuser

cart-load, die Ladung

case: in such a case, in diesem Falle; case of high treason, die Hochverrathssache

cast (a shadow), werfen; to be cast away (driven on shore), an den Strand treiben

Castilian, castilianisch

castle, das Schloß

cathedral (of Strasburg), der Münster

catholic, adj., katholisch

cattle, das Vieh; not a herd of cattle, keine Herde Vieh; a group, no matter of what cattle, eine Gruppe von welcher Art sie auch sei

cauliflower, der Blumenkohl

cause, vb., (to make necessary), veranlassen; (to order, to make), lassen; (to act so that), bewirken

cause, sb., die Ursache; to plead a cause, eine Sache führen; . cause (of failure), der Grund; (subject, of an argument), der Gegenstand

causeway batteries, die Chaussee-Batterien

cavalier's cloak, der Reitermantel

celebrated, adj., berühmt

celebrity (fame), der Ruhm

cell, die Zelle

Central Arabia, · Mittelarabien (neut.)

centre, der Mittelpunkt; centre battalion, das Centrum; centre (of an army), das Centrum

centurion, der Centurion

century, das Jahrhundert

certain, gewiß

certainly, gewiß

chain-pier, die Kettenbrücke

chair, der Stuhl

champion, der Kämpe

change, vb., verändern; changed the whole face (of the battle) = (the battle) assumed another aspect, nahm eine andere Gestalt an

change, sb., die Veränderung

character (attribute), der Charakter; (person), die Persönlichkeit; (one's) character, der Ruf

charger (war-horse), das Schlachtroß

charity, die Wohlthätigkeit

Charles, Karl; Charles the Great, Karl der Große

charlock, der Ackersenf; wilder Senf

charming (manner), einnehmend

check: to operate as but a slight check upon, nur geringen Einhalt thun

checkered fortune, abwechselnder Erfolg

cheer (to encourage), ermuthigen

cherish: the memory of Joseph II. was long and fondly cherished, Joseph II. stand lange in theurem Andenken

chicken, das Hühnchen; prairie chicken, das amerikanische Feldhuhn

chief (of a staff), der Chef

chiefly, vorzüglich, hauptsächlich

chieftain, der Häuptling

child, das Kind

child's, kindlich

chin, das Kinn

chivalry, das Ritterthum. (See also p. 57, n. 1)

chlamys, die Chlamys

choice (flowers), schönst choice, sb., die Wahl; through (from choice), aus freier Wahl; to make a choice, wählen

choose, wählen; who might have chosen = to whom it might occur, dem es beigefallen wäre

chopped, gehackt

Christian, adj., christlich

Christmas-day, der Weihnachtstag

chronicle, bie Chronit
church, bie Kirche
circular, *adj.*, treisförmig
circumstance, ber Umstand; (incident), ber Zwischenfall
citizen, ber Bürger
city, bie Stabt
civilization, bie Civilisation
claim, *vb.*, reclamiren
claim, *sb.*, ber Anspruch
class, bie Klasse
classificatory, classificirenb
clattering (the), bas Gerassel
clean, *vb.*, reinigen
clear, klar; clear (knowledge), genau
clearly (show), beutlich
clergy, bie Geistlichkeit
cliff, bie Klippe
climb (a hill, a mountain), erklimmen; to climb up, hinaufklettern
cling to, sich anklammern
cloak: cavalier's cloak, ber Reitermantel
close, *adj.*, (to come to close quarters), angreifen; to be in close attendance on him, sich stets um ihn befinben
close, *vb.*, (the gates closed), sich schließen; to close upon, sich schließen über
close to, *adv.*, neben
closely (muffled), bicht; closely engaged (in busiuess), sehr stark in Anspruch genommen
closing (ranks), geschlossen
cloud, bie Wolte
cloudless, unbewöltt
cluster of heights, bie Berggruppe
coarse, roh
coast, bie Küste
coat, ber Rock
cogency, ber Zwang
cogent, triftig
cold, kalt
coldly: it (the wind) blew coldly upon the soldiers = the soldiers felt its keenness (Schärfe)
collar round his neck, bas Halsband
colony, bie Kolonie

colour, bie Farbe
column of attack, bie Angriffskolonne
combatant, ber Kämpfer
combine, verbinben
come, kommen; ages to come, bie künftigen Zeiten; to come down, herabkommen; to come forth (to creep out), herauskriechen; to come on (to rain), anfangen; to come out (from under), hervorkommen; to come out iu front (of a position in battle), vorrüden hinaus; to come up (to his assistance), kommen herbei; to come up to it, vor bemselben ankommen; to come upon (to fall upon, to attack), überfallen; (to chance upon), aufstoßen; we, coming upon some break, inbem wir auf irgenb eine Abwechselung stießen
   come (*omitted*): come and live, wohnen; come to settle, sich niederlassen
comedy, bas Lustspiel
comer: first comer, ber Erste Beste; against all comers, gegen alle Welt
command (to govern), beherrschen; (to order), befehlen; to be commanded (to), ben Befehl erhalten
   command, *sb.* (leadership), bie Anführung; to have at his command, ihm zu Gebote stehen
commandaut, ber Commanbant
commander (in chief), ber Felbherr; (of a corps), ber Befehlshaber
commanding (in manner), ehrfurchtgebietenb; commanding officer, ber Commanbant
commence, anfangen
commercial town, bie Handelsstadt
commission (as officer), bie Offizierstelle; first commission, bie Ernennung zum Offizier
commit (to send), schiden; commit (a fault), begehen
commou (Bedouin), gemein; common (colour), gewöhnlich; common (room), gemeinschaftlich

Commons (House of), baš Unter=
haus

communicate (ideas by speech),
ausbrüden

companion, ber Gefährte; (friend),
ber Freunb

company, bie Gefellfchaft; (of
guards), bie Compagnie; (of
soldiers), bie Truppe

competitor, ber Mitwerber

complain of, fich beflagen über

complete, vollftänbig

complying with the habit, bem
Gebrauch nachfommenb

compose (an alphabet), bilben; to
be composed of, beftehen aus

composition (elaboration), bie Aus=
arbeitung; (of an essay), bie Ab=
faffung. (See p. 30, n. 1, and p.
62, n. 6)

Compound Expressions, two, having the same subordinate member, 93, n. 16

comprehend, verftehen

comprehension, ber Verftanb

conceal, verbergen

conceive (imagine), fich benten

concentration, bie Concentration

conception (geometrical), ber Be=
griff

concerning: (such questions) concerning it, barüber

conciliate (the hearts, win them
over), winnen

condescending, herablaffenb

condition (state), bie Lage; ber Zu=
ftanb; (position), bie Stellung;
improving the condition of the
poor, bie Pflege ber Armen

Conditional mood, used (1) in
clauses expressing supposition,
48, n. 9; (2) in adverbial clauses
of time, 96, n. 11; (3) for the
present participle after but for,
55, n. 7; (4) instead of the conjunctive, 74, n. 16

conduct (to lead, to bring to),
führen; to conduct out of the
town, zur Stabt hinaus führen
conduct (behaviour), bas Be=
tragen

confidence, bas Vertrauen

confidently, muthig

confine (to limit), befchränfen

conform (one's self to), fich an=
fchließen

confound: to be confounded
(with), verwechfeln (mit)

confusion, bie Verwirrung

conjointly, gemeinfchaftlich

Conjunctive mood, use of, 26, n.
16; 29, n. 3

conquer, befiegen; conquered, adj.,
befiegt

conqueror (victor), ber Sieger.
(See p. 36, n. 1)

consequence, bie Folge; mighty in
its consequences, folgenreich

consider (well), erwägen (see p. 71,
n. 13); I, considering however,
ba ich in Erwägung zog; consider
(as, expressed or understood),
betrachten als; anfehen als (see p.
85, n. 2); consider necessary,
für nöthig halten

considerable (share), bebeutenb;
considerable (degree), hoch

consideration, bie Rückficht

consist (of), beftehen (aus)

conspicuous: to appear conspicuous, zeichnen fich befonbers aus

Constantine the Great, Conftantin
ber Große

constellation, bas Sternbilb

constraint, ber Zwang

Construction, characteristics of
German, Int. xiv. I.

Construction, elliptical, 35, n. 13

consume (one's life) = to pass,
bahinbringen

contain, enthalten; (a town) containing 100 inhabitants, bie 100
Einwohner hat

contemplate (doing something),
beabfichtigen

continent, ber Kontinent; (world),
bie Welt

continue (to last), bauern; to continue to walk on, weiter fchreiten.
(See p. 37, n. 17)

contrary, bas Gegentheil; very much
the contrary, ganz im Gegentheil;
on the contrary, hingegen

contrast, ber Gegenfatz

contribute, beitragen

contrivance (arrangement), die
Vorrichtung

contumacious, troßig; most contumacious, äußerst troßig

convenient, bequem

conveniently, mit Bequemlichkeit

conversation, die Unterhaltung

convey: to take and convey
(a prisoner to anyone), überliefern

convince, überzeugen

cook: well-cooked, sorgfältig zubereitet

cooperate, zusammenwirken

copy, vb., abschreiben; (to repeat),
wiederholen

corn, das Korn; (Indian corn),
der Mais

coronation, die Krönung

corpse, die Leiche

correct (precise), bestimmt

corresponding (change), entsprechend

cost, vb., kosten

Cottonian (Library), Cottonisch

could, see can

counter-march, der Contremarsch

country, das Land; (native land),
das Vaterland (see p. 9, n. 39);
surrounding country, die Umgegend; country round, die Umgegend; an extent of country, eine
Landstrecke

couple: married couple, das Ehepaar

courage, der Muth

courageous, muthig

course (of his speech), der Verlauf

court, der Hof; Court noble, der
Höfling

courteous, höflich

courteously, höflich

courtesy, feiner Anstand

cove, die Bucht

cover, vb., bedecken

cover (protection), der Schuß

cradle, die Wiege; from their
cradles, von der Wiege an

crater, der Krater

crawl, kriechen

create (discontent), hervorrufen

crest (of a hill), der Gipfel

crew: boat's crew, die Schiffsmannschaft

Crimean War, der Krim-Krieg

crisp (hair), kraus

critical, kritisch

cross, vb., übergehen; (to cross, to
ford a river), durchwaten

cross-bow, die Armbrust

cross-bowman, der Armbrustschütz

crowd, vb., (to flock towards),
strömen
    crowd (number of people),
    die Menge; crowd of men (the
    whole of them), der ganze Haufe;
    die Männer

crown, sb., die Krone

crowned, adj., gekrönt

cry (of a hound), das Gebell; cries
(shouts), das Geschrei (sing.)
    cry out, ausrufen

crystal, der Krystall

cultivate (land), bauen; (a science,
&c.), sich befleißigen

culture, die Bildung

curds, der Quarg; der Quark

curiosity, die Neugier; from curiosity, aus Neugier

curious (wishful), begierig

current, sb., die Strömung

current, adj., im Umlauf

curule, curulisch

custody, der Gewahrsam

custom, der Gebrauch; die Gewohnheit

customary, gebräuchlich

cut, schneiden; (features liberally
cut, gebildet; (nose finely) cut,
geschnitten; to cut away (the
ground), abtragen; to cut (down),
umhauen; to cut up (paper, &c.),
zerschneiden; to cut up (an animal), zerlegen

cutlet, die Kotelette

ba, or bar, when added to prepositions, 97, n. 2

daily, täglich

dance, der Tanz

danger, die Gefahr

Dante, Dante

Danube, die Donau

dare: if he dared, wenn er den
Muth dazu hätte

dark, buntel; (gloomy), büfter
dark (nightfall), bas Dunfelwerben
darkness, bie Finsterniß
dash away (to take flight), fort=
 stürzen
Date, place of, in German, 98, *n.* 1
Dative, idiomatic use of, 85, *n.* 15
dawn, *sb.*, bie Dämmerung
dawn, *vb.*, grauen; as the day
 dawned, bei Tagesanbruch
day, ber Tag; day *on which an event
 occurs, when not governed by a
 preposition is in the accusative
 case*, e.g., the next day we went,
 ben nächsten Tag gingen wir; all
 that day, ben ganzen Tag; at this
 day (up to this day), bis auf
 biesen Tag; in our own days, in
 unserer Zeit; in the days of
 Charles II., unter Karl bem zwei=
 ten; day's journey, bie Tagereise
daytime: in the daytime, am Tage
dead, *adj.*, tobt; the dead (of
 night), *sb.*, bie Stille
deal (to treat with), unterhandeln
deal: a good deal of, viel
dear, theur
dearest, *sb.* (*plur.*), bie Theuersten
death, ber Tob; he is fairly frightened to death, es überfällt ihn
 eine wahre Tobesangst; (became)
 a question of life and death,
 zur Lebensfrage
debate, *vb.*, bebattiren; (to dispute),
 streiten
debate, *sb.*, bie Debatte
debated question, bie Streitfrage
decaying (fire), erlöschenb
decide, entscheiben
declare, erllären; declare itself
 free, sich für frei erllären; (to
 testify), bezeugen
decline (of an empire), bas Sinten
deed: in deeds of charity, in ber
 Ausübung ber Wohlthätigteit
deep, tief; deep (potation), start
defeat, *vb.*, schlagen
defence, bie Vertheibigung; to make
 defence (for the purpose of
 making a defence), zur Verthei=
 bigung; (men) for defence, als
 Vertheibiger

defend (a place), vertheibigen; defend (a passage of arms), auf=
 nehmen
definition, bie Definition
defy, Trotz bieten
degree, ber Grab
delicious, löstlich
delight, *sb.*, bie Freube
delight, *vb.*, entzücken
delivery: for delivery, zur Bestel=
 lung
demagogue, ber Demagoge
demand, *sb.*, bie Forberung
demand, *vb.*, forbern
demur, *sb.*, (hesitation), ber Auf=
 enthalt
department (of knowledge), bas
 Fach
depend (on), verlassen (auf)
dependent, abhängig
deportment (in public), bas Be=
 nehmen
depose (kings, &c.), entthronen
depths of forest, bas Walbesbicticht
derive: to be derived, herstammen
descend, absteigen
descend from (to be derived from),
 herstammen von
describe, beschreiben
descry, erblicken
desert, *sb.*, bie Wüste
desert, *vb.*, verlassen
design, with the design (object),
 zu bem Zweck
designate, bezeichnen
despondency, bie Verzweiflung
destined: to be destined (to meet)
 sollen
destroy, zerstören; vernichten
detection, bie Entbeckung
deter, abhalten
determine (to resolve), beschließen;
 entschließen; (to settle about), be=
 stimmen (über); determined by
 (sentiment), bestimmt burch
develope: to be developed, sich
 entfalten; strongly developed,
 start ausgeprägt
devote themselves, sich wibmen
devoted (addicted to), ergeben
devotion (to a duty), bie Hinge=
 bung

I

devout, fromm

diadem (of the Caesars), die Krone

dial, das Zifferblatt

dialect, der Dialekt

dictatorial, bictatorisch

die, sterben

dies, *use of the abbreviated form*, 90, n. 18

different, verschieden

difficult (to do), schwer; difficult (road), schwierig

difficulty, die Schwierigkeit; (trouble), die Mühe; (fix), die Verlegenheit

dignified, würdevoll

dilapidation, die Verstümmelung

diligence (coach), der Eilwagen

dine, speisen; essen; (at noon, *expressed or understood*, zu Mittag)

dining-room, der Speisesaal

dinner, das Mittagsmahl

direct, *vb.* (to drive, *understood*), fahren lassen; direct (a camel, &c.), lenken; to be directed (to be ordered), den Befehl erhalten

direction, die Richtung; the directions which he had directed him to give = the order (Befehl) which he had given him for delivery (zur Bestellung)

disappear, verschwinden

disaster, das Unheil

discipline, *vb.*, biscipliniren

discomfiture (of an army), die Niederlage

discontent, die Unzufriedenheit

discover, entbecken; (to invent), erfinden; is discovered (by them *understood*, they, *and not the thing discovered, being the chief subject of the narration*), sie entbeckten; is discovered (is found), man findet

discovery, die Entbeckung

discuss (to talk over), besprechen

disgrace, die Schande

disguise (to hide), verbergen; (to live) in disguise, (hidden), verborgen

dish (earthenware), die Schüssel; (food), das Gericht; die Speise

dismay, die Angst; (the pilot) in dismay, in seiner Angst

dismounted, vom Pferde abgestiegen

disordered (troops), in Unordnung gerathen

display, die Entfaltung

disputed (boundary), streitig; streitiggemacht

distance, die Ferne; die Entfernung; for the distance of 15 leagues, 15 Meilen weit

distant, fern; entfernt; very distant, sehr weit entfernt; distant only 20 miles = which lies only 20 miles distant (weit)

distinct, verschieden

distinctly, beutlich

distinguish: to be distinguished (from), sich unterscheiden; easily distinguished, leicht zu erkennen

distress, die Noth

distressed, bebrängt

district, der Landstrich; der District

disturb, stören

divide (to separate from), trennen; still hold divided sway, noch immer gemeinschaftlich beherrschen

divisible, theilbar

division (*mil.*), die Division

do, *trans. vb.*, thun; to do (work), verrichten; to do (a service), leisten; (to accomplish anything), (etwas) vollbringen; to do (anything to a person), anthun; (nothing was) done = undertaken, unternommen

     do, *intrans. vb.*, (to succeed), gelingen

docile (in temper), sanft

docility (of temper), die Sanftheit

doctrine, die Lehre

dog, der Hund

dome, die Kuppel; gigantic dome, der Riesendom

Don John of Austria, Don Juan b'Austria

dose, die Dosis

doubt: no doubt, ohne Zweifel

doubtful, zweifelhaft

doubtless, ohne Zweifel

dough, der Teig

doughty, tapfer

down (the way down), hinunter;
to go down, hinunter gehen; to
bear down to the ground, zu
Boden werfen; to lay down (anything), niederlegen; cut down,
umhauen; to push down (from),
herabbrängen; looking down over
the multitude, hinweg die Menge
übersehend; took us down with
him = went with us

downright (decided), entschieden

downs, das Hügelland

downy, flockicht

drag, ziehen

draw (into a fine thread), ausbehnen

draw back, zurückziehen

dream: he will never dream (of),
es fällt ihm nicht im Traume ein

dreamlike, traumhaft

dress, vb., sich kleiden

dress (clothing), die Kleidung. (See
also p. 78, n. 18)

dried, adj., getrocknet

drink, das Getränk

drive: to drive from (displace),
verdrängen aus; to drive (anyone) from, austreiben; to drive
along, dahin fahren; driven (by
fears), getrieben

drizzling rain, der Nebelregen

drop (a theory), aufgeben; to drop
(on one's knees), fallen

drove, der Trieb; not a drove of
sheep, kein Trieb Schafe

drown, ertrinken

Dub: hill of Dub, der Dubhügel;
Dub ridge, der Rücken des Dubhügels

dubious, zweifelhaft

duchess, die Herzogin

dues, die Abgaben (plur.)

duke, der Herzog

dull (stupid), dumm

dun-coloured, dunkelfarbig

Durham militia, die Durhamer Miliz

during, während

dusk, die Dämmerung; die Dämmerstunde; at dusk, in der Dämmerung; about dusk, ungefähr in der
Dämmerstunde

dust, der Staub

Dutch, adj., holländisch

dwelling, eine Wohnung

Dyak, der Diak

each, jeder, jede, jedes; the skeleton of each (of the two), die
beiden Skelette; as each has her
own individuality = as the individuality of each (einer Jeden);
each other, einander; to each
other (mutually), sich gegenseitig;
each other's, gegenseitig

eager, begierig

ear, das Ohr

early, früh; early (poet), alt; early
(philosophers), ältest

earth, die Erde; (ground), der
Boden

earth-bank, der Damm

earthen, irden

earthquake, das Erdbeben

ease of manner, die Leichtigkeit im
Vortrag (masc.)

easily, leicht

east (towards the east), nach Osten

Eastern Arabia, Ostarabien (neut.);
Eastern Court (Roman), ost-
römischer Hof

easy, leicht; nothing so easy, nichts
leichter

eat, essen

eating-room, das Eßzimmer

eccentrically-minded, excentrisch

echo: shout echoed by the Franks
without = shout in which the
Franks joined from without;
to join in (a shout), einstimmen

economy, die Sparsamkeit

edge (brink), der Rand; water's
edge, der Rand des Wassers; edge
(of a ravine), der Abhang

Edinburgh, Edinburg (neut.)

education, die Erziehung

Edward, Eduard

effect, sb., die Wirkung; (result),
die Folge

effect, vb., bewerkstelligen

effort, die Anstrengung

egg, das Ei; hard-boiled (eggs),
hartgekocht; not hard-boiled, weich-
gekocht; hard eggs and boiled
eggs, hart- und weichgekochte Eier;
scrambled eggs, Rühreier

Egyptian, *sb.*, der Ägypter

eight, acht; eight thousand; achttausend

eighteen, achtzehn

either . . . or, entweder . . . oder; on either side, zu beiden Seiten

elastic, *adj.*, elastisch

Elbe, die Elbe

elder (of a church, of a sect), der Älteste; Elder Frederick, Ältester Friedrich

elderess, die Älteste

Elector of Saxony, der Churfürst von Sachsen

electrical, elektrisch

elegance, die Anmuth

element, das Element; (essential condition), der Umstand; das Moment

elephant, der Elephant

eligible (situation), passend

elongate, verlängern

eloquent, beredt

embarrassment, die Verlegenheit

emigrant's team, das Auswanderergespann

eminence (height), die Anhöhe

eminently, außerordentlich

emit (light), ausstrahlen

emperor, der Kaiser

Emphasis, of Verbs, how expressed in German, 34, *n.* 13

empire, das Reich

empirical, empirisch

employing: by employing, durch die Anwendung

emprise, die Aufgabe

empty, leer; (clear), frei

enable, in den Stand setzen; möglich machen

encamp, campiren

enclosed (ground), umzäunt

encompass, einschließen

encounter (fight), der Kampf; das Gefecht

encourage, ermuthigen; ermuntern; (to promote), befördern

end, *trans. vb.*, ein Ende machen; *intrans. vb.*, enden; as the reading of the Gospel ended, so wie das Evangelium verlesen war

end (of a table), das untere Ende

endeavour, *vb.*, sich bestreben

endeavour, *sb.*, das Bestreben

endurance (of ill), das Ertragen

endure, ertragen

enemy, der Feind (*see p.* 14, *n.* 5); enemy's fire, das feindliche Feuer

energetic, energisch; kraftvoll

energy, die Energie

engage (*mil.*), angreifen; auf einen Kampf einlassen; to be engaged (in battle), kämpfen; closely engaged (in business), sehr stark in Anspruch genommen; to keep actively engaged, beschäftigen; to engage one's self (to), sich binden

engine (of war), die Maschine

England, England (*neut.*)

English, *adj.*, englisch

English, *sb.*: the English, die Engländer. (*See p.* 73, *n.* 17)

enjoy genießen

ennui, die Langeweile

enormous, ungeheuer

enough, genug

enrol one's self, sich aufnehmen lassen

ensign, der Fähnrich; to make him an ensign, ihn zum Fähnrich ernennen

enter (a room), eintreten; (through the gates), durchkommen; never, perhaps, entered (the gates), kam wohl nie durch; enter (after a struggle), gelangen (in)

enterprise, das Unternehmen

entertain him with a solo, ihm ein Solo vorspielen

entertainer (the host), der Wirth

entertainment (banquet), das Gastmahl

enthusiasm, der Enthusiasmus; die Begeisterung

entirely (new), ganz; entirely (concealed), gänzlich

entitle (help to), verhelfen

entrance, der Eingang; (entry), der Einzug

entrust, anvertrauen

epithet (expression), der Ausdruck

equal (in appearance), ähnlich

equally, gleich

erect, *vb.*, errichten

eruption, der Ausbruch

es, (1) *supplies the place of the Object, Gr. Int. xx. V., and* 17, *n.* 7 ; (2) *used as grammatical subject,* 81, *n.* 10

escape (by flight), *sb.*, die Flucht

especially, besonders

establish (one's self) on a platform, das Plateau besetzen

estate, das Besitzthum

esteem, die Achtung

estimate (opinion), die Meinung

Etna, der Etna

euer, *when written* Ew., 40, *n.* 10

European, *adj.*, europäisch

even, selbst ; (than), noch ; even then, schon damals ; even though, und wenn ; not even (a rumour), nicht einmal

even tenor (of their lives), der ruhige Gang

evening, der Abend ; in the evening, am Abend ; at six in the evening, um sechs Uhr des Abends evening party, die Abendgesellschaft

event : at all events, auf alle Fälle

eventually (ultimately), schließlich

ever, jemals ; than ever, als je (*see* p. 17, *n.* 5) ; for ever, auf immer

every, jeder, jede, jedes ; every consideration, alle Rücksichten (*plur.*) ; every man, ein Jeder ; every one, Jeder, Jede, Jedes ; every one of the sciences, sämmtliche Wissenschaften ; (slopes) on every side, auf jeder Seite ; (beleaguered) on every side, von allen Seiten

everybody, Jedermann

everything, Alles

everywhere, überall

evidence : to be evidence of, beweisen

evidently, augenscheinlich

exaltation (of sentiment), der Aufschwung

examine, untersuchen ; besichtigen ; (the place) when examined, bei genauer Untersuchung

example, das Beispiel

exceeding, *adj.* übermässig

exceedingly, äußerst

excel, sich auszeichnen ; excelling in = although he excelled in . . ., obgleich er sich in . . . auszeichnete

excellent, vortrefflich ; ausgezeichnet

excentricity, die Excentricität

except (to the exclusion of), ausgenommen ; (unless), außer

excessive, übermäßig

exchange one dress for another, eine Kleidung mit einer anderen vertauschen

excitement, die Aufregung

exclaim, ausrufen

exclusively, ausschließlich

excuse, *sb.*, die Entschuldigung

execute (work), ausführen ; execute (a solo), vortragen

exemplary, exemplarisch

exercise (bodily), die Leibesübung ; (riding, walking, &c.), die Bewegung ; religious exercises, die Andachtsübungen (*plur.*)

exhausted, *adj.*, erschöpft

exhibit (traces of), an sich tragen

exhibition (of prowess), die Kundgebung

existence (life), das Leben ; das Dasein ; (of a place), das Dasein

existing condition (of things), der Thatbestand

expand into, sich ausdehnen zu

expect, erwarten

experienced, erfahren

expert, *adj.*, gewandt

explain, erklären

exploring party, die Expedition

expose one's self (to criticism, &c.), sich blosstellen

express, ausdrücken ; (to denote), bezeichnen ; (to manifest), bezeigen

expressive, ausdrucksvoll

extend, sich erstrecken

extent of country, eine Landstrecke

externally : such, externally, was the youth, so war das Äußere des Jünglings

extinct : become extinct, aussterben

extirpate, vernichten

extraordinary, außerordentlich

extravagance (poetical), die Überschwänglichkeit

extremely, äußerst

extremity: reduced to extremities, aufs Äußerste getrieben

exuberance (of spirit), das Übergefühl

eye, das Auge; to the public eye, öffentlich

eye-witness, der Augenzeuge

face, das Gesicht; (mask), die Maske; (aspect), die Gestalt

fact, die Thatsache; das Factum. (See p. 48, n. 8)

faculties, die Geisteskräfte (*plur.*)

fail: if he fails, wenn es ihm nicht gelingt; he will not fail to have words at his command, so ist es gewiß, daß ihm die Worte zu Gebote stehen werden

failure (of a plan), das Mißlingen; their failure = the failure of their plan; (ill-fate), das Mißgeschick (see p. 32, n. 4); failure (of an attempt to), der vereitelte Versuch

fair (harbour), ruhig; in a fair way, auf gutem Wege

fairly (properly, perfectly), vollständig; he is fairly frightened to death, es überfällt ihn eine wahre Todesangst

fall, *sb.*, der Fall

fall, *vb.*, fallen; to make (troops) fall back, zurückdrängen; to fall (on one knee), sich niederlassen; shame fall on those, Schande treffe diejenigen; to fall off, herabfallen; to fall to (to set to), sich daran machen

fallacy, der Trugschluß

falter, stocken

familiar, vertraut

familiarly, vertraulich

family, die Familie

famous, berühmt

fancy: may fancy himself perusing, könnte glauben, daß er lese

far, weit; as far as (the gate), bis zu; far beyond (one's compre-

hension), viel zu hoch für; so far from being evidence, weit entfernt zu beweisen

farm (farm-house), das Farmhaus

farmer (tiller of the soil), der Landmann

farther on, weiterhin

fascinating, bezaubernd

fashion, die Mode; in a fashion = to a certain degree (der Grad)

fate, das Schicksal

father, der Vater

fatherland (original home of a people), das Heimathland

fatigue, *sb.*, (that which fatigues), die Anstrengung

favour, *vb.*, begünstigen

favour, *sb.*, die Gunst; in favour (of), zu Gunsten

favourable, günstig

fears: driven by their fears, von Furcht (*sing.*) getrieben

feathery, gefiedert

feature (of a face), der Zug; play of features, das Mienenspiel; (detail), der Umstand

federal, föderirt

feeble, schwach

feed (animals, insects, &c.), füttern

feel, fühlen (felt in, see n. 15, p. 3)

feeling, das Gefühl; act of generous feeling, die großmüthige Handlung

fellow-feeling, kamerabschaftliches Gefühl

fellow-student, der Mitschüler; der Kollege

female Majesty, königliche Frau

festival, das Fest

fetch, holen

feud: border feud, die Grenzfehde

feudal, feudal

few, wenig; few (days, words, &c.), einige

fibre, die Faser

field, das Feld

fierce, wild

fifteen, fünfzehn

fifteenth, fünfzehnte

fifty, fünfzig

fight, *sb.*, der Kampf; fight of infantry, das Infanteriegefecht

fight, *vb.*, fechten
figure (of a man), die Gestalt
file (into a room), sich begeben
final, endlich
find, finden; find again, wieder=
finden; find out, entdecken; find
outside (in front of), vorfinden;
find the way back, den Weg wie=
derfinden
fine (hair), fein; dünn
finish (one's prayers), verrichten
fire, das Feuer
fireside: by the fireside, am Herde
firm, fest
first, *adj.*, erst; *adv.* erst; zuerst; at
first, zuerst; in the first place,
vor allem; from first to last
(throughout), durchaus
first-comer, der Erste Beste
fir-wood (forest), der Tannenwald
fissure, der Spalt
five, fünf; five (o'clock), fünf Uhr;
five hundred pounds, fünfhundert
Pfund
fix: (celebrity had) fixed all eyes
upon him = drawn the eyes of
all upon him, die Augen Aller auf
ihn gezogen
flame, die Flamme
flank attack, der Flankenangriff
flat (the plain), die Ebene; (insipid),
schal
flax plant, der Flachs
flee back, zurückfliehen
flesh: rosy flesh, rosiger Teint
flexible, biegsam
flicker about, hin und her flackern
flight, die Flucht; (of arrows), der
Schauer; (of steps), die Flucht
float in the air, in der Luft schweben
flock, die Herde; flocks and herds,
die Herden
flood (of melted butter), der
Strom
flour, das Mehl
flower, die Blume
flowery, blumreich
fly: (the news) had flown, hatte
sich verbreitet
fodder, das Futter
follow, folgen; to follow one to
church, einem in die Kirche folgen

follower, der Begleiter
following (next), nächst
fondly: the memory of Joseph
II. was long and fondly cherished, Joseph II. stand lange in theur=
em Andenken
food, die Nahrung; die Speise; (the
various dishes), die Speisen
(*plur.*). (See p. 65, *n.* 6)
foot, der Fuß; at the foot, am Fuß;
on foot, zu Fuß; underneath the
foot, unter den Füßen
for, *conj.*, denn. (See p. 89, *n.* 8)
for, *prep.*, für; (in order to), um
(zu); (for use as), als; for (an
hour), während; (on account of),
wegen; (exchange one dress) for
(another), mit; for (twenty
miles on either side), auf; for
any long period, auf längere Zeit;
for (ever), auf; for delivery,
zur Bestellung; for instance, zum
Beispiel; (order) for a movement, zu einer Bewegung; (drop
on their knees) for a prayer, zu
einem Gebet; required for rest,
zum Ausruhen nötig; for some
foray, zu einem Raubzug; for (*expressing duration of time*), see
p. 59, *n.* 2; continued for thirty
days, dauerte dreißig Tage; for
many hours, viele Stunden lang;
for months together, Monate
lang; to live for some months,
einige Monate verleben; remained
for some weeks, blieb einige
Wochen; for a time, einige Zeit;
without waiting for the time,
ohne die Zeit abzuwarten; for the
distance of 15 leagues, 15 Meilen
weit; to stretch for miles, sich
meilenweit erstrecken; forgive me
for what I have done, vergebt
(*in addressing a king*) mir, was
ich gethan habe; for my own part,
was mich betrifft; we hope for
health, wir hoffen Gesundheit
foray, der Raubzug
forbid, verbieten
force, die Kraft
force (troops), die Truppen (*plur.*);
(so great) a force, eine Truppen=

maſſe; whole of his forces, ſeine Geſammtmacht

force (compel), zwingen; force (their way), erzwingen

forced march, der Eilmarſch

ford, die Furt

foreboding, die Ahnung

forefather, der Vorvater

foreign, fremd; foreign countries (abroad), das Ausland

foremost (of them), der Vorderſte

forest, der Wald; depths of forest, das Waldesdickicht

forget, vergeſſen

forgive, vergeben; forgive me (in addressing a king), vergebt mir

fork, die Gabel

form, sb., die Form; forms of vegetation, Pflanzenformen

form, vb., bilden; (mil.), ſich anſtellen

formally, förmlich; to call formally upon, einen förmlichen Beſuch machen

former, früher; ehemalig

formerly, früher

Formica fusca, die ſchwarzgraue Ameiſe; Formica rubescens, die röthliche Ameiſe

forth: to come forth (to creep out), herauskriechen; to stand forth (forming) an oasis, eine Oaſe bilden

fortified, feſt; befeſtigt

fortress, die Feſtung

fortunately, zum Glück

fortune, das Glück; (wealth), das Vermögen; checkered fortune, abwechſelnder Erfolg

forty, vierzig

forward: to be forward (in pursuing) = to venture forward, ſich vorwagen

found, vb. in fin., gründen

foundation-stone, der Grundſtein

founder, der Begründer

four, vier

fourteenth, vierzehnte

frame (bodily), der Körperbau

frame (his version), vb., machen

France, Frankreich (neut.)

Frankish, fränkiſch

frankly, freimüthig

fraternal, brüderlich

Frederick, Friedrich

free, frei; to set free, loslaſſen

freezing, das Gefrieren

French (man), der Franzoſe; (language), das Franzöſiſch or das Franzöſiſche

French, adj., franzöſiſch

frequent, häufig

frequently, oft

fresh, friſch; (new), neu

friend, der Freund

friendless, freundlos

frighten: he is fairly frightened to death, es überfällt ihn eine wahre Todesangſt; to frighten away, verſcheuchen

frightful, ſchrecklich

from, von; aus; from (that moment), von ... an; (two miles) from the Alma, weit von der Alma entfernt; (out), aus; (Schiller's flight) from (Stuttgart), aus; (in conjunction with verbs), aus—; (owing to), aus; (obeys) from a sort of, aus einer Art von; from first to last = throughout, durchaus; from month to month, monatlich; judging from, zu urtheilen nach; (shone) from beneath it (fem.), unter derſelben hervor

from (omitted): from fifty to sixty, fünfzig bis ſechzig

front, die Fronte; in front of, vor; in front of (a river), diesſeits

frontier, die Grenze

fruit, die Frucht

fruit-tree, der Obſtbaum

fulfil: (all that remained) to be fulfilled = to be done, zu thun

full, voll

fully: more fully, beſſer

functionary, der Beamte

für, when used with adjectives, 92, n. 14

furiously, heftig

furnish (with), verſehen; (a house), einrichten

further, weiter; entfernt; (the side) furthest from Horitz, die von

Horitz am weitesten entfernt liegt;
(longer time), länger; (more),
mehr; still further (still more),
noch mehr
further (our aims), *vb.*, fördern
fury, bie Wuth
future, bie Zukunft
Future Tense, English emphatic,
how rendered in German, 38,
n. 22
Gaelic, bas Gälisch; old Gaelic, bas
Altgälisch
gaily, fröhlich
gain (a victory), winnen
gait, ber Gang
gallant (brave), tapfer
galling, lästig
Galloway men, Männer von Galloway
gallows, ber Galgen
game, bas Spiel
gamekeeper, ber Förster; ber Jäger.
(*See p.* 26, *n.* 13)
gape open, aufklaffen
garden, ber Garten
garlic, ber Knoblauch
gate, bie Thür; (of a fortress or
town), bas Thor
gathering, bas Sammeln
gaudy, bunt
Gaul (a native of), ber Gallier
gay, heiter
gaze (vulgar), *sb.*, bie Angafferei
gaze at, besehen
gegenüber, place of the prep., *see
p.* 61, *n.* 14
general, *sb.*, ber General
general (universal), allgemein;
in general, im Allgemeinen; (for
the public), öffentlich; general
appearance = appearance in
general (im Allgemeinen); general staff, ber Generalstab
generally, gewöhnlich; (for the
most part), meistens
generation, bie Generation
generous: act of generous feeling,
bie großmüthige Handlung
Genitive, (1) place of, in common
prose, 14, *n.* 4; (2) with proper
nouns, 3, *n.* 11 (*a*); *n.* 15; (3)
used to express time, 78, *n.* 5

Genitive, rendering of objective,
62, *n.* 12
Genitive, partitive, generally rendered by von, 6, *n.* 26 (*b*); 87,
n. 8
genius, bas Genie
gentian, ber Enzian
Gentile, ber Heibe
gentle, milb
gentleman, ber Herr; (husband),
ber Ehemann
geometry, bie Geometrie
German (language), bas Deutsch *or*
bas Deutsche
German, *adj.*, beutsch
Germanic, germanisch
get, bekommen; get beyond the
reach, aus bem Bereich kommen;
get off (away from a place),
bavon kommen; get over (to over-
come), überwinden; to get possession (*mil.*), sich bemächtigen; get
through, burchgehen; burchkom-
men; get to, erreichen; get under
arms, ins Gewehr treten
gigantic dome, ber Riesendom
give, geben; (to offer), anbieten;
give (hints), machen; (to cause),
machen; gives him no regret,
macht ihm keinen Kummer; give
(attention), schenken; give (into
one's hands as a prisoner), überliefern; give the alarm (*military*),
zu ben Waffen rufen; give thanks
again, von Neuem banken; give
up, aufgeben; give up (a prisoner), ausliefern; give assurance
of, versichern baß
gladly, mit Freuben
glancing, *adj.*, glänzenb
glass, bas Glas; (the various articles made of glass), bas Glasgeschirr
glittering, glänzenb
gloomy, büster
glorious, glorreich
glory, ber Ruhm
go, gehen; wollen (*see p.* 70, *n.* 16);
while (he) goes, im Gehen; (to
travel), reisen; go back, zurückgehen; go forth (from home),
fortwandern; go forward (to ad-

vance), vorrücken; go from home,
verreisen; go in secret, sich heim=
lich aufmachen; go on (to proceed), fortfahren; to go ou picking up, immer auflesen; go out,
ausgehen; go out (to come out
from a house), heraustreten; go
to (the battle-field), sich begeben
auf; to set a-going, in Bewegung
bringen; to be going on, statt=
finden

God, der Gott

gold: land of gold, das Gold=
land

gold, *adj.* golden

golden, golden

good, *sb.*, das Gute
good, *adj.*, gut; wohl (*see p.
75, n.* 4); good deal of, viel;
good supply, genug; tender,
good (offices), freundschaftlich;
well and good, so mag es hin=
gehen

good-humoured, gutgelaunt

good-will, das Wohlwollen

goose, die Gans

Gospel, das Evangelium

gossip, *vb.*, schwatzen

Goth, der Gothe

govern (to influence), beeinflussen

government, die Regierung

governor, der Gouverneur

gory, blutig

grace, die Gnade; (of movement),
die Grazie; (of manner), die Lie=
benswürdigkeit

graceful, zierlich

graciously, gnädig

gradually, allmählich

grain of musk, das Gran Moschus

grammar, die Grammatik

Grammar School, die Gelehrten=
schule

grand, großartig; grand (tussle),
tüchtig; groß

grand-duke, der Großherzog

grandson, der Enkel

grange, das Gehöft

granite hill, der Granithügel

grape, die Weintraube

grass: tops of the grass, di Gras=
spitzen

grassy, rasenbewachsen

grateful, dankbar

gratifications, der Genuß (*sing.*)

gratify (the public interest), Ge=
nüge thun

grave, ernst

gravity, die Gravität

gravy, die Sauce

graze, weiden

grease, das Fett

great, groß; great (ability), bedeu=
tend; great (lord), vornehm;
great distance, weite Entfernung;
great deer (*plur.*), das Hochwild
(*sing.*)

greatly, bedeutend

Greek (*adj.*), griechisch

green, *adj.*, grün

green, *sb.*, das Grün

groan, das Gestöhne

ground, der Boden; (*mil.*) der Ter=
rain; open ground (*mil.*), freies
Feld; on the ground (for the
reason), auf Grund; stand its
ground, sich behaupten; to bear
down to the ground, zu Boden
werfen; groundless (claim), un=
begründet

group, die Gruppe

grow, wachsen; erwachsen; grow up,
erwachsen; grown (fully grown),
ausgewachsen

growth (mode of growth), das
Wachsthum; (thriving), das Ge=
deihen

guard (the men on guard), die
Wache; guard (escort), die Wache;
guards, die Garden; (the king's),
die Leibwache; brigade of guards,
die Garden=Brigade
guard (a ford), bewachen

guest, der Gast

guidance, die Leitung

guide, *sb.*, der Führer

guide, *vb.*, führen

guild, die Gilde

gum resin, das Harz

gun (cannon), die Kanone

gust, der Windstoß

Gustavus, Gustav

haben, aux v. when omitted, *p.* 12,
n. 47 (*e*)

habit, die Gewohnheit; (custom),
der Gebrauch; die Sitte; (knack),
die Fertigkeit
hair, das Haar
half, halb; half a mile, eine halbe
Meile; one half (or part of the
men), die Einen
half-grown, halb ausgewachsen
half-savage, halbwild
hallow, heiligen
hand, die Hand; hand of man, die
Menschenhand; (wrote) with her
own hand, eigenhändig; night is
at hand, die Nacht rückt heran;
(cross-bow) in hand, in der Hand;
(omitted), on the right hand, zur
Rechten; hand (of a watch, meta-
phorically), der Weiser
handle (a subject), behandeln
handsome, schön
hang back (to tarry), zögern
happen (in a certain connection),
sich fügen; (at a place), sich zutragen
happy, glücklich
harass, belästigen
harbour, sb., der Hafen
harbour (one's self), Zuflucht suchen;
(to give shelter to), Zuflucht gewähren
hard (blow), stark
hardly, kaum
harmless harmlos
harmony, die Harmonie
harnessed, geharnischt
haste, die Eile
hasten, sich beeilen
hat, der Hut
hatch, ausheden
hate, vb., hassen
hautboy-player, der Hoboist
have, aux. vb., haben; sein; it
might have cost him his life,
es hätte ihm das Leben kosten können; had or could have run before him, war ihm vorangegangen,
oder hätte ihm vorangehen können;
he having (done so and so), nachdem er; as if it had (been made),
als wäre es; has been taken,
wurde genommen; you had better
(let it alone), du thätest besser;
to have to, müssen

have, tr. vb., haben; (at command),
stehen; have the best of the
struggle, die Oberhand bekommen; have mercy, sich erbarmen; (such questionings) had
they concerning it, stellten sich
darüber auf; have recourse, Zuflucht nehmen
he, er
head, der Kopf; (of a table), das
obere Ende; at the head (of an
army, &c.), an der Spitze; to take
it into one's head, sich vornehmen
headstrong, eigenwillig
health, die Gesundheit
hear, hören; I have never heard of
(such and such a thing being
done), ich habe nie davon gehört,
daß —
hearer, der Zuhörer
hearing (the), das Gehör
heart, das Herz
heat (of an argument), der Eifer
heath, die Heide
heather, die Heide
heaven, der Himmel; (glittering
guides) of heaven, am Himmelszelt
heavenly harmonies (the harmony
of the spheres), die Harmonie der
Sphären; heavenlier glow (of
blue), tiefere Himmelsbläue
heavy, schwer
Hebrew (language), das Hebräisch
heed: to take heed of (to trouble
about), sich kümmern um
height (of a man), die Größe;
heights (hills), die Hügel (plur.);
cluster of heights, die Berggruppe
heir, der Erbe
help (each other to the food),
reichen (see p. 27, n. 12); (need)
some help (to food) = something handed, etwas gereicht
helpless, hülflos
Henry, Heinrich
her, poss. adj., ihr, ihre, ihr
herb, das Kraut
herd, die Herde
hereditary, erblich

hero: naval hero, der Seeheld
hero-lay, das Heldenlied
herself, selbst; sich
hesitation (in speech), das Stocken
hide, verbergen
high, hoch; high (voice), laut; high above, hoch über; überragend; high altar, der Hochaltar
highlander, der Hochländer
Highness, Hoheit (*fem.*)
hilarity (of the crowd), der Jubel
hill, der Hügel
hill of Dub, der Dubhügel
hill-fort, die Bergfeste
hill-side, der Hügelabhang
himself, sich; selbst; he himself, er selbst; than himself, als er
hind leg, das Hinterbein
hint, die Andeutung; (warning), die Warnung
hippopotamus, der Hippopotamus; das Nilpferd
his, sein, seine; (*part of a title*), Se. = Seine (see p. 39, *n.* 17); (*when the context clearly shows whose*), der, die, das; slipped over his head, ihm über den Kopf gezogen; at his side, zur Seite; a friend of his, einer seiner Freunde
historical, historisch
history, die Geschichte
hither, hierher
hold, halten; (an army), festhalten; (a festival), begehen; hold lands (by feudal tenure), Güter tragen zu Lehen; hold sway, beherrschen
holder (householder) der Bewohner; all the holders, alle Bewohner
hollow, der Hohlweg
holy, heilig
home, die Heimath; (stopping place), der Aufenthaltsort
homely (simple), einfach
home-made wine, der Obstwein
homestead, die Heimstätte
hominy, Hominy
honour, *sb.*, die Ehre
honour (with one's presence), beehren. (*See p. 35, n.* 3)
hope, *sb.*, die Hoffnung

hope, *vb.*, hoffen
hopeless, hoffnungslos
hospital, das Hospital
hospitality, die Gastfreundschaft
Horace, Horaz
horn, das Horn
hornblower, der Hornbläser
horrible, schrecklich
horse, das Pferd; troop of horse, der Trupp Reiter
horseman, der Reiter
host = army, das Heer
hostile, feindlich
hostility, die Feindschaft
hot (dispute), heftig
hotel, das Hotel
hound, der Hund
hour, die Stunde; for many hours, viele Stunden lang; within an hour, binnen einer Stunde
house, das Haus
how, wie
however, *conj.*, jedoch; (still), indessen; considering, however, to ich in Erwägung zog however, *adv.*, wenn auch; however grand (their titles), wie großartig auch; however humiliating it (may sound), so demüthigend es auch
huge, riesig
human, menschlich
humble (lowly), niedrig; humble (forms of vegetation), unter
humiliating, demüthigend
hundred, hundert; hundred thousand, hunderttausend
hunger, der Hunger; (to die) of hunger, vor Hunger
hunt, *sb.*, der Jagd
hunting, das Jagen
husband: the King her husband, ihr königlicher Gemahl
hussar, der Husar
hyacinth, die Hyacinthe
I, ich
idea, die Idee
ideal, *sb.*, das Ideal
ideal, *adj.*, ideal
idiom, das Idiom
if, wenn; (*omitted*), see p. 48, *n.* 9; (though), ob; as if to = al

though it would, als ob es wollte; (in case), falls; as if (from), gleichsam; as if it had, als wäre es ill (qualified), schlecht; to bear ill will, übel wollen

imagine, sich denken

immediate (close), unmittelbar

immediately, sofort; sogleich; (so soon as), so wie

imminent, nahe bevorstehen

impatient, ungeduldig

impel, anspornen

imperfect, unvollkommen

imperial, kaiserlich

implicit, unbedingt

implore, anflehen

importance, die Wichtigkeit; of importance, wichtig; of such importance, so bedeutend

important, wichtig

impose (an obligation), auferlegen; imposing (in appearance), imponirend

impossible, unmöglich

impression, der Eindruck

imprisonment, die Gefangenschaft

improve, verbessern; bereichern; assiduously improve (one's abilities), durch Fleiß pflegen

improvement, die Ausbildung

in, in; an; auf; aus; bei, &c.; in 1624, im Jahre 1624; (to observe) in them, an ihnen; in the afternoon, am Nachmittag; in such a place, an einem solchen Ort; to take an interest in, Antheil nehmen an; in our island, auf unsrer Insel; (produced its effect) in (minds), auf; in a manner, auf eine Weise; one (m.) in a troop, einer aus einem Trupp; (instinct discovered) in (the ants), bei; in (the present state), bei; in (a word), mit; (end) in (a fight), mit; in a few days, nach einigen Tagen; in fifty minutes more, nach fünfzig Minuten; in the days of Charles, unter Karl; in the reign, unter der Regierung; in the meanwhile, unterdessen; in stature, von Gestalt; in memory of, zur Erinnerung an; in part, zum Theil; in the time, zur Zeit; in alarm, voll Bestürzung; in front of, vor; (this side of a river), diesseits; in public, öffentlich; in question, betreffend; in search of, um . . . aufzusuchen; in short, kurz; in sight, sichtbar; in silence, schweigend; in some way (understands), gewissermaßen; in the first place, vor allem; in the midst, inmitten; in which = where, wo; to ride in, hineinreiten

incapable, unfähig

incognito, das Inkognito

inconvenient, unbequem

increase, vb., zunehmen; (to extend), erweitern; the storm increases (in violence), der Sturm nimmt überhand

indescribable, unbeschreiblich

indeed, in der That; wirklich; (to be sure), freilich

indefatigable, unermüdlich

independence, die Unabhängigkeit

independent, unabhängig

Indian (American), der Indianer. (See p. 44, n. 6)

Indian, adj. indisch

India-rubber, das Gummi Elasticum

indicate (mark), bezeichnen

indication (idea), der Begriff

indifferent, gleichgültig

individuality, die Individualität

inductive, induktiv

indulgent to, nachsichtig gegen

infamy, die Schande

infancy, die Kindheit

infantry, die Infanterie; infantry reserves, die Infanteriereserve; fight of infantry, das Infanteriegefecht

inferior (not so good), schlechter

infidel, der Ungläubige

Infinitive, accusative with, (1) how construed in German, (2) used with sehen, hören, &c., Gr. Int. xvii., III., &c.

Infinitive, preceded by as, and referring to the demonstr. so, 4, n. 18.

Infinitive, preceded by *as if*, 89, *n.* 5

Infinitive, without zu after auxil. verbs of mood, 11, *n.* 45 (*b*)

inflict upon, zufügen (*dat.*)

influence, der Einfluß; die Einwirkung; (where reason) was admitted to influence, Eingang fand

inform, mittheilen

information, die Kunde; (news), die Nachricht

ingenious (clever), genial

ingenuity, der Geist

inhabitant, der Einwohner; der Bewohner; (aborigines), die Ureinwohner

inherit, erben

injure, beschädigen

injury, die Kränkung

injustice, die Ungerechtigkeit

inquire respecting, forschen nach

inspire with, einflößen (*dat.*)

instance (example), das Beispiel; for instance, zum Beispiel; (case), der Fall

instant, der Augenblick; in an instant, im Augenblick

instantly, sofort; sogleich

instead, anstatt

instinct, der Instinkt

instructive, lehrreich

intend, beabsichtigen; intended to have given, hätte geben wollen; but if the expression is intended (to), soll aber der Ausdruck

intention, die Absicht; das Vorhaben

intercept, auffangen

interest (in knowing), das Interesse; (in a person's affairs), die Theilnahme; to take an interest in, Antheil nehmen an

interesting, interessant

interlace: their shields interlaced, die Schilde zusammengehalten

into, in; to expand into, sich ausdehnen zu; to introduce into (a country), bringen nach; to sink into, sich senken; sink into (graduate into), sich entfalten zu; to make (rice) into pilaws, Pilaws daraus bereiten; to turn (one thing) into (another), vertauschen mit

introduce (as a companion), gesellen; introduce into (a country), bringen nach

invent, erfinden

Inversions, not admissible in *dependent sentences*, 3, *n.* 15 (*b*)

inveterate(ly), eingewurzelt

invisible, unsichtbar

invitation, die Einladung

invite, einladen

involve (in an affair), verwickeln; involve (a battalion in a retreat), mitziehen (hinein)

Ireland, Irland (*neut.*)

Irish, *adj.* irisch

Irish Sea, die Irische See

iron, *adj.* eisern

irritate, aufregen

island, die Insel

Isle of Man, die Insel Man

issue (from), hervorbrechen (aus)

it, es; er; sie; der—, die—, dasselbe; (anything done, said, &c.), dies; it is true, das ist wahr; of it (masc.) = of the same, desselben; jealous of it, eifersüchtig darauf; it was their pride, sie waren stolz darauf; it puzzled me (*in consequence*), so zerbrach ich mir den Kopf darüber; it is, it was, &c. (*omitted*), *see p.* 34, *n* 13; it is the slaves which determine, bestimmen die Sklaven, but it was to the sailor alone aber erst für den Seemann; it was about dusk when he arrived = he arrived there about dusk; it is (*followed by the past part.*) man (*followed by 3rd pers. pres indic.*); it may be, man kann; it may be (*followed by past part.*) man könnte

its, sein, seine; ihr, ihre; its velocity, dessen Schnelligkeit; (*omitted*): (running) between its low banks, zwischen niedrigen Ufern

itself: the throne, itself the chair = the throne, formerly the chair; formerly, ehemalig

Jack, Hans

jaw, der Kinnbacken; jaws, der Rachen (*sing.*); (carry) in their jaws, im Munde

jealous, eifersüchtig

jeopardy, die Gefahr

jerks: angry jerks of the head, heftige Kopfbewegungen

John, Johann

join (to border), grenzen

journal, das Journal

journey, die Reise; a day's journey, eine Tagereise

jousts, das Turnier

joy, die Freude

joyful (growth), fröhlich

joyous, freudig

judgment, das Urtheil

judicial system, die Gerichtsbarkeit

jump, springen

just, *adv.* gerade; (had) just (been elected), soeben; just the same (undisturbed), ruhig

just, *adj.*: it was the just boast of Schiller, Schiller war mit Recht stolz darauf

keenly (debated), lebhaft

keenness, die Schärfe

keen-sighted, scharfsichtig

keep, halten; keep (a garden trim), erhalten; keep actively engaged, beschäftigen; to keep from it, abhalten davon; keep order, Ordnung halten; keep sacredly, heiligen; keep silence, stillschweigen

kidnapper, der Menschenräuber

kill, töten; the bodies of the killed, die Getödteten

killing, *sb.*, die Tödtung

kind (of food, &c.), die Art; all kinds, jede Art

kindle, anfachen; anzünden

kindly (quickly taken root), schnell

kindness, die Freundlichkeit; die Güte; to show (*understood*) kindness to the poor, den Armen Gutes thun

king, der König; the King her husband, ihr königlicher Gemahl; proclaimed king, zum König ausgerufen; the Books of Kings, die Bücher der Könige

kingdom, das Königreich; das Reich; das Land; (animal and vegetable), das Naturreich

knead, kneten

knee, das Knie; drop on their knees, auf die Kniee fallen

knee-deep, knietief

kneel, knieen; kneel in prayer, betend knieen

knife, das Messer

knight, der Ritter

knock up (to build a hut), zusammenzimmern

knoll, der Hügel

knot of trees, die Baumgruppe

know, wissen; (to be acquainted with), kennen; who (*plur.*) knew the English = to whom the English were known, denen die Engländer bekannt waren; nothing is known, nichts ist bekannt; it is well known, es ist bekannt; (to have experienced), erleben

knowledge, das Wissen; (science), die Wissenschaft; knowledge (of), die Erkenntniß

Kowrgané, Kowrgané

labour, die Arbeit

lack: there is no lack (of), es fehlt nicht (an)

lady, die Dame; (*omitted*), my lady Queen, meine Königin

lance, die Lanze

land, *sb.*, das Land; (native land), das Vaterland; land of gold, das Goldland; Land of Promise, das gelobte Land; lands (landed property), Ländereien; to hold lands (by feudal tenure), Güter tragen zu Lehen; rise of land, die Erhöhung

land, *vb.*, landen; ans Land steigen

language, die Sprache; (*omitted*), (translated) into the German language, ins Deutsche

large, groß; large (features), kühn

largely: very largely, in großer Menge

larva, die Larve

last, letzt; from first to last (throughout), durchaus

last (to last), anhalten
lastly, schließlich
late, spät; late (years), letzter
Latin, *sb.*, das Lateinisch *or* das Lateinische
Latin, *adj.* lateinisch
Latinise, latinisiren
latter, der Letztere
laugh at, sich lustig machen über
law, das Gesetz
lawless, zügellos
lawyer, der Abvokat
lay, legen; lay down (anything), niederlegen; lay open (the road), frei machen
lay (song), das Lied
lazy, faul
lead, führen; lead up, upwards, hinaufführen; lead behind them, mit sich führen; lead the way, vorangehen; lead (the way, as guide), zeigen
leaf, das Blatt
league (3 English miles), say die Meile (4·63 English miles) *or* die französische Meile
learn (to come to know), erfahren
leave, lassen; leave behind, zurücklassen; leave (a place), verlassen; to be left (to spare), übrig bleiben
    leave (permission), die Erlaubniß
leben (life), when not used in the plural, 5, *n.* 25 (*c*)
lecture, die Vorlesung
loe, die Leeseite
left, link; left (hand, *expressed or understood*), die Linke; on the left, zur Linken; links
leg: hind leg, das Hinterbein
Legaspi: of Legaspi, des Legaspi
legitimate (official), officiell
length: at length, endlich
Lepanto, Lepanto
less, weniger; minder
let (land), vermiethen; (land) which would let well, das sich gut vermiethen ließe
    let it alone, es bleiben lassen
letter (of the alphabet), der Buchstabe

liberally cut (features), edel gebildet
liberty, die Freiheit; to set at liberty, in Freiheit setzen
library, die Bibliothek
licensed, autorisirt
lie (to rest), liegen; lie at the mercy (of), sich in der Gewalt befinden; lie down, sich niederlegen
lie, *sb.*, eine Lüge
life, das Leben; (way of living), die Lebensweise; (biography), die Biographie; sign of life, das Lebenszeichen; (became) a question of life and death, zur Lebensfrage
light, *sb.*, das Licht
light (a fire), *vb.*, anzünden
Ligurian, *sb.*, der Ligurier
like, *adj. and adv.*, ähnlich; gleich; (as), wie; and the like, und dergleichen; to look like, aussehen wie; plant-like, pflanzenartig. (*See* p. 83, *n.* 8)
like, *vb.*, mögen; to like the best, am liebsten mögen
likely: any person likely = any person who is likely (die allenfalls möchte)
liken, vergleichen
limb, das Glied
limited, *adj.*, beschränkt
line, die Linie; (a row), eine Reihe; (the enemy's line or position), die Stellung
lion, der Löwe
lip, die Lippe; upper lip, die Oberlippe
liquor (drink), das Getränk
listen, horchen
literature, die Literatur; of literature, literarisch
little (small), klein; (in value), gering; a little after (midnight), bald nach
live, leben; (to dwell), wohnen; (to spend one's time), verleben; (to enjoy), sich erfreuen (*gen.*)
Livonia, Liefland (*neut.*)
loaf, das Brod
lodge (of a forester), das Försterhaus

lofty, hoch

log, das Klotz

lone, einsam

lonely, einsam

long, *adj.*, lang

long (*adv. of time*), lange; long before, lange ehe; long ago, längst; no longer a position, keine Position mehr

look (upon, at), *vb.*, ansehen; (to view, to examine), besehen; look (towards), hinblicken; look after (to take charge of), Acht geben auf; look like, aussehen wie; looking down over the multitude, hinweg die Menge übersehend

   look, *sb.*: to wear a look, aussehen

lord: his lord, King Edward, sein Herr und König Eduard; (master, ruler), der Beherrscher; a great lord, ein vornehmer Herr

lose, verlieren

loss, der Verlust

loud, laut

Louvain, Löwen

love, *sb.*, die Liebe; love of music, die Liebe zur Musik

   love, *vb.*, lieben; he would have best loved to make his appeal, er hätte am liebsten appelliren mögen

low, niedrig

loyal, loyal

luck, das Glück

lucky, glücklich

lump, das Stück

Lusiads, die Lusiaden

lustrous, glänzend

luxury (in the way of food), der Leckerbisse

maddening, *adj.*, bis zur Raserei treibend

magician's spell, das Zauberwort

magistrate, der Magistrat; (Roman dignitary), der Staatsbeamte

Magna Charta, die Magna Charta

magnificent, herrlich

magnitude (importance), die Bedeutung

maiden speech, eine Erstlingsrede

main road, die Hauptstraße

maintain, nähren; (an opinion), behaupten

majesty, die Majestät; his Majesty, Se. Majestät; your Majesty, Ew. Majestät; female Majesty, königliche Frau

make, machen; make (nests, cells, &c.), bauen; make (savoury dishes), bereiten; make (rice) into pilaws, Pilaws daraus bereiten; make (a request to), anstellen; make (a resistance), leisten; make a choice, wählen: make appeal, appelliren; (in order) to make defence, zur Vertheidigung; make one's way (to a place), kommen; make one's way up, hinaufgehen; make prisoner, zum Gefangenen machen; make no answer, nichts antworten; make towards, eilen nach; make (troops) fall back, zurückdrängen; make use of, benutzen; first voyage *that was made* round the world (*omit in translating* "that was made")

man, der Mann (*see p. 65, n. 16*); der Mensch (*see p. 3, n. 14*); (anyone), Jemand; every man, ein Jeder; old man, der Greis; two men, zwei Männer; sixty men, sechzig Mann; two hundred men, zweihundert Männer; armed men (soldiers), gewaffnete Mannschaft; his men (military), seine Leute; the men (some of them), die Einen; sufficient men (sufficiently manned), hinlängliche Mannschaft; man's estate, das Mannesalter; the hand of man, die Menschenhand

mankind, die Menschheit

manner, die Weise; (presence), das Wesen; ease of manner, die Leichtigkeit im Vortrag; in a manner, auf eine Weise; to answer in a manner most contumacious, äußerst trotzig antworten

many, viele; many things (various subjects), vielerlei

marauding, die Plünderung

K

march, *sb.*, ber Marſch; forced march, ber Eilmarſch

march, *vb.*, marſchiren

Marianne Islands, bie Marianen

mark (a trace), bie Spur; mark (of animality), baß Merkmal
　　mark (to denote), bezeichnen; (to characterise), characteriſiren; (to distinguish), kennzeichnen

marked (distinct), beſtimmt

market, ber Markt, ber Jahr= markt

married couple, baß Ehepaar

marry, heirathen

marsh, ber Moraſt, ber Sumpf; marsh of Curragh, Curragh= marſch

martial, kriegeriſch

martyrdom, baß Märthrerthum

marvellous, wunderbar

mass (church service), bie Meſſe

masses (of troops), Truppen

massive (brow), gewölbt

mast, ber Maſt

master, ber Herr

mastery, bie Herrſchaft; to obtain mastery of, in Gewalt zu be= kommen

materials (for baking, &c.), bie Sachen (*plur.*)

matter: a group, no matter of what cattle, eine Gruppe von welcher Art ſie auch ſei

mauvaise honte, bie Befangenheit; bie falſche Scham

may (to be able), können; (express- ing a supposition), bürfen; it may be (suspected), man kann; may be said, man kann ſagen; may be reached (by them, *ex- pressed or understood*, they *being the chief subject of the narra- tion*), ſie könnten erreichen; might (*expressing a supposed possi- bility*), *see p.* 71, *n.* 10; we might (possibly), wir würden; whatever it might be, waß immer eß auch ſei; it might have cost him his life, eß hätte ihm baß Leben koſten können

Mayflower (the ship), bie Mahflower

mazy, verſchlungen

meal: during meals, während beß Eſſens

mean, *vb.*, meinen; (to signify), bebeuten

means, baß Mittel (*sing.*), or bie Mittel (*plur.*); by no means, burchauß nicht

meantime, unterbeſſen

meanwhile, unterbeſſen; in the meanwhile, unterbeſſen

measure, baß Maß; measures (means), bie Maßregeln (*plur.*)

measurer, ber Meſſer

measuring, baß Außmeſſen

meat, baß Fleiſch

mechanically, mechaniſch

medicine, bie Arznei

meet (together), ſich verſammeln; (one another), zuſammentref= fen

melt, ſchmelzen

member, baß Glied

memory, baß Gebächtniß; (remem- brance of a person), baß Anben= ken; in memory of, zur Erinner= ung an; memories = past his- tory, hiſtoriſche Vergangenheit

mention, erwähnen

merchant, ber Kaufmann

mercy: to lie at the mercy (of), ſich in ber Gewalt befinden

mere, bloß

merely, bloß

merit, *sb.*, baß Verbienſt

merit, *vb.*, verbienen

Mesopotamia, Southern, Süb=Me= ſopotamien

Mesopotamian, meſopotamiſch

mess (a prepared dish), baß Gericht

messenger, ber Bote

metamorphosed (to be), ſich ver= wanbeln

meteor, baß Meteor

microscope, baß Microſkop

Middle Ages, baß Mittelalter; middle height, bie Mittelgröße

midnight, *sb.*, bie Mitternacht

midnight, *adj.*, mitternächtlich

midst: in the midst, inmitten; in ber Mitte; from the midst (rise), auß ber Mitte

might, *see* may

mighty in its consequences, folgen=
reich

migrate, fortziehen

migration, die Wanderung

Milan, *adj.*, Mailänder

mile, die Meile; to stretch for
miles, sich meilenweit erstrecken

military, militärisch; kriegerisch; military guild, die Schützengilde

militia, die Miliz

milk, die Milch

mind, der Geist; (disposition), das
Gemüth; to be the mind of most
people = most people like
(mögen)

mind (to trouble about), sich küm=
mern um

mine, mein, meine, mein

miner (gold - digger), der Gold=
gräber

mineral kingdom, das Mineralreich

mingle with (persons), sich an=
schließen; (to unite with), sich
vereinigen mit

minister, der Minister; minister of
peace, der Friedensbote; Minister
of State, der Staatsminister

minstrel, der Minnesänger

minute, die Minute; in a few
minutes, in wenigen Minuten;
in fifty minutes more, nach fünf=
zig Minuten

mirage, die Luftspiegelung

misled (to be), sich irre leiten
lassen

missile, das Wurfgeschoß

mistake, der Fehler

mistress (lady), die Dame

misuse, mißhandeln

mix, mischen; vermischen

mode of growth, das Wachsthum

model, das Muster

modern, modern; modern (history),
neu; modern painters, die Maler
der Neuzeit; in modern times,
in neuerer Zeit

modesty, die Bescheidenheit

modulate (to refine), verfeinern

Moesian, mösisch

molest, belästigen

moment, der Augenblick; der Mo=
ment; without a moment's pre-

paration, ohne irgend welche Vor=
bereitung

monarch, der Monarch; (to be)
crowned the monarch, zum König
gekrönt

Monday, der Montag; on Monday
(*omit* on *at the beginning of a
sentence when translating*)

money (treasure), der Schatz

monk, der Mönch

monotony, die Einförmigkeit

month, der Monat; month of October, der Monat Oktober; for
months together, Monate lang;
from mouth to month, monatlich

moon, der Mond

moored (in harbour), vor Anker
liegen

morass, der Morast

morbidly, auf krankhafte Weise

more, mehr; one minute more,
nach einer Minute; the more . . .
the more, je mehr . . . desto mehr

morning, der Morgen; (dawn), der
Tagesanbruch; this morning, heute
Morgen; in the morning, des
Morgens; morning, as it dawned,
showed the place to be = as the
morning dawned it was discovered that the place was

morning prayers, die Morgenan=
dacht (*sing.*)

Moses, Moses

Mosstrooper, der Grenzräuber

most, meist (*see p.* 91, *n.* 6); (extremely), äußerst; most striking,
am auffallendsten; for the most
part, größtentheils

mother, die Mutter

motion, die Bewegung

mount *or* mount on (a horse), be=
steigen. (*See p.* 39, *n.* 1)

mountain, der Berg; mountains
(range, group of), das Gebirge
(*sing.*)

mountain air, die Bergluft

mouth, der Mund; (of a river), die
Mündung

move (to retreat rapidly), fliehen

movement, die Bewegung

mow (to pass over), überfahren

much, viel; to leave much, viel

K 2

übrig laſſen; (we do not love them) much, ſehr; (quite), gänzlich; very much the contrary, ganz im Gegentheil

muffled, gehüllt

Mulacha, bie Mulacha

mutilation, bie Berſtümmelung

multiply (themselves), ſich vermehren

multitude, bie Menge; (of the people), baß Bolf

murky, trüb

muscular, mußfulöß

music, bie Muſif

musician, ber Muſifer

musk, ber Moſchuß

mutual sufferings inflicted = the sufferings which were inflicted upon both parties (beiben Parteien zugefügt wurden)

my, mein, meine, mein

myself: to myself, mir ſelbſt

mysteriously, geheimnißvoll

Names of Materials, not used in the plural, 8, *n.* 36 (*c*)

Names, common, when used without an article, 28, *n.* 6

Names, proper, see *Proper Names*

name, *sb.*, ber Name; village of that name, baß genannte Dorf

name, *vb.*: (a squire) named —, Namenß; to name after, benennen nach

namely, nämlich

napkin (table), bie Serviette

narrate, erzählen

narrative, bie Erzählung

narrow, eng; ſchmal

nation, bie Nation

national, national

native, *sb.*, ber Eingeborne

native (hills), heimatlich; native tongue, bie Mutterſprache

natural, natürlich

naturally, von Natur

nature, bie Natur

Nausites, bie Nauſiten

naval hero, ber Seeheld

near, nah; unweit; (situated near), bei; near him (self), bei ſich; near (the village), in ber Nähe (beß Dorfeß); near (your house),

nahe bei; near (the road), nahe an; nearest (tho wall), zunächſt

nearly, beinahe; (almost), faſt

neat (maid-servant), ſauber; neat (dwelling), hübſch

necessary, nöthig

necessity, bie Nothwendigfeit; there was a necessity, bie Nothwendigfeit war vorhanden

neck, ber Halß

need, *vb.*, brauchen; need I say, brauche ich zu ſagen; need (some help to food), etwaß gereicht haben wollen; must needs, müſſen

neigh, *sb.*, baß Wiehern

neighbour, Nachbar, ——in

neighbourhood, bie Gegend

neighbouring, benachbart

nerve, ber Nerv or bie Nerve

nervous, nervöß

nervousness, bie Ängſtlichfeit

nest, baß Neſt

Netherlands, bie Niederlanbe

Neustria, Neuſtrien

never, nie; he will never dream (of), eß fällt ihm nicht im Traume ein

new, neu

new (the), baß Neue

new-fashioned, neumobiſch

New America, Neu-Amerifa

New England colony, bie Kolonie in Neu-England

news, bie Nachricht

next (*when rendered by* folgenb *and when by* nächſt, *see p.* 68, *n.* 12); next day, ben folgenben Tag

night, bie Nacht; by night, zur Nachtzeit, in ber Nacht; (nightfall), ber Abenb
night (foray), nächtlich

nine, neun

Nineveh, Nineveh

no, *adj.*, fein; to make no answer, nichtß antworten; no doubt, ohne Zweifel; a group, no matter of what cattle, eine Gruppe von welcher Art ſie auch ſei; by no means, burchauß nicht; no one, Keiner, Keine, Kein; Niemanb; no self-esteem could disguise

= the best opinion of ourselves could not disguise

no, *adv.*, nein; no longer, nicht länger; no longer a position, keine Position mehr

noble: Court noble, ber Höfling

nobody, Niemand

noise, ber Lärm

nominal, nominell

nook, ber Winkel

noon, ber Mittag; at noon, um bie Mittagsstunde

noose, bie Schlinge

nor (*preceded by* neither), noch; (*when not preceded by* neither), auch nicht. (*See p.* 42, *n.* 7)

North, ber Norben; (towards the north), nach Norben

Northumberland, Northumberlanb

north-west, norbwestlich; 15 miles to the north-west (of it), 15 Meilen norbwestlich (babon) entfernt

nose, bie Nase

not, nicht; not any, kein; not a tree, kein Baum; not a word (is spoken), kein Wort; (it) could not but, mußte natürlich; that he was not dealing with a messenger, baß er mit keinem Boten unterhanble; not far (from the shrine), unweit (bes Schreines); not to woman or child, weber einer Frau noch einem Kinb

notable, notorisch

nothing, nichts; nothing equal to it, nie was Ähnliches

Nouns, plural of, ending in ium, 91, *n.* 14

Nouns, Abstract, (1) used with def. article, 1, *n.* 1; 8, *n.* 35 (*a*); (2) used in the singular only, 12, *n.* 47 (*c*)

Nouns, used in the singular only, (1) when denoting unlimited plurality, 6, *n.* 28; (2) when used as terms of weight, measure, or number, 7, *n.* 32 (*d*)

Nouns, collective, generally require the verb and pronoun in the singular only, 72, *n.* 3

Nouns, compound, see *Substantives*

novice, ber Neuling

now, jetzt; nun; (then), bann

number (of troops), eine Masse; a great number of, eine große Menge

Numidian, *sb.*, ber Numibier

o'clock: four o'clock, bier Uhr

oar, bas Ruber

oath: my oath is to you (the king), Euch habe ich meinen Eib geleistet

obeisance: to bend in obeisance, sich tief verneigen

obey, gehorchen; obey (as guide), (als ihrem Führer) folgen

object (purpose), bie Absicht; ber Zweck; the object was, bies hatte zum Zweck

Object (place of the), supplied by es, Gr. Int. xx. V.

obligation, bie Verpflichtung

oblige (compel), zwingen; (to make necessary), nöthigen; to be obliged, müssen

obliterate, vertilgen

obscure (unobserved), unbeachtet

observe (to perceive), wahrnehmen; (to make a remark), bemerken; (notice), bemerken; sich merken

observer, ber Beobachter

obtain, bekommen; erlangen; obtain (the name), erhalten; cannot be obtained, ist nicht zu haben; that obtained for him, burch welchen (Umstanb) er erhielt

occasion (opportunity), bie Gelegenheit; (cause for), bie Veranlassung

occasion (to cause), verursachen; veranlassen

occasional: an occasional quarrel = occasionally (gelegentlich) a quarrel

occasionally, gelegentlich; bann unb wann

occupation, bie Beschäftigung

occupy (*mil.*), besetzen; occupied (in thought), bebacht

occur, vorkommen; (to happen), geschehen

of, von; aus; an; auf, &c.; allure it out of the path, es vom Wege abloďen; food consists of (aus); points of steel, Spißen aus Stahl: (what has become) of his rider, aus seinem Reiter; (remind me) of those, an die; want of practice, der Mangel an Übung; there is no lack of, es fehlt nicht an; (glittering guides) of heaven, am Himmelszelt; in memory of, zur Erinnerung an; (battle) of (*followed by the name of a place*), bei; (*followed by the name of a river, mountain, &c.*), an; e.g. die Schlacht bei Leipzig, die Schlacht an der Alma; an anecdote of, eine Anekdote in Bezug auf; jealous of it, eifersüchtig darauf; out of his grace, in seiner Gnade; (the greatest) of (the Greeks), unter; of style, über den Stil (Styl); to take heed of (to trouble about), sich kümmern um; of hunger, vor Hunger; (love) of music, zur Musik; (union) of (the Roman and the Teuton), zwischen; of it (*masc.*) = of the same, desselben; by way of, als; to rid (one's self) of (anything), abschütteln; (at the moment) of reaching, wo er erreichte; I have never heard of (such and such a thing being done), ich habe nie davon gehört, daß ——

of (*omitted*): the town of Drumble, die Stadt Drumble; bit of land, das Stück Land; name of Moses, der Name Moses; (the more) it feels of pleasure, fühlt es Freude; a flight of steps, eine Flucht Stufen; troop of lions, Trupp Löwen; regiment of volunteers, Regiment Freiwilliger

of, *not transl.* (1) *after the common names*, Insel, Land, Stadt, Königreich, &c., 5, *n.* 24 (*a*); (2) *after names of number, weight, or measure*, 4, *n.* 20, *and n.* 21 (*a*)

of, (1) before names of materials of which a thing is made, 1, *n.* 3; (2) before names of places and countries, 9, *n.* 40

(*c*); (3) after the word 'battle,' 49, *n.* 1; (4) as partitive genitive, 87, *n.* 8

off: to fall off, herabfallen; to throw off (a rider), abwerfen

offence (fault), das Vergehen

offer, *sb.*, das Anerbieten

offer (to do anything), sich erbieten

office (official position), das Amt; offices (kind help), die Dienste (*plur.*)

officer, der Offizier (*see p.* 74, *n.* 14); commanding officer, der Commandant

often, oft

oil, das Öl

old, alt; old man, der Greis; old (the, and the new), das Alte

olfactory nerve, der Geruchsnerv or die Geruchsnerve

on, an; auf; bei; zu, &c.; on the railroad, an der Eisenbahn; (hand) on the (dial of a watch, &c.), am; on (the way), auf; on paper, auf dem Papier; an enemy on the watch, ein Feind, der auf die Gelegenheit lauerte; straight on, gerade aus; on the side of (a river), bei; on (his return), bei; on (this occasion), bei; (taken root) on, in; on their roots (stand), mit den Wurzeln; reflecting on, nachdenken über; to be in close attendance on him, sich stets um ihn befinden; on every side, von allen Seiten; dependent on, abhängig von; on either side, zu beiden Seiten; on foot, zu Fuß; on the right, zur Rechten; on account (of), wegen; on the contrary, hingegen; on the left, links; on their part, ihrerseits; farther on, weiterhin; to continue to walk on, weiter schreiten

on (*omitted*): on the 2nd April, den 2ten April; on Monday (*omit* on *at the beginning of a sentence in such cases when translating*)

once, einmal; at once, fofort; all
at once (suddenly), plötzlich
one, ein, eine, ein; a good one
(*masc.*), ein guter; no one, Nie=
mand; Keiner, Keine, Kein; every
one, Jeder, Jede, Jedes; any one,
Jemand; one of them, einer der=
felben; one by one, je einer;
with one (a person), mit Je=
mand; with one hand, mit der
einen Hand; a thousand to one,
taufend gegen eins; a rule, but
one that (is neglected), eine
Regel, die aber ——
    one, *used after an adjective,
not expressed in German, see p.
19, n.* 10
    one (*omitted*): one hundred
warriors, hundert Krieger
onion, die Zwiebel
only, nur; (merely), bloß; (had
been) only a few months, erst
einige Monate
    only, *adj.*, einzig
onwards: to pace onwards, weiter=
fchreiten
open, *adj.*, offen; (clear), frei
    open, *vb.*, öffnen; an abyss
opened, ein Abgrund fich öffnete;
a valley opening on to the sea,
ein Thal das der See gegenüber lag;
open one's lips, fprechen
operate as but a slight check upon,
nur geringen Einhalt thun
opiate, das Opiat
opinion, die Meinung
opportunity, die Gelegenheit
oppose, gegenüberstehen
opposite, jenfeitig: entgegengefetz; of
the opposite kind, des Gegen-
theils
opposition: an attitude of opposition to, eine feindliche Stellung
gegen; without opposition, un=
gehindert
oppression, die Unterdrückung
or, oder; forty or fifty, vierzig bis
fünfzig
orator, der Redner
order, *vb.*, den Befehl geben; to order
to advance, vorrücken laffen
    order, *sb.* (command), der Be=

fehl; by order, to the order (of),
auf Befehl
    order (in order), die Ordnung;
to put all in the best order,
Alles aufs befte zufammenstellen
    order (of chivalry), der Orden
orderly (soldier-servant), die Or=
donanz
ordinance, die Verordnung
organist, der Organist
organize, organifiren
origin, der Urfprung
original: an original Magna Charta,
ein Original der Magna Charta
originally, urfprünglich
other, ander; each other, einander;
to each other (mutually), fich
gegenfeitig; somewhere or other,
an dem einen oder dem anderen Ort
otherwise, fonft
ought: no one ought, Niemand
follte
our, unfer, unfere, unfer; according
to our strength, nach eigenen
Kräften
ourselves: as best pleases ourselves, wie es uns am beften ge=
fällt
out, aus; out of = from, von;
allure it out of the path, es vom
Wege abloden; to conduct out of
the town, zur Stadt hinaus führen;
out of his grace, in feiner Gnade;
come out (from under), hervor=
kommen; set out (on a journey)
fich aufmachen
outlaw, der Geächtete
outside (in front of), vor,
over, über; over (a desert), durch;
looking over, überfehend; (to
take an oath) over (a corpse),
an; to tower over, emporragen;
to watch over, bewachen
overboard, über Bord
overcast, trüb
overflowed with (crowded with),
gedrängt voll von
overhead, über dem Haupte
overpassed, zurückgelegt
overpast, vorbei; (till the fury) was
(should be) overpast, fich- gelegt
hätte

owe, verbanfen; owing (to), in Folge

own, eigen; busy with his own affairs (*i.e.* eating and drinking), mit fidj felbft befdjäftigt; with her own hand (wrote), eigenhändig; for my own part, was mich betrifft; tell their own tale, für fidj felbft fprechen; as each has her own individuality = as the individuality of each

    own (*omitted*): his own education, feine Erziehung; of my own age, von meinem Alter; in our own days, in unferer Zeit

pace onwards, weiterfchreiten

Pacific Ocean, der Stille Ocean

pain, der Schmerz

paint, malen

painting (the), das Gemälde

palace, der Palaft

palliation, die Erleichterung

paper, das Papier; on paper, auf dem Papier

paralyse, lähmen

parent plant, die Mutterpflanze

parish, das Kirchfpiel

park, der Park

parliament, das Parlament

part, der Theil; in part, zum Theil; for the most part, größtentheils; for my own part, was mich betrifft; on their part, ihrerfeits

    part (*referring to a hill-side*), die Seite

partake: (a sheep), of which they partake, an deffen Gemuß fie Theil nehmen

Participial Constructions, (1) changed into a regular clause with a conjunction indicating time; (2) changed into a relative clause; (3) changed into a regular sentence, introduced by da; (4) changed into attributive adjectives; (5) turned by finite verbs and connected by und; (6) rendered by adverbial expressions; (7) when used also in German, and how expressed in common prose, Introd. xv., &c., II. *a—g;* (8) implying concession, 48, *n.* 1; (9) introduced by ohne daß, 88, *n.* 4

Participial Constructions, English passive, expressed by the supine in the active form, 45, *n.* 20

Participle, present, implying concession, how turned, 43, *n.* 1

particular, befonder

partly, theils; theilweife

party, die Partei; evening party, die Abendgefellfchaft; exploring party, die Expedition; (of soldiers), die Truppe

pass, gehen; (to carry from one to the other), bringen; pass (the surf), durchfchiffen; and (they) passing the surf, indem fie die Brandung durchfchiffen; pass for, gelten; pass on (to drive along), dahin fahren; pass over the killed and the wounded, über die Getödteten und Verwundeten dahinfchreiten; pass through, durchgehen; paffiren; passing through (the streets) and back again, durch (die Straßen) hin und zurückgehen; (many days) passed, vergingen; words passed = words were addressed to (gerichtet an)

    pass (road), der Paß

passage (in a book), die Stelle; passage of arms (between knights), der Ritterkampf

passion, die Leidenfchaft; (propensity), der Trieb

Passive Voice, (1) use of, 1, *n.* 4 (*b*); changed into the *active voice,* 2, *n.* 8; (2) changed into Reflective form, 10, *n.* 41 (*b*); (3) used impersonally, 5, *n.* 22 (*b*); (4) rendered by man, 79, *n.* 8

past (above the altar), über

pasture, der Weideplatz *or* die Weideplätze (*plur.*); country of pastures, wiefenreiches Land

patches of wood (trees), die zerftreut liegenden Gehölze (*plur.*)

path, der Pfad; der Weg

pathway, der Pfad

patience, die Geduld

patient, geduldig

patiently, gebulbig

patriarchal, patriarchalifch

patrician, ber Patricier

patron (saint), ber Schußheilige

pay attention (to), barauf achten

peace, ber Friede; minister of peace, ber Friedensbote; time of peace, Friedenszeiten (*plur.*)

peaceful, friedlich

peace-loving, friedliebenb

peach, ber Pfirfich

peasant, ber Bauer

peasantry, bie Bauern (*plur.*)

peat digger, ber Torfgräber

peculiar, eigenthümlich; (special), befonber

pedant, ber Pebant

penalty, bie Strafe

people (persons in general), bie Leute; (the commonalty), bas Volt (*see p.* 41, *n.* 11); (men), bie Menfchen

peppery (words), fcharf

perceive (notice), bemerten

perfect, vollftänbig; (precise), genau; (to be) perfect in, vollftänbig ausgebilbet; perfect (itself *or* one's self), fich ausbilben

perfectly, vollftänbig; vollfommen

perform (a dance), auffühzren

performer on the violin, ber Violinspieler

perhaps, vielleicht; never, perhaps, entered (the gates), tam wohl nie burch

period, bie Zeit; bie Periobe; for any long period, auf längere Zeit

periodical (publication), bie Zeitschrift

perish (to die), fterben

permanent, permanently, bleibenb

permit, geftatten

persist, beftehen barauf

person, bie Perfon; (anyone), Jemanb

personage, bie Perfon

personal, perfönlich

peruse, lefen

phenomenon, bas Phänomen

Philippine Islands, bie Philippinen

philosopher, ber Philofoph

physic, bie Arznei

physiology, bie Phyfiologie

phytology, bie Phytologie

pick up, auflefen; (to find, and take possession of), aufgreifen

picture (of a person), bas Portrait

pie (fruit pie), Pie

piece, bas Stück; piece of land, bas Stück Land; flowery piece (of land), blumreicher Boben

pilaws, Pilaws

pile up, aufhäufen

pilgrim, ber Pilger

pillow, bas Kopffiffen

pilot, ber Lotfe

pitch (highest pitch of indignation), ber Grab

pity: and it would be a pity, unb bas wäre Schabe

place (locality), ber Ort; (to put a thing), ber Plaz; in the place where, an ber Stelle wo; in the first place, vor allem

place, *vb.*, fezen; to place (in prison), unterbringen; to be placed, ftehen; fich befinben; to take place, ftattfinben; place before, vorftellen; place (upon), legen; place upon (the heab), auffezen; placing themselves in procession, inbem fie eine Procefsfion bilbeten

plain, bie Ebene

plain (rule), fchlicht

plan, ber Plan; plan of attack, ber Angriffsplan

plane (*geom.*), bie Ebene

planet, ber Planet

plank, bas Brett

plant, bie Pflanze; parent plant, bie Mutterpflanze

planted (ground), bebaut

plant-like, pflanzenartig

plate, ber Teller

plateau, bas Plateau

platter, bie Schüffel

plead a cause, eine Sache führen

pleasant, angenehm

please: if he pleases, wenn es ihm fo gefällt; to be graciously pleased (to), fich gnäbig herablaffen (zu)

pleasure, die Freude
pledge (any one's health), trinken
plentiful (provinces), gesegnet
plenty (of the food), eine Menge
ploughed, gepflügten
plougher, der Pflüger
pluckily, muthig
plunder : without stopping to plunder, ohne sich mit Plündern aufzuhalten
plunge, sich stürzen; plunge through (wade through), durchwaten
poem, das Gedicht
poet, der Dichter
poetry (the art), die Poesie
point, der Punkt ; (of a weapon), die Spitze ; (subject), das Ding
policy (tactics), die Strategie
poison, das Gift
polish, vb., poliren
politeness, die Höflichkeit
politician (statesman), der Staats= mann
politics : of politics, politisch
pony, das Pony
poor (the), die Armen
poor, adj., arm
Pope, der Papst
popinjay, der Vogel
popular tradition, die Volkssage ; to hold sway in popular tradition, das Reich der Volkssage beherr= schen
population, die Bevölkerung
port (haven), der Hafen
portrait, das Porträt
possess, besitzen
possession, der Besitz ; in posses- sion, im Besitz ; to get possession (in war), sich bemächtigen
possible, möglich
post (to post a sentinel), postiren
post-horses (special), die Extrapost
postilion, der Postillon
potation (draught), der Zug
potato, die Kartoffel
pound, das Pfund ; fifty pounds, fünfzig Pfund
pour, gießen
power (force), die Kraft
practical, praktisch
practice, die Übung

practise (to carry into practice), ausüben
prairie, die Prairie
prairie breeze, der Prairiewind ; prairie chicken, amerikanisches Feldhuhn ; prairie rose, die Prairierose ; prairie sea, das Prairiemeer ; prairie soil, der Prairieboden ; prairie stream, der Prairiestrom
prayer, das Gebet ; morning pray- ers, die Morgenandacht (sing.)
preach, predigen
precede, vorangehen
precious, kostbar
precipitous, steil
prefer, vorziehen
Prefixes, inseparable, advantages of, p. 35, n. 3
premeditate : carefully premedi- tated, planmäßig vorbereitet
preparation, die Vorbereitung
prepare, bereiten
Prepositions, (1) joined to the de- monstrative da, or dar, 97, n. 2 ; (2) two —, used to express di- rection, 23, n. 12
presence, die Gegenwart ; (of mind), die Geistesgegenwart ; (personal ap- pearance), persönliche Erscheinung ; in the presence of John, in Ge= genwart Johanns
present, adj., gegenwärtig ; present (name), jetzig ; present time (at present), jetzt ; present on this occasion, bei dieser Gelegenheit zu= gegen
　　present (to show) one's self, sich zeigen ; present (a stick to, at), vorbehalten
preserve, bewahren ; aufbewahren ; preserved (well), gut erhalten ; preserved by tradition, durch Tradition auf uns gekommen
press upon (to crowd upon), ein= bringen auf
pressing, adj., bringend
pretend, sich stellen als ob ; (assert), behaupten
pretty (strongly developed), ziem= lich
prevent, verhindern

previous (occasions), früher

price, der Preis

pride: it was their pride, sie waren stolz darauf

prince, der Fürst; Prince (Napoleon), Prinz. (*See also p.* 80, *n.* 13)

princely, fürstlich

principal thoroughfare, die Hauptstraße

principally, vorzüglich

principle, der Grund

prison, das Gefängniß

prisoner, der Gefangene; to make prisoner, zum Gefangenen machen; to take prisoner, gefangennehmen

private conversation, die Privatunterhaltung

probability, die Wahrscheinlichkeit

proceed, fortfahren; proceed (towards), sich begeben (zu)

proceedings (of people), Thun und Lassen

process (proceeding), das Verfahren

procession, die Procession

proclaim king, zum König ausrufen

produce (of the earth), das Erzeugniß

produce (to show), zeigen; (bring forward), vorbringen; produce (an effect), hervorbringen

profession (of a creed), das Bekenntniß

professional or other office, irgend ein Beruf oder Amt

profile, das Profil

profound, tief

progress, der Fortschritt

promise: Land of Promise, das gelobte Land

promising, *adj.*, vielversprechend

promotion, die Beförderung

Pronoun, possessive, repetition of, 53, *n.* 5

Pronoun, relative, (1) not omitted in German, 5, *n.* 23; (2) when to use der, die, das, for welcher, &c., 68, *n.* 10

pronounce, aussprechen

pronunciation, die Aussprache

proper, eigentlich

Proper Names, declension of fo-

reign, (1) ending in a sibilant, 3, *n.* 15 (*a*); 9, *n.* 40 (*b*); 54, *n.* 7; (2) not ending in a sibilant, 9, *n.* 40 (*b*)

Proper Names, place of, used in the genitive, 3, *n.* 11 (*a*)

Proper Names of Countries, preceded by adjectives, 66, *n.* 14

proportion (number), die Anzahl

proportioned: boldly proportioned, in kühnen Proportionen

prose, die Prosa

prospect, die Aussicht

protection, der Schutz

provided (that), wenn nur

province (country), das Land

provisions (*plur.*), die Vorräthe (*plur.*)

prudently, vorsichtiger Weise

Prussian, *adj.*, preußisch

public, öffentlich; in public, öffentlich; public gaze (vulgar), die allgemeine Angafferei

publicly, öffentlich

pump-room, die Trinkhalle

punishment, die Strafe

pupa, die Puppe

pupil (of the eye), die Pupille. (*See p.* 42, *n.* 6)

purchase, *vb.*, kaufen

purely (ideal), rein

purse, die Börse

pursuit, die Verfolgung

push down (from), herabdrängen

put a ball (from a gun) through his head, ihm eine Kugel durch den Kopf jagen; put all in the best order, Alles aufs beste zusammenstellen; put all to rights, Alles in Ordnung bringen; put in action, thatsächlich ausführen; he was put under a week's arrest, ihm wurde eine Woche Arrest auferlegt

puzzle (one's self), den Kopf darüber zerbrechen

quadrillion, die Quadrillon

quadruped, der Vierfüßler

qualify: to be qualified (suited to), sich eignen (dazu)

quality, die Eigenschaft; rice of an inferior quality, eine schlechtere Art Reis quantity of light, bie Lichtmaſſe

quarrel, *sb.*, ber Zank

quarter (of a town), ber Stabttheil
    quarter (troops in a town),
    einquartieren; (in a position),
    ſtationiren

queen, bie Königin

question, bie Frage; debated question, bie Streitfrage; (became) a
question of life and death, zur
Lebensfrage; (subject) in question, betreffenb

questioning, *sb.*, Fragen (*plur.*)

quickly, raſch

quiet, ruhig; quiet (means), frieb-
lich

quietly, ruhig

quite, ganz; to be quite sufficient,
vollſtänbig ausreichen; quite as
(promising), ebenſo

race (of man), bie Raſſe

rage, *vb.*, wüthen

railings, bie Gitter

railroad, bie Eiſenbahn

rain, ber Regen

raising: by raising (earth-banks,
&c.), burch bie Errichtung

rally, ſich verſammeln

ranged in a line, in einer Reihe auf-
geſtellt

rank, ber Rang; ranks (of the
troops), bie Reihen

rapidly, raſch

rare, ſelten

rarely, ſelten

rather, lieber; rather above, etwas
über

ravine, ber Hohlweg

reach (a place), erreichen; the road
by which the place was reached,
ber Weg, welcher nach bem Orte
führte
    reach (out of any one's), ber
    Bereich

read, leſen

reader, ber Leſer

reading: as the reading of the
Gospel ended, ſo wie bas Evangelium verleſen war

ready, bereit; (prompt), raſch; ready
to, im Begriff zu; (to be) the
more ready (to), um ſo mehr

real (genuine), wahrhaft

really, wirklich; really affords, in
Wirklichkeit barthut

realm, bas Reich

reason, bie Vernunft; (cause), bie
Urſache; reason (for), ber Grunb

reasonably, mit Grunb

reasoning (sequence of thought),
ber Gebankengang

receipt (of dues), bie Einnahme

receive, erhalten; (a person), emp-
fangen; (doctrines), annehmen;
(hospitality), genießen

recite, herſagen

reckon, *intrans.*, rechnen; *trans.*,
berechnen

recollection, bie Erinnerung; (of
the points in an argument),
bie Faſſung

recommence, von Neuem anfangen

recommend: his character recommended him to the esteem =
he won, through his character,
the esteem (to win, ſich erwerben)

record, *sb.*, (portrayal), bie Schilberung

record (as a trait), *vb.*, anführen

recourse: to have recourse, Zuflucht nehmen

recover one's self, ſich ſammeln

recreation, bie Zerſtreuung

red-cabbage, ber rothe Kohl

redoubt, bie Reboute

red-shirted miners, bie Golbgräber
mit ihren rothen Hemben

reduced to extremities, aufs Äuſ-
erſte getrieben

reeds (*plur.*), bas Schilf (*sing.*)

refer to (a person for an opinion),
befragen

referee, ber Schlebsrichter

reflect, zurückwerfen; (think), ſich
überlegen; nachbenken; reflect on
(to blame), tabeln; some passages reflecting on, einige Stellen
gegen

Reformation (the), bie Reformation

refuge, bie Zuflucht

refuse, ſich weigern

regard, *vb.*, anſehen

regiment, das Regiment; regiment of volunteers, Regiment Freiwilliger

region, die Gegend

regret, der Kummer

regulate, reguliren

reign, die Regierung; in the reign, unter der Regierung
    reign, vb., regieren; herrschen

relate, erzählen; is related by Voltaire, Voltaire erzählt; (to report), mittheilen

relations (between nations), die Verhältnisse (plur.)

relative (relation), der Verwandte

release, befreien

relief: (lances) stood in relief, stark abstachen

religious, religiös; religious exercise, die Andachtsübung

remain, bleiben; all that remained, Alles was übrig blieb

remarkable, merkwürdig

remember, sich erinnern

remind (one of), erinnern (an)

remote, entfernt

removed (distant from), entfernt

remuneration, die Belohnung

renowned, berühmt

rent, die Miethe; der Miethzins

reoccupy, Besitz wiedernehmen

repast (the time for), die Mahlzeit

repeat, wiederholen

reply (to a person), antworten; erwidern

report, sb., der Bericht
    report (to anyone), mittheilen

represent (to show), bezeichnen; the advance, represented by = the advance as it was represented by

representation (performance), die Aufführung; (on paper), die Figur

republic, die Republik

reputation, der Ruf

require (to need), bedürfen (governs gen.); to be required, nöthig sein; required for, nöthig zu; (materials) as required, wie sie gebraucht werden

research, die Forschung

resembling, adj., ähnlich

reserve: infantry reserves, die Infanteriereserve

residence (of a private individual), die Wohnung. (See p. 95, n. 5)

resin, das Harz

resistance, der Widerstand

resolve, beschließen

respect, die Achtung; in this respect, in dieser Hinsicht

responsibility, die Verantwortlichkeit

rest, vb., ruhen
    rest, sb., das Ausruhen
    rest (of them), die Übrigen; (everything else), alles Andere

restore, wiederherstellen

result, die Folge

resume (their rounds), wiedermachen

retain, beibehalten

retake (by conquest), zurückerobern

retaliation (reprisals), die Repressalien (plur.)

retire (from danger), flüchten

retreat, sb., der Rückzug; movement of retreat, die rückgängige Bewegung
    retreat, vb., sich zurückziehen

retreating, adj., (flying), fliehend

return, sb., die Rückkehr
    return, vb., zurückkehren; (swing back), zurückschnellen; return home, heimkehren, nach Hause zurückkehren; every article is returned to its place, jedes Stück befindet sich wieder in seinem Platz; to be returned to Parliament, ins Parlament gewählt werden

reveal, entdecken

revelation, die Enthüllung

revenge: vow of revenge, das Rachgelübde

reverence, die Verehrung

reverential tradition = traditional reverence, traditionelle Ehrfurcht

Rhine, der Rhein

rice, der Reis

rich, reich; (soil), üppig

riches (treasures), Schätze (masc. plur.)

rid (one's self) of (anything) abschütteln

ride, *vb.*, reiten; as he rode along (he), als beim Dahinreiten; ride away, fortreiten; to ride in, hineinreiten; ride off, davonreiten; ride out (to ride forth), fortreiten

rider, der Reiter

ridge, der Rücken

right, *adj.*, recht; right (hand, *expressed or understood*), die Rechte; on the right, zur Rechten; rechts; to be right, Recht haben; put all to rights, Alles in Ordnung bringen

rigorous, streng

ring (resound), erschallen

ringing (the), das Geklirr

ripe, *adj.*, reif; *vb.*, reifen

rise of land, die Erhöhung; (of a Republic), die Entstehung

rise, *vb.*, aufstehen; (from a seat), sich erheben; (from the midst), emporragen; (a sound) rose, herausscholl; rise into (bold hills), übergehen in; rising tier above tier, in aufsteigenden Reihen; rising and falling (waves), auf= und niederwogend

rising (of sun, stars, &c.), der Aufgang

risk (danger), die Gefahr

river, der Fluß; river side, das Ufer

   Rivers, names of, gender of, p. 82, *n.* 1

road, der Weg; road, die Straße; main road, die Hauptstraße; ten mile of road, die zehn Meilen Weges

roar out (a groan), ausstoßen

roast (roasted), *adj.*, gebraten

rock, der Fels; = rocks, Felsen

rocky, felsig; Rocky Mountains, das Felsengebirge

roll out (dough), ausrollen

Roman, *sb.*, der Römer; *adj.*, römisch

   Roman Catholic, *adj.*, katholisch

romantic, romantisch

Rome, Rom; at Rome, in Rom

room, das Zimmer; (space), der Raum; der Platz

root, die Wurzel

rope (tow-rope), das Tau

rose, die Rose; prairie rose, die Prairierose; Roses (Lancaster and York), die Rosen

rosy, rosig

rough, roh

roughly (built), roh

rough-woolled, hartwollig

round, *prep.*, um; the country round, die Umgegend

   round (of a policeman, &c.), die Runde; round (of visits to patients) of 30 miles. eine Praxis, die sich auf dreißig Meilen in die Runde erstreckt

rouse (to startle), aufschrecken; rouse to indignation, entrüsten

routed (to be), zersprengt werden

Roxburgh, Roxburgh

royal, königlich; (princely), fürstlich

rude (idiom), roh

rugged, rauh

ruins, Ruinen (die Ruine, *sing.*)

rule, die Regel; (custom), der Gebrauch

rumour, das Gerücht

run before (precede), vorangehen; the argument ran high, der Streit wurde laut; run (a boat) on shore, stranden lassen; (stream) running (between), dahinfließend; swift running (river), reißend

rush in (following a leader), nachstürzen; rush out at, losstürzen auf

Russian, *adj.*, russisch

Sabbath, der Sabbath

sacredly: to keep sacredly, heiligen

saddle, der Sattel; saddled (in their stables), gesattelt stehen

safely, glücklich; to be safely moored (in a harbour), sicher vor Anker liegen

said (aforesaid), besagt

sail, *sb.*, das Segel

   sail, *vb.*, segeln; after some hours' sailing = after they had sailed some hours; sail (from), absegeln sailor, der Matrose; (mariner), der Seemann; (navigator), der Seefahrer

saint, der Heilige; Saint Lazarus, der heilige Lazarus

  St. Paul's Cathedral, die Paulskirche

  St. Peter, basilica of, die Peterskirche

saintly, fromm

sally forth, forteilen

saltness (salt taste), der Salzgeschmack

same: at the same time, zu gleicher Zeit; it is all the same to him, es gilt ihm gleich; just the same (undisturbed), ruhig

  same (omitted): to that same castle, zu jenem Schloß

sand, der Sand

sandal, die Sandale

sanguinary (warlike), kriegerisch

satisfaction, die Befriedigung

satisfied, zufrieden

satisfy = to be able to satisfy (hunger), stillen können

savage, sb., der Wilde

save (rescue), retten; save (the country), retten

savoury, schmackhaft

Saxon, adj., sächsisch

Saxony, Sachsen

say, sagen; (remark), bemerken; it is said, they say, rendered by sollen. (See p. 11, n. 45 (a))

saying (the), der Ausspruch

scanty (families), wenig

scarce short of = almost border upon, fast angrenzen

scarcely, kaum

scentless, geruchlos

scholar (learned man), der Gelehrte

school, die Schule

schoolboy, der Schulknabe

schoolfellow, der Schulkamerad

science, die Wissenschaft

scorch up, ausdörren

score (to cut notches or furrows in), kerben

Scot, der Schotte; King of Scots, der König der Schotten; der König von Schottland

Scotland, Schottland

Scottish, schottisch

scrambled eggs, Rührei

Scriptures, die heilige Schrift

sea, die See; das Meer; prairie sea, das Prairiemeer .

  sea-green, seegrün; sea-mew, die Möwe; sea-shore, die Küste; sea-side, die Meeresküste

seal, das Siegel

search: in search of it, um es zu suchen or aufzusuchen

season, die Jahreszeit; (parliamentary), die Session

second (num.), zweite; on the 2nd April, den 2ten April; John the Second, Johann der Zweite

secluded, abgelegen

secret, das Geheimniß; in secret, heimlich

secure, vb., (to gain), erwerben

sedgy, schilfig

see, sehen; see (a spectacle), ansehen; (witness), zusehen; (to notice), bemerken; who, seeing a change as he rode along, der, als er beim Dahinreiten eine Veränderung bemerkte; (to catch sight of), erblicken; to be seen (in hospitals), finden; (not a tree) to be seen, zu sehen; seeing the danger, da (er) die Gefahr sah

seed, der Same

seek (a fortune), versuchen; seek out, aufsuchen

seem, scheinen

sein, aux. v., when omitted, p. 12, n. 47 (e)

seize, ergreifen; (an opportunity), ergreifen; (a place, a position, mil.), sich bemächtigen

select, wählen

self-dubbed, selbsternannt

self-esteem, eine gute Meinung von sich selbst

semi-barbarous, halbbarbarisch

semi-circular, halbkreisförmig

send, senden; schicken; send (grace), angedeihen lassen

sensation (feeling), das Gefühl

sense (feeling), das Gefühl; (consciousness), das Bewußtsein sensibility, bie Reizbarkeit; (timid-ity), bie Schüchternheit

sensitive, senfitiv

sensitiveness, bie Empfinblichkeit

sensuous, sinnlich

Sentences, dependent (1) express-ing a *condition*, and preceding a *principal* clause, 2, *n.* 7; (2) require the inflected verb to be placed at the end, 3, *n.* 12 (*b*); (3) do not admit of inversions, 3, *n.* 15 (*b*)

sentiment, bas Gefühl

sentry, sentries, bie Schilbwache

servant-maid, bas Dienstmädchen

serve, bienen; (at table), aufwarten; (to be sufficient for the pur-pose), genügen

service, ber Dienst

set (him to watch), lassen; set ago-ing, in Bewegung bringen; set at advantage, Vortheile gewähren; set free, loslassen; set at liberty, in Freiheit setzen; (the point from which it) set out, ausging; set out (on a journey), sich aufmachen; set to work, sich an bie Arbeit machen; set up a claim to, einen Anspruch auf (etwas) machen

setting (of sun, stars, &c.), ber Untergang

settle, sich niederlassen; settle (the habit), verleihen

settlement (on land), bie Nieber= lassung; acquiesced in their set-tlement = settled peacefully (to settle, sich niederlassen)

settler, ber Ansiebler

Seven Weeks' War (Austro-Prus-sian), *known as* 'the Seven Days' War,' ber siebentägige Krieg

seventeenth, siebzehnte

several, mehrere

severe: to be severe upon, streng bestrafen

severed (isolated), *adj.*, isolirt

severity, bie Strenge

sex (fair sex), bas schöne Geschlecht

shade, ber Schatten

shadow, ber Schatten

Shakers (religious sect), bie Shaker (*plur.*)

shall: should (supposing, assum-ing that), sollte; sollten

shame, bie Schanbe

shanty (log-hut), bas Blockhaus

share, *sb.*, ber Antheil

share, *vb.*, theilen; (one's inten-tions), eingehen

sheep, bas Schaf

sheer (nothing else than), bloß

Sheikh, ber Scheik, ber Scheich

shelter one's self, Schutz finden

shepherd, ber Hirt

shepherd's dog, ber Schäferhunb

shield, ber Schilb

shine, scheinen; (the eyes), leuchten

ship, bas Schiff

shipwrecked, *adj.*, schiffbrüchig

shoot down (rays from the sun), herabsenden

shop, ber Laben

shore, bas Ufer; to run (a boat) on shore, stranden lassen

short, kurz; in short, kurz; short of = border upon, angrenzen; to be short of both sleep and food, weber Schlaf noch Nahrung genug haben

shoulder, bie Schulter

shout, ber Ruf

show, zeigen; showed (the place to be) = it was discovered (that the place was), es zeigte sich (baß, u.s.w.); (to produce), vorzeigen; to be shown (to be evident), sich kundgeben

shrewdness, ber Scharfsinn

shrine, ber Schrein

shut up (to confine), einsperren

shyness, bie Scheu

Sicani, bie Sicanier

sick (the), bie Kranken

side, bie Seite; (of a hill, of a volcano), ber Abhang; to set at the king's side, sich neben ben König setzen; on the side of (a river), bei
side (*omitted*): to his master's side, zu seinem Herrn

sight: in sight, sichtbar; in the sight of all, Angesichts Aller; to spring into sight = to appear suddenly, plötzlich erscheinen

sign, das Zeichen; sign of life, das
Lebenszeichen; (sign-board), das
Schild

signature, die Unterschrift

signify: what does it signify, was
liegt daran

silence: in silence, schweigend; still=
schweigend

silent, still

silver fir, die Silbertanne

similarly (headstrong), ebenso

simple, einfach

simples (medicinal herbs), Heil=
kräuter (das Heilkraut)

simplify, vereinfachen

simply (merely), bloß

since, seit (*gov. dat.*); (as), da

single (the one, the only), einzig;
(not double), einfach; single man
(bachelor), der Junggesell; I am
a single man, ich bin Junggesell

singular, eigenthümlich

sink into, sich senken; (graduate
into), sich entfalten zu

sinner, der Sünder

Sire, Sire

sister, die Schwester

sit, sitzen; sit down, sich setzen; sit
at the king's side, sich neben den
König setzen; sit (at the receipt
of dues), beaufsichtigen

situated, to be, sich befinden

situation (employment), die Stelle;
(state of affairs), die Lage

six, sechs; six hundred, sechshundert;
six (o'clock), sechs Uhr

sixty, sechzig

size, die Größe

skeleton, das Skelett; the skeleton
of each (of the two), die beiden
Skelette

sketch, die Skizze

skill: trial of skill, die Kunstprobe

skull, der Schädel

sky, der Himmel

slaughter (in battle), das Ge=
metzel

slave, der Sklave; to make them
slaves, sie zu Sklaven machen
slave-making, *adj.*, knechtend;
slave-making instinct, der In=
stinkt Sklaven zu machen

slay, töten; (with a blow), erschla=
gen; (an animal for food),
schlachten

sleep, *sb.*, der Schlaf; *vb.*, schlafen

sleeve, der Ärmel

slight, *adj.*, gering; slight attention = slight degree (geringer
Grad) of attention
slight, *vb.*, verachten

slightly aquiline (nose), leichtge=
bogen

sling, die Schleuder

slip (over the head), ziehen

slope, der Abhang

slumber, der Schlummer

small, klein; small (effort), gering;
small (rise of land), sanft

snail, die Schnecke
snail-picker, der Schneckensamm=
ler

snaky, schlangenartig

snow, der Schnee

snuff-box, die Dose, die Schnupfta=
bakdose

so, conj., when placed before principal sentences, *p.* 2, *n.* 7
so, *adv.*, so; (in this manner),
auf diese Weise; (consequently),
also; demgemäß; (he is) so described, als solcher beschrieben;
so far from (being evidence),
weit entfernt (zu beweisen); so
truly a = such a, ein solcher, &c.;
either naturally so, or, entweder
von Natur, oder
so, conj., so; and so (the rule
is this), demnach; so (that, provided that), wofern nur, wenn nur.
(See *p.* 18, *n.* 17)

soak (to steep), tunken

society, die Gesellschaft

soft (breeze), sanft; (pleasant),
freundlich

soil (ground), der Boden; prairie
soil, der Prairieboden

soldier, der Soldat; 100,000 soldiers, hunderttausend Mann

soldiery, Soldaten

sole, solely, einzig

solemn (feast), feierlich

solemnity (keeping the feast), die
Festlichkeit

L

solitary, einzeln
solitude, die Einsamkeit
sollen, used for *it is said; they say*, *p.* 11, *n.* 45 (*a*)
solo, das Solo
some, einige; some time, einige Zeit; (a small quantity), ein wenig; (any one person or thing, any kind of), irgend ein *or* eine (*see p.* 60, *n.* 5); some (certain) movements, irgend eine Bewegung; some other, ein ander (*masc.*); some dog, ein Hund; for some foray, zu einem Raubzug; of some exemplary severity, von einer exemplarischen Strenge; some alien group, eine fremdartige Gruppe; in some way (understands), gewissermaßen
somehow, irgendwie
sometimes, zuweilen; manchmal
somewhat, etwas
somewhere or other, an dem einen oder dem anderen Ort
son, der Sohn
song, das Lied
sort, die Art
soul, die Seele
sound, *sb.*, der Laut; der Klang; (part of the sea), die Meerenge
sound, *vb.*, (a statement may sound), klingen
sour, sauer
South, der Süden; (towards the south), nach Süden; South Sea, die Südsee
southern, südlich; Southern Mesopotamia, Süd-Mesopotamien
sovereign (king), der König
Spain, Spanien (*neut.*)
Spaniard, der Spanier
Spanish, *adj.*, spanisch
speak, sprechen; so to speak, so zu sagen
spear, die Lanze
species (of ant), die Art
speck: without a weed to speck them = free from every weed
spectacle, das Schauspiel
speculate (about anything), (darüber) nachdenken; speculate on (to try to imagine), grübeln über

speech (discourse), die Rede (*see p.* 31, *n.* 12); (a maiden speech), eine Erstlingsrede
speedily, rasch
speedy, schnell
spell: magician's spell, das Zauberwort
spend (one's time), zubringen; spend itself (in the service), sich erschöpfen
sphere, die Sphäre
spirit, der Geist; (animal spirits), das Dasein
spiritual, geistlich; spiritual (ideas), abstrakt
spirt out (to manifest itself), sich Luft machen
spoil, verderben
sport, die Jagd; active sports, die Leibesübungen
spot (place), der Ort; die Stelle
spread (over a wide extent), sich ausbreiten; to spread (a wave over), ausbreiten
spring, *sb.*, der Frühling; (blossoming time being) principally spring, vorzüglich im Frühling spring of water, der Brunnen spring, *vb.*: (the race) from which he sprang, aus welcher er stammte; to spring into sight = to appear suddenly, plötzlich erscheinen
springy (turf), elastisch
spur (on to), anspornen
square, *sb.*, der Square. (*See p.* 67, *n.* 15)
squash (kind of pumpkin), der Kürbiß
squire, der Edelmann; (vassal), der Vasall; (in attendance), der Page
stab, erstechen
stable, der Stall
staff (*mil.*), der Stab; staff officer, der Stabsoffizier
stag, der Hirsch
stage (degree), das Stadium. (*See p.* 91, *n.* 14) stage-coach, die Postkutsche
stake: are not at stake, stehen nicht auf dem Spiele

stammer, ſtammeln

stamp, *vb.*, ſtempeln

stampede, bie Flucht

stand, ſtehen; stand forth (forming) an oasis, eine Oaſe bilben; stand in relief, ſtarł abſtechen; stand its ground, ſich behaupten

star, ber Stern

stare at, anſtaunen

stark, ſtarr

start (by coach, train, &c.), abfahren

State, ber Staat; Federal States, bie Föberirten Staaten

stately (building), prächtig

stature, bie Statur; bie Geſtalt; in stature, von Geſtalt

stay, bleiben; stay (in sight), nicht verſchwinben, it stayed patiently (spread out on the mountain), es lag gebulbig ba

steadfast, ſtanbhaft

steel, ber Stahl

steep, *adj.*, ſteil; steep (of a hill), *sb.*, ber Abhang

steer, ſteuern; (with oars), lenłen

step, ber Schritt; (of the stairs), eine Stufe; steps (footprints, tracks), bie Spuren

stepdame (*used as an adj.*), ſtiefmütterlich

steward (on an estate), ber Verwalter

stick, ber Stoď

still (yet), noch; (for all that), bennoch

stimulate, anregen

stir (to excite), aufregen

stop, ſtehen bleiben; ſich aufhalten; (when on the march), Halt machen

storm, *sb.*, ber Sturm; a storm of snow and rain, ein Sturm von Schnee und Regen begleitet storm (a redoubt), *vb.*, ſtürmen

story (legend), bie Sage

straight on, gerabe aus

stranded, geſtranbet

strange, ſeltſam

Strasburg, Straßburg; Strasburg gates, Straßburgs Thore

stratagem (of war), bie Krieglіſt

stream: prairie stream, ber Prairieſtrom

street, bie Straße

strength, bie Kraft; bie Stärłe; (*mil.*), bie Macht; according to our strength, nach eigenen Kräften (*plur.*)

strengthened (with the time) = became stronger (ſtärłer)

stretch (to extend), ſich ziehen; ſich ausbehnen; stretch for miles, ſich meilenweit erſtreden

stretching (of elastic, &c.), bas Ausziehen

strictly, ſtreng

strike: it strikes me, es will mir ſcheinen

striking (remarkable), auffallenb; most striking, am auffallenbſten

strip of land, ber Laubſtrich

strive, ſtreben

strong, ſtarł; strong (castle), feſt

strongly, ſtarł

structure, bas Gebäube; (of a plant), ber Bau

struggle: to have the best of the struggle, bie Oberhanb bełommen

study, *sb.*, (learning), bas Stubium; studies, bie Stubien study (elegance), *vb.*, ſich befleißigen

stupid, bumm

sturdy (independent), trotzig

style, ber Stil *or* Stył; (chronological), ber Styl; 11th December, old style, 11ten Dezember, alten Styles

Styrian, *adj.*, ſteleriſch

subject (for an essay), bas Sujet; ber Gegenſtanb

Subject, grammatical, use of, *p.* 81, *n.* 10

submissive, unterwürfig

submit, ſich unterwerfen

subordinate, untergeorbnet

substantial, ſolib; etwas Wirłliches

Substantives, compound, (1) advantage of forming, 22, *n.* 3; (2) formed without any connecting link, or by means of the gen., 59, *n.* 10; 72, *n.* 1 and 10; (3) formed with adjectives, 59, *n.*

9; (4) mode of writing two compounds having the same subordinate member, 93, *n.* 16

Substantives, (1) frequentative, how formed, 15, *n.* 4; (2) gender of abstract—, formed from adjectives, 92, *n.* 7

[See also *Nouns*]

suburb, bie Vorſtabt

succeed each other, auf einanber folgen

success, baß Gelingen

successfully, mit Erfolg

such, ſolĉ; ſo; of such importance, ſo bebeutenb; such a (powerful), ein ſo; in such a case, in bieſem Falle; on such an occasion, bei bieſer Gelegenheit; such as, wie; such works as, Werke wie; such things, bergleiĉen

suddenly, plötzliĉ

suffer, leiben; suffer (disaster), betroffen ſein

sufficient, hinlänngliĉ; to be sufficient, ausreiĉen

sufficiently, genug

suggest (when asked for an opinion), meinen

suggestion (the point of view suggested), bie Anſiĉt

summit, ber Gipfel

sumptuous, präĉtig

sun, bie Sonne

sunbeam, ber Sonnenſtrahl

sup, ſpeiſen zu Abenb

superhuman, übermenſĉliĉ

Superlative, relative, of adverbs, *p.* 87, *n.* 1

supersede, verbrängen

superstition, ber Aberglaube

Supine, (1) definition of, and its general use, 2, *n.* 9 (*a*); (2) with *verbal forms* in -*ing* preceded by *of*, *instead of*, *for*, or *without*, 7, *n.* 31 (*a*); (3) with verbs expressing that something *can* or *should* be done, 9, *n.* 38; (4) with befehlen, 89, *n.* 1; (5) not used after aux. verbs of mood, and ſehen, hören, etc., 11, *n.* 45 (*b*); 37, *n.* 4

supply, *vb.*, liefern

supply, *sb.*: a good supply genug

support, *sb.*, bie Unterſtützung

support, *vb.*, unterſtützen; (to supply food for), nähren

suppose, annehmen

supposed, *adj.*, vermeintliĉ

suppress, unterbrüĉen

sure: then he was sure, bann warb es ihm zur Gewißheit

surf, bie Branbung

surface, bie Oberfläĉe

surgeon (medical man), ber Arzt. (*See p.* 77, *n.* 11)

surprise, *vb.*, in Erſtaunen ſetzen

surrender (a prisoner), ausliefern; if not surrendered (a town), wenn bie Übergabe niĉt erfolgte

surround, umgeben

surrounding country, bie Umgegenb; surrounding poor, bie Armen in ber Umgegenb

survivor, ber Überlebenbe

suspect (assume), annehmen

suspend (around the neck), hängen

suspense (anxious uncertainty), bange Ungewißheit

sustain, aufreĉt erhalten

Suttum, Suttum

swallow up, verſĉlingen

sway (the sceptre), führen

swear, ſĉwören; swear allegiance, ben Lehenseib leiſten

sweep: (warriors) swept over = streamed over, ſtrömten über; sweep bare (the table, to clear it), abbeĉen

sweeping (lines of Greek art), geſĉwungen

sweet (air), friſĉ; (nice), ſĉön

swell: the sea swells, bie See geht hoĉ

swift, ſĉnell; swift running (river), reißenb

swim, ſĉwimmen

swimming, baß Sĉwimmen

sword, baß Sĉwert

sycophant, ber Sĉmeiĉler

sympathy, bie Sympathie

symptom, baß Zeiĉen

syrup, ber Fruĉtſaft. (*See p.* 28, *n.* 14)

system, bas Syſtem

table, ber Tiſch; (writing table), ber Schreibtiſch; to serve at table, bei Tafel aufwarten

tail, ber Schwanz

tailor, ber Schneider

take, nehmen; (to accept), anneh= men; take (advice), befolgen; (an opportunity), ergreifen; take and convey (a prisoner to any- one), überliefern; take amiss (to be angry with), zürnen; take (by conquest), erobern; take heed of (to trouble about), ſich kümmern um; take into one's head, ſich vornehmen; take place, ſtattfinden; take off (one's hat), abnehmen; take (one to), bringen; take root, Wurzel faſſen; take the hint (take warning), es zur Warnung dienen laſſen; take upon one's self, übernehmen; took us down with him = went with us

taking: worth taking, bes Nehmens werth

tale, bie Erzählung; (the event nar- rated), bas Ereigniß; tell their own tale, für ſich ſelbſt ſprechen

tall, groß; tall-grown, groß ge= wachſen

tapping (trees for their sap), sb., ber Einſchnitt

target (targe), bie Tartſche

tart, bie Torte

task, bie Aufgabe

taste (for), bie Vorliebe

tea, ber Thee

team: emigrant's team, bas Aus= wanderergeſpann

tear through (with shot and shell), zerſprengen; tear up (bread), brechen

Telegraph (name of a hill), ber Telegraph

tell, ſagen; tell their own tale, für ſich ſelbſt ſprechen; as we are told, wie uns berichtet wird

temple, ber Tempel

tempting, adj., verführeriſch

tend (to care for), pflegen; tend to (irritate), beitragen bazu

tender, good (offices), freundſchaft= lich

tenor: even tenor (of their lives), ber ruhige Gang

term (expression), bas Wort; ber Ausbruck. (See p. 2, n. 9)
   term (to name), nennen

terrible, ſchrecklich

terrified (to be), erſchrecken

terror, ber Schrecken

Teuton, ber Teutone

Teutonic, teutoniſch

than, als; wie

thanks: to give thanks again, von Neuem banken; without (formal) thanks, ohne Förmlichkeiten

that, dem. pron. and adj., ber, bie, bas; jener, jene, jenes; ber—, bie—, or basjenige; bieſer, bieſe, bieſes; of that which, von bem, was; from that moment, von bem Mo= ment an; von bieſem Augenblicke an; that is = namely, nämlich
   that, rel. pron., (a river) that had steep banks, beſſen Ufer ſteil waren; (the circumstance) that obtained for him, burch welchen er erhielt; all that (had oc- curred), Alles. was
   that, conj., baß (see p. 33, n. 17; p. 34, n. 13; and p. 45, n. 19); (in order to), um

the, ber, bie, bas; the (more), je; abounds with the (superstition), voll von jenem
   the (omitted): all the (hold- ers), all the (Numidians), alle; in the presence, absence, &c., in Gegenwart, &c. (See also p. 76, n. 10)

their, ihr, ihre, ihr; ber, bie, bas, &c.; their father, beſſen Vater; their aid, bie Hülfe berſelben; from their cradles, von ber Wiege an; with their shields over their heads, bie Schilbe über ben Köpfen; slept with their swords under their pillows and their horses saddled in their stables, ſchliefen, bas Schwert unter bem Kopfkiſſen, während bie Pferde geſattelt in ben Ställen ſtanden; their lives, bas

Leben (*no plural in this sense*);
tell their own tale, für sich selbst
sprechen; laid down their knives
and forks, legten Messer und Ga=
beln nieder

them, sie; ihnen; one of them,
einer derselben; some of them,
einige derselben; which forbids
them from engaging their infantry = which forbids their
infantry to engage

themselves, sich; they themselves
being so many, während ihrer so
viele waren

then, *adv.*, dann; (at that time),
damals; (hereupon), hierauf
   then, *conj.*, (therefore), also

thence, von da aus

thenceforth, von da an

theoretical, theoretisch

theory, die Theorie; (opinion), die
Meinung

there, dort; da; (in, at that place),
daselbst

there is, es ist; es gibt (*see p.* 25,
n. 7); when there is no butter,
wenn keine Butter vorhanden ist;
there is no lack of, es fehlt nicht
an; there is nothing to describe, es läßt sich nichts beschreiben;
there is reason (to suppose),
man hat Grund; while there is
still room, da noch Raum bleibt;
there is (throughout history),
es herrscht; there was a necessity,
die Nothwendigkeit war vorhanden;
(he) finding there were no sentries, da er keine Schildwache fand
   there (*omitted*): (years) afterwards there rode, später ritt; in
that castle there lived, in diesem
Schlosse lebte; on either side
there grew up, zu beiden Seiten
erwuchs

therefore, deshalb; daher

these, diese

they, sie; they themselves being
so many, während ihrer so viele
waren; they were baffled = their
plans were frustrated

thick (forest), dicht

thin (loaf), dünn

thing, das Ding; (undefined), Et=
was; (matter, affair), die Sache
(*see p.* 70, *n.* 1); many things
(various subjects), vielerlei

think, denken; (believe, conclude,
imagine, &c.), glauben; (consider), erwägen; (to judge a
thing to be), halten für; think it
necessary, es für nöthig halten;
think of (doing anything), ge=
denken zu (*see p.* 15, *n.* 3); think
little of, gering achten; thinking
to himself, bei sich denkend

third, dritte

thirteenth, dreizehnte

thirty, dreißig; Thirty Years' War,
der dreißigjährige Krieg

this, dieser, diese, dieses; (referring
to something done, doing, or to
be done), dies; this (morning,
evening, &c.), heute; an example
of this, ein Beispiel hievon; and
so the rule is this:—, demnach
wäre Folgendes die Regel:—

thorn (bush), der Dornbusch

those, jene; (*rel. pron.*), die

though, wenn auch; obgleich; ob=
wohl; as though, als ob; even
though, und wenn

thought, der Gedanke; thoughts
(views, opinions), Ansichten;
peaceful thoughts, friedliche Ge=
müthsstimmung

thousand, das Tausend; a thousand
to one, tausend gegen eins; one
hundred thousand, hunderttau=
send

thread, der Faden

threaten, drohen; bedrohen

threatening, *adj.*, drohend

three, drei; three hundred, drei=
hundert; three times, dreimal

throne, der Thron

through, durch; through choice,
aus freier Wahl

throughout, hindurch

throw, werfen; throw away, weg=
werfen; throw off (to unseat a
rider), abwerfen

thrust, der Stoß

Thuringia, Thüringen

Thuringian, *adj.*, Thüringer

Thursday, ber Donnerstag; every Thursday, jeben Donnerstag

thus, so

thy, bein, beine, bein

tide, bie Strömung

tier, bie Reihe; rising tier above tier, in aufsteigenben Reihen

till, bis

Time, (1) duration of, expressed by the accusative, 59, *n*. 2; (2) point of —, expressed by an with the dative, 88, *n*. 15; by the genitive, 79, *n*. 5

time, bie Zeit (*see p*. 13, *n*. 50 (*a*); time of peace, Friebenszeiten (*plur*.); time of war, Kriegs= zeiten (*plur*.); at the present time, jetzt; at the time (just then), im Augenblicke; by this time, jetzt; nun; schon

time, bas Mal; several times, mehrere Male; eight times, acht= mal

tint, bie Farbe

title (name), ber Name

titled (aristocratic), vornehm

Titles, English, not translated, *p*. 31, *n*. 7

to, zu, an, auf, in, &c.: (in order to), um; (Carlyle) to (Goethe), an; to go to (the battle-field), sich begeben auf; (surrender) to the orders, auf Befehl; to the sound (of a bell), auf ben Klang; (attention) to, auf; (to set up a claim) to, (to confine) to (three languages), auf; (en-gaged himself) to (the militia), bei; from fifty to sixty, fünfzig bis sechzig; (as far as), bis an; to the top, bis auf ben Gipfel; but it was to the sailor alone, aber erst für ben Seemann; lost to us, für uns verloren; (towards), gegen; (indifferent, sensitive) to, gegen; (observed) to me, gegen mich; (gentle) to his friends, einen Freunden gegenüber; to fol-low one to church, einem in bie Kirche folgen; the news had flown to = the news had spread itself in; to great distances,

in weite Entfernung; (to journey, go, drive, &c.) to (a place), nach; 15 miles to the north-west (of it), 15 Meilen norbwestlich (bavon) entfernt; to the west, westwärts

together, zusammen; for months together, Monate lang

Tom: Jack or Tom, Hans ober Peter

tomato, ber Liebesapfel

Tombora (mountain), ber Tombora

tongue: native tongue, bie Mutter= sprache

too, zu; (also), auch

top (of a hill), ber Gipfel; tops of the grass, bie Grasspitzen

tortoise, bie Schilbkröte

tow, *vb*., bugsiren

towards (move towards), zu; mako towards, eilen zu; towards the end, gegen Enbe

tower, *sb*., ber Thurm

tower, to tower over, empor= ragen

town, bie Stabt; the town of Guatelma, bie Stabt Guatelma

Town-house (the Town Hall), bas Rathhaus

trace (with a pencil), zeichnen; (to follow traces of), verfolgen; trace back, verfolgen

track (path), ber Pfab

tract (place), bie Stelle; (of ground), eine Strecke; upland tract, bas Hochlanb

tractable: to be tractable (to one's voice), aufhören

trade, ber Hanbel

tradition, bie Trabition; (on that spot) which tradition, welche bie Trabition; bie Sage; times of tradition, bie Sagenzeit; to hold sway in the popular tradition, bas Reich ber Volkssage beherrschen

traditional, als Sage bekannt

tragedy, bas Trauerspiel

train (from the cradle), *vb*., er= ziehen

trait, ber Zug

trampling (a), bas Getrampel

transept, bas Transept

transfer back, zurückbringen

transgress, sich schuldig machen;
transgress again, sich desselben
Vergehens schuldig machen

translate, übersetzen

translation, die Übersetzung

transplant, verpflanzen

travel, *vb.*, reisen; (miners) travelling in search of, die reisten um
. . . aufzusuchen

treasure, der Schatz

treasury, die Schatzkammer

treat (of), sprechen (von)

tree, der Baum; a knot of trees,
eine Baumgruppe

tremendous (groan), schrecklich

trial, das Gerichtsverfahren; trial of
skill, die Kunstprobe

tribe, der Stamm

trick, der Streich

trifling, *adj.*, geringfügig

trim (garden), zierlich

Trojan, *adj.*, trojanisch

troop, der Trupp; troop of horse,
der Trupp Reiter
    troops, die Truppen (*plur.*);
    troops of the line, die Linientrup-
    pen; (an army), eine Armee

trouble, *sb.*, die Mühe

trouble one's self with, sich beküm-
mern um

true, *sb.*, das Wahre
    true, *adj.*, wahr; (faithful),
    treu; (real), eigentlich

truffles, die Trüffeln (*plur.*)

trumpet, die Trompete

trumpeter, der Trompeter

truth, die Wahrheit; in truth, in
der That

try, versuchen; try (before a judge),
vor Gericht stellen

tumultuous, stürmisch

turf, der Rasen

turn (an opportunity to account),
ausbeuten; (one thing into another), vertauschen; turn aside,
ablenken; turn back, zurückkehren;
turn loose, loslassen; turn out
(on guard), ins Gewehr treten;
turn over (to hand over), überliefern; turned their backs (fled),
flohen; turn to ruin, vernichten;
turned twenty, über zwanzig

turn, *sb.*: by turns, abwechselnd

turnkey, der Gefängnißwärter

tusk, der Hauzahn

tussle, der Kampf .

twenty, zwanzig; at the age of
twenty, im Alter von zwanzig
Jahren

twenty-fifth, fünf und zwanzigste

twenty-four, vier und zwanzig

twenty-seven, sieben und zwanzig

twice, zweimal

twist, drehen

two, zwei; the two kingdoms, die
beiden Reiche; two hundred, zweihundert

Tyrol, Tyrol; to go to the Tyrol,
nach Tyrol gehen

Ulphilas, Ulphilas

um, precedes the *supine*, p. 2, n.
9 (*a*)

unable, nicht im Stande; to be unable, nicht können

unavoidable, unvermeidlich

unbounded, unbegrenzt

uncle, der Onkel

unconnected, unzusammenhängend

unconscious (not suspecting), nicht
ahnend

under, unter; to get under arms,
ins Gewehr treten; under the
sand, in dem Sand; (fall) under
(the weight), durch

underneath, unter

undertake (to take in hand), sich
daran machen

undertaking, das Unternehmen

understand, verstehen; (to discover),
entdecken

undomesticated (unsociable), un-
gesellig

undoubtedly (indisputably), unstreitig

unexampled, beispiellos

unfathomable (depths of forest),
undurchdringlich

unfortunate, unglücklich

uniform, *sb.*, die Uniform

uniform (rule) = general (custom),
allgemein

uniformity, die Gleichförmigkeit.
(*See p.* 91, *n.* 5)

union, bie Verbindung; bie Vereini=
gung
United States, bie Vereinigten
Staaten
unknown, fremb; unbekannt
unless, außer; es sei denn; wenn nicht
unlet, unvermiethet
unlike, unähnlich
unmeaning, unbebeutenb
unnecessary, unnüß
unparalleled, adj., beispiellos
unprincipled, gewissenlos
unquestionable, unstreitig
unsurpassed, unübertroffen
until, bis
up, auf; (upwards), hinauf; up to
(the time), bis zu; to come up
(to), kommen herbei; lead up,
hinaufführen
upland, bas Hochlanb; upland tract,
bas Hochlanb
upon, auf; upon (a subject), über;
upon which, worauf; (slaughter
wrought) upon (troops), unter;
upon the day, am Tage; upon
him, bei sich; to call upon him,
ihm einen Besuch machen; to close
upon, sich schließen über; to look
upon, ansehen; to take upon
one's self, übernehmen; to operate as but a slight check upon,
nur geringen Einhalt thun
upper lip, bie Oberlippe
Urceola Elastica, bie Urceola
Elastica
urge, bringen
use, sb., ber Gebrauch; to make use
of, benußen
use (for anything), vb., brau=
chen
useful, nüßlich
usual, üblich; gewöhnlich
usually, gewöhnlich
utterance, ber Ausspruch; volubility
of utterance, bie Zungengeläufig=
keit
utterly, gänzlich
Valens, (indeclin.), Valens
valley, bas Thal
valour, bie Tapferkeit
valuable, werthvoll
Van Eyck, Van Eyk

vanish, verschwinden
various, verschieden
vary (to sound contradictory),
lauten verschieben
vast, groß; mächtig; ungeheuer
vastness, ungeheure Größe
vedette, bie Vebette
vegetable (kind of), bie Gemüseart;
vegetable kingdom, bas Pflan=
zenreich
vegetation: forms of vegetation,
Pflanzenformen
velocity, bie Schnelligkeit
venal, feil
venture, vb., wagen
ver, use of insep. prefix, p. 96, n.
14
verbal, mündlich
   Verbal Forms in -ing, transl.
   of, (1) when preceded by *of*,
   instead of, *for*, or *without*, 7, n.
   31 (a); (2) when used substantively, 15, n. 1
   Verbs. I. (1) When conjugated with sein; (2) omission of
   aux. verbs of tense, haben and
   sein, 12, n. 47 (e); (3) use of aux.
   — of mood, 52, n. 1
   II. (1) Use of the passive
   voice, 1, n. 4 (b); (2) use of
   active voice instead of passive
   voice, 2, n. 8; (3) use of the
   reflective instead of passive
   voice, 10, n. 41 (b)
   III. Government of — of
   choosing, appointing, &c., Gr.
   Intr., xviii.; 36, n. 4
   IV. (1) Verbs governing a
   direct and indirect object, 5, n.
   22 (b); (2) government of insep. comp. —, 2, n. 9 (b); (3)
   government of sep. comp. verbs,
   compounded with an, auf, bei,
   &c., 5, n. 25 (a); (4) government of — denoting motion,
   24, n. 10; (5) government of
   — denoting want, 87, n. 10
   V. (1) Place of finite —
   containing *assertion*, 2, n. 5 (b);
   3, n. 12 (a); (2) place of —
   in dependent sentences, 3, n.
   12 (b)

VI. Intransitive —, how transformed into transitive ones, 29, *n.* 14

Verbs, upon which the objective clause or the supine depends, followed by a preposition, 97, *n.* 2

Verfaſſung, *when used for* composition, p. 62, *n.* 6

verily, wirflich

version (translation), bie Überſetzung

very, *adv.,* ſehr; (extremely), äußerſt; very distant, ſehr weit entfernt; very largely, in großer Menge; very much the contrary, ganz im Gegentheil

very, *adj.:* the very ideal (personified), baß verförperte Jbeal; the very model, ein wahreß Muſter (*see p.* 37, *n.* 3); as the very name declares, wie ber Name ſchon bezeugt; the very top, ber Gipfel ſelbſt. (*See p.* 23, *n.* 5)

vessel (boat), baß Boot; (for cooking), baß Gefäß

vestige, bie Spur

victory, ber Sieg

view, bie Ausſicht; width of view (mental), umfaſſenbe Anſchauungsweiſe

vigilant, vorſichtig

village, baß Dorf

violate (to oppose a custom), entgegenhanbeln

violet, baß Beilchen

violin: performer on the violin, ber Violinſpieler

vinea, bie Laufhaſſe

virtue, bie Tugenb

Visigoth, ber Weſtgothe

visit, *vb.,* beſuchen

Vladimir column, bie Wladimir-Colonne

vociferously, laut ſchreienb

voice, bie Stimme

volcano, ber Vulcan

volubility of utterance, bie Zungengeläufigfeit

voluntarily, freiwiſſig

volunteer, ber Freiwiſſge

vorangehen, gov. dative, *p.* 5, *n.* 25 (*a*)

vow of reveng

voyage, bie Rei

wafted, to b

wafted (to),

wait for, abwar

wake, wecfen

walk, gehen,

weiter ſchreite

wall, bie Mauer

its walls, an

want, *sb.,* baß

ber Mangel (

war, ber Krieg

War, ber brei

of war, Krie

warm, warmly

warrior, ber

Held

Wartburg (th

war-whoop, ba

waste, *vb.,* verg

watch: an en

(to), ein Fein

helt lauerte

watch, v

bewachen; wa

watch for, a

watchful, wach

watch-tower,

water, baß W

water, ein

water's ed

Waſſerß

water-laden,

wave, bie Wo

Grasweſſen

wavy, weſſenfö

way (manner)

life, bie Lebe

ber Übergan

to lead the

make one's

weak, ſchwach;

weapon, bie W

wear, tragen;

ſehen

we, wir; as

berichtet wir

weed, baß Unk

week, bie Wo

eine Woche

weight (press

Weimar, Weimar (*neut.*)

welcome, willkommen

well, *sb.*, der Brunnen

well, *adv.*, gut; wohl (*see p.* 75, *n.* 4); (finely), fein; well and good, so mag es hingehen; well aware, überzeugt; well cooked, sorgfältig zubereitet; well examine, genau besichtigen

well-ascertained, völlig-erwiesen

Welsh, *adj.*, wallisisch

west (towards the west), nach Westen; to the west, westwärts; West Cliff, die Westklippe

western, westlich

westward, westwärts

wet, naß

what, was; what (you write) about, worüber

whatever it might be, it was —, was immer es auch sei, so war es —; at whatever risk, auf jede Gefahr hin

wheaten bread, das Weizenbrod

when (*see p.* 41, *n.* 9 *and p.* 50, *n.* 22), als; wenn; (whereupon), worauf; (just then), da; when examined, bei genauer Untersuchung; the time, when, die Zeit, wo; even when most resembling = even the most like, selbst die ähnlichsten; it was about dusk when he arrived = he arrived there about dusk

when (*omitted*): when hindered he assumed, aufgehalten, nahm er

whence (from which), von dem, von der

where, wo; advanced to where . . ., schritt bis zu dem Platze vor, wo . . .; (in minds) where, bei denen

wherewith, womit

whether, ob; whether to direct or impel, sei es um zu lenken oder anzuspornen

which, welcher, welche, welches; der, die, das; in which = where, wo; of which, wovon; of which = whose, dessen; deren; on the highest of which = on whose highest point; each of which,

von denen jeder; of that which, von dem, was; on which, worauf; (a race) on which (affection is thrown away), bei der; to which (this led), wohin; which being so, und da dies der Fall ist

Whig, Whig

while, indem; während; da; while there is still room, da noch Raum bleibt; while (he) goes, im Gehen; (*omitted*): I have, while in England, ich habe in England. (*See p.* 36, *n.* 12)

whilst, indem; während

whirr, *vb.*, schwirren

whisper, *sb.*, das Flüstern

white, weiß

whither, wohin

who, der, die, das; welcher, welche, welches

whole, ganz; whole of the, sämmtlich (*adj.*); whole of his forces (*mil.*), seine Gesammtmacht

whose: (trees) whose seeds = the seeds to which the trees owed their existence, die ihr Dasein dem Samen verdankt

why, warum; (in that case), nun

wide, breit; far and wide, weit und breit; wide (extent of country), groß

width of view (mental), umfassende Anschauungsweise

wife, die Gemahlin

wild, wild; (growing wild), wildwachsend

wilderness, die Wildniß

will, *vb.*, (to have a will to), wollen; *aux. vb. of fut. tense*, werden; (one only symptom) will it give, giebt es

will, *sb.*: to bear ill will, übel wollen

William, Wilhelm

will-o'-the-wisp, das Irrlicht

wind, der Wind

winding road, sich hinwindende Straße

wine, der Wein

wing, der Flügel

wise: to be wise, weise sein

wish, *vb.*, wünschen

wistfully, ſehnſüchtig

with, mit; with (the army, his regiment, &c.), bei; (to live) with (anyone), bei; (together with), ſammt; (a few men) and the Ligurian with them, ſammt bem Ligurier; (to build a hut) with (logs, &c.), aus; (a feeling) with, für; with the design, zu bem Zweď; to abound with, voll ſein von; overflowed (crowded) with, gebrängt voll von; with his name stamped upon it, worauf ſein Name geſtempelt war; with her own hand (wrote), eigenhänbig; entertain him with a solo, ihm ein Solo vorſpielen

with, *omitted in all such cases as:* an emigrant's team with the women under the awning, ein Auswanberergeſpann, bie Frauen unter ber Plane; slept with their swords under their pillows, ſchliefen, bas Schwert unter bem Kopfkiſſen; &c.

within, in; within an hour, binnen einer Stunbe; within the entrance, am Eingang

without, *prep.*, ohne; without a moment's preparation, ohne irgenb welche Vorbereitung; without a weed, frei von jebem Unkraut; without opposition, ungehinbert; was without result, hatte keine Folge

within (*adv.*) = from without, von außen

witness (to see), ſehen; (to notice), wahrnehmen; (to be present at), beiwohnen

witty, witzig

wohl, expressing probability, place of adv., *p.* 41, *n.* 6

wolf, ber Wolf

woman, bie Frau

wonderful, wunberbar; (extraordinary), außerorbentlich

wont: as was his wont, wie gewöhnlich

wood (timber), bas Holz; (forest), ber Walb

wooden, hölzern

woodland: (country) of woodlands, walbig

woodless, walblos

wool, bie Wolle

word, bas Wort; word of command, bas Commanbowort; in a word, mit einem Wort; words (*connected terms, having a coherent meaning*), Worte; (*unconnected*), Wörter; no words, not a word (being spoken), kein Wort

work, *sb.*, bie Arbeit

work, *vb.*: set to work, ſich an bie Arbeit machen; (stimulate) to work, zum Arbeiten; (the slaughter)wrought upon(troops, by artillery), angerichtet unter

worker (ant), ber Arbeiter

world, bie Welt

worse (than his reputation), ſchlimmer

worshipful (*ironical*), hochlöblich

worth, ber Werth; worth taking, bes Nehmens werth

would, *see* will

wounded (men), bie Verwunbeten

wrecked (to be), Schiffbruch (*masc.*) leiben

write, ſchreiben

writer (author), ber Verfaſſer

writing (style of composition), bie Schreibweiſe

wrought, *see* work

year, bas Jahr; (£500) a year, bes Jahres; a year's journey through, ein Jahr in

yet, boch; (but), aber; (nevertheless), bennoch

yield (to produce), liefern

you, Sie; Euch (*see p.* 90, *n.* 12); (*used by a king in addressing a subject*), Er, Ihn, Ihm; bu, bich, bir (*see also p.* 71, *n.* 16); (anyone), man (*nom.*), Jemanb, Niemanb. (*See p.* 38, *n.* 4)

young, jung

Your Majesty, Ew. Majeſtät

youth, ber Jüngling

Ziethen Hussars, Ziethen'ſche Huſaren

zone = girdle, ber Gürtel

zoologist, ber Zoolog

RICHARD CLAY AND SONS, LIMITED, LONDON AND BUNGAY.

A CATALOGUE

OF

EDUCATIONAL WORKS

Published by

GEORGE BELL & SONS.

————— >•••••—————

CONTENTS.

4 YORK STREET, COVENT GARDEN, LONDON, W.C.

GRAMMAR-SCHOOL CLASSICS.

A Series of Greek and Latin Authors, with English Notes.
Fcap. 8vo.

Cæsar : De Bello Gallico. By George Long, M.A. 4s.

———— Books I.-III. For Junior Classes. By G. Long, M.A. 1s. 6d.

———— Books IV. and V. 1s. 6d. Books VI. and VII., 1s. 6d.

———— Books I., II., and III., with Vocabulary, 1s. 6d. each.

Catullus, Tibullus, and Propertius. Selected Poems. With Life.
By Rev. A. H. Wratislaw. 2s. 6d.

Cicero : De Senectute, De Amicitia, and Select Epistles. By
George Long, M.A. 3s.

Cornelius Nepos. By Rev. J. F. Macmichael. 2s.

Homer : Iliad. Books I.-XII. By F. A. Paley, M.A., LL.D.
4s. 6d. Also in 2 parts, 2s. 6d. each.

Horace : With Life. By A. J. Macleane, M.A. 3s. 6d. In
2 parts, 2s. each. Odes, Book I., with Vocabulary, 1s. 6d.

Juvenal : Sixteen Satires. By H. Prior, M.A. 3s 6d.

Martial : Select Epigrams. With Life. By F. A. Paley, M.A., LL.D.
4s. 6d.

Ovid : the Fasti. By F. A. Paley, M.A., LL.D. 3s. 6d. Books I·
and II., 1s. 6d. Books III. and IV., 1s. 6d. Books V. and VI., 1s. 6d.

Sallust : Catilina and Jugurtha. With Life. By G. Long, M.A.
and J. G. Frazer. 3s. 6d., or separately, 2s. each.

Tacitus : Germania and Agricola. By Rev. P. Frost. 2s. 6d.

Virgil : Bucolics, Georgics, and Æneid, Books I.-IV. Abridged
from Professor Conington's Edition. 4s. 6d.—Æneid, Books V.-XII., 4s. 6d.
Also in 9 separate Volumes, as follows, 1s. 6d. each :—Bucolics—Georgics,
I. and II.—Georgics, III. and IV.—Æneid, I. and II.—III. and IV.—V.
and VI.—VII. and VIII.—IX. and X.—and XI. and XII. Æneid, Book
I., with Vocabulary, 1s. 6d.

Xenophon : The Anabasis. With Life. By Rev. J. F. Macmichael.
3s. 6d. Also in 4 separate volumes, 1s. 6d. each :—Book I. (with Life,
Introduction, Itinerary, and Three Maps)—Books II. and III.—IV. and V.
—VI. and VII.

———— The Cyropædia. By G. M. Gorham, M.A. 3s. 6d. Books
I. and II., 1s. 6d.—Books V. and VI., 1s. 6d.

———— Memorabilia. By Percival Frost, M.A. 3s.

A Grammar School Atlas of Classical Geography, containing
Ten selected Maps. Imperial 8vo. 3s.

Uniform with the Series.

The New Testament, in Greek. With English Notes, &c. By
Rev. J. F. Macmichael. 4s. 6d. The Four Gospels and the Acts, separately.
Sewed, 6d. each.

CAMBRIDGE GREEK AND LATIN TEXTS.

Aeschylus. By F. A. Paley, M.A., LL.D. 2s.
Cæsar: De Bello Gallico. By G. Long, M.A. 1s. 6d.
Cicero: De Senectute et De Amicitia, et Epistolæ Selectæ.
    By G. Long, M.A. 1s. 6d.
Ciceronis Orationes. In Verrem. By G. Long, M.A. 2s. 6d.
Euripides. By F. A. Paley, M.A., LL.D. 3 vols. 2s. each.
Herodotus. By J. G. Blakesley, B.D. 2 vols. 5s.
Homeri Ilias. I.-XII. By F. A. Paley, M.A., LL.D. 1s. 6d.
Horatius. By A. J. Macleane, M.A. 1s. 6d.
Juvenal et Persius. By A. J. Macleane, M.A. 1s. 6d.
Lucretius. By H. A. J. Munro, M.A. 2s.
Sallusti Crispi Catilina et Jugurtha. By G. Long, M.A. 1s. 6d.
Sophocles. By F. A. Paley, M.A., LL.D. 2s. 6d.
Terenti Comœdiæ. By W. Wagner, Ph.D. 2s.
Thucydides. By J. G. Donaldson, D.D. 2 vols. 4s.
Virgilius. By J. Conington, M.A. 2s.
Xenophontis Expeditio Cyri. By J. F. Macmichael, B.A. 1s. 6d.
Novum Testamentum Græce. By F. H. Scrivener, M.A., D.C.L.
    4s. 6d. An edition, with wide margin for notes, half bound, 12s. EDITIO
    MAJOR, with additional Readings and References. 7s. 6d. (*See page* 15.)

CAMBRIDGE TEXTS WITH NOTES.

*A Selection of the most usually read of the Greek and Latin Authors, Annotated for
Schools. Edited by well-known Classical Scholars. Fcap. 8vo. 1s. 6d. each,
with exceptions.*

> ' Dr. Paley's vast learning and keen appreciation of the difficulties of
> beginners make his school editions as valuable as they are popular. In
> many respects he sets a brilliant example to younger scholars.'—*Athenæum.*
> ' We hold in high value these handy Cambridge texts with Notes.'—
> *Saturday Review.*

Aeschylus. Prometheus Vinctus.—Septem contra Thebas.—Aga-
    memnon.—Persae.—Eumenides.—Choephoroe. By F.A. Paley, M.A., LL.D.
Euripides. Alcestis.—Medea.—Hippolytus.—Hecuba. — Bacchae.
    —Ion. 2s.—Orestes.—Phoenissae.—Troades.—Hercules Furens.—Andro-
    mache.—Iphigenia in Tauris.—Supplices. By F. A. Paley, M.A., LL.D.
Homer. Iliad. Book I. By F. A. Paley, M.A., LL.D. 1s.
Sophocles. Oedipus Tyrannus.—Oedipus Coloneus. — Antigone.
    —Electra.—Ajax. By F. A. Paley, M.A., LL.D.
Xenophon. Anabasis. In 6 vols. By J. E. Melhuish, M.A.,
    Assistant Classical Master at St. Paul's School.
——— Hellenics, Book I. By L. D. Dowdall, M.A., B.D. 2s.
——— Hellenics, Book II. By L. D. Dowdall, M.A., B.D. 2s.
Cicero. De Senectute, De Amicitia, and Epistolæ Selectæ. By
    G. Long, M.A.
Ovid. Fasti. By F. A. Paley, M.A., LL.D. In 3 vols., 2 books
    in each. 2s. each vol.

Ovid.   Selections.   Amores, Tristia, Heroides, Metamorphoses.
By A. J. Macleane, M.A.
Terence.   Andria.—Hauton Timorumenos.—Phormio.—Adelphoe.
By Professor Wagner, Ph.D.
Virgil.   Professor Conington's edition, abridged in 12 vols.
'The handiest as well as the soundest of modern editions.'
Saturday Review.

PUBLIC SCHOOL SERIES.

A Series of Classical Texts, annotated by well-known Scholars. Cr. 8vo.

Aristophanes.   The Peace.   By F. A. Paley, M.A., LL.D.   4s. 6d.
—— The Acharnians.   By F. A. Paley, M.A., LL.D.   4s. 6d.
—— The Frogs.   By F. A. Paley, M.A., LL.D.   4s. 6d.
Cicero.   The Letters to Atticus.   Bk. I.   By A. Pretor, M.A.   3rd
Edition. 4s. 6d.
Demosthenes de Falsa Legatione.   By R. Shilleto, M.A.   7th
Edition. 6s.
—— The Law of Leptines.   By B. W. Beatson, M.A.   3rd
Edition. 3s. 6d.
Livy.   Book XXI.   Edited, with Introduction, Notes, and Maps,
by the Rev. L. D. Dowdall, M.A., B.D. 3s. 6d.
—— Book XXII.   Edited, &c., by Rev. L. D. Dowdall, M.A.,
B.D. 3s. 6d.
Plato.   The Apology of Socrates and Crito.   By W. Wagner, Ph.D.
12th Edition. 3s. 6d. Cheap Edition, limp cloth, 2s. 6d.
—— The Phædo.   9th Edition.   By W. Wagner, Ph.D.   5s. 6d.
—— The Protagoras.   7th Edition.   By W. Wayte, M.A.   4s. 6d.
—— The Euthyphro.   3rd Edition.   By G. H. Wells, M.A.   3s.
—— The Euthydemus.   By G. H. Wells, M.A.   4s.
—— The Republic.   Books I. & II.   By G. H. Wells, M.A.   3rd
Edition. 5s. 6d.
Plautus.   The Aulularia.   By W. Wagner, Ph.D.   5th Edition.   4s. 6d.
—— The Trinummus.   By W. Wagner, Ph.D.   5th Edition.   4s. 6d.
—— The Menaechmei.   By W. Wagner, Ph.D.   2nd Edit.   4s. 6d.
—— The Mostellaria.   By Prof. E. A. Sonnenschein.   5s.
Sophocles.   The Trachiniae.   By A. Pretor. M.A.   4s. 6d.
—— The Oedipus Tyrannus.   By B. H. Kennedy, D.D.   5s.
Terence.   By W. Wagner, Ph.D.   3rd Edition.   7s. 6d.
Theocritus.   By F. A. Paley, M.A., LL.D.   2nd Edition.   4s. 6d.
Thucydides.   Book VI.   By T. W. Dougan, M.A., Fellow of St.
John's College, Cambridge. 3s. 6d.

CRITICAL AND ANNOTATED EDITIONS.

Aristophanis Comoediae.   By H. A. Holden, LL.D.   8vo.   2 vols.
Notes, Illustrations, and Maps. 23s. 6d. Plays sold separately.
Cæsar's Seventh Campaign in Gaul, B.C. 52.   By Rev. W. C.
Compton, M.A., Head Master, Dover College. 2nd Edition, with Map
and Illustrations. Crown 8vo. 4s.
Calpurnius Siculus.   By H. C. Keene, M.A.   Crown 8vo.   6s.

Catullus. A New Text, with Critical Notes and Introduction by Dr. J. P. Postgate. Foolscap 8vo. 3s.

Corpus Poetarum Latinorum. Edited by Walker. 1 vol. 8vo. 18s.

Livy. The first five Books. By J. Prendeville. New Edition, revised, and the notes in great part rewritten, by J. H. Freese, M.A. Books I., II., III., IV., and V. 1s. 6d. each.

Lucan. The Pharsalia. By C. E. Haskins, M.A., and W. E. Heitland, M.A. Demy 8vo. 14s.

Lucretius. With Commentary by H. A. J. Munro. 4th Edition. Vols. I. and II. Introduction, Text, and Notes. 18s. Vol. III. Translation. 6s.

Ovid. P. Ovidii Nasonis Heroides XIV. By A. Palmer, M.A. 8vo. 6s.

———— P. Ovidii Nasonis Ars Amatoria et Amores. By the Rev. H. Williams, M.A. 3s. 6d.

———— Metamorphoses. Book XIII. By Chas. Haines Keene, M.A. 2s. 6d.'

———— Epistolarum ex Ponto Liber Primus. By C. H. Keene, M.A. 3s.

Propertius. Sex Aurelii Propertii Carmina. By F. A. Paley, M.A., LL.D. 8vo. Cloth, 5s.

———— Sex Propertii Elegiarum. Libri IV. Recensuit A. Palmer, Collegii Sacrosanctæ et Individuæ Trinitatis juxta Dublinum Socius. Fcap. 8vo. 3s. 6d.

Sophocles. The Oedipus Tyrannus. By B. H. Kennedy, D.D. Crown 8vo. 8s.

Thucydides. The History of the Peloponnesian War. By Richard Shilleto, M.A. Book I. 8vo. 6s. 6d. Book II. 8vo. 5s. 6d.

TRANSLATIONS, SELECTIONS, &c.

Aeschylus. Translated into English Prose by F. A. Paley, M.A., LL.D. 2nd Edition. 8vo. 7s. 6d.

———— Translated into English Verse by Anna Swanwick. 4th Edition. Post 8vo. 5s.

Calpurnius, The Eclogues of. Latin Text and English Verse. Translation by E. J. L. Scott, M.A. 3s. 6d.

Horace. The Odes and Carmen Sæculare. In English Verse by J. Conington, M.A. 11th edition. Fcap. 8vo. 3s. 6d.

———— The Satires and Epistles. In English Verse by J. Conington, M.A. 8th edition. 3s. 6d.

Plato. Gorgias. Translated by E. M. Cope, M.A. 8vo. 2nd Ed. 7s.

Prudentius, Selections from. Text, with Verse Translation, Introduction, &c., by the Rev. F. St. J. Thackeray. Crown 8vo. 7s. 6d.

Sophocles. Oedipus Tyrannus. By Dr. Kennedy. 1s.

———— The Dramas of. Rendered into English Verse by Sir George Young, Bart., M.A. 8vo. 12s. 6d.

Theocritus. In English Verse, by C. S. Calverley, M.A. 3rd Edition. Crown 8vo. 7s. 6d.

Translations into English and Latin. By C. S. Calverley, M.A. Post 8vo. 7s. 6d.

Translations into English, Latin, and Greek. By R. C. Jebb, Litt.D., H. Jackson, Litt.D., and W. E. Currey, M.A. Second Edition. 8s.

Folia Silvulæ, sive Eclogæ Poetarum Anglicorum in Latinum et Græcum conversæ. By H. A. Holden, LL.D. 8vo. Vol. II. 4s. 6d.

Sabrinae Corolla in Hortulis Regiae Scholae Salopiensis Contexuerunt Tres Viri Floribus Legendis. Fourth Edition, thoroughly Revised and Rearranged. Large post 8vo. 10s. 6d.

LOWER FORM SERIES.
With Notes and Vocabularies.

Virgil's Æneid. Book I. Abridged from Conington's Edition. With Vocabulary by W. F. R. Shilleto. 1s. 6d.

Cæsar de Bello Gallico. Books I., II., and III. With Notes by George Long, M.A., and Vocabulary by W. F. R. Shilleto. 1s. 6d. each.

Horace. Book I. Macleane's Edition, with Vocabulary by A. H. Dennis. 1s. 6d.

Frost. Eclogæ Latinæ; or, First Latin Reading-Book, with English Notes and a Dictionary. By the late Rev. P. Frost, M.A. New Edition. Fcap. 8vo. 1s. 6d.

———— **A Latin Verse-Book.** An Introductory Work on Hexameters and Pentameters. New Edition. Fcap. 8vo. 2s. Key (for Tutors only), 5s.

———— **Analecta Græca Minora,** with Introductory Sentences, English Notes, and a Dictionary. New Edition. Fcap. 8vo. 2s.

Wells. Tales for Latin Prose Composition. With Notes and Vocabulary. By G. H. Wells, M.A. 2s.

Stedman. Latin Vocabularies for Repetition. By A. M. M. Stedman, M.A. 2nd Edition, revised. Fcap. 8vo. 1s. 6d.

———— **Easy Latin Passages for Unseen Translation.** Fcap. 8vo. 1s. 6d.

———— **Greek Testament Selections.** 2nd Edition, enlarged, with Notes and Vocabulary. Fcap. 8vo. 2s. 6d.

CLASSICAL TABLES.

Latin Accidence. By the Rev. P. Frost, M.A. 1s.

Latin Versification. 1s.

Notabilia Quædam; or the Principal Tenses of most of the Irregular Greek Verbs and Elementary Greek, Latin, and French Construction. New Edition. 1s.

Richmond Rules for the Ovidian Distich, &c. By J. Tate, M.A. 1s.

The Principles of Latin Syntax. 1s.

Greek Verbs. A Catalogue of Verbs, Irregular and Defective. By J. S. Baird, T.C.D. 8th Edition. 2s. 6d.

Greek Accents (Notes on). By A. Barry, D.D. New Edition. 1s.

Homeric Dialect. Its Leading Forms and Peculiarities. By J. S. Baird, T.C.D. New Edition, by W. G. Rutherford, LL.D. 1s.

Greek Accidence. By the Rev. P. Frost, M.A. New Edition. 1s.

LATIN AND GREEK CLASS-BOOKS.
See also Lower Form Series.

Baddeley. Auxilia Latina. A Series of Progressive Latin Exercises. By M. J. B. Baddeley, M.A. Fcap. 8vo. Part I., Accidence. 5th Edition. 2s. Part II. 5th Edition. 2s. Key to Part II., 2s. 6d.

Baker. Latin Prose for London Students. By Arthur Baker, M.A. Fcap. 8vo. 2s.

Church. Latin Prose Lessons. By Prof. Church, M.A. 9th Edition. Fcap. 8vo. 2s. 6d.

Collins. Latin Exercises and Grammar Papers. By T. Collins, M.A., H. M. of the Latin School, Newport, Salop. 7th Edit. Fcap. 8vo. 2s. 6d.

———— **Unseen Papers in Latin Prose and Verse.** With Examination Questions. 6th Edition. Fcap. 8vo. 2s. 6d.

Collins. Unseen Papers in Greek Prose and Verse. With Ex-
amination Questions. 3rd Edition. Fcap. 8vo. 3s.
—— Easy Translations from Nepos, Cæsar, Cicero, Livy,
&c., for Retranslation into Latin. With Notes. 2s.
Compton. Rudiments of Attic Construction and Idiom. By
the Rev. W. C. Compton, M.A., Head Master of Dover College. 3s.
Clapin. A Latin Primer. By Rev. A. C. Clapin, M.A. 1s.
Frost. Eclogæ Latinæ; or, First Latin Reading Book. With
Notes and Vocabulary by the late Rev. P. Frost, M.A. New Edition.
Fcap. 8vo. 1s. 6d.
—— Materials for Latin Prose Composition. By the late Rev.
P. Frost, M.A. New Edition. Fcap. 8vo. 2s. Key (for Tutors only) 4s.
—— Materials for Greek Prose Composition. New Edition.
Fcap. 8vo. 2s. 6d. Key (for Tutors only), 5s.
Harkness. A Latin Grammar. By A. Harkness. Post 8vo. 6s.
Holden. Foliorum Silvula. Part I. Passages for Translation
into Latin Elegiac and Heroic Verse. By H. A. Holden, LL.D. 12th Edit.
Post 8vo. 7s. 6d.
—— Foliorum Silvula. Part II. Select Passages for Trans-
lation into Latin Lyric and Comic Iambic Verse. 3rd Ed. Post 8vo. 5s.
—— Foliorum Centuriæ. Select Passages for Translation
into Latin and Greek Prose. 10th Edition. Post 8vo. 8s.
Jebb, Jackson, and Currey. Extracts for Translation in Greek,
Latin, and English. By R. C. Jebb, Litt. D., LL.D., H. Jackson, Litt. D.,
and W. E. Currey, M.A. 4s. 6d.
Key. A Latin Grammar. By T. H. Key, M.A., F.R.S. 6th
Thousand. Post 8vo. 8s.
—— A Short Latin Grammar for Schools. 16th Edition.
Post 8vo. 3s. 6d.
Mason. Analytical Latin Exercises. By C. P. Mason, B.A.
4th Edition. Part I., 1s. 6d. Part II., 2s. 6d.
Nettleship. Passages for Translation into Latin Prose. By
Prof. H. Nettleship, M.A. 3s. Key (for Tutors only), 4s. 6d.
'The introduction ought to be studied by every teacher.'—*Guardian.*
Paley. Greek Particles and their Combinations according to
Attic Usage. A Short Treatise. By F. A. Paley, M.A., LL.D. 2s. 6d.
Penrose. Latin Elegiac Verse, Easy Exercises in. By the Rev.
J. Penrose. New Edition. 2s. (Key, 3s. 6d.)
Preston. Greek Verse Composition. By G. Preston, M.A.
5th Edition. Crown 8vo. 4s. 6d.
Pruen. Latin Examination Papers. Comprising Lower, Middle,
and Upper School Papers, and a number of Woolwich and Sandhurst
Standards. By G. G. Pruen, M.A. Crown 8vo. 2s. 6d.
Seager. Faciliora. An Elementary Latin Book on a new
principle. By the Rev. J. L. Seager, M.A. 2s. 6d.
Stedman. First Latin Lessons. By A. M. M. Stedman, M.A.
Second Edition, enlarged. Crown 8vo. 2s.
—— First Latin Reader. With Notes adapted to the Shorter
Latin Primer and Vocabulary. Crown 8vo. 1s. 6d.
—— Easy Latin Exercises on the Syntax of the Shorter and
Revised Latin Primers. With Vocabulary. 3rd Edition. Cr. 8vo. 2s. 6d.
—— Notanda Quædam. Miscellaneous Latin Exercises on
Common Rules and Idioms. Fcap. 8vo. 1s. 6d. With vocabulary 2s.
—— First Greek Lessons. [*In preparation.*
—— Easy Greek Passages for Unseen Translation. Fcap.
8vo. 1s. 6d.

Stedman.   Easy Greek Exercises on Elementary Syntax.
                                                    [*In preparation.*
——— Greek Vocabularies for Repetition. Fcap. 8vo. 1s. 6d.
Thackeray. Anthologia Græca. A Selection of Greek Poetry,
   with Notes. By F. St. John Thackeray. 5th Edition. 16mo. 4s. 6d.
——— Anthologia Latina. A Selection of Latin Poetry, from
   Nævius to Boëthius, with Notes. By Rev. F. St. J. Thackeray. 5th Edit.
   16mo. 4s. 6d.

Donaldson.   The Theatre of the Greeks.   By J. W. Donaldson,
   D.D. 10th Edition. Post 8vo. 5s.
Keightley.   The Mythology of Greece and Italy.   By Thomas
   Keightley. 4th Edition. Revised by L. Schmitz, Ph.D., LL.D. 5s.
Mayor.   A Guide to the Choice of Classical Books.   By J. B.
   Mayor, M.A. 3rd Edition. Crown 8vo. 4s. 6d.
Teuffel.   A History of Roman Literature.   By Prof. W. S.
   Teuffel. 5th Edition, revised by Prof. L. Schwabe, and translated by
   Prof. G. C. W. Warr, of King's College. 2 vols. medium 8vo. 15s. each.

CAMBRIDGE MATHEMATICAL SERIES.

Arithmetic for Schools.   By C. Pendlebury, M.A.   6th Edition,
   with or without answers, 4s. 6d. Or in two parts, 2s. 6d. each. Part 2 con-
   tains the *Commercial Arithmetic*. Key to Part 2, for tutors only, 7s. 6d. net.
   EXAMPLES (nearly 8000), without answers, in a separate vol. 3s.
   In use at St. Paul's, Winchester, Wellington, Marlborough, Charterhouse,
   Merchant Taylors', Christ's Hospital, Sherborne, Shrewsbury, &c. &c.
Algebra.   Choice and Chance.   By W. A. Whitworth, M.A.   4th
   Edition. 6s.
Euclid.   Newly translated from the Greek Text, with Supple-
   mentary Propositions, Chapters on Modern Geometry, and numerous
   Exercises. By Horace Deighton, M.A., Head Master of Harrison College,
   Barbados.   New Edition, Revised, with Symbols and Abbreviations.
   Crown 8vo. 4s. 6d. Key, for tutors only, 5s. net.
          Book I.   ...   .   1s. | Books I. to III.   ... 2s. 6d.
          Books I. and II. ... 1s. 6d. | Books III. and IV.   1s. 6d.
Euclid.   Exercises on Euclid and in Modern Geometry.   By
   J. McDowell, M.A. 4th Edition. 6s.
Elementary Trigonometry.   By J. M. Dyer, M.A., and Rev.
   R. H. Whitcombe, M.A., Assistant Masters, Eton College. 2nd Edit. 4s. 6d.
Trigonometry. Plane. By Rev. T. Vyvyan, M.A. 3rd Edit. 3s. 6d.
Geometrical Conic Sections. By H. G. Willis, M.A. 5s.
Conics.   The Elementary Geometry of.   7th Edition, revised and
   enlarged. By C. Taylor, D.D. 4s. 6d.
Solid Geometry.   By W. S. Aldis, M.A.   4th Edit. revised. 6s.
Geometrical Optics.   By W. S. Aldis, M.A.   3rd Edition. 4s.
Rigid Dynamics.   By W. S. Aldis, M.A.   4s.
Elementary Dynamics.   By W. Garnett, M.A., D.C.L. 5th Ed. 6s.
Dynamics.   A Treatise on.   By W. H. Besant, Sc.D., F.R.S.   2nd
   Edition. 7s. 6d.
Heat.   An Elementary Treatise.   By W. Garnett, M.A., D.C.L. 5th
   Edition, revised and enlarged. 4s. 6d.
Elementary Physics.   Examples in.   By W. Gallatly, M.A.   4s.

Elementary Hydrostatics. By W. H. Besant, Sc.D., F.R.S. 15th Edition, rewritten. Crown 8vo. 4s. 6d. Key 5s. net.

Hydromechanics. By W. H. Besant, Sc.D., F.R.S. 5th Edition. Part I. Hydrostatics. 5s.

Mathematical Examples. By J. M. Dyer, M.A., Eton College, and R. Prowde Smith, M.A., Cheltenham College. 6s.

Mechanics. Problems in Elementary. By W. Walton, M.A. 6s.

Notes on Roulettes and Glissettes. By W. H. Besant, Sc.D., F.R.S. 2nd Edition, enlarged. Crown 8vo. 5s.

CAMBRIDGE SCHOOL AND COLLEGE TEXT-BOOKS.

A Series of Elementary Treatises for the use of Students.

Arithmetic. By Rev. C. Elsee, M.A. Fcap. 8vo. 14th Edit. 3s. 6d.

—— By A. Wrigley, M.A. 3s. 6d.

—— A Progressive Course of Examples. With Answers. By J. Watson, M.A. 7th Edition, revised. By W. P. Goudie, B.A. 2s. 6d.

Algebra. By the Rev. C. Elsee, M.A. 8th Edit. 4s.

—— Progressive Course of Examples. By Rev. W. F. M'Michael, M.A., and R. Prowde Smith, M.A. 4th Edition. 3s. 6d. With Answers. 4s. 6d.

Plane Astronomy. An Introduction to. By P. T. Main, M.A. 6th Edition, revised. 4s.

Conic Sections treated Geometrically. By W. H. Besant, Sc.D. 8th Edition. 4s. 6d. Solution to the Examples. 4s.

—— Enunciations and Figures Separately. 1s.

Statics, Elementary. By Rev. H. Goodwin, D.D. 2nd Edit. 3s.

Mensuration, An Elementary Treatise on. By B. T. Moore, M.A. 3s. 6d.

Newton's Principia, The First Three Sections of, with an Appendix; and the Ninth and Eleventh Sections. By J. H. Evans, M.A. 5th Edition, by P. T. Main, M.A. 4s.

Analytical Geometry for Schools. By T. G. Vyvyan. 5th Edit. 4s. 6d.

Greek Testament, Companion to the. By A. C. Barrett, M.A. 5th Edition, revised. Fcap. 8vo. 5s.

Book of Common Prayer, An Historical and Explanatory Treatise on the. By W. G. Humphry, B.D. 6th Edition. Fcap. 8vo. 2s. 6d.

Music, Text-book of. By Professor H. C. Banister. 15th Edition, revised. 5s.

—— Concise History of. By Rev. H. G. Bonavia Hunt, Mus. Doc. Dublin. 12th Edition, revised. 3s. 6d.

ARITHMETIC. *(See also the two foregoing Series.)*

Elementary Arithmetic. By Charles Pendlebury, M.A., Senior Mathematical Master, St. Paul's School; and W. S. Beard, F.R.G.S., Assistant Master, Christ's Hospital. With 2500 Examples, Written and Oral. Crown 8vo. 1s. 6d. With or without Answers.

Arithmetic, Examination Papers in. Consisting of 140 papers, each containing 7 questions. 357 more difficult problems follow. A collection of recent Public Examination Papers are appended. By C. Pendlebury, M.A. 2s. 6d. Key, for Masters only, 5s.

Graduated Exercises in Addition (Simple and Compound). By W. S. Beard, C. S. Department Rochester Mathematical School. 1s. For Candidates for Commercial Certificates and Civil Service Exams.

A 2

BOOK-KEEPING.

Book-keeping Papers, set at various Public Examinations. Collected and Written by J. T. Medhurst, Lecturer on Book-keeping in the City of London College. 2nd Edition. 3s.

A Text-Book of the Principles and Practice of Book-keeping. By Professor A. W. Thomson, B.Sc., Royal Agricultural College, Cirencester. Crown 8vo. 5s.

Double Entry Elucidated. By B. W. Foster. 14th edition. Fcap. 4to. 3s. 6d.

A New Manual of Book-keeping, combining the Theory and Practice, with Specimens of a set of Books. By Phillip Crellin, Accountant. Crown 8vo. 3s. 6d.

Book-keeping for Teachers and Pupils. By Phillip Crellin. Crown 8vo. 1s. 6d. Key, 2s. net.

GEOMETRY AND EUCLID.

Euclid. Books I.–VI. and part of XI. A New Translation. By H. Deighton. (See p. 8.)

—— The Definitions of, with Explanations and Exercises, and an Appendix of Exercises on the First Book. By R. Webb, M.A. Crown 8vo. 1s. 6d.

—— Book I. With Notes and Exercises for the use of Preparatory Schools, &c. By Braithwaite Arnett, M.A. 8vo. 4s. 6d.

—— The First Two Books explained to Beginners. By C. P. Mason, B.A. 2nd Edition. Fcap. 8vo. 2s. 6d.

The Enunciations and Figures to Euclid's Elements. By Rev. J. Brasse, D.D. New Edition. Fcap. 8vo. 1s. Without the Figures, 6d.

Exercises on Euclid. By J. McDowell, M.A. (See p. 8.)

Mensuration. By B. T. Moore, M.A. 3s. 6d. (See p. 9.)

Geometrical Conic Sections. By H. G. Willis, M.A. (See p. 8.)

Geometrical Conic Sections. By W. H. Besant, Sc.D. (See p. 9.)

Elementary Geometry of Conics. By C. Taylor, D.D. (See p. 8.)

An Introduction to Ancient and Modern Geometry of Conics. By C. Taylor, D.D., Master of St. John's Coll., Camb. 8vo. 15s.

An Introduction to Analytical Plane Geometry. By W. P. Turnbull, M.A. 8vo. 12s.

Problems on the Principles of Plane Co-ordinate Geometry. By W. Walton, M.A. 8vo. 16s.

Trilinear Co-ordinates, and Modern Analytical Geometry of Two Dimensions. By W. A. Whitworth, M.A. 8vo. 16s.

An Elementary Treatise on Solid Geometry. By W. S. Aldis, M.A. 4th Edition revised. Cr. 8vo. 6s.

Elliptic Functions, Elementary Treatise on. By A. Cayley, D.Sc. Demy 8vo.   [*New Edition Preparing.*

TRIGONOMETRY.

Trigonometry. By Rev. T. G. Vyvyan. 3s. 6d. (See p. 8.)

Trigonometry, Elementary. By J. M. Dyer, M.A., and Rev. R. H. Whitcombe, M.A., Asst. Masters, Eton College. 4s. 6d. (See p. 8.)

Trigonometry, Examination Papers in. By G. H. Ward, M.A., Assistant Master at St. Paul's School. Crown 8vo. 2s. 6d.

MECHANICS & NATURAL PHILOSOPHY.

Statics, Elementary. By H. Goodwin, D.D. Fcap. 8vo. 2nd Edition. 3s.

Dynamics, A Treatise on Elementary. By W. Garnett, M.A., D.C.L. 5th Edition. Crown 8vo. 6s.

Dynamics, Rigid. By W. S. Aldis, M.A. 4s.

Dynamics, A Treatise on. By W. H. Besant, Sc.D., F.R.S. 7s. 6d.

Elementary Mechanics, Problems in. By W. Walton, M.A. New Edition. Crown 8vo. 6s.

Theoretical Mechanics. Problems in. By W. Walton, M.A. 3rd Edition. Demy 8vo. 16s.

Structural Mechanics. By R. M. Parkinson, Assoc. M.I.C.E. Crown 8vo. 4s. 6d.

Elementary Mechanics. Stages I. and II. By J. C. Horobin, B.A. 1s. 6d. each. [*Stage III. preparing.*

Theoretical Mechanics. Division I. (for Science and Art Examinations). By J. C. Horobin, B.A. Crown 8vo. 2s. 6d.

Hydrostatics. By W. H. Besant, Sc.D. Cr. 8vo. 15th Edit. 4s. 6d.

Hydromechanics, A Treatise on. By W. H. Besant, Sc.D., F.R.S. 8vo. 5th Edition, revised. Part I. Hydrostatics. 5s.

Hydrodynamics, A Treatise on. Vol. I., 10s. 6d.; Vol. II., 12s. 6d. A. B. Basset, M.A., F.R.S.

Hydrodynamics and Sound, An Elementary Treatise on. By A. B. Basset, M.A., F.R.S. Demy 8vo. 7s. 6d.

Physical Optics, A Treatise on. By A. B. Basset, M.A., F.R.S. Demy 8vo. 16s.

Optics, Geometrical. By W. S. Aldis, M.A. Crown 8vo. 3rd Edition. 4s.

Double Refraction, A Chapter on Fresnel's Theory of. By W. S. Aldis, M.A. 8vo. 2s.

Roulettes and Glissettes. By W. H. Besant, Sc.D., F.R.S. 2nd Edition, 5s.

Heat, An Elementary Treatise on. By W. Garnett, M.A., D.C.L. Crown 8vo. 5th Edition. 4s. 6d.

Elementary Physics, Examples and Examination Papers in. By W. Gallatly, M.A. 4s.

Newton's Principia, The First Three Sections of, with an Appendix; and the Ninth and Eleventh Sections. By J. H. Evans, M.A. 5th Edition. Edited by P. T. Main, M.A. 4s.

Astronomy, An Introduction to Plane. By P. T. Main, M.A. Fcap. 8vo. cloth. 6th Edition. 4s.

Mathematical Examples. Pure and Mixed. By J. M. Dyer, M.A., and R. Prowde Smith, M.A. 6s.

Pure Mathematics and Natural Philosophy, A Compendium of. Facts and Formulæ in. By G. R. Smalley. 2nd Edition, revised by J. McDowell, M.A. Fcap. 8vo. 2s.

Elementary Course of Mathematics. By H. Goodwin, D.D. 6th Edition. 8vo. 16s.

A Collection of Examples and Problems in Arithmetic,. Algebra, Geometry, Logarithms, Trigonometry, Conic Sections, Mechanics, &c., with Answers. By Rev. A. Wrigley. 20th Thousand. 8s. 6d. Key. 10s. 6d.

FOREIGN CLASSICS.

A Series for use in Schools, with English Notes, grammatical and explanatory, and renderings of difficult idiomatic expressions.
Fcap. 8vo.

Schillers's Wallenstein. By Dr. A. Buchheim. 6th Edit. 5*s.*
Or the Lager and Piccolomini, 2*s.* 6*d.* Wallenstein's Tod, 2*s.* 6*d.*
———— Maid of Orleans. By Dr. W. Wagner. 3rd Edit. 1*s.* 6*d.*
———— Maria Stuart. By V. Kastner. 3rd Edition. 1*s.* 6*d.*
Goethe's Hermann und Dorothea. By E. Bell, M.A., and E. Wölfel. New Edition, Revised. 1*s.* 6*d.*
German Ballads, from Uhland, Goethe, and Schiller. By C. L. Bielefeld. 5th Edition. 1*s.* 6*d.*
Charles XII., par Voltaire. By L. Direy. 7th Edition. 1*s.* 6*d.*
Aventures de Télémaque, par Fénelon. By C. J. Delille. 4th Edition. 2*s.* 6*d.*
Select Fables of La Fontaine. By F. E. A. Gasc. 19th Edit. 1*s.* 6*d.*
Picciola, by X. B. Saintine. By Dr. Dubuc. 16th Thousand. 1*s.* 6*d.*
Lamartine's Le Tailleur de Pierres de Saint-Point. By J. Boïelle, 6th Thousand. Fcap. 8vo. 1*s.* 6*d.*

Italian Primer. By Rev. A. C. Clapin, M.A. Fcap. 8vo. 1*s.*

FRENCH CLASS-BOOKS.

French Grammar for Public Schools. By Rev. A. C. Clapin, M.A. Fcap. 8vo. 13th Edition. 2*s.* 6*d.* Key to Exercises 3*s.* 6*d.*
French Primer. By Rev. A. C. Clapin, M.A. Fcap. 8vo. 9th Ed. 1*s.*
Primer of French Philology. By Rev. A. C. Clapin. Fcap. 8vo. 6th Edit. 1*s.*
Le Nouveau Trésor; or, French Student's Companion. By M. E. S. 19th Edition. Fcap. 8vo. 1*s.* 6*d.*
French Papers for the Prelim. Army Exams. Collected by J. F. Davis, D. Lit. 2*s.* 6*d.*
French Examination Papers in Miscellaneous Grammar and Idioms. Compiled by A. M. M. Stedman, M.A. 4th Edition. Crown 8vo. 2*s.* 6*d.* Key. 5*s.* (For Teachers or Private Students only.)
Manual of French Prosody. By Arthur Gosset, M.A. Crown 8vo. 3*s.*
Lexicon of Conversational French. By A. Holloway. 3rd Edition. Crown 8vo. 3*s.* 6*d.*

PROF. A. BARRÈRE'S FRENCH COURSE.

Junior Graduated French Course. Crown 8vo. 1*s.* 6*d.*
Elements of French Grammar and First Steps in Idiom. Crown 8vo. 2*s.*
Précis of Comparative French Grammar. 2nd Edition. Crown 8vo. 3*s.* 6*d.*
Récits Militaires. From 1792 to 1870. With English Notes, for Candidates for the Army Exams. Crown 8vo. 3*s.*

F. E. A. GASC'S FRENCH COURSE.

First French Book. Crown 8vo. 116th Thousand. 1*s*.

Second French Book. 52nd Thousand. Fcap. 8vo. 1*s*. 6*d*.

Key to First and Second French Books. 5th Edit. Fcp. 8vo. 3*s*. 6*d*.

French Fables for Beginners, in Prose, with Index. 16th Thousand. 12mo. 1*s*. 6*d*.

Select Fables of La Fontaine. 18th Thousand. Fcap. 8vo. 1*s*. 6*d*.

Histoires Amusantes et Instructives. With Notes. 17th Thousand. Fcap. 8vo. 2*s*.

Practical Guide to Modern French Conversation. 18th Thousand. Fcap. 8vo. 1*s*. 6*d*.

French Poetry for the Young. With Notes. 5th Ed. Fcp. 8vo. 8·.

Materials for French Prose Composition; or, Selections from the best English Prose Writers. 21st Thous. Fcap. 8vo. 3*s*. Key, 6*s*.

Prosateurs Contemporains. With Notes. 11th Edition, revised. 12mo. 3*s*. 6*d*.

Le Petit Compagnon; a French Talk-Book for Little Children. 14th Edition. 16mo. 1*s*. 6*d*.

An Improved Modern Pocket Dictionary of the French and English Languages. 47th Thousand. 16mo. 2*s*. 6*d*.

Modern French-English and English-French Dictionary. 5th Edition, revised. 10*s*. 6*d*. In use at Harrow, Rugby, Westminster, Shrewsbury, Radley, &c.

The A B C Tourist's French Interpreter of all Immediate Wants. By F. E. A. Gasc. 1*s*.

MODERN FRENCH AUTHORS.

Edited, with Introductions and Notes, by JAMES BOÏELLE, Senior French Master at Dulwich College.

Daudet's La Belle Nivernaise. 2*s*. 6*d*. *For Beginners.*

Clarétie. Pierrille, by Jules Clarétie. 2*s*. 6*d*. *For Beginners.*

Hugo's Bug Jargal. 3*s*. *For Advanced Students.*

Balzac's Ursule Mirouët. 3*s*. *For Advanced Students.*

GOMBERT'S FRENCH DRAMA.

Being a Selection of the best Tragedies and Comedies of Molière. Racine, Corneille, and Voltaire. With Arguments and Notes by A. Gombert. New Edition, revised by F. E. A. Gasc. Fcap. 8vo. 1*s*. each; sewed, 6*d*.

CONTENTS.

MOLIÈRE:—Le Misanthrope. L'Avare. Le Bourgeois Gentilhomme. Le Tartuffe. Le Malade Imaginaire. Les Femmes Savantes. Les Fourberies de Scapin. Les Précieuses Ridicules. L'Ecole des Femmes. L'Ecole des Maris. Le Médecin malgré Lui.

RACINE:—Phédre. Esther. Athalie. Iphigénie. Les Plaideurs. La Thébalde; ou, Les Frères Ennemis. Andromaque. Britannicus.

P. CORNEILLE:—Le Cid. Horace. Cinna. Polyeucte.

VOLTAIRE:—Zaïre.

GERMAN CLASS-BOOKS.

Materials for German Prose Composition. By Dr. Buchheim.
14th Edition. Fcap. 4*s.* 6*d.* Key, Parts I. and II., 3*s.* Parts III. and IV.,

Goethe's Faust. Part I. Text, Hayward's Prose Translation, and Notes. Edited by Dr. Buchheim. 5*s.*

German. The Candidate's Vade Mecum. Five Hundred Easy Sentences and Idioms. By an Army Tutor. Cloth, 1*s.* *For Army Exams.*

Wortfolge, or Rules and Exercises on the Order of Words in German Sentences. By Dr. F. Stock. 1*s.* 6*d.*

A German Grammar for Public Schools. By the Rev. A. C. Clapin and F. Holl Müller. 5th Edition. Fcap. 2*s.* 6*d.*

A German Primer, with Exercises. By Rev. A. C. Clapin. 2nd Edition. 1*s.*

Kotzebue's Der Gefangene. With Notes by Dr. W. Stromberg. 1*s.*

German Examination Papers in Grammar and Idiom. By R. J. Morich. 2nd Edition. 2*s.* 6*d.* Key for Tutors only, 5*s.*

By Frz. Lange, Ph.D., Professor R.M.A., Woolwich, Examiner in German to the Coll. of Preceptors, and also at the Victoria University, Manchester.

A Concise German Grammar. In Three Parts. Part I., Ele-mentary, 2*s.* Part II., Intermediate, 2*s.* Part III., Advanced, 3*s.* 6*d.*

German Examination Course. Elementary, 2*s.* Intermediate, 2*s.* Advanced, 1*s.* 6*d.*

German Reader. Elementary, 1*s.* 6*d.* Advanced, 3*s.*

MODERN GERMAN SCHOOL CLASSICS.
Small Crown 8vo.

Hey's Fabeln Für Kinder. Edited, with Vocabulary, by Prof. F. Lange, Ph.D. *Printed in Roman characters.* 1*s.* 6*d.*
—— The same with Phonetic Transcription of Text, &c. 2*s.*

Benedix's Dr. Wespe. Edited by F. Lange, Ph.D. 2*s.* 6*d.*

Hoffman's Meister Martin, der Küfner. By Prof. F. Lange, Ph.D. 1*s.* 6*d.*

Heyse's Hans Lange. By A. A. Macdonell, M.A., Ph.D. 2*s.*

Auerbach's Auf Wache, and Roquette's Der Gefrorene Kuss. By A. A. Macdonell, M.A. 2*s.*

Moser's Der Bibliothekar. By Prof. F. Lange, Ph.D. 3rd Edition. 2*s.*

Ebers' Eine Frage. By F. Storr, B.A. 2*s.*

Freytag's Die Journalisten. By Prof. F. Lange, Ph.D. 2nd Edition, revised. 2*s.* 6*d.*

Gutzkow's Zopf und Schwert. By Prof. F. Lange, Ph.D. 2*s.*

German Epic Tales. Edited by Karl Neuhaus, Ph.D. 2*s.* 6*d.*

Scheffel's Ekkehard. Edited by Dr. H. Hager. 3*s.*

DIVINITY.

By the late Rev. F. H. Scrivener, A.M., LL.D., D.C.L.

Novum Testamentum Græce. Editio major. Being an enlarged
Edition, containing the Readings of Bishop Westcott and Dr. Hort, and
those adopted by the Revisers, &c. 7s. 6d. (*For other Editions see page 3.*)

A Plain Introduction to the Criticism of the New Testament.
With Forty Facsimiles from Ancient Manuscripts. 4th Edition, revised
by Rev. E. Miller, M.A. 8vo. [*In the press.*

Codex Bezæ Cantabrigiensis. 4to. 10s. 6d.

The **New Testament for English Readers.** By the late H. Alford,
D.D. Vol. I. Part I. 3rd Edit. 12s. Vol. I. Part II. 2nd Edit. 10s. 6d.
Vol. II. Part I. 2nd Edit. 16s. Vol. II. Part II. 2nd Edit. 16s.

The **Greek Testament.** By the late H. Alford, D.D. Vol I. 7th
Edit. 1l. 8s. Vol. II. 8th Edit. 1l. 4s. Vol. III. 10th Edit. 18s. Vol. IV.
Part I. 5th Edit. 18s. Vol. IV. Part II. 10th Edit. 14s. Vol. IV. 1l. 12s.

Companion to the Greek Testament. By A. C. Barrett, M.A.
5th Edition, revised. Fcap. 8vo. 5s.

Guide to the Textual Criticism of the New Testament. By
Rev. E. Miller, M.A. Crown 8vo. 4s.

The Book of Psalms. A New Translation, with Introductions, &c.
By the Rt. Rev. J. J. Stewart Perowne, D.D., Bishop of Worcester. 8vo.
Vol. I. 8th Edition, 18s. Vol. II. 8th Edit. 16s.

—— Abridged for Schools. 7th Edition. Crown 8vo. 10s. 6d.

History of the Articles of Religion. By C. H. Hardwick. 3rd
Edition. Post 8vo. 5s.

History of the Creeds. By Rev. Professor Lumby, D.D. 3rd
Edition. Crown 8vo. 7s. 6d.

Pearson on the Creed. Carefully printed from an early edition.
With Analysis and Index by E. Walford, M.A. Post 8vo. 5s.

Liturgies and Offices of the Church, for the Use of English
Readers, in Illustration of the Book of Common Prayer. By the Rev.
Edward Burbidge, M.A. Crown 8vo. 9s.

An **Historical and Explanatory Treatise on the Book of**
Common Prayer. By Rev. W. G. Humphry, B.D. 6th Edition, enlarged.
Small Post 8vo. 2s. 6d.; Cheap Edition, 1s.

A Commentary on the Gospels, Epistles, and Acts of the
Apostles. By Rev. W. Denton, A.M. New Edition. 7 vols. 8vo. 9s. each.

Notes on the Catechism. By Rt. Rev. Bishop Barry. 9th Edit.
Fcap. 2s.

The Winton Church Catechist. Questions and Answers on the
Teaching of the Church Catechism. By the late Rev. J. S. B. Monsell,
LL.D. 4th Edition. Cloth, 3s.; or in Four Parts, sewed.

The Church Teacher's Manual of Christian Instruction. By
Rev. M. F. Sadler. 43rd Thousand. 2s. 6d.

TECHNOLOGICAL HANDBOOKS.

Edited by Sir H. Trueman Wood, Secretary of the Society of Arts.

Dyeing and Tissue Printing. By W. Crookes, F.R.S. 5s.

Glass Manufacture. By Henry Chance, M.A.; H. J. Powell, B.A.; and H. G. Harris. 3s. 6d.

Cotton Spinning. By Richard Marsden, of Manchester. 4th Edition, revised. 6s. 6d.

Chemistry of Coal-Tar Colours. By Prof. Benedikt, and Dr. Knecht of Bradford Technical College. 2nd Edition, enlarged. 6s. 6d.

Woollen and Worsted Cloth Manufacture. By Professor Roberts Beaumont, The Yorkshire College, Leeds. 2nd Edition. 7s. 6d.

Silk Dyeing. By G. H. Hurst, F.C.S. With numerous coloured specimens. 7s. 6d.

Cotton Weaving. By R. Marsden. [*Preparing.*

Bookbinding. By J. W. Zaehnsdorf, with eight plates and many illustrations. 5s.

Printing. By C. T. Jacobi, Manager of the Chiswick Press. 5s.

Plumbing. By S. Stevens Hellyer. 5s.

Soap Manufacture. By W. Lawrence Gadd, F.I.C., F.C.S. 5s.

BELL'S AGRICULTURAL SERIES.

The Farm and the Dairy. By Prof. Sheldon. 2s. 6d.

Soils and their Properties. By Dr. Fream. 2s. 6d.

The Diseases of Crops. By Dr. Griffiths. 2s. 6d.

Manures and their Uses. By Dr. Griffiths. 2s. 6d.

Tillage and Implements. By Prof. W. J. Malden. 2s. 6d.

Fruit Culture. By J. Cheal, F.R.H.S. 2s. 6d.

Others in preparation.

HISTORY.

Modern Europe. By Dr. T. H. Dyer. 2nd Edition, revised and continued. 5 vols. Demy 8vo. 2l. 12s. 6d.

The Decline of the Roman Republic. By G. Long. 5 vols. 8vo. 5s. each.

Select Historical Documents of the Middle Ages. Collected and Translated by Ernest F. Henderson, Ph.D. Small post 8vo. 5s.

The Intermediate History of England. For Army and Civil Service Candidates. By H. F. Wright, M.A., LL.M. Crown 8vo. 6s.

Historical Maps of England. By C. H. Pearson. Folio. 3rd Edition revised. 31s. 6d.

England in the Fifteenth Century. By the late Rev. W. Denton, M.A. Demy 8vo. 12s.

Feudalism: Its Rise, Progress, and Consequences. By Judge Abdy. 7s. 6d.

History of England, 1800–46. By Harriet Martineau, with new
and copious Index. 5 vols. 3s. 6d. each.

A Practical Synopsis of English History. By A. Bowes. 9th
Edition, revised. 8vo. 1s.

Lives of tne Queens of England. By A. Strickland. Library
Edition, 8 vols. 7s. 6d. each. Cheaper Edition, 6 vols. 5s. each. Abridged
Edition, 1 vol. 6s. 6d. Mary Queen of Scots, 2 vols. 5s. each. Tudor and
Stuart Princesses, 5s.

History and Geography Examination Papers. Compiled by
C. H. Spence, M.A., Clifton College. Crown 8vo. 2s. 6d.

For other Historical Books, see Catalogue of Bohn's Libraries, sent free on
application.

PSYCHOLOGY AND ETHICS.

The Student's Manual of Psychology and Ethics. By F. Ryland, M.A., late Scholar of St. John's College, Cambridge. Specially
adapted for London Examinations. Fifth Edition, with Lists of Books
for Students, and Examination Papers. 3s. 6d.

Ethics: An Introductory Manual for University Students. By
F. Ryland, M.A. 3s. 6d

DICTIONARIES.

WEBSTER'S INTERNATIONAL DICTIONARY of the
English Language. Including Scientific, Technical,
and Biblical Words and Terms, with their Significations, Pronunciations, Etymologies, Alternative
Spellings, Derivations, Synonyms, and numerous
illustrative Quotations, with various valuable literary
Appendices and 83 extra pages of Illustrations grouped
and classified, rendering the work a COMPLETE
LITERARY AND SCIENTIFIC REFERENCE-BOOK. *New*
Edition (1890). Thoroughly revised and enlarged
under the supervision of Noah Porter, D.D., LL.D.
1 vol. (2118 pages, 3500 woodcuts), 4to. cloth, 31s. 6d.; half calf, 2l. 2s. ;
half russia, 2l. 5s.; calf, 2l. 8s.; full sheep with patent marginal Index,
2l. 8s.; or in 2 vols. cloth, 1l. 14s.; half russia, 2l. 18s.
Prospectuses, with specimen pages, sent free on application.

Kluge's Etymological Dictionary of the German Language.
Translated from the 4th German edition by J. F. Davis, D.Lit., M.A.
(Lond.). Crown 4to. half buckram, 18s.

Dictionary of the French and English Languages, with more
than Fifteen Thousand New Words, Senses, &c. By F. E. A. Gasc. With
New Supplements. 5th Edition, Revised and Enlarged. Demy 8vo.
10s. 6d. IN USE AT HARROW, RUGBY, SHREWSBURY, &c.

Pocket Dictionary of the French and English Languages.
By F. E. A. Gasc. Containing more than Five Thousand Modern and
Current Words, Senses, and Idiomatic Phrases and Renderings, not found
in any other dictionary of the two languages. New edition, with addi-
tions and corrections. 49th Thousand. 16mo. Cloth, 2s. 6d.

ENGLISH CLASS-BOOKS.

Comparative Grammar and Philology. By A. C. Price, M.A., Assistant Master at Leeds Grammar School. 2s. 6d.

The Elements of the English Language. By E. Adams, Ph.D. 25th Edition. Revised by J. F. Davis, D.Lit., M.A. Post 8vo. 4s. 6d.

The Rudiments of English Grammar and Analysis. By E. Adams, Ph.D. 19th Thousand. Fcap. 8vo. 1s.

A Concise System of Parsing. By L. E. Adams, B.A. 1s. 6d.

Examples for Grammatical Analysis (Verse and Prose). Selected, &c., by F. Edwards. New edition. Cloth, 1s.

Questions for Examination in English Literature. With brief hints on the study of English. By Professor W. W. Skeat, Litt.D. Crown 8vo. 2s. 6d.

Ten Brink's History of English Literature. Vol. I. Early English Literature (to Wiclif). Translated by H. M. Kennedy. 3s. 6d. Vol. II. (Wiclif, Chaucer, Earliest Drama, Renaissance). Translated by W. Clarke Robinson, Ph.D. 3s. 6d.

Notes on Shakespeare's Plays. By T. Duff Barnett, B.A. MIDSUMMER NIGHT'S DREAM, 1s.; JULIUS CÆSAR, 1s.; HENRY V., 1s.; TEMPEST, 1s.; MACBETH, 1s.; MERCHANT OF VENICE, 1s.; HAMLET, 1s.; RICHARD II., 1s.; KING JOHN 1s.; KING LEAR, 1s.; CORIOLANUS, 1s.

GRAMMARS.

By C. P. Mason, Fellow of Univ. Coll. London.

First Notions of Grammar for Young Learners. Fcap. 8vo. 75th Thousand. Revised and enlarged. Cloth. 1s.

First Steps in English Grammar for Junior Classes. Demy 18mo. 54th Thousand. 1s.

Outlines of English Grammar for the Use of Junior Classes. 87th Thousand. Crown 8vo. 2s.

English Grammar, including the Principles of Grammatical Analysis. 34th Edition. 143rd Thousand. Crown 8vo. 3s. 6d.

Practice and Help in the Analysis of Sentences. 2s.

A Shorter English Grammar, with copious Exercises. 49th to 53rd Thousand. Crown 8vo. 3s. 6d.

English Grammar Practice, being the Exercises separately. 1s.

Code Standard Grammars. Parts I. and II., 2d. each. Parts III., IV., and V., 3d. each.

Notes of Lessons, their Preparation, &c. By José Rickard, Park Lane Board School, Leeds, and A. H. Taylor, Rodley Board School, Leeds. 2nd Edition. Crown 8vo. 2s. 6d.

A Syllabic System of Teaching to Read, combining the advantages of the 'Phonic' and the 'Look-and-Say' Systems. Crown 8vo. 1s.

Practical Hints on Teaching. By Rev. J. Menet, M.A. 6th Edit. revised. Crown 8vo. paper, 2s.

Test Lessons in Dictation. 4th Edition. Paper cover, 1s. 6d.

Picture School-Books. With numerous Illustrations. Royal 16mo. The Infant's Primer. 3d.—School Primer. 6d.—School Reader. By J. Tilleard. 1s.—Poetry Book for Schools. 1s.—The Life of Joseph. 1s.— The Scripture Parables. By the Rev. J. E. Clarke. 1s.—The Scripture Miracles. 1s.—The New Testament History. 1s.—The Old Testament History. By the Rev. J. G. Wood, M.A. 1s.—The Life of Martin Luther. By Sarah Crompton. 1s.

BOOKS FOR YOUNG READERS.

A Series of Reading Books designed to facilitate the acquisition of the power of Reading by very young Children. In 10 vols. cloth, 6d. each.

Those with an asterisk have a Frontispiece or other Illustrations.

*The Old Boathouse. Bell and Fan; or, A Cold Dip.

*Tot and the Cat. A Bit of Cake. The Jay. The Black Hen's Nest. Tom and Ned. Mrs. Bee.

*The Cat and the Hen. Sam and his Dog Redleg. Bob and Tom Lee. A Wreck.

*The New-born Lamb. The Rosewood Box. Poor Fan. Sheep Dog.

} *Suitable for Infants.*

*The Two Parrots. A Tale of the Jubilee. By M. E. Wintle. 9 Illustrations.

*The Story of Three Monkeys.

*Story of a Cat. Told by Herself.

The Blind Boy. The Mute Girl. A New Tale of Babes in a Wood.

*Queen Bee and Busy Bee.

*Gull's Crag.

} *Suitable for Standards I. & II.*

Syllabic Spelling. By C. Barton. In Two Parts. Infants, 3d. Standard I., 3d.

GEOGRAPHICAL READING-BOOKS.

By M. J. BARRINGTON WARD, M.A. *With numerous Illustrations.*

The Child's Geography. For the Use of Schools and for Home Tuition. 6d.

The Map and the Compass. A Reading-Book of Geography. For Standard I. New Edition, revised. 8d. cloth.

The Round World. A Reading-Book of Geography. For Standard II. New Edition, revised and enlarged. 10d.

About England. A Reading-Book of Geography for Standard III. With numerous Illustrations and Coloured Map. 1s. 4d.

The Child's Geography of England. With Introductory Exercises on the British Isles and Empire, with Questions. 2s. 6d.

ELEMENTARY MECHANICS.

By J. C. HOROBIN, B.A., Principal of Homerton Training College.

Stage   I. *With numerous Illustrations.* 1s. 6d.
Stage II. *With numerous Illustrations.* 1s. 6d.
Stage III.   [*Preparing.*

BELL'S READING-BOOKS.

FOR SCHOOLS AND PAROCHIAL LIBRARIES.

Post 8vo. Strongly bound in cloth, 1s. each.

*Adventures of a Donkey.
*Life of Columbus.
*Grimm's German Tales. (Selected.)
*Andersen's Danish Tales. Illustrated. (Selected.)
*Uncle Tom's Cabin.
* Great Englishmen. Short Lives for Young Children.
} *Suitable for Standard III.*

Great Englishwomen. Short Lives of.
Great Scotsmen. Short Lives of.
Parables from Nature. (Selected.) By Mrs. Gatty.
Lyrical Poetry. Selected by D. Munro.
*Edgeworth's Tales. (A Selection.)
*Scott's Talisman. (Abridged.)
} *Standard IV.*

*Poor Jack. By Captain Marryat, R.N. Abgd.
*Dickens's Little Nell. Abridged from the ' The Old Curiosity Shop.'
*Oliver Twist. By Charles Dickens. (Abridged.)
*Masterman Ready. By Capt. Marryat. Illus. (Abgd.)
*Gulliver's Travels. (Abridged.)
*Arabian Nights. (A Selection Rewritten.)
} *Standard V.*

*The Vicar of Wakefield.
Lamb's Tales from Shakespeare. (Selected.)
*Robinson Crusoe. Illustrated.
*Settlers in Canada. By Capt. Marryat. (Abridged.)
*Southey's Life of Nelson. (Abridged.)
*Life of the Duke of Wellington, with Maps and Plans.
*Sir Roger de Coverley and other Essays from the Spectator.
Tales of the Coast. By J. Runciman.
} *Standards VI., & VII.*

* These Volumes are Illustrated.

Uniform with the Series, in limp cloth, 6d. each.

Shakespeare's Plays. Kemble's Reading Edition. With Explanatory Notes for School Use.
JULIUS CÆSAR.   THE MERCHANT OF VENICE.   KING JOHN.
HENRY THE FIFTH.   MACBETH.   AS YOU LIKE IT.

www.ingramcontent.com/pod-product-compliance
Lightning Source LLC
Chambersburg PA
CBHW031103020726
47495CB00007B/2029